# THE AMBITIOUS CITY

# THE AMBITIOUS CITY

## SCOTT THORNLEY

RANDOM HOUSE CANADA

PUBLISHED BY RANDOM HOUSE CANADA

Copyright © 2012 Scott Thornley

www.randomhouse.ca

Random House Canada and colophon are registered trademarks.

This book is a work of fiction. Names, characters, places and incidents
either are the product of the author's imagination or are used fictitiously.
Any resemblance to actual persons, living or dead, events or locales is
entirely coincidental.

**Library and Archives Canada Cataloguing in Publication**

Thornley, Scott
The ambitious city / Scott Thornley.

Also issued in electronic format.

ISBN 978-0-307-35928-5

1. Title.

PS8639.H66A43 2012          C813'.6          C2011-908140-7

Front cover image: Shin Sugino
Cover concept and art direction: Scott Thornley
Cover design: Kirk Stephens
Cover imagework: Mark Lyle
Printed and bound in the United States of America

10 9 8 7 6 5 4 3 2 1

Wesley Gordon Woods, OBE (1915–2008)

*Classical scholar and linguist, Anglican priest,*
*bomber navigator, British cultural attaché,*
*artist and birder—my uncle and mentor.*

"Show me a hero and I'll show you a tragedy."

*F. Scott Fitzgerald*

# PROLOGUE

**R**EFERRED TO LOCALLY as The Grave, the steel company's dock dropped five storeys to the thick muck of the harbour below, its nickname a less than subtle nod to Dundurn's history. Or at least to the history of a myth that had arisen shortly after the dock was completed back in 1926. Competing mobs in the city, it was said, were dropping their cemented dead into the harbour off that dock. Over time, as the bay grew more polluted with human waste and industrial runoff, no one would willingly venture into the water to check it out. The police were happy to simply call it a myth.

Sheltered from the noise of several suction pumps that had been running night and day for four months, Howard Ellis, principal engineer for the *Hamilton-Scourge* Project, sat in his "room with a view"—the only trailer of six at the dredging site whose windows faced Dundurn Bay. The others looked out onto the red-brown chaos of cranes, elevators and an ever-changing parade of mud-caked men and diesel-belching heavy equipment hauling the day's sludge away to God-knows-where.

The city hadn't seen a project of this magnitude since the completion of the Sky-High Bridge in 1958. And before that, you'd have to look all the way back to the industrial development of the waterfront in the early 1900s. Three books lay fanned out neatly at the end of the long worktable dominating Ellis's trailer. One contained architectural renderings, another, construction tendering documents—the largest of the three—and the last was the one Ellis would flip through the way he used to flip through the Eaton's catalogue, longing for his parents to get him the blue CCM bike. This last volume brought the project to life in a way the drawings and dock-bottom scans couldn't. He'd studied it so many times he had committed the opening paragraph to memory:

> It was just after midnight on Sunday, August 8, 1813; the schooners *Hamilton* and *Scourge*—dangerously top-heavy, overloaded with men and munitions—were anchored miles offshore of Forty Mile Creek. They were part of an American squadron assembling to engage the British fleet, lying off Burlington, the next day. Men were asleep on deck and below, propped up against cannons, shot boxes and barrels of gunpowder, when a sudden squall tore through the otherwise still night. In less than five minutes, both ships sank, carrying all but a dozen to a watery grave, where they remain to this day—three hundred feet below the surface of Lake Ontario.

Ellis stared out over the bay again, trying to imagine the day when the two warships, raised from the depths, would arrive on his site. The fireboats would spray great plumes of water, the freighters and tugs would sound their horns, bunting would fly from the Burlington Bridge and the steel company's rusting cranes, and the

Royal Dundurn Yacht Club's sails and powerboats would fill the bay. Mingled with the horns and ships' whistles would be thousands of cheers and huzzas from the crowd. And he'd be right there to guide the schooners in.

Maybe, he thought, if the bigwigs got off their butts, they'd even have a fleet of tall ships—a grand escort flotilla of sail. *Certainly it'll be a historic day for Dundurn*, he thought, *but it'll also be a day of unprecedented glory for Howard Ellis . . .*

As he took the Thermos of coffee out of his briefcase, a young man from the tech trailer burst through the door. "Here ya go, Mr. Ellis," he said, handing him a large manila envelope, and left as quickly as he had come. Once a week Ellis received outputs that gave him an accurate picture of what was beneath the toxic soup that had lain undisturbed for almost a century off the harbour's eastern wharf. It was so dense that their scanning equipment could penetrate only three feet or so beneath the surface. He'd managed to find a place on the wall for all the grainy, gridded printouts, and he looked them over now before opening the envelope of new scans.

Ellis filled his mug and sat back to enjoy the first coffee of the day while he studied the latest printouts. What he saw caused him to spill his drink. He bolted out of his chair, grabbed the scans, and ran to find the engineer, two trailers away in number four. If he was going to believe it, Ellis would have to see what was on the computer monitor for himself.

# 1.

"**B**IKER SLAYINGS — SEARCH INTENSIFIES in Cayuga." The headline was terse and grim, the story short on details because the crime scene on the farm in Cayuga was locked down until the full extent of the mayhem could be uncovered. So far the police had found seven dead bikers, two from a shotgun blast to the face and one from a less messy gunshot. Three were dead from blunt-force trauma or broken necks, and one had his throat cut through to the spine. MacNeice's colleague Detective Superintendent John Swetsky had been given the lead, and within hours he had seconded most of the available homicide detectives in the city. Most, but not all. Swetsky and his team had been at it now for two weeks, and MacNeice had decided it was time to see if there was anything he could do to help.

The cruiser blocking the driveway moved aside when the uniform inside recognized the heavy Chevy approaching. Driving slowly down the long lane, MacNeice counted three more cruisers, two police buses and four unmarked cars, one of which belonged to Michael Vertesi, the young detective inspector who reported to him. Behind the farmhouse there was a large black trailer—a mobile forensics unit borrowed from the Mounties and fitted out by Dundurn's own forensics team. And beyond that, the city's only EMS-CS, a cold-storage van known irreverently as the ice cream truck. As MacNeice parked the Chevy, Vertesi and his other report, DI Montile Williams, emerged from the farmhouse.

"You know, for bikers, they keep a very tidy house," Vertesi said, peeling off his latex gloves. "What brings you out here, boss?"

"Just wanted to see if I can help. Swetsky's emptied the division—I thought I heard crickets in there this morning. Where can I find him?"

"In the barn, checkin' inventory," Williams said. "They got more equipment than Dundurn Streets 'n' Sanitation."

As MacNeice headed towards the barn, he could see two lines of cops walking the open field, looking for evidence. So far the daily reports had said they'd found almost four hundred spent rounds from a variety of weapons, mostly in and around the buildings and on the driveway.

The bodies had been buried between the barns, piled like cordwood six feet down, each sealed in plastic. Forensics was examining them for DNA, after which they'd be shipped to the coroner's lab. He could hear the high-speed hum of the forensic unit's exhaust fans. As he hadn't eaten anything, he decided to avoid going near the trailer.

Three rows of equipment filled the massive space inside the main barn—everything from recreational 4x4s to Bobcats, tractors and posthole diggers—and that was just what he could make out while standing on the threshold. He heard the big man coming before he actually saw him; Swetsky emerged from the farthest row carrying a clipboard.

"Mac! What brings you to Sherwood Forest? Have you been pushed into this one?"

"No, but since you've cleaned out the department, I thought I'd offer a hand too. How are you doing?"

"It's a serious mop-up. I gave 'em each a floor of the farmhouse and put Palmer in the basement, where he belongs."

"Have you worked out who the Damned Two Deuces were at war with?"

"No—so far all the bodies are D2D. The rest cleared out after they buried them. I heard there was a Quebec gang down here, but I haven't seen any evidence to prove it."

"I've read the reports. Other than the shrink-wrapped bodies, the place seems pretty clean."

"Yeah, well, we're cataloguing all this shit"—Swetsky nodded towards the tractor beside him—"and there's more in the other barn. Believe it or not, some of it's legit. We're also making sure we have all the bodies."

MacNeice's cell rang and he looked down at the call display. "I have to take this." Back out in the sunlight, he answered.

"Mac," a familiar voice said. "Jesus, it's been a long time. Are you okay?"

He could hear gulls calling and wind buffeting the microphone on the other end. "I'm fine, Bob. Where are you?"

"What do you know about the *Hamilton-Scourge* Project?"

Driving back to the city, MacNeice recalled that the last time he'd seen Bob Maybank, Dundurn's popular mayor, was at Kate's funeral. It seemed that not a day went by when he didn't see the mayor on television or in the papers, but in the flesh, the last time had been at the cemetery. MacNeice was impressed that he had made the trip up north to watch her ashes being interred. It wasn't that he didn't like the mayor—he did. They'd grown up together, played on the same teams and at times dated the same girls. He even admired what Bob was doing for Dundurn. But four years was a long time between calls. There were friends of his and Kate's who had made themselves scarce after she died, and Maybank was one of those. The urgency in his voice had been palpable—he'd called today because he needed something.

Weaving swiftly through traffic as he descended the mountain, MacNeice thought about the waterfront regeneration project the mayor had mentioned. In 2012 the country would mark the 200th anniversary of the War of 1812, and if Maybank could pull this off, it would inject new revenue into the city, both through construction and afterwards, when the tourists arrived. Specifically what it was going to be MacNeice wasn't sure. Like many people in Dundurn he'd been skeptical that the feds and the province would invest heavily in a city known nationwide for its dead or dying manufacturing sector. Industry, it was understood, was the city's only reason for being. In the much sought after "new economy," it seemed to be accepted that Dundurn would be collateral damage.

Maybank had given quirky instructions on how to find the trailer: "Go past the blast furnace, past all the long rows of rusty red buildings, all the way to the end of life as you know it—and then turn left." MacNeice pulled up next to the shiny black Lincoln Town Car and looked out to the bay, where the cormorants were diving for lake fish dumb enough to come through the canal. Stepping out of the Chevy and walking over to the wooden steps of the first trailer, he noticed the fusion of smells, dominated by oil and chemicals and topped off with marine decay—it wasn't unpleasant. But then, the wind was blowing the sulphur fumes from the steel plant up over the city and not over the water.

The door to the trailer swung open and Mayor Bob stepped out with his winning smile, firm handshake and shoulder clasp. "Mac, welcome to the future—the Museum of the Great Lakes. Come on inside; it smells like rat shit out here. In a couple of years, though, it'll be all candy floss and coconut oil, I promise you."

"Stop campaigning, Bob. I'm here, and you've already won the election."

"Ah, but the secret is—to never stop." He smiled broadly and opened the door for MacNeice.

Waiting for them inside were three people introduced as Julia Marchetti, Maybank's head of communications, Terence Young, the project architect, and Howard Ellis, the project's principal engineer. MacNeice shook their hands and looked back at Maybank for an explanation.

"We have a great opportunity with this project, Mac. We have the support of all three levels of government, as well as the United States Congress and Senate and the U.S. Navy—they're responsible for marine war graves. They all know this will be unique in North America and in the world."

"Raising the two ships and gifting them to Dundurn was signed into law decades ago," Young said enthusiastically, "but the technology to do it didn't exist back then. What's keeping those ships and everything on them in mint condition is the temperature down there—it's just above freezing year-round. Bring them up, and in a few weeks they'll disintegrate right before your eyes." He moved his hands as if to say *poof*. "Today we have the technology to refrigerate them, from the bottom of the lake to their arrival here. Imagine a huge aquarium—one-inch-thick plate glass, shrouded in blue light. To be precise, they'll be in the same conditions as now, but on view forever."

As Maybank slid an aerial site view across the table and opened the architectural renderings, MacNeice said, "Excuse me, but I'm a homicide detective. You need to get to the point, Bob—what am I doing here?"

For a moment the mayor looked angry. Then he smiled and said, "Okay, Mac, here's the point. In a routine check of the scans showing the bottom of the wharf, Ellis discovered something." He nodded to the engineer.

Ellis came over to MacNeice. "Once we'd dropped the wall on the bay side and began pumping the water out, we started making weekly scans of the progress: bird's-eye views of the dock. That wall behind the mayor represents scans from the past four months. As you can see, there's nothing unusual."

MacNeice looked over at the wall. The soft blue-grey scans all looked the same.

Ellis began laying prints on the table. "These are the latest scans— the time frame is seven days." He laid them down in sequence. The first two looked the same as those on the wall, but numbers three to five were different. "You can see forms emerging here, here, here, here and here." He put another print down and pointed to a rounded lump. "We're pumping sludge day and night; this was yesterday morning and that form is getting clearer. I mean, it's still below the surface but it'll be dry on the bottom by tomorrow." He put the last output on the table with a modest flourish. "This is from this morning." MacNeice could feel Maybank's eyes on him, waiting for a reaction.

The scan revealed four long columns lying on their sides, two circular and two square. They could now see that the rounded lump was an automobile—an old automobile. MacNeice picked up the print and studied it closely. "Looks like it's from the thirties."

"Very good, Mac," said the mayor. "I'm told it's a 1935 Packard 120 sedan."

"Those columns are what, seven or eight feet long?" MacNeice asked Ellis.

"The square ones are concrete—six feet, six inches, by scale to the output. And the round ones—where you can just make out a spiral pattern—those are eight-foot Sonotubes filled with concrete."

"Sonotubes . . . like poster tubes?"

"Exactly. They're used as formwork for concrete columns. However"—Ellis pointed at the end of a round-sectioned column—"construction columns are reinforced with steel rods, but these appear to be solid concrete." He moved away to let MacNeice draw the conclusion that everyone else in the trailer had already reached.

MacNeice looked over at the mayor, who nodded. "Howard thinks the square columns may have been down there for half a century or more. But the Sonotubes are recent. If you look at the one on the right, the wrapping is unwinding in that gunk."

"What's this got to do with me, Bob?" MacNeice was staring at the sequence of prints.

"Julia, can you, Ellis and Young leave us for a moment, please." The mayor waited till they had closed the door behind them. "You're the best, and I need you. This project is too important to the city for it to be derailed by this kind of drama. Our funding depends on everything going smoothly."

"Chain of command, Bob."

"I'm the mayor, for fuck's sake!" Maybank snapped. "Tell me what you need and I'll make things happen. Start by telling me what we should do now, for chrissakes. If this becomes a crime scene, the media will be all over us."

"If it's a crime scene, it's their job to be all over you. And if it's a crime scene you'll have plenty of cops down here too."

"I don't want plenty of cops. I want you." The mayor leaned towards him over the table. "I'm just trying to do what's best for this city, Mac, and if that car and some of those columns have been down there for more than half a century, how is turning this into a media circus going to help Dundurn? We've been Canada's armpit all our lives. This project will get us off our knees and back into the game."

"Quit mixing your metaphors and grab that aerial view of the site."

When Maybank set the large colour print down in front of him, MacNeice put his finger on a rail line located at the northwest corner of the wharf. "As fast as you can, get City Works to erect a tent, say thirty by fifty feet, right here. Make sure it has sides and air conditioning; in fact, get a refrigeration truck and park it there"—he tapped the image. "You'll need twenty-four-hour security you can trust, but don't use the police." He picked up a pen and drew the rectangles of the tent and the truck. "Use your cranes to lift the columns up onto the carts that run on that track, and roll them into the tent. Put the Packard in there too."

He put the pen down on the drawing. "One more thing. You've already lost the media game, Bob. Every one of those workers grew up around here, or has heard from those who did. They're the same stories you and I grew up with—about the mob, the bay, the cement overshoes. You've cleared them from the site but you can't clear their heads of what they're sure is happening here."

"What do you recommend I do, then?"

"If I were you, I'd ask Julia Marchetti to write a terrific story about how it's part of the great history of Dundurn—a tough steel city born of the same spirit of daring and survival that two hundred years earlier inspired our country to victory in the War of 1812. Dundurn is our Bronx, or Brooklyn; it was never a quiet, innocent town."

"You made up that shit just now?"

MacNeice smiled, looked briefly out the window and headed for the door.

"But Mac, you'll do the investigation for me, right?"

"I can't promise that. We're short-staffed, and you know that— you approved the Police Services budget. I can't give you a commitment. Get that tent up, get those things in there, get a couple of men you can trust with jackhammers, and then call me."

———

Back at his desk, MacNeice went online to read more about the *Hamilton* and the *Scourge*. One of the schooners had originally been British, and as often happened in times of conflict, it had been captured and renamed. Its origin wouldn't have been lost on the crews, however; the figurehead on the *Scourge* was its original namesake, Lord Nelson. The *Hamilton*'s was the goddess Diana, though she looked to MacNeice more like a character out of *Pride and Prejudice*. The photographs of the shipwrecks were notable for their absence of wreckage. Both ships were upright, their masts still in position, cutlasses, sabres and boarding axes all neatly stowed. While the cannons had rolled about with the impact of the squall, they looked ready to roll back on command.

For the men caught below, there had been no hope. The water had rushed through the gun ports, over the sides and down the hatches, blocking their escape. Those who'd been on watch or sleeping on deck were likely washed overboard, where their only chance for survival was to swim for it or climb aboard the only lifeboat, itself full of water. Some knew how to swim but many others did not, and since the only floating debris was another man struggling to stay afloat, the loss of life was high.

He googled the recovery research that had been done when they were found, and was surprised to learn that the *Mary Rose*, King Henry VIII's flagship, was the first reference. When he and Kate were in Britain on their honeymoon, she had taken him to see it, or what was left of it, in an enormous permanent tent. The huge, skeletal remains rested under a perpetual shower of polyethylene glycol, a water-based wax solution. People in yellow rain gear climbed about on scaffolding doing research or checking for further decay, as the visitors looked on, somewhat bewildered, from the dry side of a Plexiglas wall. "She'd be sawdust in no time if they stopped," a young Australian seaman explained.

"The worms are dormant now, but they'd spring to life like maggots on a carcass if it stopped rainin' in there."

MacNeice shut down the computer. He had no interest in thinking about his honeymoon.

As he drove home along Main Street and up the narrow mountain road to the stone cottage, thoughts of his past ricocheted around his brain. As quickly as he'd hunt one down and banish it, another would appear. Parking in front of the cottage, he suddenly remembered making love to Kate on an island in Georgian Bay. Her flesh had seemed so alive to his touch and so smooth against the moss, lichen and grey rocks. Under cedars where the lower branches were dead and the bark was flaking off, she was whole and fresh and white. He could see the shadows of the branches tracing lines across her stomach and down her legs, and how she used one arm to shield her eyes from the sun. They'd just been swimming, and droplets of water beaded her lower belly—he'd kissed those first. He remembered her groan, coming from somewhere deep inside . . .

He worked hard to turn these memories off. When such images appeared, it helped MacNeice to think of a dark, crusty scab. It's never easy to let nature take its course during healing. You're always tempted to ease the itch and pick at the edges, but you can't stop till it's bleeding again—and then it takes even longer to heal. In his kitchen he opened a bottle of wine and sat down at the table so he was facing the fridge, fearful that if he were to look out to the forest that sloped away behind his home, those northern images of Kate would flood back and he wouldn't get to sleep. Or if he did, the all too familiar nightmares would wake him again.

MacNeice had hidden or removed everything in the place that reminded him of his dead wife, but there was no place to hide from the memories born of his relentlessly acute talent for observation. He recalled the smell of the sunblock on her skin as he leaned down to kiss her belly . . . He tried thinking about the sunken ships and drowning men, and that helped, and so did Charlie Haden singing "Wayfaring Stranger" on the stereo in the living room. At last the music slowly took the images of Kate away, leaving him weary enough to head to bed.

The call came at six in the morning.

"MacNeice."

"It's Bob. Just wanted you to know it'll all be in place by noon. I'll stay away, but I want regular reports."

"I take it you've spoken to the Deputy Chief?"

"Yes. Wallace told me how busy you guys are. I'll say this only to you, Mac, but if you need any additional resources to help on this, ask me and I'll deliver—that's a promise."

"You might wish you hadn't said that."

"Just clean this up."

"I'll do what I can."

He sat up in bed, yawned several times and realized that he'd dodged a bullet by not dreaming of Kate. Swinging his feet to the floor, he thought about calling Swetsky to ask for Vertesi back, but if the car and the columns were just discarded trash, there'd be no need. He'd just have to check it out.

# 2.

**M**acNeice was parked at the south end of a large party tent. Its sides were down and three burly guys in mock cop uniforms stood outside staring at him. Two of them looked like bouncers from the Boogy Bin, moonlighting for some extra cash.

His phone rang, and when he answered, DC Wallace said, "So, who do you need down there?"

"I don't know yet. This may be nothing but decades of extreme littering."

"What are you into the mayor for?"

"I honestly don't know, sir, but I'm about to find out." MacNeice climbed out of the car as he was speaking and opened the trunk, retrieving a pocket Maglite and a Sony digital camera from his battered briefcase.

"Let me know—I mean, if it's safe for me to know. I'm just as happy being ignorant."

"I'll call." He put the camera and flashlight in his jacket pocket and shut the trunk. As he approached the tent, two of the guards stepped forward to tell him it was a restricted site.

MacNeice pulled out his shield and said, "Detective Superintendent MacNeice. I'm looking for Howard Ellis."

"Right. He told us to expect you."

The man looked as if he spent too much time in the weight room. But then, if he was what MacNeice thought he was, his job was mostly about intimidation, and in that he succeeded. His partner looked more like a hockey player than a weightlifter, so solid in his uniform that if he sneezed, he'd blow the seams. The third guard was leaning against a rail cart talking on his phone. His stomach rolled over his belt and sweat had taken over his shirt. He glanced blankly towards MacNeice as he approached the entrance, then looked away.

"That's his trailer on the other side, isn't it?" He looked across at the trailers gleaming white in the morning sun and then at his watch: 8:43 a.m.

"Yeah, the one at the end. But he's been waiting for you in here."

"You're a bouncer at the Boogy Bin, aren't you."

"Yeah, Pete Zaminsky. Do I know you?"

"No."

"This is my day job—Donny's too." He nodded in the direction of the guard standing to MacNeice's left.

Zaminsky pulled open the flap and MacNeice was hit by a wave of cool air. It was like walking into an immense, bright white bubble. The scale of the tent made the columns on their rail carts look tiny. They had been pressure-hosed and were gleaming like bones, the paper from the Sonotubes gone. The Packard, now clean, showed signs amid the rust of its original black paint finish. Towards the rear of the tent, on the left, was a refrigeration truck with its motor running; a hose ran from the truck's exhaust under the tent's curtain to the outside. The lettering over the cab read LEBLANC

BROS. FISH COMPANY. MacNeice smiled—Maybank had discovered that the city's only mobile body cooler was full of bikers in Cayuga. Luc and Patrick LeBlanc were friends of his and Bob's from high school; he wondered what Maybank had promised them to get the use of the truck.

"That's Ellis over there by the car, the guy with the white helmet."

"Who's that beside him?"

"Don't know his name, but he arrived about an hour ago with an acetylene torch."

As the bouncer turned and walked back through the opening, Ellis came towards him like a kid eager to get on with an Easter egg hunt.

"Tell me, Mr. Ellis," MacNeice asked, "has anyone touched these things beyond getting them in here and cleaned?"

"No, sir. We pressure-hosed the muck off them, but that's it. The Packard's trunk is welded shut—that's why he's here." He nodded in the direction of the torch operator. "He's a firefighter. There's something in the back seat—hard to tell what through the windows. I've been waiting for you."

The car was still remarkably intact. Even the windows, though fogged with slime, were unbroken. "Apart from the flat tires, I've seen cars in worse shape on the street. How would you explain that?"

"When we did our first sampling of the bottom, we discovered roughly ten feet of gunk—a substance somewhere between coal tar, oil and axle grease. Back in the middle of the last century, the old freighters would discharge their bilge here. It was illegal, but the environment wasn't a concern back then. This car's been encased in that stuff for more than seven decades."

"But doesn't oil rise?"

"Yeah, sure, but with all the crap floating in here and the bay pushing in more . . . Well, after a while it turned into this really heavy gunk."

"Like dinosaurs in the tar pits."

"Exactly." Ellis seemed impressed by this imaginative leap. He was much more animated than he'd been the day before with the mayor.

MacNeice looked down at the licence plate. He could see that someone had been rubbing at it with a rag.

"Massachusetts 1936," Ellis said.

There was a pop, and the torch lit up with its blue-needle flame. "Good to go," the torch operator said.

"So go," MacNeice said.

Within minutes the trunk lid was loose. The operator shut the valve on the torch and lifted the lid away from the body of the car. For a moment the trunk's contents were difficult to decipher.

"Rags?" Ellis asked.

"No. Clothes on a body, or bodies. Look here." MacNeice pointed to a hand, lying near the wheel well. He pulled out his Maglite and shone it on a shred of leathery white flesh and pale grey bones frozen in a death grip. He took out his latex gloves and put them on. Before he touched anything, he took several photos of the contents of the trunk. As the torch operator moved around to ensure the doors would open, MacNeice said to him, "You've been briefed about what you've seen here?"

"Yep, I haven't seen a thing."

After he left, MacNeice said, "Mr. Ellis, can you get me as much clean tarpaulin as you can find?"

"No problem."

"Bring it to me and then leave me alone. I'm going to be a while."

MacNeice turned back to the Packard. He took several more images of the car, the licence plate, the trunk and its contents before putting the camera back in his hip pocket. Just as the mass of cloth before him was beginning to reveal its shape—the zigzag of legs, the folded torso—his cellphone rang.

"MacNeice." He stood up and looked over at the columns resting on the rail carts.

"Williams, sir. Wallace called to say you might need Vertesi. He's pretty tied up in Cayuga, but I'm downtown today. Can I help?"

"Yes. I'm at the end of the eastern dock of the steel company. There's a large tent with a private security team outside. Tell them you're here to see me. How quickly can you make it?"

"Fifteen minutes."

"Perfect." MacNeice dialled Mary Richardson's number, but before the connection could be made, his cell rang again.

"Mac, it's Bob. Tell me what we've got."

"I don't know about the columns yet, but there's a body in the trunk of the Packard, maybe two. I'm going to bring in Mary Richardson."

"Who's she again?"

"The city's pathologist."

"Is that a good idea? I mean, I want to contain this if I can."

"You can't, Bob. We don't *contain* homicides."

"Can you give me some time, though, before this blows open?"

"I can't speak for the pathologist."

"Then keep me posted. And, please, Mac, keep it as quiet as you can."

When he got through to Mary Richardson, she agreed to come alone.

Ellis returned, carrying a bright yellow tarpaulin. He dropped it on the concrete and wiped his shirt several times, though MacNeice couldn't see any evidence of dirt or dust. He paused, perhaps waiting to be invited to stay. MacNeice turned his focus to the trunk, and in a moment he heard Ellis sigh as he walked away.

When Williams arrived, he stopped just inside the tent, put his hands on his hips and looked about in amazement. MacNeice was leaning on the rear fender of the Packard with his arms crossed.

Williams scratched his head. "Where are we, boss? And what are we doing here? Nice wheels, but it could do with a new coat of paint and some tires."

"A Packard 120, lifted off the bottom."

"What's it got to do with us?"

"Absolutely nothing. There's a body or two in the trunk, but they've been down there, nestled in the muck, since this thing was new." Seeing that Williams was still confused, he went further. "Those columns over there—there might be bodies in them too."

"No shit."

"The concern isn't about the square columns. The two round ones at the end are more recent."

"Okay, I get it, this is a crime scene. But we've got our own pack of evildoers, so why are we here?"

"It's a favour, for now."

"Favour? 'Pick up my dry cleaning' is a favour. 'Come and check out these dead bodies we found in the bay'? Man, that's takin' some liberties in favourland. What do you want me to do?"

"Put your gloves on. Let's roll out the tarpaulin." MacNeice had gotten used to the young black detective's sense of humour; he accepted it in part because he found him to be intelligent and intuitive. MacNeice took one end of the bright yellow nylon tarp and Williams took the other, spreading it out flat on the pier.

Both men took off their jackets, folded them neatly and laid them at the far end of the tarp. Then they rolled up their shirt sleeves as they walked over to look in the trunk.

"Nice suit. Pinstriped, I think," Williams said, looking inside.

MacNeice took the right side, where the hand was, while Williams cradled the zigzag legs. "On three." It was surprisingly light but difficult to lift, the bones shifting and moving within the fabric. The left foot, still in its shoe, came off and fell back into the trunk.

Williams looked over at MacNeice. "Sorry, I lost the foot."

"No problem, I've lost his head. And look—he wasn't alone." He nodded back at the trunk, where another skeleton lay.

They laid the body gently on the yellow tarpaulin, still in its fetal position. The bones sagged with a soft clacking and then were silent. They went back to the trunk. The man's skull was lying against the frame, its jaw wide open. There was no skin or hair, just sad grey bone. MacNeice lifted it out, laid it in the correct position above the body and returned to the car. Williams had retrieved the foot and shoe and laid it beside the pant leg.

The other remains were female, wearing what had been a red and yellow striped summer dress. Judging by it and the shoes—which probably had been cherry red—she was young, in her late teens or twenties. There were shreds of leathery white flesh on the arms and legs. And her hands, like his, resembled frozen claws.

Williams tilted his head to look at the body.

Beside him, MacNeice said, "One summer morning, a long time ago, this girl woke up, put on that pretty dress and went out for the day, feeling terrific."

"Probably thought she'd ride up front too," Williams said softly.

Leaning into the trunk, MacNeice could see that the fabric on its roof had been torn—or clawed—not eroded by time and submersion. The car was beautifully made; they had been alive when they went into the trunk.

"Spooning," Williams said.

"Spooning? Ah, yes . . . Well, let's get her out of there." Behind her body was a small red handbag, its straps intact.

When they had the two lying side by side on the bright tarp, it was possible to imagine them as two young people in summer . . . but you had to squint really hard.

MacNeice took more photographs. "See what you can find inside the car," he told Williams. He squatted next to the dirty grey suit and white bones. He patted the jacket's exposed hip pocket—nothing. Nothing in the inside pockets or the pants pockets, and the fabric disintegrated with the intrusion.

"Got a big square case in the back seat," Williams called.

MacNeice took the purse and opened it. There wasn't much. With his pen he moved things about—a cigarette package, a tortoiseshell lighter with a flip top, lipstick, a small hand mirror and a membership card. He lifted it out. Brown, badly stained and fragile, it registered a Rosemary McKenzie for Wonderland, the outdoor dance palace that had stood for years at Parkdale and Main, in the city's east end. No wallet, keys or any other identification beyond the dancehall card.

"Jesus H—Boss, there's a kid in this thing!"

Williams stood back from the case lying open on the concrete and started to pace back and forth.

MacNeice walked over. At first glance it did look like a child of five or six. MacNeice looked more closely, then started to laugh.

"Tell me what's funny about that!" Williams was angry.

"It's a dummy, Montile. A ventriloquist's dummy."

"What the hell . . ." Williams came closer, too relieved to attempt to cover his embarrassment.

MacNeice closed the lid and rubbed the nameplate riveted on top. "The dummy's name is Archie. And here—look, below it—the ventriloquist . . ." He leaned back so his shadow didn't obscure the small capital letters. CHARLIE 'CHAS' GREENE. BOSTON, MASS.

"So that sorry fucker over there is probably Chas Greene."

"You've heard of him?"

"Nope."

"Someone can do the research on it. Not us."

Neither man had noticed that Mary Richardson had arrived. She was only a few feet from the tarpaulin when she spoke. "Gentlemen, can you introduce me to your friends here?"

MacNeice shot to his feet, embarrassed that someone could get that close without his noticing. "I believe her name is Rosemary McKenzie, and if this is his dummy, then he was Charlie Greene. They were in the trunk of the Packard."

"How long?"

"I assume since 1936 or 1937. I was hoping you could tell me."

"Not my job." She put down the black case and turned to look at the columns beyond him. "What have you got over there, Detective?"

"I'm not sure, but there are possibly more bodies in those columns."

"What do you want me to do?"

"Well, for starters, check out these two. We'll crack open these columns. The two round ones at the end are very recent."

"These two likely died of drowning or asphyxiation. I'll take a look but, for the record, I don't appreciate being called down here for this. I do wonder at your priorities, Detective." She was opening up her bag and retrieving what looked like large cutting shears.

"It's a favour for a friend." MacNeice walked over to the opening of the tent and asked the bouncer to find Ellis and the jackhammer operator.

The bouncer tried to look around MacNeice, curious to know what the woman with the black bag was doing.

"Ask them to come now," MacNeice said.

Williams was leaning across the front seat from the driver's side when MacNeice returned. "A Borsalino hat, a map of New York State and, best of all, the ownership, buried in the glove compartment," he called. "If it's his car, he's not Charlie Greene, he's Chaim Greenblatt."

"So Greene was his stage name," MacNeice said.

"Yeah, I guess so. Chas or Chaim—easy choice to make, especially in those days."

Richardson had cut off the tie and cut away what was left of the shirt, trousers and boxers, which were still intact. Before them was a skeleton, partly covered by what looked like white leather, and inside, bits of blackened, dried meat.

"Remarkable," Richardson said.

"How so?"

"Well, I would have expected bones, but flesh . . . and innards in any form"—she pointed with the end of the shears to the black mass inside the pelvis—"well, that's truly amazing. That trunk was an air-tight tomb."

"It was."

"She's in slightly better shape." Richardson nodded towards the remains of the girl. "An interesting study for Sheilagh Thomas, the medical anthropologist at Brant."

MacNeice reached for his notepad, and then realized it was in his jacket.

"Not to worry, Detective, I'll call her for you. Let me open the dress, and then, unless you have something else for me, I've got work to do back at the lab."

"Just the round columns, Doctor." On cue, the tent cover opened and Ellis appeared, with a huge man carrying a jackhammer over his shoulder as effortlessly as a teenager carries a baseball bat. MacNeice pointed in the direction of the two farthest columns and said, "We'll do the two at the end first." Ellis kept looking back at the scene unfolding around the Packard, while the man carrying the jackhammer appeared completely disinterested. MacNeice went back to Richardson, who was kneeling, shears in hand.

"She had lovely panties on. Pity to cut them," she said.

"Not the way she thought they'd come off when she put them on," MacNeice said under his breath. As Richardson cut, lacy fragments fell into the pelvis, where blackened ropelike masses lay. Next she cut the brittle straps of the bra and leaned closer.

"Thirty-four B. You can see the tag through the ribcage."

"When did they start sizing brassieres?"

"That's a good question. I have no idea."

"What's that around her neck?"

"A locket. I'll leave that to you. It's in the shape of a heart. Sweet. That mass lying on the bottom of the dress . . ."

"Yes?"

"Her heart. The clumps on either side that look like large dried teabags, those are her lungs. Not much else to talk about, I'm afraid, though Dr. Thomas will no doubt be fascinated by both of them."

# 3.

NTRODUCED SIMPLY AS August, the Lithuanian with the solemn eyes wheeled the jackhammer generator into place next to the first column. He handed MacNeice a thick black marker. "You, show me where to cut."

MacNeice took the marker and made a line straight across the middle of the column. August flipped up the operating panel on the generator, put on his goggles and helmet and waved to MacNeice and Ellis. "Stand back. When I stop hammer, you can come."

"Do you want my helmet, detective?" Ellis asked.

"I'll be fine, thank you." They walked fifteen feet away and watched as August attached the power cord. As the jackhammer rattled noisily to life, MacNeice resisted the urge to put his hands over his ears. August made the first incision, holding the hammer at chest height.

"Incredible, eh? He uses it like a scalpel," Ellis shouted over the din.

MacNeice smiled briefly and nodded.

A minute later, August pulled away the jackhammer and let it idle. He waved to MacNeice to come forward. To his eye, there was nothing to be seen in the concrete but more concrete. "Nothing there?"

"Yes, something there," August said, pointing to the column.

"How can you tell?"

"Too soft, not right. Come out like angel cake. You want send lady away?"

"Oh no, she's here to see this. Don't worry, that's her job." .

"Bad job," he said, looking at Richardson. "Okay, stay back. I work both sides."

If they weren't so clearly horrific, some scenes could be hysterically funny. The sight of a large male torso suspended between two jagged sections of concrete—legs protruding from Bermuda shorts buried in one end, head and shoulders in the other—sent Montile Williams into peals of laughter, which faded quickly when he caught the whiff of decomposition.

MacNeice could see that Ellis was upset by what he considered disrespectful behaviour, so he asked him to leave. The fact was, Ellis had no place being there anyway.

"Like popping out of cake," August said. "You want me do top or bottom? Or go to next column?"

"Do the feet now, then the head. Ellis said you can use that like a scalpel—well, now's the time. Once we've freed him, we'll move on to the next one."

August was soon carving around the legs, and again the concrete broke away easily from the body. One, then the other leg dropped, causing the whole torso to sag. It was difficult to tell if this was a fat man with skinny legs or a slim man whose torso had expanded from the terrible gases and decay bottled up within. Judging by the lack of stress on the Bermuda shorts, he assumed it was the former, but the smell suggested that both theories could be accurate.

Great chunks of concrete now littered the surface of the dock.

MacNeice heard Williams choke back another laugh. He turned to him, warning, "Don't start, not again." He took out his camera and shot several frames. Looking over to Richardson, he asked, "How long do you think he's been in there?"

"Not long—a year, maybe more. I'm not going to do an autopsy here, MacNeice. Let me get him to the lab."

"If there's a body in that other column, we'll take them to the morgue in the fish truck."

August started the jackhammer, then etched a controlled line lengthwise up the body. On his second pass, the right side gave way, revealing a chest, shoulder, arms and part of the neck. He continued to etch and drill, and in minutes the body was lying flat on the cart. August brushed away the larger fragments, put down the jackhammer and went to reposition the generator near the other round column.

There was a large-calibre entry wound in the forehead of a tall, fat man in his mid- to late fifties. He wore a yellow shirt, stained black with gore, atop jungle-patterned Bermuda shorts. A rope was attached to his arms, looping around his wrists and tethered to his neck before extending above his head, presumably to hold him in place while the concrete was poured. His tongue, like a large bubble of brown chewing gum, filled the space between the lips of his open mouth.

"Know him?" Williams asked, looking down at the face.

"No, but I don't think he was a dentist," MacNeice said, taking several more images, full-body and close-up.

"Meaning?" Richardson asked.

"Meaning he looks like central casting's ideal for a heavy."

Richardson put down her bag and was soon measuring the size of the entry wound—.44 calibre—and inspecting the mouth, eyes and ears. "My guess, eighteen months."

"You want to draw next one?" August asked as MacNeice and Williams approached the remaining column.

"No, do it just as you did the first," MacNeice said.

"Thanks to the city for the air conditioning, boss, but if there's another one in there, I need to get something to cover my nose." Williams said. The terrible stench had drained all the humour out of him. August looked back at MacNeice. "I do other two later. Need to eat lunch away from here."

"Thank you, August. And please don't talk about what you've seen."

"Not interested in this. Not healthy talk." He lowered his goggles and started the hammer.

The second body hadn't fared as well as the first. The man was wearing a black T-shirt and slacks; judging by the long black hair and lanky body, he appeared to be a man in his thirties. His face had been removed back to the ears—sheared off. No forehead, eyes, nose, mouth or chin; even the interior of his skull had been emptied. The rope used to suspend him for pouring the concrete was attached to his arms from behind, which had forced his shoulders so far forward they'd dislocated. The hands and feet had also been removed, and the flesh on the inside of both forearms had been sliced off down to the bone.

"Tattoos?" Williams said.

"Probably. An identifier, like the face and hands." MacNeice turned to Richardson, who was retrieving a large magnifying glass from her case. "Odd—they didn't mind us identifying the first one but they don't want us to know who this was."

"We'll do what we can with what we've got." Richardson studied the arm and then lifted it up to study the severing wound at the wrist. "An electric knife."

Williams's head snapped towards her.

"A double-bladed carving knife, like you would use on a large turkey. Serrated blades that saw back and forth at high speed. I think he was bled clean before he was inserted into the tube. The other one, not."

"Butchered with his clothes on," Williams said.

MacNeice started taking photos, recording the mutilation in detail as well as wider shots of the remains.

"If I can interrupt, gentlemen, I'd best be getting back. I don't have a car—Junior dropped me—but I'm open to suggestions."

MacNeice told Williams to give Richardson his keys and to follow in the fish truck when they got the bodies loaded. The pathologist packed up and without another word left the tent. MacNeice patted the pockets of the cadaver's pants and noted that he had no ID either. They cut two sections from the tarp, wrapped each body as carefully as possible and laid them in the near-freezing fish truck. As Zaminsky opened the tent to let the truck out, MacNeice's phone rang. Stepping out the north-end door to the bay, he inhaled deeply for the first time in a while.

"MacNeice," he said, watching a lake freighter make its way slowly through the canal, gulls circling in its wake, hoping to find something churned up by the props.

"What have you got?" the mayor asked.

"Two recent homicides in the round columns. If we're true to form, there'll be two more in the square columns, but they'll be much older. Dr. Sheilagh Thomas from the university will be here to collect those, and two from the trunk of the car."

"Christ, it's a cast of thousands. Can I get time before this blows up?"

"No. LeBlanc's Fish just left with the two freshest. It'll soon be out of the bag, if it isn't already. Just stay ahead of it. Don't try to massage it."

"Or sugarcoat it." The mayor was getting the picture.

"There's no sugarcoating these guys. One has a huge hole in his forehead and the other doesn't have a forehead—or a face, hands or feet. Richardson guesses they've been down there roughly eighteen months. Isn't that when you started pitching this project?" He was looking down at the broken surface of the dock, marvelling at the tiny flowering plants growing through cracks in the concrete.

"Jesus, yes. Okay, try to keep a lid on it for a day or so."

MacNeice put the phone back in his pocket and looked for the freighter, but it was gone. He thought about what would happen if the cops stopped Williams—in LeBlanc's truck, with two corpses instead of lake trout in the freezer. It made him smile as he entered the tent again. The air conditioners seemed to be whining, struggling to rid the place of the heavy smell of rotting men. As he walked over to get his jacket, he glanced back at the two bodies on the tarp. Asleep, deeply asleep.

Outside, MacNeice walked to the edge of the dock. The vertical drop made him feel nauseated, and the two-by-four construction barrier gave him very little confidence that he wouldn't fall in. All activity below had ceased; there were a few large puddles, but otherwise the dock was more or less dry and flat. Grey gulls were spiralling downward and landing on the rough slate floor, where they walked about searching for food. It suddenly occurred to him what a massive volume of space this was. From there it didn't take long before he was wondering how much concrete it would take to build the new Museum of the Great Lakes.

As he was leaving, he told Zaminsky that it was okay to admit a Dr. Sheilagh Thomas and August the jackhammer man, but no one else. If there were issues, he was to call at once. MacNeice handed him a card. "By the way, who called in your firm?"

"We're brought in by the insurers of this project. We were told that security had to be trusted. We can be trusted."

"I don't doubt it. Keep it tight."

"Word." It looked as if Zaminsky would go for a high-five, but he settled for a handshake.

# 4.

DRIVING WEST ALONG King Street, MacNeice realized he was famished and headed to Marcello's. Stopped at a light, he took out the black CD wallet and flipped through the leaves till he found the Brahms piano concerto. It was Kate's favourite. He kept it near him for a myriad of reasons, and today it had the right mood, a river of melody that never failed to carry him somewhere else. Music was a gift—he had given her jazz, she had given him classical, and both remained a safe haven and neutral territory.

Pulling into the parking space behind the restaurant, he turned off the engine and waited as the piano made its entrance. MacNeice left the car and went inside, the music lingering in his head.

"Calamari and pasta pomodoro," he said, when Marcello came to take his order. "Tell me something, March, strictly between us. When an Italian mobster kills someone, is it normal, or even conceivable, that they'd remove the face, hands and feet before sinking him in concrete?"

"Some Italians would. Calabrians, no. We prefer a shot to the head and then just walk away. You want Shiraz or something lighter to go with the calamari? I'll order them grilled, not *fritti*—you okay with that?"

"Grilled's fine and Shiraz will do."

"Yeah, so in my town, San Giorgio, there are white circles. Yeah, you see them around in every kind of place—outside the bakery, city hall, the police station, the church—wherever."

"What are they for?"

"They mark where someone was shot. Just shot—*bang!* The shooter walks away. But to cut someone up, that's Naples. Neapolitans, they like chopping people up—making a statement."

"A statement?"

"Yeah, you see bits, chunks, of someone you knew—maybe you were related to them or loved them—and you think twice about life. But you know, the Russian mobs are worse than any in Naples. I'll get the Shiraz. Sparkling water too?"

"Perfect."

MacNeice was wrestling with the idea that someone would go to the trouble of sinking a body into the bay knowing that someday it would come up again to bring the "statement" home. *That's patience—a concrete time capsule with no fixed opening date—just sublime patience and serendipity. That's sophisticated.* If the plan for the steel company's eastern dock had been known, then known too was the moment—give or take—of the opening of the time capsule. It was brilliant, and twisted.

As Marcello passed by, MacNeice stopped him. "Tell me, if I were to ask someone from Naples the same question, is it possible they'd agree? Or would they say something like, 'Not us, no. But those crazy Calabrians—man, they're the worst'?"

"Yeah, probably." Marcello erupted in a full body laugh and slapped his shoulder, then carried on to the kitchen.

After lunch, feeling somewhat renewed, MacNeice headed down to the morgue. As Richardson was about to be inundated with bodies from Cayuga, he was counting on first-come, first-served for the pair from the waterfront.

Walking along the white-tiled subterranean corridor always made him uneasy, but as he neared the double stainless doors, he could hear classical music—Bach, one of the Brandenburg concertos. He leaned his shoulder into a door and went in. Richardson swung around from the gurney and greeted him. "Just in time. Right, Junior?"

"Right," said Junior, with his creepy smile that suggested he liked his work too much. MacNeice had never seen Richardson's young lab assistant when he wasn't wearing his whites and those tall grey rubber boots. Clearly his job included hosing the gore from the red-tiled floor, which was spotless and glistening wet.

He wasn't looking forward to seeing "No-Face," as Richardson had dubbed him, but this time at least he was no-face down.

Returning from her office, where she'd turned down the music, she said, "We've found something I think you'll find interesting." She pulled the long hair away from the base of the skull, where she'd shaved a patch to reveal a small blue tattoo. Nine numbers—177126619—a serial number. On the lower back there was also a small scar from an entry wound, probably a .22 calibre; Richardson thought it had been there for years. She was guessing the contents of No-Face's stomach—beer and a cheeseburger—but would confirm that with further analysis.

"Anything else?" MacNeice asked.

"He had an impressive hood ornament," Junior said under his breath, and snickered.

"I'm sorry?"

"He was very well endowed, Detective," Richardson answered, shooting a withering look Junior's way.

"Right. Anything on Bermuda Shorts?"

"Not yet."

As he left the building, MacNeice thought about how even brilliantly committed homicides could be undone by equally brilliant twists of fate. No one would think to check under a man's hair for a hidden tattoo . . . and that's when it hit him. The tattoo had likely been put there at a time when it would be visible. *He's a convict or a soldier—a man living among men with shaved heads.*

Sitting in the Chevy, he took out his phone and punched in a number. "Swetsky, it's Mac."

"Whaddya need, brother?"

"Two men. I've got a couple of bodies dredged up from the bay."

Swetsky covered the mouthpiece and yelled at someone. MacNeice pulled the phone away; he disliked the sensation that his right ear was underwater.

"You've got Williams. You want Vertesi back too?"

"If possible, yes."

Swetsky covered the phone again during another short burst of yelling, and then he was back. "No problem. I'll make do with Palmer and the two DIs from the west end. Truth is, I got so many cops out here it's hard to get any police work done. I'm more a traffic cop than a detective."

"I can imagine. It's a huge case, Swets."

"We'll be okay. I'll send Vertesi back tonight."

Driving back to Division, MacNeice made two more calls, the first to Wallace to tell him he had reassigned the two DIs, and the second to Bob Maybank, to collect on his promise. He wanted immediate resources to hire a researcher and would let the mayor know when he'd found one. Maybank listened quietly, and when MacNeice had finished his pitch, he said, "Done."

He had no sooner pulled into the division parking lot than he turned around, put the red cherry on the dash and sped along Main

Street, heading back to the eastern dock. As he entered the worksite, he stowed the cherry under the dash. It was 5:16 p.m., and he could see Ellis walking to his car, briefcase and white helmet in hand. MacNeice pulled up beside him just as he reached his silver Volvo. He cranked down his window.

"Question for you, Ellis."

"What is it?" He seemed impatient to get going.

"How much concrete will this project use?"

"That's a big question. The easy answer is, a lot. A lot of concrete." He opened the door and put his briefcase and helmet on the passenger seat.

"Has the contract been assigned to a local firm?"

"There are several kinds of concrete needed on this project, and three firms won the bids to provide them. For a better idea of how they're split, you should go see the model in Terence Young's office. He'll give you all the details you need." Ellis told him where to find the architect's office and got into his car.

The reception room was a symphony of black leather and chrome, with models of buildings on stands like art in a museum. But Young's office was even more of a statement: dark grey walls, a sleek low desk, black leather sofa, matching armchairs and a wall of glass that overlooked the bay.

"What do you want to know about the project, Detective?" Young asked, leaning against his desk.

"I have a basic knowledge of what this project is, but I need more detail."

Young went on at length about the new technology that would allow them to lift the ships and transport them in their refrigerated state. He moved to a large grey model of the eastern wharf. "The wharf is 380 yards long, 100 feet wide and 60 feet deep. The building you're looking at will rise another five storeys above grade for a total of ten storeys." The ships would be housed in large tanks of fresh water kept at the same temperature as their current resting place.

"Tell me more about the actual building."

"Well, as the name suggests, the Museum of the Great Lakes will be an orientation and interpretive history centre that places the War of 1812 in the larger context of what was happening in the world beyond—Napoleon, Wellington, even Beethoven—to get North Americans to understand that this was much bigger than a regional conflict." He swung out the end of the model table, which split lengthwise to reveal cutaways on both sides. "It'll be like Santa's Village—you go through the development of human life on the lakes, the whole history of the war, and then you arrive at the ships, housed in this huge water tank." A light came on in the model schooner aquarium, enveloping the ships in ghostly blue-grey. Hundreds of tiny plastic figures lined the glass wall, looking at the ships from three levels. In scale they appeared only yards away from the wrecks.

"Santa's Village . . . and Beethoven."

"Sure, he composed 'Wellington's Victory' in 1813, as the crews on these ships were living and dying."

While MacNeice did find it fascinating, he had come for another reason. "Tell me about the concrete contracts. I understand there are three firms involved. Was it an open bid?"

"To everyone within fifty miles. The government wanted it to be local for all kinds of reasons, job creation being one, but also environmental. The winning bids went to Mancini Concrete, not far from here, McNamara in Waterdown and ABC Canada–Grimsby." These companies would supply Smith-Deklin, the subcontractor that had won the bid for pouring. "It'll take thousands of tons of concrete to complete this project, and the steel company will benefit as well, perhaps even more."

"By supplying structural steel?"

"That certainly, but also the rebar for the concrete. This will be a major undertaking simply because of the enormous water tank and the robust structure required to maintain its integrity."

"Who were the losers in the concrete competition?"

"DeLillo, out of Buffalo–Fort Erie. They were scooped by ABC and probably weren't too happy about it. ABC's also American; they bought up a failing business in Grimsby in order to bid."

"Isn't there an international law against disturbing marine war graves?"

Young smiled and said those issues had disappeared when Ronald Reagan signed into law—and Congress approved—an agreement that Canada could raise the ships. "Once his signature was in place, there was and is no erasing it, even though it's now decades later." The President had stipulated that the remains of the crews would be repatriated to either Arlington or Annapolis for burial with full military honours.

MacNeice studied the model, peering into the various floors of exhibits on early North America, the Aboriginal and French halls, the United Empire Loyalists, who had swept through the area to claim land in the wake of America's Declaration of Independence from Britain. Slab after slab—floors, walls, exterior walls—the place was a marvel of concrete. Even the solar energy panels, curved to capture the sun's movement across the sky, were mounted on concrete wings.

Later, in his living room, MacNeice poured himself a double grappa and studied the tall, slender bottle of clear liquid against the light. Over the past four years grappa had become his most constant evening companion. Tonight he considered how appropriate that was—a forty-proof salvation wrung from the last dregs of the vine—such pleasure, born of such pain.

# 5.

THEY HAD BEEN fighting, he couldn't remember about what, but it was enough of a fight to separate them in a town neither of them knew. It was dark; there was no moon and MacNeice thought he knew the way back. There was something intangible and threatening about the place, and the more MacNeice walked, staying to the middle of the road, the more he felt it. He had lost her but was counting on her sense of direction—besides, there'd be no point in retracing his footsteps, he told himself, since he couldn't see where he'd been anymore than where he was going. It was strange to be in town without any streetlights. *A blind man sees nothing*, he said to himself.

At a cul-de-sac, MacNeice discovered a dirt path. It was well worn, or so it felt underfoot. Walking slowly along the path, opening his eyes as wide as possible in an attempt to allow more light in, he came to a waist-high wire fence. Beyond it, the ground dropped off vertically to a ledge fifteen or twenty feet below. Beyond that he could see nothing. Looking around for another way out, he discovered an irregular and very narrow path between a dark brick wall—perhaps it was a building—and the fence. He pushed on the fence and found that it was barely secured by posts in the ground on either side. It was as if someone had been working it loose.

MacNeice knelt down, both to keep his imagination from throwing him over the fence and to collect his thoughts. He could go back, but to what? He'd never felt such a fear of the unknown, as a cop or as a tourist. He tried to steady his breathing and kept looking for some light, some sense of what lay beyond the narrow path.

He remembered hiking with his father when he was ten. They had gone out hunting for grouse. Miles from their cottage, a storm descended on them, and the late October afternoon suddenly became as dark as midnight. His father said, "Use the sky, Mac. Use the sky. Shapes will appear and you won't be frightened."

He stared again, trying to find it, but there seemed to be no distinction between the earth and the sky, just the flimsy wire fence and the darkness beyond. He studied the brick wall to see if anything was lurking in the shadows, and that's when he heard it.

Someone was coming up behind him, running wildly, breathing heavily, as if they'd been running for a long time—away from or towards someone. The sounds grew louder but he still couldn't see anything. MacNeice stiffened for the impact and waited. He told himself that he'd stand up quickly and start swinging his fists; he told himself he'd have to push back, or the runner's forward momentum would carry them both over the edge.

He clenched his fists, widened his eyes and was about to throw himself at the runner when he suddenly saw that it was Kate. He let out a yell, but she was on him and past him so fast that she hit the fence and toppled over into the void. The sound of her breathing stopped when she fell.

MacNeice leapt up in time to see her land on her stomach, close to the edge. She was stunned by the fall, and she turned to look at him. But before he could call out, "Don't move!" she rolled the wrong way and disappeared over the edge without a sound.

MacNeice screamed and tore at the fencing till it came away in his hands.

He awoke in a sweat, breathing heavily in the blackness of his bedroom. Instinctively he reached over to Kate's side of the bed. Gasping for air, he wept, and couldn't make out whether it was because of the dream or because she wasn't there.

When he'd calmed down enough that the dream had faded to being just a dream, he sat in bed wondering what to make of it. It was a mug's game trying to figure these things out, but still, he wondered.

It was the only dream in which he'd actually seen her, even if only in the moment when she ran past him and fell, and again, briefly, on the ledge before she disappeared. For years, in countless other dreams, he would hunt for her, catch a glimpse of her as she turned a corner—just her leg or her back, perhaps—but when he got there, she would be gone. Or he'd smell her perfume, hear a door shut, see the shiver of the window sheers, just feel her presence, but he'd never actually see her. This one was more terrifying because he could have saved her and didn't. What's the only conclusion one could draw from such a dream? He wondered, but in truth he knew the answer—he'd failed her.

He looked at the clock radio—4:10 a.m. Rather than risk sliding back into the dream and picking at the scab again, he got out of bed, went into the washroom and turned on the shower.

# 6.

**M**ACNEICE ARRIVED AT Division early, to find both men waiting in his cubicle. It was clear from the look of disbelief on Vertesi's face that Williams had been describing the previous day's drama on the dock. MacNeice dropped his jacket on his chair and went to retrieve the large whiteboard from the storage room. Sliding it into place, he picked up a red marker and wrote CONCRETE.

Vertesi opened his notebook.

"Concrete," MacNeice said as he wrote it on the whiteboard. "The *Hamilton-Scourge* Project is going to need a lot of concrete. We've got three winning bids. I want to know all about them, and about the loser, and who approved the bids." Below it, he wrote *Winners: Mancini—Dundurn, McNamara—Waterdown, ABC-Grimsby—New York*. Below, separated by a line, *Loser: DeLillo—Fort Erie–Buffalo*.

"You think in an economy where nobody's pouring concrete, the mob is still in the concrete business?" Williams asked.

"I think the waterfront project is like heavy rain hitting a dry creekbed. In short order, life springs up everywhere. Within a week or two there are wildflowers, weeds, tadpoles and snakes, all competing for a piece of it. And you look at it and think the creek always looked that way."

"Out of interest, how much concrete are we talking about?" Vertesi asked.

"Thousands of tons."

"I know the Mancini family," Vertesi said. "I'll talk to Alberto. He's the founder and still the CEO."

"I thought you might know them," MacNeice said. "Also, I think we're going to need a researcher, and I was thinking about Ryan, the young tech-head downstairs."

"Aces! He's going out of his mind with those forensics geeks. He built a whole rig of computers and they have him looking up chemical formulas. Definitely give him a shot," Williams said.

Turning back to the whiteboard, MacNeice transcribed the tattoo numbers from his notebook. While there might be more bodies in the square columns, they would focus on the two freshest. Assuming the mutilation of the second body was done to eliminate the possibility of identification, and not strictly for the thrill of carving someone up, the discovery of the tattoo was significant.

"Williams, start researching serial numbers for the Canadian military and prison systems, and if they don't pan out, go to their American equivalents. Send images of Bermuda Shorts to police forces across North America. I'll make the call to Wallace concerning Ryan before I head down to see what's popped out of the other two columns."

"Just a question, boss—how can you hire someone in the middle of a hiring freeze?" Williams asked.

MacNeice smiled. "Let's just say I have a genie. I don't know for how long or for how many wishes, but I intend to use him while I can. Strictly speaking, however, this is a temporary redeployment of existing personnel, not a new hire."

# 7.

THE FRONT OFFICE of Mancini Concrete was as Vertesi had imagined it would be: a wooden counter against which, over the years, countless heavyset men had stood and negotiated tonnage rates and delivery schedules, wearing away the plywood surface and its bullnose edge to raw pine. Behind the counter were four grey solid metal desks cluttered with paper, large binders, Rolodexes, ancient computers, coffee mugs, telephones, cellphones and desk calendars. On three of the desks sat model cement trucks with Mancini's logo in red block letters on the driver's door and on the white ready-mix drum. Covering everything—including, Vertesi thought, the men who staffed the desks—was a thin dusting of fine powder, likely unavoidable given the busy yard outside, with trucks coming and going from six in the morning till six at night. Along one wall of the office was a shelving unit with a work surface lost under dusty rolls of blueprints and flattened architectural drawings that looked as if they'd gone undisturbed for years. The scene put Vertesi in mind of images of Pompeii and its inhabitants after the volcano.

A fifth desk, set apart from the others and closest to the back wall, had on it a telephone, a laptop and mouse pad and a red model Ferrari as large as the cement trucks, its yellow stallion logo visible to Vertesi from fifteen feet away; he assumed it was the desk of Alberto's only son, Pat. Though they were contemporaries, they weren't friends. Michael Vertesi had gone to the local Catholic high school, while Pat Mancini had gone to St. Michael's in Toronto for the hockey program and from there to Junior A. He was big and fast, and it was assumed by everyone that he'd have a long career in the NHL. Pat had been typecast as a heavy, but after several stellar seasons and one too many concussions, he—or the NHL—had called it quits. No one knew the exact details, but he had quietly come back to work in his family's concrete business. Friends—Italian hockey fanatics—told Vertesi that Mancini had been miscast, that he was actually a finesse player who just happened to be big. On the ice he was targeted as a goon. For them that was an insult to the Italian community of Dundurn.

Catching the eye of one of the salesmen, Vertesi asked, "You leasing Ferraris now?" He nodded in the direction of the back desk.

"That? Nah, that's Pat's toy car. We stick to concrete here."

Vertesi registered the man's disdain and could easily imagine how he would resent the owner's son—a young man who'd never worked in the business—suddenly taking over the best desk and installing a model of a $250,000 car on it. As he was thinking about the impact that would have on these men who spent their lives covered in dust, the door to the back office opened. Pat Mancini motioned for him to come through. Without acknowledging the detective, the concrete salesman at the counter lifted the movable section and with his foot swung the lower door open. "Thank you," Michael said, to no response. He walked past another salesman sitting at his desk, who glanced up at him, a dusty black telephone cradled on his shoulder.

"How you doin'? Pat Mancini." Mancini reached out and took Vertesi's hand in his steely grip.

"I'm doing okay. We've met before. I'm Michael Vertesi." Vertesi walked into the office as Alberto stood to greet him from behind his desk. He had a full head of white hair, a sculpted face with bright blue eyes and deep lines from his cheekbones to his jaw. He was wearing a grey suit, a white shirt and a narrow blue tie that made his eyes seem even brighter.

"Michael, how's your dad?" They shook hands and exchanged brief pleasantries about Christmas visits past, then the older man offered Vertesi one of the two chairs in front of the desk. Pat sat in the other. Beige blinds covered the windows; a desk lamp and two standing lamps provided light quite different from the sunlight and fluorescent brightness of the front office. This could have been anywhere but a concrete yard. The walls were dressed in dark oak panelling with a variety of framed industry and civic awards hanging side by side. To the left was a leather sofa with two matching club chairs arranged around a coffee table on an Oriental carpet. On the table were two used espresso cups, a small plate of chocolate wafers and a vase with six red roses. Near the desk stood an elegant wooden trolley with several types of glasses and three rows of wine and spirits. There wasn't a computer in the room.

Mancini sat with his arms on the desk, one hand resting gently over the other. "I heard you were shot last year, but I see you've recovered."

"Yes, I have."

"I remember," Pat said. "A shotgun to the gut, right?" His lip tugged down on the left side; he nodded briefly and shifted in his chair.

"In the side, yes, but I'm fine."

"A mangia-cake called Michael a wop!" Alberto said to his son.

"No shit?" Pat leaned forward, a wide grin on his face. Michael could see a thin white scar, a lazy S across the bottom of his chin.

"No shit." Vertesi took out his notebook and pen to indicate this wasn't a social call.

"Well, you give my regards to your pop, Michael, and your mother."

"I will, sir. Thank you."

"What did you want to discuss?"

"The *Hamilton-Scourge* Project for the eastern wharf, and the bid to supply concrete."

"What do you want to know about it?"

"Well, sir—"

"Please, call me Alberto." His smile was as gentle as the Pope's and he opened his hands in the same manner—showering grace on the flowers of the church.

"Thank you, Alberto." He couldn't help but be touched and was certain his face showed it. Long ago, when their families would get together after Mass on Sundays, he had been taught to address his elders formally, and nothing had changed—until now. "We've found bodies at the bottom of the wharf, two of them recent, the others decades old."

"So it's true!"

"If you mean the urban myth, yes, it's true."

"What's that got to do with us, Michael?" Alberto's hands were relaxed, but the top one rose slightly with the question.

"Two of the bodies were dumped in concrete columns at roughly the same time as the bidding for this project was happening."

"What's your point?" Pat asked. He looked quickly at his father as if to measure how aggressive he should be, but there was no help there. Alberto could have been listening to the weather report from Saskatoon.

"Because our families know each other, Alberto, I thought I'd ask you if—"

"If I'd offed the guys and dumped them there." No longer the Pope, Alberto spoke with icy sarcasm.

"No, sir, I want to know if there was anything you noticed during the bidding that might have led to these men being killed."

"Son, this isn't the twenties. We're all businessmen. We compete. We win, lose, break even, score big or don't score at all. It's business, and at night we all go home for dinner." Nothing about the father appeared defensive or insecure.

"Maybe I'm a bit slow, but are you accusing my dad of killing people?" Pat Mancini turned in his chair so he was more or less facing Vertesi. There was an unfocused energy about the man, as if he had difficulty sitting still, or difficulty living in his own skin.

Vertesi looked directly at the son and answered. "No, Pat, not at all." Turning back to the father, he asked, "There are three suppliers, two in addition to Mancini. Do you know the principals of the other firms?"

"McNamara, yes. 'The Irish' we call them. The other is an American firm; they won a portion strictly for the . . . what do you call it?" He looked to his son, whose face was blank. "The optics. Politics. The Americans have a stake in this show, since the two ships were technically theirs, so they won a third. But they bought a Canadian business in Grimsby that was going under, so their piece is good for both countries."

"Is that substantial?"

"In this economy, supplying a third of a project this size is huge," Pat said, looking at his father.

"Look, we couldn't have handled the whole project and kept it on schedule," Alberto said. "I don't even think the Irish and Mancini together could have done it. Remember, the city's got a deadline they're trying to hit. We needed a third supplier."

"Are you happy with the third they've chosen?"

The old man unfolded his arms and made the slow slicing

movement with his hands that all Italian males revert to in conversation. "I don't make the rules, Michael . . ."

"Do you know if McNamara felt the same way, or whether they might have been more concerned about an American supplier taking a third of the project?"

"Well, Americans aren't doing the work; they're just taking the profit."

"What are the chances that ABC Canada's parent company will shut down the Grimsby operation when this project is finished and take its principal assets back to head office in New York State?"

"We're in the concrete business, not the speculation business. Apart from the quarry, there wasn't enough to keep them going before ABC came in. It's anybody's guess." He checked his watch, then pulled down his sleeve.

"Was another contender for the purchase of the Grimsby operation edged out by ABC?"

"He asks good questions, Patrizio, you see that?" Alberto smiled at his son before turning back to Vertesi. "*Si, si,* now you have an interesting path to follow. But you must do your homework." Alberto stood up. "I'm sorry, I have to go to a meeting outside the office. If you have any more questions, call me." He walked over to the vase of roses, chose one, snapped its stem and inserted the bloom in his jacket buttonhole, dropping the broken stem into the bin under his desk. He looked every inch the distinguished president of a concrete firm.

"One last question: is there a legitimate fourth competitor for this project within fifty miles of the site?"

Coming around the desk, Alberto took Vertesi's hand in both of his. "Not precisely, no." With a hand on Vertesi's shoulder, he led him to his office door. "Pat will see you out. *Ciao,* Michael, and take care of yourself."

Pat stood up to usher Vertesi to the front door. "You park outside?"

"Yes, just to the left."

"You'll need a car wash after this; it's a bitch on a good paint job. You driving standard issue?"

"All the way."

"What is it now? A beefed-up Chevy, or have they sucked you into driving a hybrid for the *optics* of it?"

"Not yet—a Chevy it is. Thank you, Pat. Good to see you back in town."

"Yeah, not much choice. Did I know you?"

"Not really, just when we'd go to your place around Christmas time. When we were kids."

"Sure as shit aren't kids anymore. Mike, a word to the wise: we take care of our own, no complaints that way. *Ciao* for now." Pat shook his hand, harder this time, and held the door open for a second after he left. Vertesi could feel the younger Mancini's eyes still on him as he waited in his car for two cement trucks to turn into the driveway of the yard.

# 8.

MacNEICE PARKED THE Chevy next to an old Land Rover, one of the ones built before the company decided to become groovy. On the hood the pale blue paint was worn down to the primer, and the interior was a mess. The back seat was littered with papers, a tennis racquet, a pair of white scuffed court shoes, a hand shovel, some whisks and brushes, several binders with the university logo on the cover, and on the floor, at least a dozen paper coffee cups. On the front passenger seat were six or seven CDs without covers; he couldn't make out what they were. To finish it off, a jiggly plastic Hawaiian girl with a lei and a grass skirt was mounted on the dash under the rear-view mirror. MacNeice smiled. *No Good Housekeeping Seal for this puppy*, he thought. He put on his jacket and walked over to the tent. A new team of security guards was stationed outside, looking considerably keener than the last, which wasn't saying much. MacNeice pulled out his badge and the guard on the door nodded and opened up for him, adding perfunctorily, "She's expecting you."

Once inside, he let his eyes adjust to the brightness. What was left of the two round columns had been taken away to the lab for examination; the bodies next to the Packard were gone, and there were obvious signs that August had opened the square columns. Next to the third rail cart, a woman in worn, baggy jeans and a T-shirt stood looking at him. She was slim, with a mop of grey-brown hair that looked as if she spent as much time at the hairdresser as she did at the car wash.

"Detective Superintendent MacNeice. This is your show, I understand." She had dancing eyes, a smoker's voice—low, gravelly and strong—and an unmistakable British accent. *What is it*, he thought, *with female Brits and dead bodies?*

"What do you make of it so far?" she said, and then added, "Sheilagh Thomas, by the way. Pleased to meet you finally. Mary thinks you're the brightest bulb on the homicide tree."

MacNeice shrugged off the compliment. "I was going to ask you that very question, Doctor. What do you make of them?"

"P.F., they've been at the bottom roughly seventy to eighty years, died at the same time more or less, and what you see on the rail trolleys is only what came away from the concrete—"

"P.F.?"

"Oh, simply *post facto*—and I should also tell you I think their age at time of death was roughly twenty-eight for Harry here"—she patted a thigh bone—"and perhaps thirty-two for Arthur. Though once we get the matter cleaned off the concrete and we scope these bones, I'll be more exact. If you can imagine taking off a leg cast and everything but the bones comes away with the plaster—well, that's roughly what happened to these chaps."

"Any indication of a prior wound or assault?"

"You mean other than Harry's massively crushed skull and Arthur's split head? No, but I should have thought that was sufficient to do the job in any case."

"What do you need from me?" he asked.

"Well, for starters, what's your objective here? The people who put these men in concrete are surely themselves long underground, or somewhere else in the bay. We may be able to discover something interesting that would help in an investigation, but investigate what, or whom?"

"I have the distinct impression you're about to make a proposition, Sheilagh—mind if I call you Sheilagh?"

"You are a bright one. I usually insist on 'gorgeous,' but Sheilagh will do. A proposition—exactly so. The university would like to take ownership"—she waved a hand at the skeletal remains as if she were presenting a plate of smoked salmon—"to relieve you of Harry and Arthur for the study and enlightenment of the next generation—actually only the second generation—of medical anthropologists. Of course, you—and by 'you' I mean the police and City of Dundurn—will be the first to know what we find, and we will spare no effort in uncovering all that there is to, um, uncover."

"I can't speak for the City—"

"I beg to differ. I've already spoken to the mayor's office, and the word is 'Whatever MacNeice wants to do with them will be in the City's interest.' So you see, I'm here to ply you with reason, and later with wine, if necessary, to appeal to you to let me have them."

"Well, then, on behalf of the good people of Dundurn, I bequeath Harry and Arthur to the university."

"Splendid. I'll toddle off to the Rover for the paperwork." She bowed slightly, which seemed as odd as it was charming, and then walked cheerfully towards the entrance.

If Richardson's humour was dry, Thomas's was considerably wetter. She was wearing tan hiking boots scuffed and stained from years of digging holes and spilling God-knows-what on the leather. He wanted to believe it was from creating an English country garden in Dundurn, but he doubted it.

When she returned, she said, "It's a bit of a tip inside; took me a while to find it."

"I did notice a lot of coffee cups."

"Ha! You imagine that I'm trucked up on caffeine, Detective. I drink only tea, water, wine and single-malt Irish whiskey. And I refuse, I stubbornly refuse, to drink tea from a paper cup."

Seeing the confusion on his face, she explained. "The cups are for samples. Human samples." She shoved Harry's leg bones back from the edge of the cart, saying, "No, no, don't get up," and put down her binder. Flipping the pages, she came to a photocopied form with the university's logo on top. She wrote the details of what she was taking ownership of on the appropriate lines and checked the caveats concerning distribution of any discoveries found during study. She signed the bottom above her name, which was printed on the form, and dated the signature before handing the pen to MacNeice.

"Do I need to read it?" he asked.

"I wouldn't. Do you mind if I smoke?"

"No. Was this written by the university's legal department?"

"By me." She smiled.

He bent over, mindful of the leg bones just beyond the page, and signed.

She looked down at his signature. "Thank you, Iain."

"Don't call me Iain."

"Right. Mac it is. I'll be in touch once I have something on these two and the two from the trunk. We'll do that work outside this contract, so they're still the City's property. But we'd be happy to discuss ownership of them as well." She flipped the binder closed. "Until then, *bonne chance* and Godspeed." She bowed again and then offered her hand. For such a strong, almost masculine woman, her hand was soft and her handshake worthy of royalty—gentle and firm, with a brief pause before a quick release.

"One last thing. Why did you call them Harry and Arthur?"

"It's more human than 'John Doe One' and 'John Doe Two,' or any number. Being an optimist, I can imagine them as aliases that will eventually get put aside for their real names. Of course, if we can't discover them, they'll each have a number in perpetuity."

"I see. Well, goodbye, Sheilagh." As he was leaving, he glanced at the skulls of Harry and Arthur and noted, like most other skulls he'd seen, they appeared to be smiling.

# 9.

RETURNING TO DIVISION, MacNeice discovered the researcher, Ryan, lying on his back under a desk surrounded by boxes. Above him was the most bizarre array of computers that MacNeice had ever seen. Together they looked like castoffs from *Mad Max*—found objects cobbled together with wire, tape and hope—but then the electric-blue screens came to life above the keyboards and the joystick on its plastic camouflage control platform.

Williams was on the phone, pen in hand, and he looked up when MacNeice arrived. He nodded and slid his chair over far enough to kick Ryan's foot.

The young man bolted upright, nearly slamming his head into the underside of the desk. "Sorry, sir. I was just connecting all the bits and hooking into the division's server. I'll have everything up and running in about five minutes."

"Good to see you, Ryan. I understand you built this . . . what would you call it?"

"I did, from scratch, sir, with a lot of orphan parts people thought were broken but were just misunderstood. You could call it a home-made supercomputer. I call it the Millennium Falcon, because it's not pretty but will hit warp speed in no time at all."

"That seems like what we need. Is it legal?"

"Grey area, sir. But I promise you she'll do the job for us. I've saved a whack of gear from going to some landfill in Southeast Asia."

"Right. Well, I'll leave you to it."

When Williams got off the phone, he explained that even though he'd made his calls as a homicide detective, he hadn't been able to determine the origin of the serial number. Since prisons were con-trolled by the federal government, he'd had to call Ottawa. After following up on several referrals, he discovered that the person who had the authority to answer the question was away from her desk. Trying the back door and calling the prisons directly hadn't worked, as there was no way of confirming over the telephone that Williams was who he said he was. Going through channels would take time, but it was—as he was told more than once—the proper way to make such a request.

When Williams had pointed out that all he wanted was confir-mation of how many elements there were in a convict's serial number and whether they were numeric, alphabetic or a combina-tion of both, he was left with static on the line, so he finally hung up. "But I did look up someone I put in Kingston—seven digits, not eight—so No-Face wasn't in our system. The Canadian military wasn't any better: all requests have to flow through the Department of National Defence. So far, no one has returned my call."

"I might be able to help," Ryan said from under the desk.

"Do you know someone?" Williams asked.

"No, but I'm pretty good at finding things out."

"You're on," Williams said, raising his eyebrows at MacNeice.

"Vertesi called after his meeting at Mancini. He's going to drop in on ABC-Grimsby."

MacNeice turned to the whiteboard. Williams had put up photos of No-Face and Bermuda Shorts, the couple from the Packard and even Archie the dummy. Photos for the two from the round columns would have to wait for Dr. Thomas, but MacNeice picked up the marker and added *Two male skeletons, estimated 70 years in the bay.*

"Okay, I'm ready to roll," Ryan said, climbing out from under the desk and sitting down in front of the trio of screens, each of which appeared to be blinking or processing different information. MacNeice handed him a sticky note with the serial number on it and went back to his desk to call Richardson.

Behind him he could hear the young man's fingers clicking rapidly on the keyboard. He listened, enjoying the rhythm of it, until Richardson came on the line. "Anything on Bermuda Shorts, Mary?"

"But for the hole in his head, no other markings, scars, tattoos or even birthmarks. However, what he had eaten is a visual and olfactory match to the other chap. I'm guessing bacon cheeseburger and beer."

"Any indication whether he was tortured before he was killed?"

"Negative on Bermuda."

"And the other one, can you determine the order in which he was mutilated?"

"Actually, yes. I'm almost certain his feet were removed first, followed by his hands, the flesh on the forearms and finally his face."

"Christ almighty."

"Yes. There's every likelihood he was unconscious by that time, from shock and blood loss."

"Every likelihood, but not a certainty . . ."

"No. He may have had an incredibly strong constitution, and there's also the possibility that the butcher moved quickly to ensure he'd be conscious. Why do you ask?"

"I wanted to know if the mutilation was done after he was dead from the head wound, because that would suggest the rest was strictly a way to erase his identity."

"And if it wasn't?"

"Tells me that he'd done something or knew something that his killer believed warranted such butchery."

When he got off the phone, Ryan's key tapping seemed to be going faster.

"You should come and see this, boss," Williams said, sitting to Ryan's left.

The central screen appeared to be scrolling several columns of information on its own—very quickly. Lines of text and numerals filled the screen from top to bottom before blinking and beginning again.

"Here we are," Ryan said.

"Where? Where are we?" Williams asked.

Ryan clicked the Return key. "Turns out it's not Canadian—17712619 is a U.S. Army serial number."

Williams snapped his head up to look at MacNeice, who turned to the photo of the faceless man on the whiteboard.

Ryan entered something else and again information started filling the screen. Less than ten seconds later he said, "The serial number belonged to Master Sergeant Gary Robert Hughes, a martial arts specialist of the Second Infantry Division's Second Brigade combat team."

"With long hair, in a concrete column in Dundurn Harbour?" Williams shook his head in disbelief.

"Keep going," MacNeice said.

Ryan dug deeper into files that MacNeice felt certain weren't accessible to the public. The way the young man's hands moved from the keyboard to the joystick reminded MacNeice of a musician working a Hammond B3 organ.

"Hughes received an honourable discharge in 2008 after serving fourteen years. He was thirty-four years old." More clicking, and moments later: "Upon discharge, his residence was in Georgia, near the Fort Benning base. But he moved to upper New York State that December."

"Is this legit?" Williams asked.

"The information? Oh yeah, it's legit." Ryan nodded several times but didn't look away from the screen.

"Keep going," MacNeice said.

Ryan moved the joystick and clicked the keys several times, and suddenly the second screen lit up. "Last known address for Sergeant Hughes is 3245 Trail Road, Tonawanda, New York." *Click, click, click.* "There's his phone number."

"I'll call from Swetsky's office," MacNeice said, wrote down the number and left the cubicle.

Williams got out of his chair and went to the whiteboard. "Great work, Ryan, though we probably shouldn't know how you did it . . ."

Ryan said, "Thank you, Detective, but it wasn't that hard, due to the fact that the military database security system is massively out of date."

"Meaning you broke through their firewall?"

"More like I was rooting around in the files they store in the basement . . . But yes, I broke in."

"Let's keep that down low."

"Yes, sir. In a minute I should be able to give you a photograph of what he looked like—I mean, with a face."

Williams wiped *No-Face* from the board and wrote *Gary Robert Hughes* below the image. Looking at Bermuda Shorts, he asked,

"Can you disappear the bullet hole in this guy's forehead?"

"Easy."

The phone rang five times before it was picked up. "Hi—sorry, I was out in the yard—who's calling?" The woman was out of breath.

"Who am I speaking to, please?" MacNeice asked. His pen was poised above a clean page in his notebook.

"Sue-Ellen Hughes. Can I help you?"

"Ms. Hughes, I'm Detective Superintendent MacNeice of the Dundurn Police Department."

"Dundurn . . . You mean, up in Canada?"

"Yes."

"I don't understand—"

"Can you tell me your relationship to Gary Robert Hughes?"

MacNeice could hear the woman take a deep breath and then there was silence, but for the sounds of kids playing in the background.

"Ms. Hughes?"

"Yes, yes, I'm here. Gary's my husband." He heard her take another deep breath. "What kind of detective are you?"

"A homicide detective, Ms. Hughes. We're interested in the whereabouts of Gary Hughes, as we believe he may have been a witness to a homicide here."

"I don't understand. By 'here,' you mean up in Canada?"

"In Dundurn, yes."

"But why would Gary be in Canada?"

"When did you last see your husband?"

He could hear that she had begun to weep. MacNeice waited patiently. Close to the phone, a child asked, "Mommy, what's wrong?" She told the child she had something stuck in her eye and to please go back outside, that Mommy was okay. Then she was finally able to say, "Gary left two years ago, almost to the day. He was going to meet someone about a job, and he never came home."

"Do you know where the meeting was?"

"Not far from here—a bar. I don't know what it was about. Detective, please tell me what's going on."

"You have a family?"

"Yes . . . Yes, we have three kids, four, seven and nine. The youngest and oldest are boys, and Jenny's the seven-year-old."

"What did Sergeant Hughes do for a living after he left the service?"

"Not much. Gary chased all kinds of leads trying to get a steady job."

"He found it difficult to adjust, or to find work?"

"Both. The army trained him, turned him into a weapon—he was a double black belt in two martial arts—but when he was discharged, they didn't help him with any career advice . . . And what good is a killer out of the army?"

"Did he have friends in Tonawanda?"

"Only army buddies. He came here to get trained as a carpenter, and then the economy blew apart—not just for us, but for the guys he was going into construction with. It all just faded away."

"Would they get together at your house?"

"No, only at Old Soldiers. It's a roadhouse on the outskirts of Tonawanda. Gary never drank much in the army, but up here . . . Well, it was all different."

"Did you ever meet any of his friends or go to Old Soldiers with him?" MacNeice wrote *Old Soldiers* in his book and added two question marks.

"No, my job is here with our kids."

"How are you getting by, Ms. Hughes?"

"If you mean moneywise, terrible. V.A. cut off his pension because they believe his disappearance was voluntary, which means they think he ran off with another woman—"

"And you don't?"

"Not Gary . . ." Her breathing was heavy again, and he could hear by the static that she was wiping her eyes or nose.

"Are you on welfare?"

"Yes. I had no choice."

"I apologize for upsetting you with this call."

"Please, Detective, I know you're not being straight with me"—she was sobbing into the phone now—"Just tell me, what's happened? Where's Gary?"

"I can't say any more at the moment, but I promise you we'll talk again soon." Before he hung up he heard another voice, perhaps the eldest son, asking his mother what was wrong.

MacNeice returned to the cubicle and briefed Williams. When he'd finished, he added Sue-Ellen's name to the whiteboard, noting the three kids, below her husband's. "As bad as that was, much worse is to come for Ms. Hughes."

"Here's his official portrait, sir." Ryan handed MacNeice a print-out: a head-and-shoulders portrait of a soldier standing in front of the American flag.

What struck MacNeice were the piercing eyes—dark and wise, absent of fear, malice or concern—studying the lens as if it were movement on a distant hill. His jaw was tucked in slightly and there was a clean leanness to him, the skin stretched tight over bone and sinew: a professional warrior. His mouth, while tight, betrayed neither hubris nor pride, nor a menacing suggestion of his abilities in combat. The uniform was crisp and impeccable.

The sad irony of the *Hamilton-Scourge* Project suddenly struck MacNeice. It had begun with the death of American servicemen, and now it appeared to have something to do with the death of one more, almost two centuries later. He taped the image to the white-board. "Along with those skeletons of the crews on the bottom of the lake, I'd like my genie to arrange for Gary Robert Hughes to be repatriated with full military honours, and to see that his wife gets his pension retroactively."

"Might be tough if he was up to his eyes in dirty work," Williams said.

"History's what gets reported. Depending on what we find, perhaps we'll be able to report that he was in the wrong place at the wrong time."

# 10.

A FTER MANY ATTEMPTS, Taaraa Ghosh had finally per-
fected her timing. She knew with certainty the moment
her mother would appear at the top of the stairs. As well,
she would speak to Taaraa before leaving the apartment to confirm
that she was leaving right away. It wasn't that she was worried
about her mother or that the stairs leading down from the mountain
were dangerous. She simply enjoyed sitting on the bench near the
bottom, taking a few minutes to enjoy the sounds of birds, then
looking up to see her mother crest the top of the mountain, waving
to her in wide arcs as if she were flagging down a passing ship. That
simple joy never failed to bring tears to her eyes. It was the certainty
of seeing her, and being seen by her, that overwhelmed Taaraa.

Her mother had experienced much pain in her lifetime, enough
pain for several lifetimes. And although they shopped for food
together and took the bus out to the big-box store for everything
from rice to underwear, this was always the moment—the exact
moment—she cherished most.

Taaraa imagined her mother walking quickly to the threshold of the first step and hesitating till her daughter looked up from below. Once they'd seen each other, she would descend the stairs briskly. For some reason—her mother often asked why, but Taaraa couldn't explain—Taaraa was always laughing when her mother arrived on the landing. They'd embrace and she would say, "Taaraa, daughter, why do you laugh?" The only answer that made any sense to her was "Life is funny . . ." and she'd continue laughing as they walked down the last few steps to the road.

Climbing up the stairs to the landing on this day, Taaraa was already smiling at the absurdity of their ritual: the mountain that wasn't a mountain, the Bangladeshi woman walking down and up and down hundreds of stairs to spend the day with her Bangladeshi daughter. *Life is funny*, she thought, *and it couldn't be more perfect.*

Vertesi had just finished briefing MacNeice and Williams about his visit to Mancini and ABC when a call came over his radio that a body had been discovered at the foot of the mountain, between the railroad tracks and the stairs on Wentworth. As he was just approaching Wentworth on King Street, he said he'd go up and check it out.

MacNeice walked over to the whiteboard and drew a tree diagram. He put *Smith-Deklin—Concrete Pouring* at the top. Below it he drew three lines to the concrete suppliers: *ABC, Mancini* and *McNamara.* Whether it was politics, the aggressive schedule of the endeavour, or that it was too big for one supplier, he felt certain the deaths of Gary Robert Hughes and Bermuda Shorts had something to do with the *Hamilton-Scourge* Project. Intuitively, he was also convinced that the answer was buried in the relationship among the three suppliers. To remind him later, he drew lines between the three suppliers and added two question marks.

"You think they're involved, boss?" Williams asked.

"Just a thought." He realized that if the contract had been split evenly, as Vertesi had confirmed, there was no obvious suggestion of mischief. On the other hand, the bodies hadn't been wrapped in chains or dumped in the harbour inside a refrigerator; they were encased in concrete. Two of the competing firms had been American. Below Bermuda Shorts's image he added: *American?* MacNeice put down the marker. He had long ago learned to trust his intuition, so he sat down at his desk to let the images speak to him. His cellphone rang. As he picked it up, he continued to stare at the whiteboard.

"Boss, how fast can you get up here?"

"Fast. What have you got?"

"Bad—and there's two fairly green uniforms."

"I'll be right there." MacNeice stood up and grabbed his jacket.

"You need me, sir?" Williams asked.

"No. Find out all you can about the Old Soldiers bar in Tonawanda," MacNeice said. Then he left the cubicle and ran down the corridor to the stairs.

Parking behind Vertesi's car, north of the graffiti-covered railway hut, MacNeice surveyed the scene with surprise and concern. He got out of the car and slammed the door. Traffic was still passing by, going up and down the hill. The teenagers who had likely discovered her were lining the mountain stairs above the body, and two uniformed officers were standing by. One of them was Metcalfe, a second-year kid from the east end; he had one hand over his nose and mouth, the other resting on the grip of his service weapon. MacNeice didn't recognize the second uniform, who was busying himself with keeping the traffic moving. Vertesi's car was parked just ahead of the Chevy but he was nowhere to be seen. Beyond the unmarked car was a single cruiser with flashing lights.

"Metcalfe! Clear that goddamn stair. Now!" MacNeice turned and signalled to the other cop, who was waving at the driver of a Buick to keep moving. "You want to be on traffic control? That can be arranged. This is a crime scene—close this street immediately. Secure the area. Where the hell are the paramedics? Where's Vertesi?" The young officer, whose tag read CHANG, hurried over to him.

"Sorry, sir, will do. Ah . . . the paramedics got the message wrong; they're at Wellington Street, and so are the police and firefighters. DI Vertesi, sir, he's with her—the deceased's mother."

"Okay, Chang, thank you. Is this your first?"

"First homicide? Yes, sir. It sure isn't an easy thing to see."

"No, it isn't." MacNeice motioned to the activity on the stairs and the cars slowing down to see what was happening. "Now all this—technically this is referred to as a classic clusterfuck, so get your tape and secure the area. No traffic up or down the hill, understood? And if you see people coming out of those houses, tell them to get back inside. Then call downtown and have them send officers to secure the top of the stairs and block the road at the top of the mountain. Nobody up or down on either, understood?"

"Yessir." Chang ran off to retrieve the yellow tape from his trunk. Six of the kids approached as MacNeice walked towards the scene, and three others started climbing the stairs away from him, as if what had happened had nothing to do with them.

"Metcalfe, stop those three and bring them down here. We want statements from everyone."

"That girl dead all right—tha's my statement, officer," a tall rangy teen with a sideways Bulls hat said. As his friends snickered, he added, "She soooo dead."

"All of you just corral yourselves in front of this car. I promise you we won't keep you for long."

"Right, chief. Cuz we got appointments too." Bulls hat again. Everyone giggled.

"I'm a huge Bulls fan," MacNeice said, "but I think Miami's going to wipe the floor with them this year."

"Miami? Sure. Whatever. No way for Miami." He gave a dismissive shoulder shrug and threw his right hand down with the two middle fingers folded and the others presumably forming a bull's horns.

As MacNeice had expected, one of his friends chimed in. "Yeah, man, they got some serious guns down there. The man's right, man—Miami solid."

MacNeice left them to debate basketball, a sport he had little interest in. But at least he was certain they'd hang around.

A tiny woman had Vertesi pinned to the wall of a house on the corner. She was wrapped around him and wailing. Every few seconds she'd lunge for the curb, trying to get across the street, and Vertesi would hold her back. He waved to Vertesi to stay where he was for a while.

Chang was right; it wasn't an easy thing to see. The young woman's neck had been slashed upwards, from the right collarbone to the left ear. Her stomach had four large puncture wounds forming a rough circle from the bottom of her ribcage to the top of her pubic bone. She was wearing a blue paisley cotton dress and a pale yellow cardigan. Blood was still seeping from the wound on her neck, though her heart had stopped pumping some time ago. The massive stain on the ground and the dirt, bits of leaves and grass stuck to her face and dress indicated that she had hit the ground face down and had since been turned over. Adding insult and further indignity, the contents of her intestines had emptied onto the ground between her legs. MacNeice resisted reaching for his handkerchief out of respect for the girl and her mother.

He took out his cellphone and called the dispatcher. "Betty, forget the paramedics. Send the coroner and the crime scene team. We need at least a half-dozen uniforms here to comb the area." He looked over at Vertesi, who had slid or been pulled down the wall by the woman, now sobbing on her knees and slamming her hand on the walkway. "And send someone over to care for the mother of the deceased."

"We're on it, Mac. Sorry about the snafu with directions. We still haven't figured out how that happened."

Looking down at the body, he realized she couldn't have been saved, but still he was angry. It had taken him twelve minutes to get to the scene, to find only two uniforms and Vertesi. MacNeice put his cell away. He called up to Metcalfe, who was busy taping off the stairs. "You were first here. Did you see anyone near the body?"

"Yes, sir, the mother. Those kids were on the stairs talking tough, but they didn't want to get any closer. The mother, though, she was all over the body, weeping and wailing, until Vertesi pulled her away. That was it."

"Don't touch that railing. We'll want to get prints from it, and from those kids below. A team will be here shortly to do the work. Get their names and addresses, what time they got here, what they saw, and check that they haven't been snapping pictures with their cellphones. I don't want her image all over the Internet. Get them to erase any you find and let them know they'll be charged if any do show up. You know the drill?"

"I do, sir. Sorry for the confusion." He hustled down the stairs, tapping Chang on the shoulder as he passed by.

"Chang, get over there and relieve DI Vertesi," MacNeice said. "Watch her hands. We don't want her seeing a way out of this horror by using your service weapon on herself."

"Yes, sir. I'll do my best."

Vertesi, clearly shaken, made it across the road. Straightening his tie and adjusting his jacket, he said, "Thanks for that. You know, when the dust settles on this, sometime I'd appreciate some advice on just how I should have handled this." His eyes had welled up.

MacNeice put his hand on Vertesi's shoulder. "No problem."

Looking down at the body of the young South Asian woman, MacNeice studied the neck wound again. It was deep, and the flesh had separated in a wide gash. "Backhand . . ."

"Sir?"

"Upward . . . a backhand upward slash. See how deep the entry wound is at the collarbone? It went clean through from there to the back of her neck on the left." MacNeice made the motion with his hand. "He's a right-hander, if it's a he."

"This shit's always a he, sir."

On the stomach, the four puncture wounds were each almost two inches wide and precisely placed. *Symbolic gesture*, MacNeice thought, as he squatted to look at them more closely. "Pregnant?"

"You think?"

"While there could be other reasons to stab a woman in the stomach, I can't think of any, especially after you've already killed her. Did she have a bag?"

"A small floppy backpack. The mother has it."

"Good. We'll need to take that."

Neither of them noticed the sirens till they were almost beside the scene. Suddenly the birdsong soundtrack of their discussion was replaced by flashing lights, *whoop-whoops* and whining sirens.

A forensics team of three appeared, carrying their shiny metal cases and wearing their orange Tyvek suits. Two had already put on their face masks. They stopped just short of the scene. The oldest, perhaps thirty-five, put down his case and approached the two detectives. "What can you tell us, sir?" MacNeice nodded towards Vertesi.

"Not much. She was turned over by her mother." Vertesi looked in the direction of the woman and Chang, who was holding on to her and seemed to have calmed her down. "She was the one who found her."

The forensics guy turned away from the mother to focus on the corpse.

MacNeice was still looking down at the girl. Ants had started to crawl over her face. Her eyes were open, glassed over, and appeared to be gazing sideways, as if expecting to see someone coming up the hill. "No rings on her fingers," he said.

Chang now had the woman sitting on the stoop of a nearby house. MacNeice noticed the young cop looking over at him and nodded to give him assurance that he was doing fine.

"I'll go see if we can learn anything from the mother. Does she speak English?"

"Yes, sir, though she was mostly screaming."

He walked slowly across the street. As Chang stood up to greet him, the woman went limp and slumped weeping onto the stoop.

"Thank you, Officer Chang. Stand by in case we need your help."

MacNeice sat down beside the mother and touched her shoulder gently. "May I have a word with you? It's very important that we speak . . ." The woman's head was still on her arm and she didn't respond. There was dried blood on her hands and on the side of her face. "Do you speak English?" He waited, looking over to Vertesi, who was standing several feet away.

"Of course . . . Yes, I do," she finally responded. Her voice was hoarse and sounded as if it came from deep in her chest. She rolled over and sat up, staring at the scene unfolding on the other side of the road.

"I'm Detective Superintendent MacNeice. You've already met my partner, Detective Inspector Michael Vertesi." He glanced

Vertesi's way. "We're here to find out what happened to your daughter—she was your daughter?"

"Yes, my only daughter. Her name is Taaraa, it means . . . self-luminous in Hindi." She slapped her hand softly on her face and kept it there for several seconds as she rocked forwards and back. From the amount of blood on her dress and jacket, anyone would think she was seriously wounded.

"I'm deeply sorry for your loss, but . . ." He waited for a minute or so for her response.

"I know. You must." From the pocket of her jacket she took out a gingham handkerchief and wiped her face several times. The dried blood didn't budge, except in the tracks of her tears.

"Do you know who did this to Taaraa?" he asked.

Several moments passed. It appeared to MacNeice that the woman was struggling to find something to say. "Do you know—?"

"No, I don't know."

"What is your name, please?"

"I am Radha Dutta. My daughter's name is Ghosh, Taaraa Ghosh."

"Is there a number we can call to reach your husband, Mrs. Dutta?"

"He is away today. I am alone."

"Was Taaraa in school, or working?"

"She was in college—Dundurn Nursing College. She will graduate next spring." With that she slapped both hands to her face, holding it on either side as if to keep it from exploding. The tears ran down, but she'd dropped her handkerchief. MacNeice picked it up and gently touched her shoulder before handing it to her.

"Do you live nearby, Mrs. Dutta?"

"We live on the mountain, not far from the top of the stairs."

"Were you with your daughter when it happened?"

"No, I was to meet her here. We were going shopping. Taaraa

lives in an apartment on Wentworth, near Cannon. We always meet here on the landing."

"Did she share the apartment with anyone?"

"Yes, another nursing student, a Canadian girl. It's 94 Wentworth."

"Do you have any other relatives in the city that we might contact for you?"

"No, no relatives."

"Can we call your husband?" MacNeice watched her face. She looked away, up the road to the mountain, and answered so softly that he had to ask her to repeat what she had said.

"He's looking for work. He went to Oakville. Aadesh was let go from the steel company. He'd only been there six years."

"When did they let him go?"

"In February."

"That must be hard for the family. It's a long time to be out of work."

"It is hard. But . . . we are Bangladeshi."

"Mrs. Dutta, there will be people here shortly to take care of you. Detective Vertesi and I need to find your daughter's killer. We have to take her bag with us, though it will be returned to you." She nodded as he snapped on a glove and picked the bag up by a strap. Vertesi took the small backpack. "We'll need to speak again, but for now, my deepest condolences for your loss. I promise you, we'll do everything in our power to find the person who did this to her."

MacNeice told Chang to stay with the mother and went to speak to the forensics team, who were now hard at work.

"Anything for us?" he asked the lead Tyvek.

"The knife had a blade roughly an inch and a half wide and likely six inches long—two of the stomach punctures broke through on her back. She's been turned twice. She hit the ground after the initial assault, landing on her back. That's when these were done." He pointed down to the stomach punctures. "Then he—I assume it was the perp—turned her face down. After that, the mother turned her back over again. The pathologist will confirm all that. Oh, and she had this in her hand." He held up a plastic bag with a small crumpled note in it. "A shopping list, by the looks of it. Food mostly, but she was going lingerie shopping as well."

"Where's the heel from her right shoe?" MacNeice asked.

"Haven't found it. To be honest, I hadn't noticed it was missing—and I'm surprised you did, given that her foot is almost hidden by the other leg."

"Almost." Putting his other glove on, MacNeice walked back towards the stair, looking down among the weeds, rocks and gravel. There was nothing at the foot of the stairs to suggest she had fled that way, but at the edge of the first landing he found the heel wedged between two large rocks. Picking it up, he tried to recreate what had happened. Ghosh above on the landing, sitting on the bench waiting for her mother, gazing up the stairs, unaware of someone coming up behind her. Confronted, and realizing she couldn't get past him and couldn't outrun him up the stairs, she took the only escape available and scrambled under the railing, dropping to the ground, where she lost the heel of her shoe. He turned and looked down the gravel road that led into the brush. Why didn't she run out onto the road? Panic, perhaps. He'd caught her just of out of view of the houses and the traffic.

He was studying the broken heel when Vertesi approached. "How does a guy get away from a scene like this? He must have been covered in blood," he said.

"It was calculated; he worked it out in advance." Like most people, she was probably pretty unobservant as she walked about. While her killer waited, the railway hut obscured the view from the north and the forest and bush provided cover, and not many cars took the access road in the middle of a summer afternoon. It was over in a minute or two, then he drove away, up or down the hill.

MacNeice turned to Vertesi. "Where did he park the vehicle? Make sure they cover this hill and look out for fresh tire tracks. Also, he may have thrown the knife away. They've got to search all the way up and down, both sides."

"Yessir."

"Contents of the backpack?"

"Her keys—with a rape whistle attached, a wallet, credit cards, fifty-seven dollars, some change, her hospital ID, lipstick and lip balm, a notebook—looks nursing-related, a few other incidentals, but no cellphone. I went and asked her mother about it, and she said Taaraa never went anywhere without her BlackBerry. She also said the drawstring on the bag was open when she got to her. I'll get it in for prints."

He handed Vertesi the heel. "Put a couple of uniforms to work knocking on doors and then get down to Dundurn Hospital. We want their video footage—interior and exterior—anywhere that Ghosh might have been."

"No problem. I'll also get the names of everyone we need to interview and call Williams in to assist."

MacNeice saw two women from the grief-counselling unit arrive and park on the side of the road. When they got out of their car, Metcalfe pointed them towards the mother.

"I'll be at 94 Wentworth," he said to Vertesi.

# 11.

SOME OF THE modest century homes on Wentworth had fared better than others. Built close to the street, there was little of anything natural to screen them or provide curb appeal beyond the maintenance of porch and windows. With its red-brick addition, number 94 stood out. The punched-out box erased any of the hard-won charm the neighbouring homes had managed to retain. It was 7:28 p.m. when he heard the second-floor apartment doorknob turn. He had climbed the old flight of stairs and was standing in front of the door when a young woman with an open face and loose blonde curls opened it. She was wearing a baggy Dundurn sweatshirt, basketball shorts to the knees and tangerine flip-flops. Not expecting to see someone already at the top of the stairs, she was startled and instinctively stepped back.

"I'm sorry, I didn't mean to frighten you. I'm Detective Superintendent MacNeice." He held out his card with his left hand and gently offered his right.

"I guess I didn't have time to put on my door-opening face. I'm Wendy Little. Can I help you?"

"I'm here about your roommate. Wendy, can we go inside?"

"Uh, well, sure. She's not here . . . The place is a bit of mess—I was just doing the cleaning."

"I promise you, I won't notice." A lie, of course—he took in everything: the washing on the counter overflowing a yellow plastic basket, the dishes in the sink, the flourishing rubber plant on the windowsill, the posters on the wall—the most striking of which was of the Bangladesh parliament building. There were sweatsocks on the floor in front of the sofa, and a loose DVD lay next to the remote controls. The television, while not new, sat atop a DVD player and sound system. Wendy picked up the socks and offered MacNeice the sofa; she sat on one of the two blue canvas director's chairs and then promptly stood up again. "I'm sorry, would you like coffee or tea? Or we have some pop . . ."

"I'm fine, Miss Little. Please sit down." She did, tucking her blue and white shorts tightly against her legs the way girls do with a dress.

"Miss Little—"

"Oh, please, call me Wendy." She nodded several times as if to emphasize her approval of the familiar.

"Wendy, your roommate, Taaraa Ghosh—"

"Has something happened to Taaraa?" She stood up again.

"I regret to inform you, Wendy, that Taaraa is dead."

She fell back into her chair as if she'd been struck. She covered her mouth with her hands and her eyes began to fill with tears. "No, that can't be. She left just a few hours ago to go shopping with her mom."

"She was waiting for her mother when she was killed, by the stairs at the foot of the mountain."

"Was it an accident?" She stood up again.

"No, she was murdered."

Wendy tugged at her sweatshirt and swayed a little where she stood. Her mouth opened but whatever sounds she wanted to release stayed caught somewhere deep in her stomach. After a long moment, during which he could see her working hard to control her breathing and her fear, she spoke, her voice soft, almost distant.

"But . . . who would do that? I mean, everyone loves Ghosh." Wendy wiped the tears from her eyes. "We all call her Ghosh, you know, like 'oh, my gosh.' She's the best friend I've ever had. We were going home next weekend to spend a few days with my folks in Fonthill."

"Was she seeing anyone that you know of—a boyfriend?"

"No. With this course, there's seriously no time for boys." She went into the kitchen and grabbed the roll of paper towels. She was now weeping openly, tears spilling down her face. She blew her nose hard—he was impressed and imagined it was a hangover from her country childhood, where she hadn't been taught to be ladylike. She sagged into the chair, and MacNeice waited till she had calmed a little.

"Do you know anything about her parents or whether she had any other family here?" He had his notebook open and looked down at it rather than at her.

"She didn't have any family other than her mom and her stepdad. I know she lost her father and a younger brother in Bangladesh— they were blown up in a market when she was a girl." A small pile of crumpled paper towels was growing in her lap.

"And her stepfather?"

"She got on well with him, but I never met him."

"How did she support herself in nursing school?"

"Like we all do, through the nursing program itself. We're paid to work in the hospital, so our training is very much hands-on."

"Was there anyone at the hospital, a man perhaps, that Taaraa may have fought with or had some form of relationship with?"

"Not that I know of. I mean, we were on the same shifts but in totally different wards. They move us around, you know. Right now I'm in Pediatrics and Ghosh is in Fractures."

"So at the end of your shift you would meet up for coffee or dinner?"

"Most always, sure."

"And when you didn't, where did Taaraa go?"

"Well, she didn't like going home for dinner, but she would meet her mom downtown."

"Why didn't she like having dinner at home?"

"She loved Canadian food. Give that girl a burger and she'd just light up . . . That's why coming home to Fonthill with me was such a blast for her. She'd get roast chicken or beef, apple pie, peach cobbler—she was in heaven."

"Is there anything else you can tell me about her, Wendy?"

"No, not at the moment anyways. Like, I feel pretty shaken—" The second syllable of "shaken" went up heartbreakingly, half an octave. "I've gotta call my mom . . . and, I guess, our supervisor."

"Don't worry about informing the hospital; we've taken care of it. Are you going to be okay?"

"Yeah . . . I guess so . . . I mean, I don't know what to do now."

"Don't do anything; just let it in. Before I go, I need to see Taaraa's room. Do you want to show it to me or just point me in the direction?"

"Her room is behind me. Mine's further down, closer to the bathroom. Ghosh's room isn't as nice as mine but she wouldn't take the better room, even though she found the apartment."

Ghosh's room was simple but elegant: more photos of the parliament building, a saffron-coloured silk hanging stapled to the ceiling and running along above the bed before cascading down behind the headboard. On the dresser was a framed family portrait of her as a young girl, with her mother and her long-dead father and brother.

Her clothes were neatly tucked away in her dresser—no secrets there. Nor was there anything of interest in the closet. He found nothing under the mattress or under the bed, and only a neatly folded indigo cotton nightshirt under her pillow. He took away the laptop computer. He didn't know the password, but with Ryan on board, he was certain that wouldn't be a problem.

Returning to the living room, he said, "Thank you, Wendy. There'll be a forensics team here later to go over her room more thoroughly, and you have my card if anything else occurs to you."

He went to the door. On the other side he stood there for a moment, then left once he heard the deadbolt slide shut.

# 12.

AFTER DROPPING OFF the computer with Ryan, MacNeice drove home along Main Street, longing for the comfort of his stone cottage on the hill and happy as always that some long-ago traffic engineer had set the lights to turn green just before he had to brake—as long as he maintained thirty-five miles per hour. He slipped Miles Davis into the Chevy's CD player and glanced at the clock—9:48 p.m. He hadn't eaten since lunch but had no desire for food. This was a double-grappa day.

He was pulling up to the cottage when his cellphone rang. "MacNeice," he answered as he got wearily out of the car.

"It's me, boss. The stepfather's home," Vertesi said.

"I'll be right down."

"No need. I already went to see him. He's not our man."

"How can you be sure?"

"He's in a wheelchair. He broke his back years ago, shortly after he came to Canada."

"But he worked at the steel company."

"He sat in a booth above the coiler pit for six years, doing computer programming for the inventory coming down the line."

MacNeice was happy to rule him out as a suspect. Vertesi said he was as grief-stricken as the mother and, to make matters worse, he hadn't got the job in Oakville because, the interviewer said, they couldn't take the time to train him on a new computer program. "He told me they actually said to him that they needed someone—and this is a quote, apparently—to hit the ground running."

"God, that was subtle," MacNeice said. "Anything else?"

"Dundurn General's in shock—seems like Ms. Ghosh was very popular there. I checked with Ryan, and they're pulling the video files together for him on DVDs and they've got headshots of everyone who works there, even the part-timers. They're really shocked—she was a star."

"I'm not surprised. Was Ryan able to open her computer?"

"Oh yeah, in about five minutes. He wanted you to know that she never activated email on it. Sounds weird to me, but there was no email account."

"That's interesting. Stop by her parents' house tomorrow and ask for any recent snapshots of her. Promise them they'll be returned within the day."

"Right, boss."

"I'll see you in the morning." He put the cellphone back in his jacket pocket.

MacNeice opened the cottage door, stepped inside and rested the tips of his fingers for a moment on the beautiful rump of a nude in a framed photograph. He smiled wearily, put his keys on the table below the photo and went into the kitchen for the grappa. The barrel glass would hold two shots; he poured, then lifted his glass and let the liquid slide down his throat. Looking out the window, he could see only flickering specks of light from Secord, down below. He pulled the drapes and went into the bedroom to change.

He put his jacket over the doorknob and, leaning on the low dresser that ran along the wall, kicked off his shoes without undoing the laces.

MacNeice considered having another grappa. Instead he made his way into the kitchen and put the bottle back in the cabinet. Turning to the sink, he saw his reflection in the window. "*Basta cosi,*" he said to himself. He ran water into the glass, turned out the kitchen and living room lights and went into the bedroom feeling like a condemned man.

It was a little over four years since Kate had died, and while the dreams remained as bone-grinding as ever, they were coming randomly rather than every other night. He sped through his routine—floss, brush, wash the day from his face—before peeing out as much fluid as possible so that, if a dreamless sleep should come, he wouldn't have to wake up again till morning. He closed the drapes, undressed, grabbed his ancient T-shirt from under the pillow and put it on.

He glanced at the clock radio—10:51 p.m.—and climbed into his side of the bed. The grappa had done the trick: as his body sank into the warmth, he could feel the tension seeping silently out of him and into the mattress. His eyes closed easily. "Ghosh," he whispered. And slowly the day faded and he was asleep.

# 13.

**M**acNeice arrived at Division to find another white-board already in the cubicle, with Taaraa Ghosh's name at the top in red. He greeted Ryan and the two detectives, then said, "I called Wendy Little this morning to ask her about the computer. Apparently Ghosh had everything on her BlackBerry. She thought doing emails on her computer was, as Wendy called it, a 'time suck.' She never activated it, apparently because Ms. Ghosh was entirely focused on nursing."

"Now, that's dedication," Williams said.

Dropping his jacket over the chair, MacNeice noticed her photo album with its puffed fake leather cover. Looking through the pages, he could see that they were a happy family who loved to travel around southern Ontario. There were several photos where both women had their arms around the smiling man in the wheelchair. Visiting Niagara Falls, a peach orchard, African Lion Safari, the CN Tower—each image seemed to exude a giddiness at being alive. He put the album on the filing cabinet and sat down at his desk.

He opened the police and forensics report. No knife found—*not a good sign,* he thought—two partial prints from a running shoe or hiking boot discovered near her footprints and made at roughly the same time. Some further partial footprints, this time with blood, leading to the edge of the road, where they stopped. "He took his shoes off," MacNeice said quietly. His upper body would have been the most bloodied, but he hadn't panicked. "Show me an aerial of the site."

Ryan pulled up the image on his computer. "Here you go, sir." He slid out of the way.

MacNeice studied the screen and then the outputs of the partial footprints that stopped at the road. "Blow up this section." He pointed to the middle left of the screen. With two clicks the image grew, and MacNeice looked closer. After several seconds he said, "I think we've found his way out." He reached over to where the bloody shoeprint ended and drew his finger across the road to the last house. He tapped the driveway pictured on the screen. "That's where he parked. She was looking up the stairs to the top; he parked on her blind side, arriving before her."

"I checked that house last night," Vertesi said. "It's for sale and empty. There's a paved driveway but it's all cracking, with grass and weeds coming through the concrete."

"How would he know she was going to meet her mother?" Williams asked.

"Either it was random—which I don't believe—or he knew it was her routine to meet her mother there," MacNeice said. "She left the apartment . . . Zoom out on the aerial." Ryan pulled the image back. "There, from Cannon to where Wentworth turns up the mountain. My guess—he was waiting across the street from her apartment, parked, until she came out of the house. When she did and headed south on Wentworth, he drove to that driveway and waited for her."

"There were some oil stains; it's possible they were fresh. I'll have them checked out."

"Find out whether they're oil from a car or a truck. Then look around the west side of 94 Wentworth for any similar stains." He looked again at the report; Forensics estimated the shoe size to be ten and a half to eleven. He turned the page to the fingerprints: several partials and dozens of full-on prints. They had eliminated the older prints, and after examining the fresh ones, they had determined that most were from the teenagers who had gathered there to look at the body. Ghosh's prints were found on the railing where she had jumped, but there were no fresh prints nearby. "He wears gloves. Who wears gloves in the summertime?" MacNeice said to himself.

"Boss, you'll want to see this. Ryan's just opened a link." Vertesi moved aside from the screen. "It's not good."

MacNeice and Williams both turned towards the screen. There, in colour, was a close-up of the dead girl, taken not by one of the teenagers standing on the stairs, as MacNeice had feared, but by someone standing right over her. "What is this?"

"It's the Internet, sir," Vertesi said.

"Where did it come from?" MacNeice asked.

Ryan looked up at MacNeice. "Anyone with a cellphone could push that out into the world. Judging by the image quality, it's either a BlackBerry or an iPhone."

"Hers. He took the shot while she was face up, then flipped her face down," MacNeice said, going back to his desk.

"How fast can we get that off the Web?" Williams asked.

"No can do—it's out there. Even if the service providers take it down, it's gone viral. I think there must be at least a million kids in China gawking at this image right now. Sorry."

"This is a seriously sick fuck," Vertesi said.

MacNeice put down the forensics file. "Start marking up that whiteboard. I'm at the coroner's. I'll call the Deputy Chief about the killing and let him know it's on the Web so he's ready when CNN calls. Start the interviews at the hospital—every doctor, orderly, nurse and administrator who had contact with Taaraa Ghosh."

"Will do," Vertesi called after MacNeice, who had already left the cubicle.

# 14.

**M**acNeice was seething. The damage caused by nasty or upsetting images and videos released onto the Web had become all too common around the world, committed by a sneering class of bullies who used the shelter of the Internet's anonymity to terrorize and humiliate people for their own savage amusement. For MacNeice, however, the image of a ripped-open woman defied and transcended even that level of callousness. He inhaled deeply as it occurred to him again—with this level of planning and display, what happened at the mountain stairs was probably just the beginning.

MacNeice turned the heavy Chevy into the coroner's parking lot and backed into a spot near the basement entrance. He was about to shut down the engine when he refastened his seatbelt and drove out of the lot, turning east on Barton, then right on Wentworth. It was starting to rain, and he switched on the wipers.

At the top of the hill he stopped on the shoulder where he'd parked the day before. There was a cruiser off to the side ahead of him and yellow tape still marked the crime scene. The mountain stairs remained closed to the public. He could see the uniform in the car turning to check him out, and nodded to him as he walked by. He heard the car door open behind him.

"Can I help you, sir?"

"DS MacNeice. No. Get back in your unit and out of the rain."

"Ah, sir, you're going to get soaked. I'll get you my slicker from the trunk."

"Don't bother, I'm fine." The tone of his voice caused the officer to snap the car door shut.

MacNeice walked out and stood in the middle of the road. Within seconds, two cars and a minivan had passed on either side of him.

The cop flicked on his wipers to get a clearer look. "Jesus H, this fucker's going to get smacked."

MacNeice seemed to be looking back and forth from where the body was found to the stairs. A pickup truck came around the bend and swerved to avoid the guy in the dark blue suit standing in the middle of the road. The suit was getting darker by the second.

The cop couldn't stand it anymore and reached for the radio. "Vittelli, it's Rankin. I got a situation here. Over."

"Define 'situation.' Over."

"I'm up on the Wentworth hill where the woman got whacked yesterday."

"I know. What's the situation?"

"I got a Detective Superintendent MacNeice—you know the guy? Over."

"Yeah, he's God. Don't fuck with him, Rankin. Over."

"Tell me about it. But he's standin' out in the middle of Wentworth, just staring at the hill, the crime scene. It's pissing rain and people are swerving to avoid him. What do I do? Over."

"If this guy is standing in the rain, assume there's a good reason. Over."

"Roger that. Bat-crazy. But roger that. Over and out."

Wiping the rain away from his mouth and eyes, MacNeice ran over the scenario again in his mind. She had been waiting for her mother to descend the stairs from the top of the mountain; it was a weekly ritual and her habit was to look up, not down. The killer had approached quietly from below or was waiting under the stairs. To the right was a six-foot drop onto jagged rocks, to the left, a three-foot drop down to rocks, weeds and gravel. The traffic was intermittent and the houses across the street looked deserted, so she had fled to the railing on the left and jumped to the ground, where she broke off her heel. She was now on the run and, like a terror-stricken animal, she had no thought other than to flee—tragically, in the wrong direction.

A car coming down the hill narrowly missed MacNeice. The water from its tires slashed across his shins and he heard the driver shout through the rain, "Asshole!"

She was trying to make it to the north side of the tracks, hoping to flag someone down, when he caught up to her on the edge of a dirt path obscured from the road by the railway hut. His head and shoulders might have been seen, but between the brush and the hut, she wouldn't have been seen at all. She was trapped. MacNeice followed the solid white line around the curve as a schoolbus came down the mountain towards him.

In the cruiser, Rankin closed his eyes and waited for the impact, wondering how the hell he was going to explain why he had sat there while a schoolbus took out the finest homicide cop in the city. Hearing nothing, he opened his eyes again. The bus had stopped to let MacNeice cross; the driver even flipped out his little stop sign to halt traffic in both directions. MacNeice gave a little wave of thanks when he made it to the mountain side of the road.

Rankin was breathing so heavily his windscreen had fogged up. He turned on the defroster but couldn't find MacNeice again in the downpour. He took the napkin from his muffin and wiped a clear spot in the fog; MacNeice was now standing on the side of the road, staring directly at a house across the street from him. Without looking either way, he walked across the road and stood staring down at the driveway. "He may be God, but he's totally nuts," Rankin muttered. MacNeice was squatting now, the rain coming down so hard it was zipping up all around him, but Rankin could see him touching the ground and then smelling his fingers.

He stood up, looked about and turned to stare back across the road. Rankin rubbed a larger hole in the fog. Again without looking for traffic, MacNeice made his way back down the hill. The water was running in streams along the side of the road, but he splashed through the puddles as if they weren't there. As he approached the cruiser on the driver's side, Rankin rolled down the window. "Find what you wanted, sir?" MacNeice was soaked, his hair shining black and stuck to his forehead. He had a big smile on his face.

"I did, Officer—"

"Rankin, sir. Stephen Rankin."

"Rankin, this was local talent."

"Sir?"

"Homegrown." He tapped the roof of the cruiser, smiled down at Rankin and added, "You take care now."

Rankin looked in his rear-view mirror, trying to spot where this crazy man had gone, but the back window was so fogged up he couldn't see anything. He lowered his window to check the side mirror and, sure enough, as MacNeice began his U-turn, Rankin could see he was still smiling.

Rankin's radio burped into life. "Rankin, Vittelli here. He still on the road? Over."

"Ah, nope, he's just turning down the hill. Happy as a loon. Wet as one too. Over."

"You just met a genius. Over."

"Scared the shit outta me. Over." The radio rattled with Vittelli's laughter.

# 15.

A S HE SWUNG the metal door open and entered the lab, MacNeice stopped in his tracks. Junior was slamming what looked like a kitchen knife into a doubled-over foam mattress while Mary Richardson leaned against the autopsy table on which a white plastic sheet covered, he assumed, the remains of Taaraa Ghosh. Richardson was wearing a dark grey suit and a pale blue blouse under her white lab coat, and she appeared amused by whatever her young assistant was doing.

Glancing MacNeice's way, she said, "Ah, Detective. I was expecting you earlier."

"I'm sorry. I got caught in the rain up at the mountain and had to go home and change."

With a wry smile she looked down at the clipboard she held. "Ah, the 'mountain,' yes. I prefer the term escarpment, but then, I've seen real mountains." She pushed herself away from the table, causing the body beneath the sheet to shake slightly. "Well, this young woman may have been unique for someone her age, someone so pretty . . ."

The violent thumping and grunting from the assistant in the corner distracted them both. Junior appeared, at least to MacNeice, as if he was coming unstuck. The foam innards of the mattress flew up and around him.

"Unique in what respect?" He asked, looking back at her.

"She was a virgin."

*Thump*, *thump*, grunt, *thump*, *thump*.

"Does he have to do that, whatever it is?" MacNeice asked.

"He's testing a theory. But not to worry, he's almost exhausted. Are you surprised by her virginity, Detective?"

"She seems to have been a singularly focused young woman. No, I'm not surprised."

*Thump*, grunt, *thump*, *thump*, *thump*.

Richardson decided to explain. "Junior's fascinated by the wounds to her abdomen. He believes they're not random, and he's been trying to recreate them with the mattress—so far unsuccessfully."

"There were four in a square."

"More of a diamond, the centre of which was—fairly precisely—her navel, though there isn't any indication that he knew that. Judging by the blood pattern, her dress remained in place throughout the attack."

"Can I see them?" MacNeice asked. Richardson stood away from the table and was about to pull back the sheet when he quickly corrected himself. "I mean, have you a photograph of them?"

"Junior, come here and show Detective MacNeice the printout."

Sweating, Junior came over with the photo and handed it to MacNeice. "The hard part is that you've got two cuts going one way and two the other," he said. "Doing it quickly is almost impossible. I've come close but I haven't nailed it." He demonstrated with the knife to show that the assailant would have to change his arm direction to match the angles of the entry points.

"The question is, why bother? She's already dead," Richardson said. "If this is a final *coup de grâce*, why worry about precision? His escape should have been of paramount concern at that point."

MacNeice looked down at the photo in his hand and the hair on the back of his neck stood up. "Can I borrow your pen, Doctor, and your clipboard?"

Richardson handed them over. "We've been studying these wounds for more than two hours, MacNeice, so if you see something we've not seen, I'll be very disappointed."

MacNeice clipped the print in place and put the pen on one of the entry points. He swiftly connected the four wounds, then handed it to Richardson. She said softly, "My Lord."

Richardson handed the clipboard to Junior, who looked at MacNeice and said, "No way!" After studying it again, he handed back the near-perfect drawing of a swastika.

"It's open to another interpretation, but I can't think of one," MacNeice said, retrieving the print.

"But what about the precision, and the opposing directions?" Junior asked.

"I don't know. Maybe he's ambidextrous and switched hands or shifted his body to get the angle right."

Turning to Richardson, he said, "Tell me about the neck wound. I'm interested in the angle of the cut—I'm trying to establish the killer's height."

MacNeice winced as Richardson folded back the plastic sheet to reveal Taaraa Ghosh's face, neck and upper chest. Her eyes had been closed, mercifully, but her neck, absent of blood, looked even more horrific than it had on the hill. Her mouth was open slightly, as if she were about to say something.

Richardson reached for her scalpel and, leaning over, opened the wound a little. "You see the slightly downward angle? It's so deep that you can make it out clearly. Assuming they were both standing on level ground—" She looked over her glasses at MacNeice.

"Yes, they were more or less level."

"Then you've got a man roughly six feet tall, perhaps slightly taller. He's right-handed and used a slicing uppercut."

Junior mimicked the swing with his kitchen knife, smiling at MacNeice. As if practising his stroke, he did it again.

"Enough, Junior."

Richardson pulled the sheet over the dead girl's head and put her scalpel in a shallow tray alongside several other instruments. She looked directly at MacNeice, her greying hair cut stylishly short, accenting her long, narrow face and aristocratic nose. Her skin had lost none of its peaches-and-cream colour. MacNeice wondered if his own had gone suddenly pale, because she appeared to be looking at him with concern.

As Junior walked away, still practising his backhand, Richardson raised an eyebrow at MacNeice. "One last thing, Mac, the arc of that cut, the precision of those wounds to her abdomen—the man you're looking for is very comfortable with that blade. There's no hesitation whatsoever in any of these wounds. If you get close to apprehending him, I would give him a wide berth."

"Can you describe the blade?"

"It's a hunting or military type. The blade is three-sixteenths of an inch thick and at its widest, judging by those wounds to her abdomen, it's one and three-quarters. As for the length, I can't say precisely, but since two of the thrusts exited her back, I'd guess somewhere between five and six inches. In other words, extremely nasty."

"Are you going to do a full autopsy?"

"I think not. We know exactly what killed this young woman. There's no need to put the family through any more anguish."

Richardson touched the plastic-covered shoulder and held it for a moment.

MacNeice had one last question. "Were there any bruises or marks that would indicate he held her or struck her with something other than the knife?"

"No. There was faint bruising around the abdominal entry wounds, but that would have been caused by the impact of the hilt. He didn't touch her except to wipe the blade on her dress when he'd finished."

MacNeice thanked Richardson and nodded to Junior, who was wrestling the foam mattress into a roll. He looked about the large, bright room. It took a clean efficiency to study death—all fluorescent lighting, white tile and stainless steel, except for the red-tiled floor. Even the smell spoke to the purpose of the place—a slightly acrid mix of several chemicals masking the rancid smell of human decay. Richardson's office, with its oriental carpet and low incandescent lighting, appeared to be a refuge from the clinical brightness her business demanded.

In the tiled corridor he felt the rage boiling up again, and practised deep breathing until he got behind the wheel of his car. Looking at his sketch of the swastika, MacNeice tried to imagine what else it might be. "What the hell are we into here?"

Driving uptown along King Street, he thought about the killer. If he was right about him, he was certain it wouldn't end with one death. But he couldn't shake the notion that the four punctures were more about graphic design than fascism.

# 16.

BEFORE HE'D MADE it back to Division, MacNeice received two phone calls, one from the mayor and the other from DC Wallace. Wallace had just finished a press conference about the violent death of a young woman at the foot of the mountain stairs, and the task force, under the leadership of Detective Superintendent MacNeice, that was hard at work finding her killer. The call was to find out if indeed that was true, and, if so, how quickly MacNeice thought he'd have some good news.

Bob Maybank was calling because the unions were getting overheated about not having access to the eastern wharf. They had begun pushing about when their crews could resume the work they had been hired to do. In the senior ranks of the trade unions there was currently a high degree of cooperation with and respect for the mayor. But this was tethered by piano wire to Maybank's ability to find the funds for the waterfront project. Should anything jeopardize that initiative, they would shut the city down.

MacNeice told them both in turn that the investigations had entered a quiet but productive phase, and the length of time they'd take couldn't as yet be determined. He didn't mention to either his suspicion that Taaraa Ghosh's killing was just the first, nor did he refer to the cryptic rendering of a swastika punched deep into her abdomen by a knife that was almost two inches wide. To ease union pressure, he told Maybank that the mayor could send everyone back to work once the dock had been cleared of evidence. Neither caller was satisfied with his answers.

Ryan was at his computer, scanning the DVDs from Dundurn General. "You've got two messages, sir, from Sue-Ellen Hughes. She asked that you call her back as soon as possible and said she'll call back again if you don't."

"Thank you. How are you doing?"

"I developed a crude PRA so I can scan faster." Seeing the questioning look on MacNeice's face, he clarified. "It's a pattern-recognition application that picks up her details—height, skin colour, hair, even the way she walks—and flags them so I can fly through the footage and not miss anything."

"Does it work?"

"I've got about thirty sequences from the fractures clinic. I went through them a second time without the app, and yes, sir, it works. I'm almost finished Fractures. I've got Family Practice, Maternity, the ICU, cafeteria, Emergency and parking left to do."

"Go to the emergency ward next, and then the parking lot—but show me what you've found."

"No problem. It'll come up on that screen." He pointed to the left monitor.

While he was waiting for the videos to appear, MacNeice looked more closely at Ryan's setup. The monitor he was watching had a pale blue frame with fake blood splatters near the top. The far right monitor was beige, or whatever computer companies before the Apple revolution called beige. The largest of the monitors was in the middle. It had a wide black frame with a round sticker on it, like something you'd see in a shop full of pot paraphernalia. In the middle of the sticker was MFS in black block letters; above it was BEWARE in yellow, and below, SYNDROME, also in yellow. The background was a swirl of purple and green, as if someone had put a Mixmaster into a bucket of grape and lime ice cream. Strip the colour away, however, and it could have been produced by the FBI.

"What's MFS?" MacNeice asked.

"Millennium Falcon Syndrome. It's when you stick with legacy technology because you believe nothing's faster, more powerful or cooler. Even when it means you're keeping it together with gum and string and cannibalized parts from dead falcons, you won't give up. That's MFS. Your judgment is clouded by emotion and affection—puppy love." He stood up, reached behind the centre monitor and moved a wire to the monitor on the left. "If afflicted with this disorder, you can die—tech-wise—but if you survive, you may be declared the best tech pilot around." He smiled, sat down and said, "I'm ready, sir. Ghosh was in the fracture clinic for only four days before she died. Here's all of it."

As MacNeice watched the sequences unfold, the impact her death would have on the hospital was very clear. She engaged people easily, and those she spoke to were more often than not smiling at her. Ghosh was a young woman in the thick of things, immersed in the activities of a nursing practicum. Interactions with the staff—doctors, nurses and orderlies—appeared to be cordial. Her exchanges, however brief, with patients young and old revealed a woman blessed with good humour and compassion.

"Keep going. Incidentally, the search for pattern is the basis of all scientific, psychiatric and homicide investigations."

"I didn't know that. Thanks, sir."

MacNeice went back to his desk, where an insistent red light flashed on his telephone. He had recognized in his conversation with Sue-Ellen Hughes that she was quick-minded and intelligent. Had he thought about it further, he would have known she'd start putting together the pieces of their conversation and call him if he hadn't called her. He swivelled in his chair to look at the whiteboard and the photo of Master Sergeant Hughes.

The sergeant's eyes were focused on MacNeice—he had become that distant hill. *There's probably a name for the phenomena*, thought MacNeice. He recalled touring London's National Portrait Gallery with Kate, and that several paintings there had produced the same effect. He would walk back and forth, fixed on the eyes in the painting, and no matter how far he went to the left or right, the eyes appeared to be following him. He had no doubt the same would be true of Hughes, and wondered if the young man was aware of the effect when he showed up for the photo session.

He picked up the phone and called Vertesi's cell. It rang several times before he answered.

"Yes, boss, what's up?"

"Give me a topline on the interviews."

"Well, to quote the head nurse in ICU"—MacNeice could hear him flipping the pages of his notebook—"Taaraa Ghosh was the finest nurse she'd seen in thirty years. That pretty much sums it up—she was a star, hard-working, resourceful . . . Here's another quote: 'a perfect nurse, with the sunniest disposition.' Doctors loved her too. One of the maternity ward docs told me he'd spoken to her about entering med school once she'd graduated from nursing. He said she would have made a terrific pediatrician. When I asked him how she responded, he said she was willing to consider it."

"Can Williams handle the remaining interviews on his own?"

"Phew . . . well, I'd say that with this shift and the people who were willing to come in to be interviewed, we're about halfway. Why? What do you need?"

"I want you to drive down to Tonawanda to tell the sergeant's wife what happened to him."

"Jesus, Mac. You mean literally?"

"She's smart, and she isn't likely to accept even a well-meaning obfuscation. You'll tell her that her husband was murdered and that his body was mutilated before being encased in a concrete column and dropped in the bay."

"Oh man!"

"But you'll tell her that only if necessary. Start with 'Your husband was murdered' and that he was traced by identifying the tattoo on the back of his head. She may not want to hear more." Though MacNeice didn't believe that would be the case.

"Anything else?"

"Ask her about the small-calibre bullet wound to his lower back, but other than that, no. Bring back the most recent photos of him, but don't leave until you know she has someone nearby for support. If there isn't anyone, call me and I'll ask the local police to send someone over. I don't want to tell her over the phone that he's dead."

"If she's so sharp, do you think I can keep the truth from her?"

"Keep the details from her at least. Just say you're not authorized to discuss them."

"Good, that helps. Anything else?"

"Visit Old Soldiers. Don't engage in anything that will put you at risk—is that clear?"

"Yes, sir. When do I go?"

"Right now. I'll call Mrs. Hughes and tell her to expect you within the next two hours. Let Montile know you're heading out. Lock up your weapon at home before you leave." He gave Vertesi Sue-Ellen's address and phone number and told him not to declare that he was a cop when he crossed the border—he was simply going down to visit old friends for the day.

MacNeice listened to Sue-Ellen's messages before dialling her number. When they spoke, she wanted an explanation for Vertesi's visit. When he said there were updates that were better communicated in person, her voice faltered as she asked, "What kind of updates?" He responded by saying that Vertesi would be there within two hours; following his visit, if she wanted to speak further, MacNeice would be available. He was certain it wasn't the death of her husband she feared. After two years she would have assumed the worst, even if she denied it to friends, family and herself. But the manner of his death was so grotesque there was no easy way to tell her about it. Sending Vertesi was a long-shot attempt to get her to accept the truth without hearing it.

# 17.

STEPPING INTO THE Hughes house, Vertesi could see immediately how difficult keeping it all together had been. The carpet, which must have been there long before they rented the place, was frayed from the front door through to the kitchen at the back. On the door frame of the kitchen, three sets of short horizontal lines in red, blue and green marked the heights of each child. On the living room wall their wildly coloured paint and marker sketches shared space with a large reproduction of a painting of a barn on a windswept hill. There was a television that predated flat screens by at least twenty years, and the French provincial blue upholstered sofa and chairs had deflated under the onslaught of bouncing kids.

Sue-Ellen brought a tray with mugs and a teapot, milk and sugar and four chocolate-covered cookies. She went to set it down on a small circular end table covered with magazines and children's books. Vertesi rushed to get them out of the way to make room for the tea, standing there with his arms full until finally he just set down the pile on the floor. He settled himself in a pressback rocking chair with a knitted cushion cover as Sue-Ellen, dreading what she was about to hear, sat down and held her knees.

MacNeice had been right about her. Not long after accepting his cup of tea, Vertesi was giving her the short version of what had happened to her husband. She immediately wanted more information, and he retreated: "I'm sorry but I'm not authorized to say anything more." For a moment her face flashed with anger, and then a deep sadness set in. Feeling awkward, he wrote MacNeice's phone numbers on the back of his card and put it on the table. The oldest son, who looked a lot like his father, appeared at the kitchen door with the younger ones close behind. He seemed to understand what was happening and took them out into the yard to play.

Vertesi thought about what he'd told her—that her husband had been murdered and mutilated and that his body, encased in concrete, had been dumped off a wharf into Dundurn Bay. She raised her mug, but her hands were shaking so much she put it down and didn't touch it again. Vertesi, on the other hand, welcomed the distraction; though he didn't like tea, he helped himself to a second cup. He was also grateful to MacNeice for the question about the scar on Hughes's lower back, as it seemed to distract her from the word *mutilated*.

"Gary was a wild kid," she said. "At seventeen he was in a gang. On his eighteenth birthday he was leaving a convenience store when a rival gang drove by and shot him. Gary recovered, and a few months later he went down to a recruitment centre and enlisted in the army. I met him not long after that."

The same photograph as the one on the whiteboard in Dundurn was on the mantel over the gas fireplace. Beside it were several of Hughes and the family after his discharge. She gave three of them to Vertesi.

Sue-Ellen stood in the doorway of the small white frame bunga-
low, holding the screen door open, all three kids around her, and
staring at Vertesi as he backed out of the short dirt driveway. He
waved before pulling away; the little girl was the only one to wave
back. Sue-Ellen had a brother and sister-in-law nearby and had
promised to call them when she'd pulled herself together. Vertesi
drove off slowly, looking forward to a cold beer at Old Soldiers.

When he'd gone a few blocks, though, he pulled over and studied the photos. In one, the eldest boy, Luke, was in an above-
ground pool. He was wearing a mask and snorkel and appeared
above the bright blue metal rim as if he had been diving for pearls.
Hughes was wearing a white T-shirt and knee-length green shorts.
He had the infant Sam in his arms and appeared to be pulling
Jenny, aged four or so, along the wet grass as she hugged his leg.
She was laughing hysterically; her swim goggles fallen around her
neck. Hughes, his hair in an army buzz cut, was looking into the
camera and grinning—he seemed intensely happy. In another
snapshot, Sue-Ellen and her husband were in the garden; she was
on his lap in an Adirondack chair. It was sunset and both had a
glass of white wine in their hands. Sue-Ellen had said it was their
fifteenth anniversary.

The third image was Gary—long-haired, bare-chested—in shorts,
assembling a swing. It was easy to see why he was considered a
lethal weapon. His body, though not over-packed with muscle, was
finely defined and highly tuned. He was applying a wrench to the
swing's A-frame support, the tattoo on his forearm clearly visible—
his division's shoulder patch, an Indian chief in a war bonnet contained in an arrowhead. Gary was wearing a wedding ring: a mate,
apparently, to the one Sue-Ellen was wearing as she wiped away
tears and blew her nose.

Pulling into a large, mostly empty parking lot, Vertesi circled
around a pizza restaurant, a used-furniture store and a hardware

emporium and slowly drove by Old Soldiers. Three Harleys were parked outside. He chose a spot in the middle of the lot, facing the service road he assumed would take him back to the highway.

Vertesi called MacNeice and gave him an update. "I can pretty much guarantee that he wasn't leaving that woman, as the army suggested," he said. "She's beautiful. And I don't think she's gonna believe it's him till she sees him—though that's just a guess."

"If she chooses to see him, she's owed at least that."

He told MacNeice what she'd said about the tattoo on Hughes's head, that he referred to it as a bar code, as if he was a commodity. He was most proud of the tattoos on his arms—his battalion crest on the right and the names of his kids and Sue-Ellen on the left. Vertesi also told MacNeice about the family photos he was bringing back, and ended by saying he was sitting outside Old Soldiers.

"Describe it to me."

"From the outside it's all Harleys and hurtin' music. Other than the neon signs for Pabst and Michelob, it looks like a set for a western movie. Okay to show them the official portrait of Sergeant Hughes?"

"Yes. You're an old friend and you lost track of Gary when he left the army. Someone told you to check Old Soldiers."

"Will do."

Vertesi's visit lasted less than a half-hour. He nodded to several men sitting near the darkened window; none nodded back. Standing at the bar, he ordered a light beer and tried to open a conversation with the bartender. That didn't go well—the man moved down to the end of the bar to talk to two men sitting on stools, smoking and drinking Jack Daniels, the bottle between them. Vertesi drank half the beer in one swallow and finished it with the second. Five minutes passed and the bartender came back, retrieving the empty glass. "One more for the road?" he asked. Vertesi took the question to mean that he should leave, but he ordered another. When the bartender put down the beer, he showed him the photo of Hughes. "Know him?" The man made a show of studying the image before saying "Nope."

"Strange. He used to come here all the time. Are you new?"

"Nope."

Vertesi tried again. "You don't recognize anything about him?"

"He's a master sergeant, Second Infantry Division, served with distinction in Iraq and Afghanistan."

"So you do know him."

"Nope. I know how to read a uniform and service honours." There were coughs of laughter from the smoky end of the bar.

"You made me."

"Wasn't hard, bud. You local, state or federal?"

"Neither."

"Then I don't have squat to say to you, other than 'Will that be all?'" More raspy laughing and coughing.

Vertesi finished the beer, put money on the bar to cover it, waved a salute towards the end of the bar, nodded to the bartender and left Old Soldiers.

# 18.

OTHER THAN THE rapid tap of the Falcon's keys and the irritating squeak when Ryan used the joystick, he was a quiet addition to the unit. MacNeice sat looking back and forth between the wharf and Taaraa Ghosh whiteboards. Ryan had taped Taaraa's high school graduation photo next to the one from the mountain. He felt as though the investigation was in a waiting phase—for the videos, the interviews, the forensics to arrive on the fresh oil stains from the abandoned driveway and the similar stain found across from 94 Wentworth—all he could do was wait.

He looked at the portrait of Hughes and the photo he'd taken of his body on the rail cart. Below that was a photo of both his and Bermuda Shorts's concrete columns. On a hunch, MacNeice dialed Swetsky's number. He heard the line engage and Swetsky's big voice bark something, but he couldn't make out what it was.

"Swets, is there any indication that the D2D boys were in the concrete business?"

"No, but there's all kinds of industrial equipment here. I guess there could be a cement truck hidden somewhere, but we ain't found one. Why? Whaddya got?"

"Just two men who've been in concrete for two years—at the bottom of the bay."

"Sorry, these guys preferred plastic-wrapped stiffs buried in the dirt. Concrete's too much work."

"How is it going?" He was staring at the photo of the mutilated body on the whiteboard.

"We're almost done searching and cataloguing. There's still a lot of work, including finding the guys who are above ground. But the forensics unit is shutting down—I guess the Mounties want their van back. The ice-cream truck will leave with the bodies late tonight. I heard you've got another case."

"A bad one, yes." Sergeant Hughes was looking back at him from his distant hill. "Swets, tell me how the bikers died."

"Which ones? There were the three we found above ground. Recent kills—that's how we got here in the first place. They were all shot—executed basically—in their cars."

"What about the older ones who were shrink-wrapped and buried?"

"Two snapped necks, which is no small thing—these musta been huge necks. One had his skull caved in by the heel of a boot; there's a half-moon on his forehead—the dweeb in the van says it's a size twelve. The last one, his head was almost removed with one cut; again, not an easy thing to do, given the size of the neck."

"Impressive." He was still looking at Sergeant Hughes.

"No shit. The interesting thing with all of them, they weren't worked over. Just *bingo* on the necks, *thwack* with the boot, *zip* with the blade—not a scratch otherwise. Very smooth."

It was the answer to the next question that had MacNeice running out of Division and speeding up the mountain towards Cayuga, the Chevy's red cherry clearing the way. As he sped along the concession road, he took in the immensity of the property for the first time, and all of it surrounded by an eight-foot chain-link fence topped with razor wire. There was a cruiser at the gate blocking the road into the site. Spotting MacNeice, the uniform in the cruiser flashed his lights and moved his rig out of the way. As he came alongside, MacNeice rolled down his window. "Swetsky?"

"He's expecting you, sir. He's in the first barn. Forensics knows you're coming too; they're waiting in the black van."

MacNeice drove down the road to the barn. Lit by a large grid of mercury vapour lights, the vast space had an eerie blue sharpness to it that he found vaguely unsettling. "Swetsky, where are you?" he called.

"At the back. Just keep walking."

MacNeice made his way between the rows of equipment and emerged into a large open area at the end of the barn. He shook Swetsky's hand and looked around to get a sense of the space. Running along the length of the wall was a workbench; above it a metal grid was mounted on the wall, supporting everything from motorcycle tools to heavy equipment wrenches the size of baseball bats, crowbars, hammers, huge rubber mallets and chains. Mounted on the walls at either end were jackhammers (three), chainsaws (four), nailguns (four), a brushcutter, leaf blowers (two) and drills of various makes and sizes.

"Clearly they can't resist a hardware store."

"The way hookers like skimpy underwear. Okay, here's what I've found so far. Do you know exactly what you're looking for?"

"Not exactly, but I've seen what it can do to a man's body." MacNeice looked at Swetsky's collection lying on the bench. Three smaller chainsaws, but the blade teeth were too chunky to have sliced a skull so finely. There were two electric carving knives, the kind you cut a turkey with, but they wouldn't have the strength to cut through bone, and neither box had been opened—the clear tape that held them shut was untouched. At the end of the line was a machine with a green-and-black gas tank and narrow triangular teeth on both sides of its long, flat steel shaft. "What's this thing that looks like the snout of a sawfish?"

"A hedge trimmer."

MacNeice put on his gloves and picked up the machine. "Have you seen any hedges around here?"

"Just chain link and razor wire. Do you think you've found what you're looking for?"

"I think so, but I'll get this downtown to Forensics to study its cut against what was done to the body." He put it down gently on the bench.

"It's yours. I'll log it out for you—one Chinese-made hedge trimmer. That it? Do you want to look around some more?"

When Swetsky finished filling out the paperwork for the hedge trimmer, he looked over at MacNeice, who still hadn't answered his question. He was studying the concrete floor. It sloped slightly from the sides to the middle, where there was a large metal drain cover.

"Got a Phillips screwdriver and a flashlight?" he asked.

"Sure, what size flashlight?"

"Big and bright, and a small Maglite as well." MacNeice knelt down on the floor beside the grate and waited. "Is this place on septic or connected to the town's sewage system?"

"The town. Small blessing, too—these guys are all built like Brahma bulls, and their shit must be bull-size too."

Once he had unscrewed the grille, MacNeice took the flashlight and lit the insides of the drain. It fell two feet or so to a plastic trap that sat several inches below the horizontal runoff drain. He took off his jacket, rolled up his shirt sleeve, turned on the small Maglite and put his arm as far as he could down the drain. At the bottom of the trap there were pebbles, and among them, several white fragments the size of corn kernels, one larger than the rest. "Suction."

"Suction?"

"Are there any vacuum cleaners on those shelves? Any that haven't been used at all?"

"Any particular brand? I've got six of them still in their boxes. I'd go with the English one; it's got great suction and you can see right away what's inside—it's clear plastic."

"English, please. Attach the long, narrow extension." He shone the light along the sides of the drain; it looked clean and was probably rarely used.

When Swetsky had assembled the vacuum and plugged it in, MacNeice asked him to check that the container was completely empty. It was.

"Give me the nozzle but don't turn it on till I tell you."

"Okay." He handed MacNeice the nozzle and watched as he inserted it into the drain.

MacNeice positioned the nozzle right above the kernels. "Power." The suction was tremendous, pulling the end of the plastic nozzle down to the bottom as the white bits and grey pebbles disappeared and rattled up the hose into the chamber. "Right, shut it off. Let's open the canister."

Swetsky lifted the vacuum onto the workbench and opened it up as MacNeice tore off three sections of paper towel, laying them flat on the bench. "Okay, shake them out of there."

Several pebbles bounced onto the towel. "Shake harder."

"Said the bishop to the actress." Swetsky shook the canister and rotated it so that anything caught on the lip would fall free.

"That's it," MacNeice said, and leaned over to get a closer look at the small chunks of white. "What do you make of these?"

"What do you want me to make of them?"

"Bone. I want them to be bone. Skull bone."

"Christ—you're connecting this place to the two in concrete!"

"I'm just following a hunch."

"Lemme get one of the nerds," Swetsky said and headed off towards the black van.

MacNeice walked down the second lane of the barn, where there was more equipment, appliances and furniture, all of it new. Two fibreglass mid-engine boats sat shrink-wrapped in white plastic alongside the industrial shrink-wrapping machine that had been used for more than covering boats. Stacked off to the left were six shiny slat-backed chairs made of steel. He picked one of them up and walked back to the drain, setting it down beside the hole.

"Talk to me, Hughes," he said softly.

Swetsky brought back a man wearing tan cargo pants and a madras short-sleeved shirt. He offered his hand; in the other was a beer. "Dennis Turnbull. Great to meet you, sir. I've heard a lot about you. Sorry for the casual attire—we're wrapping up tonight."

"No problem." MacNeice walked over to the paper towel.

"What have you got?" Turnbull asked.

"I'm hoping you can tell me." He pointed to the largest of the white kernels.

Turnbull leaned over. After a few moments of silence he put down his beer and said, "I'll be right back." He ran down the aisle and was gone.

"I haven't seen him move that fast since we got here," said Swetsky.

"Think skull bone."

"I am. That's exactly what I'm thinking, you macabre fuck."

Turnbull returned a few minutes later wearing latex gloves and carrying a large microscope. "Woulda been easier to carry that bit to the van than bring this here, but you know, a couple of beers and we all do wacky things, right?" He set down the heavy instrument, plugged it in and pulled a pair of tweezers from a case he carried in his pants pocket. With his head bent over the micro-scope, he focused the lens. "Hmmm. Yeah, yeah. Pretty neat. Pretty fuckin' neat." He stood up again. "Where'd you find this?"

"In the trap of the drain. What is it?"

"Bone. Human, possibly. Given the shit that went on in this place, probably human."

"May I have a look?" MacNeice asked, leaning over the micro-scope. "Finders keepers."

The white shard filled the frame and seemed almost to emit light. It was porous and creamy in colour. He stood up again and said, "Could it be skull bone?"

Turnbull was leaning against the bench, beer in hand. "Yeah, well, we're getting way ahead of ourselves, but sure, it could be. For example, it could be a pig bone"—he looked back towards the microscope—"but it looks human to me."

"Can you check out all these metal chairs for chain friction and rope burns to the finish, as well as blood, tissue or hair—and I don't mean pig. Do the same on that hedge trimmer, and then get it to Richardson's lab to test the cut with a body she has on ice."

"No problem, sir." Turnbull pulled a Ziploc bag out of his cargo pants and slid the fragments inside.

"Swets, you're not going to—"

"I know where you're headed. You want this drain excavated."

"If those fragments are human, yes."

They walked out of the barn together, Turnbull with his micro-scope and the evidence, and MacNeice with a sense that his case had just gotten clearer yet more complex. Before they left, Swetsky put a large card over the drain with DO NOT TOUCH written on it. When Turnbull walked off to the black van, MacNeice said, "Tell me about this place."

"This was the D2D country home. It's a huge property, a mile square, and as you can see, not much around it. Somebody—a lot of somebodies—came in, messed it up and left. You couldn't see it for the equipment piled in there, but check this out." Swetsky walked to the north side of the barn and pointed. The siding was full of holes—some from buckshot, others from automatic weapons and large-calibre handguns. "Hundreds. And"—he nodded over his shoulder—"there's hundreds more on that other barn."

"What have you got so far?"

"We have no idea who tipped us off, but so far we've got two D2Ds: Donald 'Bunny' Winter and Herbert 'Canny' Guenther, both originally from Edmonton. Canny got his nickname in Alberta, where he allegedly ate his his first wife—but that was never proven." From that low point, Swets went on to describe the corpses.

On his way back to Dundurn, MacNeice thought about the notes he'd taken. Big men with tattoos, mostly on the arms—snakes, a cross with a pinup model attached to it, a devil's face. One with a pair of deuces on his neck, several Harley logo tattoos on chests and backs, and one with a black rose dripping red blood over the heart. The final one was intriguing—a blue female torso in the centre of the chest, her pubic hair shaped into a fleur-de-lis. When MacNeice asked about it, Swetsky said he was more or less certain they'd find the others were local, but that one was probably a tourist from Quebec and would—as Swetsky said, pardoning the pun—"be living proof of a Montreal gang connection in the ranks of D2D." The corpse's details had been sent off to the Sûreté du Québec for possible identification.

Potentially competing interests in the concrete business; a biker gang feud that appeared to have nothing to do with concrete; two bodies encased in concrete, one a soldier whose specialty is close-quarters combat—all happening at roughly the same time . . . two years ago. MacNeice was cresting the mountain overlooking the city when he realized what Marcello was trying to say about mutilation: *People carve up people for others to see.*

That would mean, he thought, both at the time of the killing and when the body was eventually discovered. When everything identifiable is removed, a body's just a body. It can never be identified by anything other than DNA, and if you haven't any idea who you've got and don't know who you're looking for, how do you begin to find a DNA match? Killing Hughes had been a savage anonymous message undone by a small tattoo under a full head of hair. And yet he was dumped with someone who was identifiable, which meant that the mutilation had nothing to do with identification. But then, what was it about? MacNeice was turning into the parking lot of Dundurn Hospital to check on the interviews Williams was conducting, when it hit him. *Payback.*

# 19.

T WAS LATE in the afternoon, late in August. Lea Nam had finished her weight training and stretching in the Brant University athletics facility before putting on her running shoes. She was BU's finest cross-country runner and was ramping up for two track meets coming in September. She left by the gym door, setting her stopwatch to her target: the time of her previous run. She pressed Start and ran across the soccer field towards the cross-country trail.

Lea ran along the bank towards Princess Point, already ahead of her season's best time by more than a minute. All systems were functioning well, she thought, and her right hamstring, which had given her trouble over the past month or so, felt as good as new. She looked at her watch and tapped the face to increase her pace. Turning back from the point, Lea climbed the side of the ancient escarpment, the forest providing cool respite from the afternoon sun. The path was rough but familiar; there were no surprises, and she revelled in her ability to pick up speed, gaining ground as she climbed. Her heart rate and breathing were both unlaboured. Lea glanced at her watch, thinking, *UN-STOP-ABLE.*

The path followed the escarpment for more than a kilometre, up and down as the contour changed before looping back at a higher elevation. Her hamstring still felt fine. She recalled running like this as a child—the sheer joy of it, a sense that she could run forever, jumping over rocks and fallen branches like a deer or a dancer, feeling that she could pick up speed at will. Without breaking stride, at the two-and-a-half-kilometre marker she checked her watch—half a minute ahead of her previous run. "UN-STOP-ABLE!" Lea raced onto the higher path.

At the three-kilometre marker she looked down to check her time again, but before she could read the watch face, someone appeared directly in front of her, blocking the path. She saw a flash of silver and instinctively lunged to the left. Something stung her neck, but she had a bigger problem—her speed—as she tried to maintain her balance while running in the rough beside the path. She grazed a rock outcrop with her right hip; the impact pushed her onto the slope, where she tripped over broken branches and then was airborne, falling headfirst down the escarpment.

Lea instinctively threw up her arms to protect her face and head, but she began skidding and tumbling uncontrollably downwards. She felt a branch puncture her left side, knocking the wind out of her. In desperation, she stretched out her arms to grab hold of something solid. It was too late—she was in the air again and freefalling. Her feet landed first, but the momentum of her upper body sent her tumbling forward again. Her forehead hit something hard and her right eye filled with blood; she reached out, grasping at branches, but they came away in her hands. Spread-eagled on her back, she slid faster, sideways down the incline, and slammed into a tree—another rib snapped. She couldn't breathe, but she had stopped falling. Above, eighty or ninety feet up, she could see a figure backlit by the sun, still, his head a shiny black bubble. Trying to catch her breath, she pushed herself into a sitting position, wincing from the pain. When she looked up again, he was gone. Terrified, she scanned the path in either direction, but she couldn't see him.

Within minutes, three members of the men's cross-country team approached along the lower path; she could hear them talking as they ran. She tried to call out but couldn't summon enough breath to make a sound louder than a whisper. She grabbed a stick and, with great effort, threw it towards the path above, narrowly missing the front runner's face. Someone called her name. Before she blacked out, Lea again looked up to the path above—he really was gone.

Casey Mullin, a former cop and now a member of the Brant University Campus Police, met MacNeice at the doors of Dundurn General's trauma unit. Recognizing the detective, he said, "It's not a homicide but I'm glad to see you here, MacNeice."

"Sorry, I'm here on another matter. What happened at Brant?"

"Lea Nam, our cross-country superstar—she was attacked on a path in Cootes Ravine. Where she fell, the grade is roughly fifty degrees, but since she was going pretty fast, it would have been like taking a running leap off a cliff. The guys who found her said she was bleeding badly in several places, but you'll want to speak to the doctor about that. Nam mumbled something about a 'bubble-head'—they couldn't make any sense out of that. We've closed the trail and marked it for you if you want to see it."

"Is there a parking lot near the site?"

"Yeah. Well, actually, directly above it. We've closed that too. It's for overflow coming to the varsity games—empty most of the time."

"Thanks, Mullin. Let your people know I'll be coming." MacNeice walked past the three young men in BU-branded running gear and assumed they were the ones who had found the girl.

He went to the closest nursing station and asked, "Who's responsible for Lea Nam?"

The nurse looked around, then pointed with her ballpoint and said, "That's her over there—Dr. Dorothy Woodworth." She put her head down and continued her charts.

MacNeice approached the doctor, who was examining an X-ray on a screen. She was wearing blue scrubs and a surgical cap.

"Dr. Woodworth, I'm Detective Superintendent MacNeice. May I have a word?"

She gave him a quick once-over. "Be brief, Detective."

"Lea Nam. Tell me about her injuries."

"There are abrasions and contusions over most of her body, a punctured side and broken rib"—she pointed to the X-ray—"that narrowly missed going into the lung, and two cracked ribs on the other side. A nasty cut above her right eye—we've sewn that up— and then there's this slice in her sternocleidomastoid muscle." Seeing that MacNeice needed clarification on the last wound, Woodworth indicated one of two major neck muscles that rose like a V from the top of the breastbone to behind the ears.

"Do you think that cut could be a knife wound and not the result of her fall?"

"Most certainly it is, and it's not as bad as it could have been. She's a very lucky girl. I've been told she's an outstanding athlete, and it shows. We've stitched up that wound as well—it'll be very uncomfortable for her, but she's tough; she can take it."

"Is she awake? Can I speak to her?"

"She is—just. We've manipulated the rib back into place and cleaned out the puncture wound. The anesthetic has worn off but she's on Demerol for the pain, so she'll be groggy. You can have five minutes now, but you'll get better results in the morning."

"I'll take both. Can you take me to her?"

"Five minutes, Detective. Don't make me come and get you."

———

Lea was in the corner unit. A uniform from the west end was leaning against the wall but straightened up when he saw MacNeice and the doctor approaching. He held the door open for them. The blinking lights of monitors surrounded the young athlete, whose arms lay on top of the blue blanket. Two IV tubes were attached, one to her right arm, the other to her hand. Her eyes were closed; there were bandages on her forehead and neck, scrapes and small cuts on all the skin that was visible.

"Lea . . . Lea, I'm Detective Superintendent MacNeice. I'd like a brief word with you."

Dr. Woodworth stood at the bedside till the young woman opened her eyes, then, looking directly at MacNeice, she said again, "Five minutes," and left.

He waited till the young woman's eyes focused on his. "Can you tell me anything about the person who attacked you?"

It took several seconds before she spoke. He could hear the effects of the pain medication, her voice barely audible. "I . . . was running, checking my time . . . looked up . . . he was there. Something . . . something silver . . . and then I was off the path . . . I don't remember anything after that."

"Anything about him—what he looked like, what he was wearing, how tall he was?"

"Not sure . . ."

"Did you get a look at his face?"

"Don't know . . . so fast . . . going so fast . . . had to focus . . . where to run . . . He was tall, I think, and slim . . . I couldn't see his face . . . had a bubblehead . . . black, shiny bubblehead . . . maybe all black . . ."

"A bubblehead. Like a motorcycle helmet, Lea?"

"Yes . . . Black clothes." She closed her eyes. He waited for them to open again but they didn't. MacNeice left the room and the hospital. On his way to the Chevy, he called Williams and told him what was happening. The only thing the young detective said was, "One for two."

# 20.

DRIVING ONTO CAMPUS, MacNeice realized he didn't know where either the athletic facility or the parking lot was. He stopped at the curb as a jogger approached, flagging him down with his lights.

"What's up?" the young man asked. He was lanky and wore a tank top and baggy shorts to his knees.

"I'm looking for the overflow parking behind the athletic field."

"Oh yeah, where Lea got knifed."

"Exactly. How did you hear about it?"

"It's a small campus: word travels. You a cop?"

"Yes. How do I get there?"

He turned right at the end of the lane, took the next left as instructed, then passed by the athletic complex and practice field. There were two cruisers—one of them city, the other campus—blocking the entrance to the lot. On the grass beyond them was a blue police bus, used to ferry the personnel who would sweep the hill, and a black Suburban from Forensics. He drove up the curb and over the grass till he was parallel with the young cop standing outside his cruiser. MacNeice got out of the Chevy and greeted Gianni Del Bianco; his father had been a cop when MacNeice was the kid's age.

"Hi, Del. Point me in the direction of where she was attacked."

"Sure, sir. Where you see the yellow markers on the saplings—there, taped around the trunks . . ."

"I see them. Everyone down below?"

"Yes," Del said. "They're sweeping the hill. The forensics team is busy on the path. She was just below those markers when she was hit, then she went down another sixty feet or so. It's pretty vertical, but that's been taped too, about six feet either side, so you can see her path pretty clearly. She musta been flying."

"Good to see you. Say hello to your father for me."

"I will, sir, thank you."

MacNeice walked slowly into the lot. Somewhere along the escarpment a crow was calling; a few moments later a response came from farther down in the forest in the opposite direction. As he listened to the long-distance conversation, he scanned for fresh oil stains on the pavement. Nothing. He reached the space between the marked trees—still nothing.

He turned and looked across the lot to the other side. Farther to the right something was catching the light—a small black circle reflecting the evening sunshine coming uninterrupted from the west. At first he thought it was the lid of a can, but as he approached he could see it was a fresh oil stain, roughly three inches in diameter and so close to the edge of the pavement it couldn't have come from a car or a truck.

Squatting down, he dipped his index finger in the stain and held it to his nose—the sweet smell of oil and gasoline. "Two-stroke," he said to himself. The black print of a motorcycle's tire emerged out of the stain and faded to nothing, four feet or so in the direction of the lot entrance.

MacNeice walked over to the dirt path that ran along the side of the ravine just beyond the concrete barrier. There were no prints in the dust and gravel and nothing that indicated where the attacker might have descended the hill to the upper path. He walked over to the far eastern corner of the lot where the saplings were marked. Between the trees there was a narrow path that fell over rocks and tree roots. It was steep but passable. As he looked at the ground for footprints that might connect this incident to Taaraa Ghosh's murder, one of the Tyvek-clad forensics team climbed up towards him. He was carrying something in a plastic evidence bag; happy to see MacNeice above him, he held it up. He was out of breath but managed to say, "Taaraa Ghosh's BlackBerry, sir. He tossed it down the hill towards the runner. Your people found it halfway down."

"Anything else?"

"Two footprints. It's a well-worn path, but these are pretty good, and fresh. They're being checked against the one at the mountain. There's blood all the way down the hill—she was travelling so fast she was bouncing off rocks and smashing branches as she went."

"When you've put that in your truck, I want the oil stain over there." He pointed to the small circle. "Analyze it against the ones on Wentworth, both up at the mountain and down at Ghosh's apartment. How quickly can I have the results?"

"Well, we're almost done here, so I guess by first thing tomorrow, noon at the latest."

"I'll take first thing. Also, check out the tire track that leads out of the oil spill. I want to know what make of tire and, if possible, what kind of motorcycle it's on. I assume it's a two-stroke but I need to know more."

"That may take a while, sir."

"Try for noon." MacNeice turned and walked back to Del

Bianco, who was talking to a campus cop as he tossed his wind-breaker through the window of his car.

MacNeice asked, "Where do the runners come from and go to pick up the ravine trail?"

The campus cop, a man named James, pointed to the athletic facility on the far side of the field. "They come out of that side door from the gym and they head straight across the field to the cut you see between those trees. That's a paved road that leads down to Princess Point."

"Can your men check all the garbage bins on campus, especially those near the roads? I'm looking for anything that looks suspicious. Del Bianco knows how to reach me if you find anything. And lastly, please ask the young men who found Nam to speak to Del when they get back from the hospital."

"Sure thing," James said, reaching for his two-way.

Turning to the young officer, MacNeice said, "I want to know if they saw a motorcycle parked up here today, yesterday or anytime in the past week or so."

"Will do. You think he might've been scouting the trail?"

"He knew exactly where she'd be, so yes, I do."

MacNeice negotiated the steep trail at the far corner of the lot down to the path below, where there was still a lot of activity. He counted twelve uniforms, six on either side of her fall line. They were moving slowly down the incline, clinging to ropes that had been tethered to the larger trees bordering the higher and lower paths. The course of Lea's fall was clear. Dried leaves that had rested undisturbed for years had been gouged out of their slumber, and freshly broken branches and flattened bushes also defined her path. Just short of a twenty-foot vertical drop was the tree that had stopped her.

He walked over to two Tyvek kids who were on their knees concentrating on the spot where she had left the path. They were casting two clear footprints that likely belonged to the attacker. Seeing MacNeice, the older of the two said, "Hiking boots or maybe work-boots. We'll find out."

"Any idea how he got away?"

"Same way you came, sir—that path at the end. We found the same shoe print."

"Good work. Anything else?"

"Ghosh's BlackBerry. Why do you think he dumped it?"

"Because he knew we'd find it." What he didn't say was that the killer of Taaraa Ghosh wanted them to know this was his work too. MacNeice looked at the cops picking their way downward, looking more concerned about not falling than with finding anything. He walked back along the path, stepping over roots that rose out of the hardened dirt like knuckles laid bare on a forgotten battlefield. The attacker had left the trail, cutting an angle up to the vertical path, which was where they'd found the second boot print. MacNeice knelt down and studied the path he'd taken through the bush to connect with the path going up to the parking lot. He tried to imagine whether the man was panicking as he fled. There were no broken branches, and the leaves on the ground were more or less undisturbed. *He cut through just to be efficient*, MacNeice thought. *Not panicked.*

Suddenly behind him someone screamed, "Shit!" The officer at the top of the nearest ropeline had tripped and was falling. He knocked the legs out from under one of the female officers, and both began tumbling towards the next cop, who braced himself as the two ploughed into him. He sagged backwards but didn't give way. The two unscrambled themselves and with great effort regained their hold on the line.

MacNeice called down, "That officer's name, please."

Someone yelled back, "It was Nichol, sir. Constable Martin Nichol."

"Worthy of a citation, Nichol. Also, get your name on the tug-of-war team for the competition with Detroit."

"He's captain of the team, sir," someone called back. There was laughing and razzing on both sides of the line of Lea Nam's fall.

In the division parking lot MacNeice parked as he often did, close to the treeline, far away from the building. He opened the windows, hoping to catch a glimpse of a male cardinal he'd heard calling for days. Turning to a new page in his notebook, he jotted down what he knew about the slasher. He wasn't far into it when he changed tactics and wrote: *What connects a Bangladeshi-Canadian nursing student to a Korean-Canadian university athlete? Both high-achieving women, visible minorities, attacked in daylight in somewhat isolated settings. Only one cryptic swastika.* He was certain as he scanned the treeline for the bird that Nam would have suffered the same fate as Ghosh had she not fallen. *Fascist xenophobia—in Dundurn?* While there may have been closet neo-Nazis in the city, he wasn't aware of any recorded incident where they'd been cited. *Why now, why here? Who's next?* He underlined the last question.

A flash of red flew past the Chevy and landed on a branch of serviceberry. After sending its rippling call into the thick evening air, the cardinal lifted a wing and set about preening underneath it. Admiring the flame-red bird, MacNeice wrote down what he thought might be the opening line of a poem he'd get around to writing on a rainy day: *A drop of blood on a cardinal's wing may not be seen . . .* His mind freewheeling, MacNeice remembered Lea Nam's groggy reference to her attacker being all in black, with a black bubblehead. He forgot about the poem and wrote: *He's wearing black so their blood can't be seen. Is he wearing the helmet to hide or to terrorize?*

MacNeice put the notebook in his jacket pocket, closed the

windows and got out of the car. Before walking away, he looked up again at the cardinal. The bird's head swivelled towards him and, perceiving no threat, it lifted its other wing and went on preening.

Montile Williams was transcribing the day's interviews when MacNeice appeared in the cubicle. Ryan was flying through video footage with his special pattern-recognition program and only looked up to say, "The emergency ward's a Ghosh goldmine, sir. I'll have a lot to show you tomorrow."

MacNeice listened to five of the interviews Williams had recorded with the hospital staff, many of them sobbing as they spoke. And that wasn't solely because of her murder—they had been horrified to see the photograph of her corpse on the Internet.

Much of what they said had already been reported: they loved her. In each interview Williams had asked if they knew or had seen or heard of anyone at the hospital having a problem or confrontation with Nurse Ghosh, even the slightest of disagreements. In the last interview a doctor in the critical care unit said, "Look, everyone here, if asked that question about anyone else—including me—could probably fill your recorder with stories about what assholes their co-workers can be—but not Ghosh. As politically incorrect as it might be, a few of us nicknamed her Taaraa Gandhi."

As MacNeice looked up, Williams was nodding, as if to say, *What am I supposed to do with that?* "I've got eight more interviews booked for tomorrow, but I'm willing to bet they'll all be like these."

MacNeice started transcribing the observations from his notebook onto the whiteboard, about the similarities between the two women.

"Do you want me to switch to the Lea Nam case?"

"It's the same case," MacNeice said, looking back to the white-board, where a wire photo of Lea Nam accepting a gold medal had already been placed next to Ghosh. He glanced over to the second board, at Hughes in uniform, watching him, waiting. It was rare for MacNeice to feel cold, tiny shivers of panic. To the discovery of bone fragments in Cayuga, likely from the mutilated sergeant, and the fact that as of yet Bermuda Shorts had no identity, he added the certainty that Taaraa Ghosh and Lea Nam were just the beginning for the slasher. There were already more bodies than he had inves-tigators, and he could feel both cases growing, mutating into some-thing much larger.

Watching as MacNeice wrote on the boards, Williams said, "We're gettin' spread pretty thin, boss. You got any pull with that genie of yours?"

"Good question."

Ryan swung around. "Once I've finished with the hospital foot-age, I'll pitch in and research the couple in the Packard."

"Great idea—do it." He hadn't given a thought to the other bay homicides and was happy that Ryan had offered.

MacNeice could hear someone coming down the hallway—Vertesi. When he turned into the cubicle, he opened an envelope and handed the photos of Hughes and his family to MacNeice, who taped them on the whiteboard. Then he sat down at his desk while Vertesi debriefed them on the visit with Hughes's widow and his brief stopover at Old Soldiers.

"They made you," MacNeice said.

"Oh, big time, no question—for all I know, before I even got out of my rental." Vertesi stared at the whiteboards and sank lower in his chair. "God, another slasher attack. Missed his mark with this one . . . Did she give you anything?"

"Not much. He was wearing a black motorcycle helmet and he was fast with the blade, but she was faster and dodged the full stroke."

Vertesi studied the image of Nam, then sat down, shaking his head as he surveyed the two boards.

"You really think Hughes was killed by bikers?" Williams asked.

"I'm almost certain he was killed in that barn," MacNeice said.

"Judging by that family," Vertesi said, looking at the photo of Hughes and his kids, "there's no way he was a biker." He shook his head. "Those guys had snakes, Harleys and girlie tattoos. Our man had a battalion logo and the names of his family."

After a while the sound of Ryan's machine whirring away in the background—white noise—peeled away the edges of the day, leaving all three deeply fatigued. MacNeice was about to stand up when his phone rang. He answered.

"Turnbull in Forensics, sir. We just finished the lab work on that fragment—it's definitely human. We'll need more time to determine its exact skeletal origin, but the thickness and integrity of it is consistent with the skull."

"Thank you. Anything on the hedge trimmer?"

"The trimmer had been cleaned really well, probably with the pressure hose they have up there. No traces so far, but we're still looking. Once we're sure, I'll take it to the coroner's lab, cut open a coconut and compare that cut to the one on the corpse. You'll receive outputs of those soon as we're done. I'll also take the fragment so Richardson can do a DNA match to your body."

"Perfect. And the chairs?"

"One has deep abrasions on the underside and top of the seat consistent with chains restraining a bucking torso. There were similar scratches on the front legs. We're using ultraviolet photomicrography to see if there's any DNA caught in the grooves. There's nothing on the chair back, but they probably used rope around his arms and chest."

"Get the report over here as quickly as you can." MacNeice hung up and went to the whiteboard. Below *Hughes*, he wrote: *Hughes (likely) killed in the D2D barn, Cayuga. What was he doing there?*

His phone rang again; it was Turnbull calling back. "Sorry, sir. On the Ghosh file, the oil stains from the mountain driveway and Wentworth Street North sites are from the same two-stroke motor-cycle. We're not finished yet, but the one that just came in from the university has the same broad characteristics. By morning we'll have confirmation of that one for you."

"Thank you, Turnbull."

MacNeice went over to the second board and in red marker wrote: *Suspect rides a two-stroke motorcycle.* He studied the photos of Lea Nam with her gold medal and Taaraa Ghosh graduating from high school, then looked at Ghosh with her neck ripped open. He pictured the moment she had been confronted on the stairs by a stranger in black, wearing a black helmet and black visor. At first she would be confused, perhaps even angry . . .

"I'm done," he said. "First thing tomorrow, I'll go down to Dundurn General and speak to Lea Nam." He picked up his jacket, said goodnight and started to leave.

"You won't forget the genie, sir?" Williams called, turning back to his computer.

As MacNeice made the turn onto the winding road to the stone cottage, the man in the black helmet took over his thoughts. He tried to imagine what he might do next. Two women from visible minorities, one swastika. Would he attack a man next to show that he had the courage to do so, or would he continue to destroy young women, because they represented something. What? Procreation, perhaps—kill them and they couldn't produce more people like them. Or was it sexual fulfillment, even though he hadn't sexually molested either of them? Or was it that Ghosh and Nam were high-achieving women pursuing lives that were exemplary for both their sex and ethnicity—kill them and destroy hope? And what role did the police play in his scenario? Was he concerned at all about the law, or was he convinced that the force was so inept he could continue to do as he pleased? Did he hear voices in his head, the devil talking, or God? Did he know that the time would come when it would end? Was this an elaborate and grotesque road to "suicide by cop"?

# 21.

THE RAIN CAME hard, hammering the pavement and sending up clouds of steam that wrapped around his ankles, making it appear that he was floating above Wentworth Street. Cars swerved away from the lonely figure standing on the white line; occasionally someone would yell at him or hit the horn as they sped by, up or down the hill. MacNeice ignored the traffic and focused again on the stairs leading up the mountain and on the ditch to the right. He could feel the water snaking down his spine under his shirt, feel his drenched pant legs sticking to his shins with each passing car or pickup.

He heard them coming long before they passed over his head—crows, cawing through the downpour, heading for the mountain. MacNeice raised his head, squinting through the rain as they glided to the railing of the landing where Taaraa had waited for her mother. The last flew so low that he could see it look down towards him, its beady black eye shining at him, the rain splashing off its oily wings. The crow came to light just ahead of MacNeice, cranking its head sideways as if to better understand the man in the road. A truck came thundering down the mountain, its headlights catching the bird, casting its black shadow towards MacNeice. As the truck approached the crow, MacNeice thought to call out, but it was too late. The truck enveloped the bird and rumbled on past MacNeice, the rainwater slashing his legs. Unharmed, the crow turned and walked up the road, crossing to the mountain side before hopping down into the ditch where Taaraa Ghosh had died.

MacNeice wiped the water from his eyes and followed the crow. One by one the three birds that had perched on the railing lifted off and glided to the spot where the walking crow had gone. As MacNeice approached he could see them tearing at something. He paused before stepping forward: the crows were pulling at bloody strands of sinew that had been buried in the ground. Seeing MacNeice appear above the ditch, the walking crow squatted slightly, looking up at him with its beak open, revealing a bright red tongue. MacNeice expected a warning caw but heard only the splashing of the rain around him. He drew his service weapon, pointed it towards the skull of the bird and, at the last second, fired into the earth above it. Then he woke up.

Lying in bed, he realized that his T-shirt was soaking wet with sweat. He slipped it off and dropped it onto the floor. And then it came to him—*They're black coveralls, something he could easily slip on or off in a moment and appear to be someone else, just another guy on a motorcycle . . .*

MacNeice sat up, squinting at the clock radio—5:12 a.m. He considered trying to fall asleep again and decided he'd had enough of sleep, and dreams. He got out of bed, splashed his face in the sink and then climbed on his stationary bike. By 7:40 he was driving up King Street on his way to Dundurn General to speak to Lea Nam. At 8:06 he was making his way through wards where breakfast was being served, nurses were distributing painkillers and doctors were doing rounds; it was the best time to see the business side of the get-well factory.

The drapes were drawn in the room and only the upper wall light was on. Lea was sitting up, supported by the bed and several pillows. Her right eye was dark purple and swollen. The bandage from the previous day was gone, replaced by transparent adhesive closures running up at an angle away from her eyebrow. Her neck was still heavily bandaged. Her hair, blue-black and shiny, had been smoothed away from her forehead, likely by her mother, who was sitting in a chair at the far side of the bed. Seeing MacNeice, she stood up.

He offered his hand. "I'm Detective Superintendent MacNeice."

"Ruby Nam." She took his hand briefly and looked down at her daughter. "Can you tell me who did this?"

"I'm afraid I can't, not yet." Turning to the young woman, he said, "Lea, we met yesterday."

She smiled. In spite of the bruises, MacNeice was struck by how beautiful she was. "I remember. I told you about the black bubble."

"Yes. It was likely a motorcycle helmet."

"Yeah, I was out of it yesterday. But I had seen someone near the athletic centre with a black bubble helmet and a motorcycle."

MacNeice took out his notebook and pen. "Where exactly did you see him and how long ago?"

"I've been training for two big meets, so I've been on that trail every other day for the past three weeks. I can't remember which days, but I saw an orange motorcycle parked on the grass by the ravine on at least three different days. There's a parking lot at the end of the practice field—do you know it?"

"I do."

"That's where I saw him. He watched me run across the field to pick up the trail on the other side. I thought it was strange that someone was there, and every time, he was standing near his bike looking over at me."

"Tell me more about the motorcycle. Was it a scooter or a larger bike, like a Harley-Davidson?"

"Not a Harley—I'm familiar with those because there's a guy on the team who has one. No, this was smaller. Not like a scooter, though. Do you know what I mean?"

"I do. Did it have fenders?"

"I can't remember. The last time I saw him, I was on the road down to Princess Point, and it occurred to me how strange it was to keep seeing him there."

"We'll assemble a photo collection of motorcycles for you to review. Is there anything else, Lea?"

"How soon do you think—I mean, when do you think you can catch him?"

"We're committed to finding him very soon, and you've been very helpful."

Ruby Nam asked the critical question. "Do you think he'll come after my daughter again?"

"I don't think so. There are too many risks involved in making another attempt on your daughter. While she's in hospital, and even when she returns to the university, city and campus police will have her under surveillance. I'll have someone come by with the photos of motorcycles." MacNeice again offered Ruby Nam his hand, which she took, he thought, reluctantly. He smiled at Lea, turned and left the room. The cop at the door stood up as MacNeice emerged; after he'd disappeared at the end of the corridor, he sat down again.

Within two hours the cop was on his feet again, as Vertesi approached with a large manila folder. He knocked before entering the room, and seeing how dark it was, asked the woman in bed if he could turn on the overhead lights. She said, "Okay."

Vertesi introduced himself to Lea and her mother and reminded them of the reason for his visit. Using the rolling tray, he went through a series of flashcards of motorcycles, from dirt bikes to road hogs, from scooters to Japanese crotch-rockets.

She said, "Maybe," several times, but at least it was always to a similar profile: two-stroke dirt bikes and road bikes. "I'm pretty sure it was orange . . . But then, it was always sunny, so it might have been red . . . I'm sorry."

"Don't be—you're doing great. It's easy to mix them up." With each "maybe" Vertesi added to a separate pile of cards. When he'd eliminated all the "no" cards, he started going through the maybes again.

Twenty minutes later he was leaving the hospital with four bikes that qualified as maybes. One was actually blue and white, but Lea thought its profile made it a maybe. She had asked, "What kind of bikes are they?"

"All four are Japanese, but honestly, Lea, I don't know much about them. Forensics will. You've been very helpful. Tell me, did you ever hear it idling or driving away?"

"No, sorry. I remember actually thinking, the first time, maybe it had broken down."

When he returned to Division, Vertesi dropped the images off with Forensics before heading upstairs. When he reached the cubicle, Williams was leaning over Ryan's computer. Deputy Chief Wallace was in the middle of a press conference about Lea Nam, much larger than the one he'd held for Ghosh. "They're asking if there's any connection between the two attacks," Williams said.

Wallace didn't hesitate. "That hasn't been confirmed. The investigation is still in the early stages. However, nothing has been ruled out." The cluster of microphones in front of him included two sports networks among the mainstream radio stations and television channels—an acknowledgement of Nam's celebrity as an athlete. Over his shoulder to the right was MacNeice, who had made the initial announcement before turning over the micro-phone to the Deputy Chief.

When MacNeice returned to the cubicle, Williams didn't ask about the press conference but whether his boss had spoken to Wallace about additional help.

"Yes. He said, 'Speak to your genie, then tell me who you want.'"

"Damn—I thought he was the genie," Williams said.

"So I spoke to the genie."

"And?" Vertesi asked.

"He said, 'Tell your boss who you want, but remember the wage freeze.'"

"Have you got someone in mind? I mean, Swetsky's gonna be hunting for the boys who killed the bikers we found above ground, so his team's going to get bigger, not smaller. And that's before he gets to the ones wrapped in plastic."

"I do, but it's a long shot," MacNeice said.

"Fiza Aziz!" Vertesi blurted.

"Exactly."

"No way. D'ya think she'd just up and leave the university?" Williams asked. But he had to concede that, given the circum-stances, Fiza Aziz was not only the perfect candidate, she was the only candidate.

"I don't know."

"She's not happy in Ottawa, boss," Vertesi said. "We've been emailing back and forth for the past six months. Aziz was burnt out by our last case together. When the offer to teach criminology came, it just seemed like the right thing to do. But that was then . . ."

"What about the hiring freeze?" Williams asked.

"I might be able to swing calling her departure a sabbatical, a

leave of absence, or possibly even professional development
—retroactively."

"You haven't called her yet?" Vertesi asked.

"No."

Williams moved abruptly to his computer and opened the search
engine. Vertesi asked, "What's up?"

"An idea—maybe nothing. I just thought Aziz—a PhD, a detective, a member of a visible minority, a Muslim—remember the
article the *Standard* did when she was promoted to DI? It's a long
shot, but Ghosh and Nam are both overachievers." He tapped in
*Taaraa Ghosh*. The first page to appear was filled with news reports
of her murder, but halfway down the second page was an article
published three months earlier: "New Canadian Places First among
Nursing Students." It included a photograph of her smiling as she
checked the blood pressure of an elderly patient, who was also smiling. The article mentioned, among other things, the death of
Taaraa's father and brother in a terrorist bombing in Bangladesh.

Williams then entered Lea Nam's name and hit the Return
button. Again after the coverage of the recent attack came older
articles, some of them from national sources, about her triumphs—
or predicted triumphs—in cross-country.

MacNeice sat down at his desk, staring over at Williams's screen.

"So you figure our perp is reading the papers to identify his targets?" Vertesi said.

"Why not? Narrows the field. They're in the news because
they're great at something, and he's got pictures for reference. So
far he's hit two of them . . ."

"It's also something you could reverse-engineer," MacNeice said.

"How so?" Vertesi asked.

"You enter 'outstanding young immigrant women' plus
'Dundurn.' Find the articles and you find the potential targets,"
Williams answered. "Based on the first two, he's not going to take

out an immigrant mom who's in the news because her welfare cheque didn't arrive and her kid has leukemia." He looked over at Ryan. "Does that make sense?"

"The question needs refining," Ryan said.

"You know how to do it, though?"

"Yessir. Soon as I'm done with the hospital, if that's okay."

"Keep going on the hospital footage," MacNeice said.

He got up and went to Swetsky's office, where he wouldn't be disturbed. He wasn't sure Aziz would say yes to his offer. He was pretty sure she had burned out not because of their last case but because of their mutual attraction—or distraction. That distraction had led to the death of a young man, a witness to a murder whom the perpetrators wanted to silence. They'd thrown him over the railing of a hotel atrium, twenty-one storeys above the lobby; he'd smashed through a glass ceiling and blown apart at her feet. Her belief in MacNeice had been extinguished at the same time, he feared.

He laid his hand on the desk phone, working up his nerve, then picked up the receiver and dialled. The telephone rang several times before she answered. MacNeice felt a rush hearing her voice again—so steady and assured. He said hello and, after an awkward silence, asked, "Is teaching all you hoped it would be, Fiza?"

There was a long pause, during which he heard her sigh, then, at last, chuckle. "No. No, it isn't, Mac. I don't know—teaching isn't living, it's like constantly preparing for life."

"I'm not sure I understand . . ."

"I'm not sure I do either. The faculty are all criminologists, no doubt about that, and in the main they're fine people, even dedicated people, but none of them has ever smelled fear or death or experienced the brutal mayhem that we—They're concerned about tenure, Mac, and putting decks on their cottages in the Gatineaus."

"But I would have thought that brutal mayhem was exactly what you didn't want after our last outing."

"That's what I thought too."

The phone line went quiet again, and MacNeice simply waited for her to continue. He studied a snapshot tacked on the wall above the phone: a smiling Swetsky on a dock somewhere triumphantly lifting a large muskellunge for the camera. On the border he had written: *The one that didn't get away.* Was it a talisman that helped Swetsky deal with the grim realities of homicide? MacNeice realized he'd never seen the big man smile like that.

"Mac . . ."

"Yes?"

"Why are you calling?"

"To ask you to come back. Your job is open if you're interested— and we really need you here."

Aziz inhaled sharply; he could hear her chair creak as she changed positions. "You're serious?" Then she said, "Of course, you're serious."

"You must have heard about the biker killings, which have already stretched our resources to the maximum. Someone is also slashing and killing young women here, Fiza. I'm very serious."

"How much time do I have to think it over?"

"Fiza, we don't have time."

"But really, how soon would I have to get back to you? I don't want to leave them in the lurch here, no matter how much I don't think I'm suited to teaching."

"By now I mean today. *Now.*"

"Okay—tonight."

# 22.

THEY WERE ALL staring at him as he returned to the cubicle. He shrugged, then said, "We'll hear by tonight if she's coming back." All of them knew better than to push him for more detail, though Vertesi said, "Maybe we should book her a hotel until she can get her stuff moved back." MacNeice had to laugh, and they all joined in. Clearly they missed her almost as much as he did. "Let's just hold off on that," he said. "I don't want to jinx it."

Williams said, "Ryan's ready to roll four weeks of Ghosh Emerg footage."

They had set up a ringside seat for MacNeice right in front of Ryan's central monitor. Ryan was off to the side of the desk, his keyboard and joystick in front of him.

Reviewing the footage was disorienting, like watching the grooves on a baggage carousel pass by after a long flight. The scenes began at normal speed, then Ryan would move the stick forward and they'd speed up, or he'd move it back and Taaraa would walk by in slow motion. The detectives focused on the images as Ryan manipulated the joystick. They watched the changing cast of characters pass—fast, slow, normal—and after a while they sank into the rythmn of it so much that normal speed resembled crawling.

Every one of Ghosh's interactions appeared to be pleasant, professional and compassionate, whether she had her arm around an old man with a walker or was easing an extremely pregnant woman into a wheelchair or was kneeling in front of a boy with a gash on his knee.

On the third pass MacNeice said, "Wait. Rewind it. I'll tell you when to stop."

Ryan, who'd been slouching, sat up in anticipation and shoved the stick down, the images blurring by.

"Stop." MacNeice moved closer to the screen. Williams looked at Vertesi, who raised his eyebrows.

"What'ya got, boss?" Williams said.

"I'm not sure. Ryan, can you isolate this frame, then roll it all again slowly?"

"No problem." He clicked the keyboard several times and moved the mouse about. Soon the solitary image occupied a corner of the middle screen while the video footage continued to roll on the smaller monitor.

"Stop. Grab that image." MacNeice pointed to the frame.

*Click, click, click* and the second image appeared beside the first. "Let it roll, sir?"

MacNeice nodded.

Soon a third, fourth, fifth, sixth, seventh and eighth image had joined the first two in a grid on the Falcon's large monitor.

"Before you do anything else, can you label each of those images with the date and time they were captured?"

"Give me five minutes, sir," Ryan said, sliding the keyboard in front of him.

MacNeice left the cubicle to make an espresso. When he was gone, Vertesi and Williams moved closer to the screen, scanning the images.

"I think it's the guy in the light jacket." Ryan pointed to the left side of the screen. The same tall young man was either standing off to the edge of the frame or, in others, half out of the picture.

Williams shook his head slowly in admiration. "Man, the boss has an eye. All this time I was watching the people interacting with Ghosh."

Returning with coffee in hand, MacNeice asked, "What have we got?"

"The guy in a tan or grey jacket, off to the left," Williams said.

"Exactly. Who is he? Why is he there?"

"How the hell did you spot him?" Vertesi asked. "He's so far out of the action—barely in the shot."

"That's the point. He's barely there, but he's always there. Some people stand out because they keep interacting, like the staff. Others stand out because they're not, like him. He's standing or sitting among people, but apart from them. Never engaging or being engaged . . . He's just watching." MacNeice studied the eight images.

"I ran the pattern-recognition program and there's more shots of him coming in now, sir." Ryan said, clicking the keyboard. In a moment, six additional images appeared above the original eight.

"Just legs and a bit of the jacket . . ." Williams said.

"Looks like he spotted the camera," Ryan offered.

"I'm sure he did. Put the dates on those images as well." MacNeice finished his coffee and sat down.

"Should we review the fractures clinic footage again, see if he's up there?" Vertesi asked.

"He won't be if he's our man. That clinic is too deep within the hospital. He wants a nearby door to the outside and an easy escape route. We've been focused on the staff as suspects, which was the right thing to do—until he hit Lea Nam. I doubt she'd ever seen the inside of this hospital."

"Ready to roll, sir." Ryan smiled, cracking his knuckles theatrically. The eight images blinked off the screen, then back on, with date and time in a black bar at the bottom. The screen seemed to hesitate for a moment; then another six images joined the grid.

"Jesus, look at the dates!" Vertesi said. "He was there on five separate days. Who needs to be in an emergency ward for five days? And three of them consecutive."

"Can you refine the best of these images—what's the word for that?" MacNeice asked.

"Sharpen," Ryan said. "I can confuse the resolution into thinking it's sharper. And I can adjust the exposure so even a distant relative would recognize him. Give me five more minutes."

"Sir, I've got him," Ryan said a short while later, sliding his chair to the right.

Judging by the door frame behind him, the young man was just over six feet tall and slim, maybe 180 pounds. He had a long neck that supported a disproportionately large head. His face seemed too beautiful—boyish, almost pretty—to belong to someone so dangerous. *How old is he?* MacNeice wondered; it was difficult to imagine that he shaved, or had ever had a pimple. His eyes were large and wide apart; his hair was tousled and probably mousy blond, though it was difficult to be certain, since the images were in shades of grey. Was he intelligent? MacNeice studied the face again and concluded that if a cat hunting a sparrow is intelligent, then this was a very smart cat. In all but one image he was smiling. His expression reminded MacNeice of Chas Green's dummy—and it was just as frozen. In one frame, however, he seemed to be distracted, watching someone at the nurse's station, which was just out of view. When they'd looked at all the images, Ryan started again from the beginning.

"Look—his left hand in the first frame." Vertesi pointed at the screen. There was a narrow bandage wrapped tightly around the palm.

"Yeah, but it's not in the other frames," Williams said. "Can you put them all up together again?"

"Zoom in on that hand." MacNeice had turned away and was focused on the photo taped to the whiteboard of Taarraa Ghosh's stomach, with his own hand-drawn swastika connecting the wounds.

"First day, bandage. Then no bandage. He had to be scouting. What other reason could there be?" Vertesi said, turning to MacNeice. "If the security cameras were picking him up—even when he moved to get out of the frame—why wasn't Security picking him up?"

"They're looking for action. Someone punches someone, throws a chair or shoves a nurse. This guy was just Smilin' Sam, not askin' for attention and not gettin' any," Williams said. "I'll get the close-up with its date and time down to the hospital Emerg—see if they've got a record of him."

"Boss, can we send this image out across the province?" Vertesi asked.

"Not yet. Right now we have a smiling man in a waiting room. We don't know who he is or why he keeps coming back. We need the hospital report, and we need the motorcycle. Ryan, can we check out the parking lot footage?"

Ryan moved back to the centre screen. Within minutes he'd matched the dates on the frames to the corresponding times in the parking lot, and soon he was pointing to the area in the lot where motorcycles were parked.

"Okay, we're looking for a two-stroke, whatever that is," Williams said.

"Yeah, with a red or orange tank—easy to pick out in a black-and-white video," Vertesi added sarcastically.

"On the right there"—Ryan pointed—"by the edge of the lot. That's a 1986 Yamaha RZ500LC, in orange and white, or red and white. That's a hopped-up two-stroke—V4, six-speed, with 8,500 rpms of torque."

"Are you serious?" Williams looked down the line of motorcycles.

"I race dirt bikes. It's the only two-stroke in the bike pen."

"What the hell does '8,500 rpms of torque' mean?" Williams glanced over at Vertesi.

"Means it's a road bitch, sir," Ryan answered. "Built for speed, not for buying sody pops down at the mall. Its final production year was 1986. You couldn't even buy that bike in the States—it was too hot for their environmental standards even then, which is probably why Yamaha pulled it."

"Can you read the plate?" MacNeice asked.

"No, sir, he parked it broadside to the camera. But I'll scan the footage for these dates and grab him on the move."

"Who would service a bike like that, Ryan?" MacNeice asked, leaning into the screen.

"Well, the guy who owns this can probably take it apart like a junior Lego set. If it were mine, I wouldn't let anyone touch it. There are bike geeks I can ask, though . . ."

"Be discreet, but show the image to your friends. Tell them you've been promoted and you're in the market for a—what is it again?"

"An '86 RZ500LC. Does that mean I've been promoted, sir?" Ryan swung around and looked doe-eyed at MacNeice.

"I've got him, sir," Ryan said a while later, sliding off to the side.

MacNeice and the two detectives took their seats and Ryan moved the joystick forward. The biker was wearing the light jacket they'd seen on the young man in the emergency ward and had on a light-coloured bubble helmet. He drove in from the right, parking at the far end of the line of motorcycles.

"As far as he can get from the camera," Williams said.

"That helmet white or silver, Ryan?" Vertesi asked.

"Silver all the way, sir. So's the visor."

Once again the licence plate was perpendicular to the lens. "He drives into the same area every time. Watch," Ryan said as he tipped the joystick forward. The bike slid into the same spot, or the one beside it, five times. "Now here's where it gets interesting."

Ryan had cut the departure footage together. In every sequence but one, the biker backed up and drove straight ahead out of the frame—the long way out of the lot, and the sure way to avoid the camera. "Last visit, day five, he does something different." Backing out of the parking spot, he drove forward and turned left beyond the bike pen, towards the surveillance camera.

"Boy's got balls," Williams said.

"Stop the image just before he exits the bottom of the frame," MacNeice said, pointing to the screen. Ryan moved the rider slowly downfield. "Right there, stop. Can you zoom in?"

"Sure thing." Ryan clicked the keyboard and with the joystick started a slow zoom.

"Stop." MacNeice looked at the young man in the bubble helmet. The visor was mirrored but exposed his face from the bottom of his nose down.

"He's smiling," Vertesi said, shaking his head.

"Yes, and at the camera." MacNeice shook his head, disbelieving. "He's been there five days and no one has even noticed. It's like he's been given a green light on Taaraa Ghosh." MacNeice stared at the helmet; there was a highlight from the sun in the centre of it, just above the visor. "Can you blow up the helmet and reduce the glare of the sun?"

Ryan nodded. The helmet soon filled the screen, the highlight even brighter. Ryan changed the exposure until the silver looked dark grey, almost black. Now in the highlight they could see four short lines—just like the ones that had been incised in Taaraa's abdomen.

"Print that." As he glanced at Ryan, MacNeice caught sight of five empty paper cups stacked on the corner of his desk. "How long have you been here?"

Before Ryan could answer, Williams said, "Long time, boss. He was here all night."

"Christ, Ryan, you've got to go home," MacNeice said sharply.

"Tried that, boss," Williams responded for Ryan. "He's takin' the whole 'race against time' thing seriously."

"I can hear you, Detective Williams . . ." Ryan said without turning.

"What's that on your right monitor?" MacNeice asked.

"I'm tracking the bike. I know every legit garage and chop shop in the region. I've put out a cool story about how I saw this beauty RZ500 and I want to make an offer on it if I can find it."

His ingenuity and technical agility made MacNeice smile. He stood watching as each screen scrolled or stitched together something that was distinct from the others. And at last he began to understand why Ryan called the Millennium Falcon a supercomputer. It wasn't that MacNeice was a Luddite, wishing technical progress had ended with the radio and vinyl records. It was more that his thinking and his aesthetic—for want of a better word—was of another age, when one rejoiced in the beauty of the tangible, of things you could touch.

"Got any nibbles yet?" MacNeice asked.

"I've got a guy who says someone called about a crankcase for an RZ500 and he referred him to Yamaha. But Yamaha says he didn't order it through them, and they offered to trace it for me with

Yamaha Japan. They'll get back to us tomorrow if they have a name and address."

"The oil leak."

"Right on. He's got a problem he can't fix without parts."

"None of them recognize the bike?"

"No. For sure he's his own mechanic."

# 23.

LATER THAT AFTERNOON, Turnbull called MacNeice from the coroner's office. It turned out that, as he had guessed, the fragment from the drain was from the body of Sergeant Hughes. They'd failed to find DNA on the hedge trimmer but the cutting pattern matched. Junior had had way too much fun experimenting with a coconut, a plastic skull and a pig's skull—all of which proved inconclusive. Finally he'd tried slicing bone from a donor corpse, and the saw marks were identical.

MacNeice hung up the phone. Bikers and concrete companies. What was the connection? He got up, went over to the whiteboard and picked up a marker. Under the photos of Hughes, he erased the *likely* and then underlined *murdered in the D2D barn, Cayuga.*

"Whoa, boss, that's gonna have an impact on Swetsky's investigation," Williams said.

"No doubt. Michael, where do the concrete suppliers get their material?"

"Well, ABC-Grimsby has a huge quarry, and they supply Mancini as well—though Alberto Mancini didn't mention that."

"And McNamara?"

"The guy I spoke to at ABC said he thought they trucked theirs in from Orangeville."

"Further away, in other words."

"Yes, sure. But why is that important?"

"Distance is time; time is money. McNamara was at a disadvantage," MacNeice said, still staring at the photos of Hughes.

"ABC and Mancini are both Italian," Williams noted.

"Yeah, but the same guy told me Mancini had tried to buy the quarry and was beat out at the last minute by ABC. He wouldn't have been too happy about that," Vertesi said, drumming the desk with the fingers of one hand.

"It's business. He lost, then did a side deal to get the material. But where was he getting it from before?"

"I don't know."

"But Italians and bikers? I don't get the fit," Williams said.

"I do." Ryan had been working so quietly for a while that the three detectives had almost forgotten he was sitting there. "Bikers are semi-legit muscle for hire. You see them at rock shows, motocross weekends, ATV races, wrestling matches—they provide 'security.' Even when they go civilian and wear suits, they're still bikers and still only semi-legit."

"Yeah, but Italians use their own muscle," Williams said, looking over at Vertesi for confirmation.

"Not always," Vertesi said.

"Hiring an independent security contractor—probably off the books—isn't a bad idea when three levels of government are focused on your business," MacNeice said, turning back to the whiteboard.

"But aren't bikers incredibly territorial?" Williams was looking confused.

"For sure," Ryan said. "All it would take for sparks to really fly would be a rival biker gang, wearing their colours, showing up without permission."

"But Hughes wasn't a biker. Or if he was, his wife didn't know," Vertesi said.

"Who's going to war? DeLillo with ABC, Mancini with McNamara, McNamara with ABC? I'm missing the plot here." Williams wrote down the rival companies on a notepad, trying to figure out the logic. "They're all suppliers to the mayor's project, except DeLillo. McNamara's costs are higher than ABC's and Mancini's, but does that justify a war?"

"Possibly. We need confirmation that a biker gang operates out of Old Soldiers." MacNeice studied the Photoshopped image of Bermuda Shorts without the hole in his forehead. "But first, Michael, I need you to go ask the Mancinis a few more questions."

Notably absent were the pleasantries of his first visit. Vertesi was ushered into Alberto Mancini's office by one of the desk clerks. Alberto didn't offer his hand this time and waved Vertesi into one of the chairs in front of the desk; his son nodded from where he sat.

Vertesi said, "I appreciate your seeing me again at such short notice."

"You have a job to do, Michael," Alberto replied. "How can I help you?"

"I understand Mancini Concrete has a contract with ABC-Grimsby. Is that correct?"

"*Si.*"

"And that you were one of the bidders for the Grimsby quarry before ABC came along and outbid you."

"I wouldn't use the word *outbid*. I never saw the ABC bid."

"Are you suggesting ABC won it unfairly?"

"Not at all, though others might."

"Can you explain yourself, sir?"

"My father doesn't have to explain anything to you," Pat said, shifting in his chair to face Vertesi.

"Please, Patrizio," Alberto said, looking down at his hands. "We spoke before about optics and politics, Michael. Many people believe ABC won for those reasons."

"And you don't?"

"I don't care to waste my time with it. I wanted the Grimsby site so I would have access to raw materials. When we lost, I made a deal to buy the materials, so I now have what I wanted—access."

"Where were you buying them before?"

"Orangeville, North Milton, Brampton."

"Further away."

"*Si.*"

"Did McNamara try to make the same deal?"

"You'd have to ask McNamara."

"Is there any connection between Mancini Concrete and a local motorcycle club named Damned Two Deuces?"

"I don't follow you, son." Alberto's hands lifted slightly before falling slowly back to the desk.

"What the hell are you getting at?" Pat demanded, the scar on his chin appearing brighter and angrier.

"I thought you might hire bikers to manage security. Here, for example." Vertesi waved to include the whole business.

"Why would Pa need bikers to protect us? This isn't a cash business; there's nothing here worth stealing."

Vertesi stayed focused on Alberto. "You've heard about the bikers who were found dead in Cayuga?"

Alberto nodded.

"We've now linked one of the bodies from the bay to the barn on that farm."

"Yeah, a concrete crime wave—you're way outta line." Pat's voice was scornful.

"Patrizio, that's enough." Alberto's tone was firm, and his son sat back in the chair. "Michael, we don't hire bikers. I don't know any bikers, and no, we've never had a security problem."

He stood then, an Italian-Canadian patriarch secure in his position as a businessman and community leader. "If there are no further questions, I will go home to dinner."

He waited for Vertesi to stand too, and then accompanied him to the door. Pat Mancini stayed put and said nothing. Alberto shook Vertesi's hand. "Give my regards to your parents."

Stepping out of the president's office, Vertesi noticed that the four men at their desks all had their heads down, pretending to be hard at work. It was clear they'd heard Pat Mancini raise his voice.

Outside on the wooden steps, Vertesi watched the trucks coming into the yard, kicking up dust as they rumbled past him to park side by side near the silos that in the morning would load them up again. He studied the lineup of cars and SUVs in the lot near the fence, their lines softened by concrete dust. Separated from them and covered by a canvas tarpaulin was another vehicle—low and sleek, with fat wheels—Pat Mancini's car.

He tried to remember when it was that Pat had left the NHL. Almost two years ago. What was it like to follow your glory days of hockey with a job in your father's concrete yard, shaking dust off the tarp before you climb into your pretty car and cruise downtown?

Still, not many hockey players could say they'd even been to the Big Show. Pat Mancini had. He'd gone in style and played well, and would be playing still if concussions of increasing severity hadn't made that impossible. After the last one, a renowned neurologist had described his condition graphically in a widely reported interview: "It's like taking a one-of-a-kind precision instrument, smacking it five times with a sledgehammer and then expecting it to remain precise. It won't, and he won't."

And so Pat Mancini had come home to Dundurn, welcomed back into the bosom of his family but exiled from the thing he did best.

# 24.

TO ANOTHER PERSON, a dog or even a fly on the wall, the young man in the black helmet might seem odd, lost in conversation with the mirror. But he was completely alone, and to him there was nothing unusual about his habit of addressing himself in the third person. Nor was it the slightest bit strange to him when the mirror spoke back.

He enjoyed breathing inside the helmet; it made him feel invisible—not to be safe but to be dangerous, as if he were Darth Vader. It felt as if there was just him and what he could see—which was everything. Some people wanted a sound system installed in their helmet, but not Billie Dance. He enjoyed the filtered reality of the outside within the controlled world of the helmet. He could say whatever he wanted to say, call people names or laugh at them, and unless he was really loud—which was almost never—no one could hear him. The black helmet was the closest he'd come to realizing his childhood dream—born of hours of playing Dungeons and Dragons—of becoming a knight avenger, out to set things straight.

The only thing he'd lacked before now was a cause worthy of a knight avenger. Well, the truth was, his cause had been there all along, waiting for him even before he was born.

"The demographics of Canada," he told the mirror, "which were sold to the world as evidence of our happy multicultural society, changed everything."

"Huh?" the mirror image asked.

"It was like white people—who settled and tamed this country— stopped screwing to have kids in the 1960s, after the pill arrived." Lifting off the helmet, he studied his face for a moment, admiring the smooth, creamy skin and shiny fair hair of an Anglo-Saxon. "They got fat and complacent; they wanted lots of things, and they wanted someone to clean up after them and do the dirty work. Well, not at first. At first," he mused, looking down at his distorted reflection in the black bubble's visor, "they just felt sorry for immigrants of colour, many of whom couldn't, or wouldn't, learn to speak English—ever. Before long those immigrants had fucked themselves silly and had tons of kids, and the kids went to school to become somebody better than their parents, and then those kids fucked themselves silly to become somebody better than the white Canadians who had taken pity on them in the first place."

"That's not right."

"No, it's not. It's truly fucked! It wasn't until I found demographics . . ."

"Numbers?"

"Not the stuff you read in *The Economist*—the stuff that drives the stuff you read."

He had discovered the discipline of demographics in university. Billie Dance was a natural at it. His math scores were always off the charts—he could do division in his head when he was three. But school had always bored Billie, for lots of reasons.

"Gimme one!"

"Well, chess, for instance. Billie was in grade nine when he won the championship for the city, and he missed out on the provincial championships only because he got pneumonia. The absolute best, though, was when he humiliated the vice-principal, who'd been provincial junior champion when he was in grade twelve! He defeated him—crushed him—in three straight sets before the entire chess club . . . But then, that was only four people, and it's not like those friendless fuckers were going to tell anyone."

"Then what happened?"

"Nothing. That was the most challenging thing about high school, and after that he never played chess again. But when he successfully defended his master's thesis about the changing face of Canada, Billie made a breakthrough. He realized he could put demographics to work."

"How?"

"Easy. It's like cream."

"Cream rises to the top?"

"Sort of. You just keep skimming the cream off the top, because when the best of these people succeed, they get put in charge of companies that fire white Canadians; they get into government and tell us what we can do or not do; they can afford the best houses anywhere they want, but mostly they create these places that don't even look Canadian—you could be in India or Korea or China."

"And the numbers, the demographics?"

"Track the past seven decades—I've done it—and look where we're headed."

"Where?"

"To a place where white people are in deep shit. Take Toronto. You've got 150,000 people moving in every year. In four years that's a number bigger than the population of most Canadian cities. More than half of those people don't speak English as their first language.

We're going to be like the English were in India, or Africa, except those weren't their countries to begin with."

"And then what?"

"We'll be forced out, or wiped out. The only way we'll start screwing again is through intermarriage, and then you know what we've got?"

"What?"

"Population demographics won't matter anymore, because we'll be one big, muddy grey/pink/brown/yellow blob."

"A blob."

"And the history books will be burned. Who needs that shit around about the days when whites ruled? Nobody!"

"What about the Jews? Isn't this where the Jews come in?"

"That was the problem with Hitler and his band of freaks—they misidentified the problem. *We* are Jews! Don't you get it?"

"Ah, no."

"Well, go back to the Bible. Jesus—our guy—was a Jew. Ergo, we're all descendants of Jews."

"So we've wasted centuries killing Jews."

"Yup, total waste of time. They are us. That's a hyphen in *Judeo-Christian*, not a period."

"Hitler had a cool logo, though."

"Ours is cooler, not retro like the neo-Nazis'. Ours takes some intelligence to interpret, and that's what's missing with the neo-Nazis—they're dumb as dirt. Now let's get to work."

"But shouldn't we be building a following like the skinheads did?"

"No, no, no! We're not white trash like them. The Knights Templar began with eight members, eight warrior monks. The order grew to number in the thousands because of their dedication to a code. Shit, just the rumour they were coming and whole towns would clear, like rats running from a fire. We have a code and we have the dedication. People will follow us, but first we must point the way by deeds, not words."

Billie pulled his black coveralls over his jeans and T-shirt, put on the black hiking boots and slipped on the backpack with the wide padded strap. Into its Velcro sheath he slid his long blade, securing the hilt just to the left of his ribcage. Finally, and somewhat ceremoniously, he donned the black helmet.

He stood quietly in front of the mirror with his hands at his sides, angling his head to the left and then to the right. He glanced up at the clock—6:14 p.m. "Time to skim some cream!"

His right hand moved so swiftly it was hard to distinguish the downward release of the knife from the upward backhand slash.

"Christ, you're fast."

"Christ, I am."

"Let's go hunting."

"We will. Tonight. But first it's research, the terra firma of demographics." He put the knife back in the sheath and laid the backpack on the table.

"Skim some cream . . . you should do a T-shirt of that."

"Maybe I will."

"Remember when the nurse spotted you watching her and asked what you were doing? Let's not make that mistake again."

"I won't."

"Though it was cool the way you just smiled at her."

"Yeah, it freaked her out. She knew I was coming for her—she just didn't know when."

"Weird that she didn't call Security."

"They don't. Demographics, my friend. Most people think they must be mistaken, they're imagining things, or they don't want to cause trouble. Then there's their worst fear . . ."

"What's that?"

"They worry that if they're wrong, it will be so embarrassing.

They don't want to be humiliated, so they don't do anything."

"Human nature, you're saying."

"Human. Nature is something else."

"Huh?"

"You fuck with a wolf, a bear, a hyena, a snake—they don't hesitate or wonder or worry about making fools of themselves. No, this one is just human—pure and stupid simple."

# 25.

AT 9:42 P.M., MacNeice was enjoying a grappa with Marcello when his BlackBerry rang. He looked at the screen, excused himself and stepped out the back door of the restaurant into the laneway. "I'd pretty much given up on hearing from you."

Her voice was so soft MacNeice covered his other ear. "Mac, I'm coming."

"Great! How soon can you get here? We need you now, not next week or two weeks from now."

"I booked the 8:50 a.m. flight to Dundurn Regional for tomorrow morning."

MacNeice laughed and said, "I'll have you picked up and brought to Division. You'll be with us all before lunch tomorrow. And just in case you said yes, Vertesi booked you a room at the Chelsea."

"You guys don't stop, do you?"

"Fiza, we've got a man with a big knife who won't stop unless we stop him. And we've now connected one of the bodies in the bay to the biker murders Swetsky has been dealing with in Cayuga—though what the connection is we don't know. When I said we needed you, I really meant it."

Fiza laughed, long and hard, and he joined in, the knot he'd had in his stomach finally letting go.

After they hung up, he stayed outside a moment longer, watching three starlings on a telephone line chatting and shuffling to the left, then the right, as if they were dancing or perhaps deciding which had the better view of the rooftops. He was about to open the door when his cellphone rang. Without looking at the screen, he said, "Forget something?"

"It's me, boss," Williams said. "There's been another one, down at Van Wagners Beach. We're on our way now."

"I'll be right there."

MacNeice went inside to put the dinner on his tab and ran out through the back door. A quick glance at his watch told him it was 10:11 p.m.

Van Wagners Beach stretched for a mile or so along the southwest shore of Lake Ontario, not far from the canal that let lake freighters in and out of Dundurn Bay. It was a scalloped beach with breakwater piles of stone reaching out into the lake every hundred yards; they kept the sand from eroding back to the nearby highway every November, when the wind whipped up the lake. It was the closest and most popular beach destination for the city of Dundurn, a summer haunt for those who couldn't afford a cottage up north.

The sun worshippers—young families and teens—would leave when the sun fell behind the trees that lined Van Wagners Beach Road. That's when the true romantics arrived: those who wanted to make love behind the rocks, go skinny-dipping, get drunk or just enjoy the reflected glory of the sunset at their backs as they stared out at twilight on the lake.

At nine that evening, Samora Aploon, a twenty-five-year-old medical student, finished her shift at the Burger Shack. With her textbook on thoracic surgery tucked under one arm and carrying her dinner on a plastic Shack tray, she walked down the beach to the second breakwater and sat on one of the flat rocks facing away from the building. The distance would filter the noise from the burgers-and-beer crowd that descended on the Shack every night around this time, driving loud cars and even louder motorcycles. There was still enough light for her to read at least six pages while she ate.

Samora kicked off her sandals and pushed her bare feet into the still-warm sand. Opening the textbook on the rock beside her, she laid a palm-sized flat stone—the kind she'd learned to skip across the lake when it was calm—on its pages for hands-free reading. She unwrapped her fishburger, took a sip of her ginger ale and looked along the far shore that curved around Secord on its way to Niagara. She loved the purple light of twilight, so unlike the saturated buttery colours of South Africa's Western Cape, where she was from.

She was about to take a bite of her burger when he appeared from behind the rocks. She hadn't heard him approach. Suddenly she saw her face reflected in the black visor as he stopped directly in front of her. Samora stood up to ask what he wanted—and that's when he struck. The plastic cup of ginger ale flew into the rocks and ricocheted into the lazy waves, losing its top and straw, which turned in circles in the foam. She didn't have time to let go of the fishburger. It was still clutched in her hand when two young women, whose boyfriends had gone to the Shack to pick them up some beer and fries, approached with blankets and a boom box, looking for the best place to set up for the night. Both of them stood stunned for a moment at the sight of her, slashed and bleeding into the sand, and then they screamed.

———

With five cruisers parked on the road, their light bars flashing, it wasn't difficult to find the crime scene. A yellow tape barrier had been put up at the first breakwater and all along the treeline of the road to just beyond the third. MacNeice parked behind Vertesi's car.

Several uniformed police were gathered around the two women and their boyfriends, all sitting on the rocks of the first breakwater. Both girls looked his way as he crossed the beach.

"Detective Superintendent." The uniformed sergeant was first to greet MacNeice.

"What have we got here, Sergeant Matthews?"

"A young woman, Samora Aploon. She's a foreign medical student from South Africa studying here. She was almost filleted with one stroke of a knife. No one heard or saw anything until those two started to scream." He pointed in the direction of the two women. Someone had put a red-checked plastic tablecloth over the body. Vertesi was holding up a corner of it and both he and Williams were studying the body.

"Has anyone spoken to the Burger Shack staff?"

"They're pretty freaked out. Aploon was very quiet, and no one saw her outside of working hours, but they all liked her."

"Thanks, Sergeant."

Matthews nodded and walked off towards the young women, who were now standing by the rocks in the arms of their boyfriends.

With a mixture of fatigue and rage, MacNeice walked slowly over to the cheerful red-checkered vinyl. Williams helped him remove it from the body. The knife had sliced through Samora's T-shirt in the middle of the left breast and had gone right through the collarbone and into her neck, where it had ripped through to the spine. As the slasher completed his stroke, he'd taken off most of the left earlobe. Blood had sunk into the sand all around her, black in the failing light. She had fallen sideways with the impact and was lying on her back, with her feet still pushed into the sand. Her stomach had been punctured four times. She was wearing black knee-length cotton shorts with a fanny pack—nothing appeared to have been disturbed. In her right hand was the burger.

MacNeice put on his latex gloves, knelt down and unzipped the fanny pack. "Loose change, some folding money—tips—a red leather wallet, keys. No cellphone. God help us."

"Who doesn't have a cellphone? He's taken it," Vertesi said.

The night on the beach seemed like it would never end; no one knew anything, had seen anything or heard anything. If Samora had screamed, it would have been impossible to separate the sound from the general mayhem of a boozy evening at the Shack. A motorcycle tearing away wouldn't have attracted any attention either, since they were coming and going all the time.

MacNeice walked back and forth along Beach Road with his Maglite, looking for blood and oil, finding much of the latter, none of the former. But the oil was old and dried up and it was impossible to identify individual tire tracks in the loose sand and gravel of the shoulders.

It was 1:18 a.m. before the body was removed and sent to the coroner's lab. She'd almost bled out, purpling the grey sand. "Take the tablecloth too. I don't want the Burger Shack to have to deal with it," MacNeice told the coroner's retrieval team. The cheerful cloth, a dark stain now obliterating much of its checkerboard pattern, was folded neatly and laid on top of the black body bag.

MacNeice could feel the anger boiling in his men. It mirrored his own. As tired as they all were, none of them felt they could leave the scene, though there was nothing more to be accomplished by staying. Finally Williams took away the fanny pack, saying he would try to reach Samora's next of kin. Vertesi kept looking up and down the beach as if a suspect would suddenly appear, but at last he too said goodnight and walked off slowly towards his car.

"This is what defeat looks like," MacNeice said to the dark stain in the sand. He knelt down and looked out over the water, trying to capture the last thing Samora had seen as she was dying.

As he headed to his Chevy, he looked for the route the tall young man had taken—the easiest for attack and retreat. Just to the left of the rock pile, so she couldn't see him approaching, but far enough to the right that the Burger Shack staff wouldn't notice him either. And dusk was dark enough to obscure a figure dressed in black, walking as casually as if he just wanted to skip stones across the water. He knew that he shouldn't be so certain that the killer was the young man in the hospital videos, but he was. He just wished they had already found him, and that Samora Aploon had been able to finish her dinner, take her textbook, catch the bus and make it safely home.

When he got back to the stone cottage, he called the Deputy Chief's voice mail to fill him in. It was 2:30 a.m. when he finally went to bed. He picked up *The Diary of Samuel Pepys* and began where he left off, with the plague ravaging London. He read for several minutes, then, distracted by images of the young woman torn apart on the beach, he rolled out of bed, checked the clock radio—2:58—went to the kitchen and poured himself a healthy shot of grappa. When he climbed into bed again, it was 3:11. He lay there doing some deep-breathing exercises and drifted slowly off to sleep.

There were photos on the wall he recognized, poorly framed and hung crookedly. He busied himself for a while, straightening the images. But a draft from the screen door kept shifting the frames, and finally he gave up and turned instead to studying them. There he was with his parents, who looked happy.

"Camp," he said. "It was the first day of camp. I was six."

"Yeah, I thought so—you look scared shitless," Davey White said. Davey, dead since they were boys.

"I guess I was, a bit."

All his great and minor moments were there—from winning an award for bravery to marrying Kate to feeding chickadees perched on his hand behind the cottage. Surprisingly, Kate's family photos were all framed and mixed in with his. Though their parents didn't know each other well, there they were, side by side as if they were the best of friends. "Funny seeing them together . . . I mean, like this—"

"Yeah, Kate hates it. You shouldn't have done it."

He turned quickly to catch Davey's eyes. "You've seen Kate?"

"Yeah, of course. She wants to see you too—but not until you get rid of this fuckin' shrine."

"She's alive? You've really seen her!"

"I can bring her to you, Mac. She was here today. I thought you knew that."

He studied a grouping of four photos of Kate—at five, seven, ten and thirteen—all playing the violin, all with her eyes closed. "She once told me that she closed her eyes even when she was playing 'When the Saints Go Marching In.'"

"What the fuck for, to play better?"

"No, no, that wasn't it. She did it so people couldn't see her— that's what she said at the time. When I said, 'But you're playing right in front of them,' do you know what she replied?"

"No."

"'They can't see me. I'm as far away as I can get when I play. They can only see me when I open my eyes.'"

"Weird."

"Maybe . . . but it made sense to me then, and still does."

"So, do you want to see her?"

"Oh, Dave, I've been looking for her so long. I would give . . . everything."

"Okay, then, take that shit down. I'll go get her."

Davey jumped up and walked out the screen door, letting it slap shut behind him. MacNeice watched him go down the stairs with that loose-limbed *doinka doinka doinka* walk he'd always had.

He had taken down a dozen frames or so but noticed that the wall seemed to hold even more. While he didn't want to take the time to look at them, he did. Photos of the stone cottage, of them in Suffolk with her parents, of her playing onstage—all were familiar experiences, but new to him as photographs. He tried to recall taking them and couldn't. There he was being promoted to detective superintendent; he knew Kate had been there, he could remember where she stood—but he couldn't remember seeing the photograph.

On the floor, the stack of framed memories was growing, yet the wall seemed just as full as when he started. He decided the best way to deal with the situation was to put them in bags, and do it fast. He wanted Kate to come home to an empty wall. In the kitchen he opened the cupboard under the sink and took out four large black garbage bags. On the shelf he found the creamy white filler that would cover the nail holes. He congratulated himself for having all the tools necessary to erase any trace of the images, though he couldn't remember buying the filler and concluded that he must have done it a long time ago. Curious to see if it was still usable, he took a metal barbecue skewer, unscrewed the top of the tube and was about to insert the skewer when he heard the screen door open. Davey called his name. In a panic, he dropped the tube and skewer in the sink, left the bags on the counter and ran towards the hallway.

That's when he opened his eyes.

———

MacNeice knew better than most the deep disappointment of dreams. Davey White and Kate had been, for a moment, alive and well. When he woke up, both were long dead and gone. Davey had died in his teens after diving into a quarry and colliding with a submerged tractor, and Kate—four years ago, from cancer. They'd never met, but in the dream they were apparently good friends. And that didn't strike him as strange, in the dream or now, lying in bed with his eyes open.

He sat up in bed and looked at the clock radio—5:16 a.m.

He rode the stationary bike hard for an hour in the dark, staring into the forest, waiting for the light. When it came, he stopped, showered and got ready for another day. After such dreams he did all he could to narrow his focus—door, doorknob, toilet seat, shower faucet, soap, shampoo; drawer, socks, underwear; closet, pants, shirt, tie, jacket on hanger. Avoid the mirror, and when you can't, look only at the toothbrush, at the line of the razor, hands through the hair. *Avoid the eyes. The eyes hold only loss, regret, loneliness, fear.*

# 26.

AZIZ WAS STANDING silently at the whiteboard that held the photos and listed the known facts about the slasher murders. MacNeice had come and gone, to a brief press conference at which he and the Deputy Chief gave the reporters as much detail as they thought wise about the newest victim. Then, before the reporters could catch their breath, they released the photo of the young man from the hospital, describing him as a "person of interest," as well as a photocopied screen capture of his motorcycle. They then issued a call for anyone with information about how to locate the man to please come forward. When he got back, Aziz was studying the images of the young man in the emergency ward. Vertesi and Williams were shooting occasional looks at her but basically letting her be.

When she heard MacNeice come in, she turned to him. "I have an idea," she said, "though it might be a long shot and you've all probably thought of it before."

MacNeice looked over at the image of Taaraa's abdomen, then

down at his hands, hoping he had a hangnail he could busy himself with. Finding none, he looked down at the wear on the carpet and waited for the inevitable.

"What is it?" Vertesi asked.

"So far, based on those he's attacked, would we all agree he's not likely to change his type of target?"

"I think I can see where this is going," Williams said.

"He's attacked a South Asian, a Korean and a black from South Africa. If a Muslim detective who also has a PhD in criminology were to hold forth on the sick mind of a racist, he might come after her." Aziz looked directly at MacNeice, whose eyes were now focused somewhere in the vicinity of the whiteboard casters.

"Way to ease back into the job," Williams said wryly.

"You mean use yourself as bait," Vertesi added.

MacNeice stood up abruptly and asked Aziz to take a walk with him. He was already in the stairwell by the time she'd picked up her jacket. As she left the cubicle, Vertesi called after her, "Good luck, Aziz. It sounds like a scary good plan to me."

They went down the stairs to the parking lot without speaking. She took a seat on the bench near the exit door and waited. MacNeice walked back and forth for a minute or so, then stopped in front of her. He told her about the knife and how quickly the slasher struck. "Samora hadn't even dropped her fishburger, that's how fast."

"It's a solid plan," Aziz said softly.

"Fiza, I wanted to bring you up to speed, not risk your life." He leaned against one of the columns supporting the overhanging roof.

"It's solid and you know it. I'm a Muslim. Surely I'd be a prime target—an overachieving Muslim woman. Mac, it'll work."

He wondered if she felt she had something to prove. Or was she already caught up in the injustice of it and unaware of how grave the risk actually was? Had she been that bored in Ottawa? He actually said that out loud. They argued then, but the more MacNeice protested, the more it became plain to Aziz that he'd thought about the idea even before she'd offered. Yet he still refused.

Taking another tack, Aziz insisted that her status as a criminologist rather than a detective gave her an edge. She could speak credibly about the character of the killer. "I want to—what was the phrase Williams used?"

"Flush him out."

"Exactly. How could he resist me? I'm just what he wants." She looked up at MacNeice, shading her eyes from the sun that backlit him, glancing off his shoulder.

"And then?" He sat on the bench, looking down at the ants that had gathered around a discarded candy.

"That's where the team comes in, where you come in." Seeing where his eyes were focused, she gently kicked the candy into the parking lot. The ants scattered, then wandered around looking for it. MacNeice and Aziz sat for several minutes watching as the insects searched for the candy. Then one of them found it, and, mysteriously, the others followed as if nothing had happened. They looked at each other and she shrugged.

He told her again, in detail, all he knew about the tall, slim man. That he stalked his victims, knew their habits—knew exactly where they'd be at a given moment—that he struck swiftly, without warning. She smiled as he repeated himself.

"Come on, Mac. Together we can take out one psychopath with a knife."

"How?"

"I'll study the case some more. By tomorrow I'll have something close to a decent psychological profile. You call a press conference and introduce me as the city's specialist on hate crimes. That was my doctoral thesis, so it's more or less accurate."

He looked off to the treeline. "Here less than a day and you have a new position. Christ, this is risky."

"You mean because it will work, right?"

"Yes, Fiza, I think it has every chance of working."

They could sense that something had happened the moment they entered the cubicle. Ryan, Williams and Vertesi all looked sickened.

"We've got another Web image taken with a cellphone," Williams said.

Ryan pulled up the photo on screen. It was a shock for Aziz, who had yet to see any images of Samora Aploon. "This is terrorism—sheer bloody terrorism," she said, a hand involuntarily covering her mouth.

She was right, of course. The slasher was trying to scare the hell out of everyone except those who shared his beliefs. He had peeled open her T-shirt to reveal the gash from her breast—a shocking pink—to the neck, taken his photograph and then covered her up again. "He wanted that breast to be seen around the world."

"Sadly, that'll make it even more popular," Aziz said.

MacNeice turned to the whiteboards. "Print it out and put it up." On his desk was an envelope from Forensics—cold, clinical views of a young woman slaughtered on a beach. Scanning the boards, the horror of the past few days made his heart race. He thought, *Keep breathing, keep breathing.*

"Okay, Aziz," MacNeice said plainly and simply, in front of the whole team. "We'll try your plan."

Before she or any of them could respond, Vertesi's cellphone burped to life. He swung over to his desk and picked it up. "DI Vertesi, Homicide." There was a silence as he signalled MacNeice and put the cell on speaker phone. "How are you, Ms. Hughes?"

"I'm in Dundurn, at the Holiday Inn near . . . Secord and the Queen Elizabeth Highway. I'm with my brother. It's late in the day, I know, but I'm here to see Gary's body."

MacNeice nodded the way people do when they have no choice.

"All right, Mrs. Hughes, I'll pick you up at nine tomorrow morning," Vertesi said.

"Sue-Ellen, it's Detective Superintendent MacNeice. We'll bring you to the division first. It will take some time to make the necessary arrangements, and it will be very helpful—if you're willing—to interview you here."

"That's fine. I thought you might want to, but I'm also determined to see my husband." She said goodnight and hung up.

"Michael, call Richardson first thing tomorrow and let her know what's happening. She'll figure out the most compassionate way to present the remains of Sergeant Hughes to his wife. Though, for the life of me, I can't think of any."

On the way home MacNeice slipped *Solo Monk* into the CD player, hoping for calm. When his phone rang, he pushed the hands-free and said, "MacNeice."

"You know where I was earlier this evening, Mac?" The mayor's breathing was short; MacNeice could tell he was walking.

"Too late for a quiz, Bob."

"The American embassy in Ottawa, for dinner with the ambassador, the premier and some flacks from External Affairs. That place is sleek and sharp, but it's a fucking fortress—makes our city hall look like public housing."

The mayor went on to say that the session on the waterfront project had been derailed when the ambassador asked for a private conversation with him. It turned out that the ambassador had got a call from someone in Washington about the fact that the body of a veteran had been found on the very site of the project. The man's widow, a woman named Sue-Ellen Hughes, was asking questions of her government: if he'd been found dead in Dundurn, could Veterans Affairs restore her family benefits so she could feed her kids?

"So, Mac, are we sure it's her husband?"

MacNeice heard a door open and close and the ambient sounds of the night disappeared—the mayor was home.

"We're sure."

"Well, the ambassador's pissed he wasn't told by us first, and the External Affairs lackey threw me under the bus—God, I love that cliché. Anyway, I blamed it on you."

"I'd expect nothing less."

The mayor asked if he was being a smartass. MacNeice told him that he wasn't kidding. "Bob, I'm a legit alternative target for a couple of reasons: one, I don't answer to the American ambassador, and two, my responsibility is to find out who killed him and why."

Maybank told him then about the real reason for his visit to Ottawa. A groundbreaking party was being planned for the museum site at the bottom of the dock on Tuesday, September 15. "I don't want this Sergeant Hughes to be an issue—understood?"

"Well, your media guests will basically be standing on the spot where the six bodies were found. I don't think that wrapping up the Hughes case—which I certainly hope to do by then—will deter them from asking 'Is this where you found the bodies, Mr. Mayor?'"

"I'm prepared for that, sure, but it'll be better for all of us if I can say we solved it."

MacNeice heard the toilet flush and wondered if Maybank realized that such sounds could be passed through the receiver, or perhaps he knew and just didn't care.

"Just so you know, Bob, Sue-Ellen Hughes is here to identify the body tomorrow morning."

He heard a big sigh.

"It's late, Mac. I'm going to bed. Just keep me posted."

# 27.

"**S**HE'S HAVING A coffee in number three, sir, and her brother is with her. He and Gary served together. He didn't say a word on the way over here, just sat in the back seat looking out the window." Vertesi took off his jacket and put it over his chair.

"I'll join you, Michael, but so we don't overwhelm her, Fiza and Montile, you're behind the mirror."

"She's very strong, but I really don't think she's prepared for this."

MacNeice waited a minute for Vertesi to get settled with notebook and pen. Looking through the interview room's narrow sidelight window, he studied the brother. He was wearing a loose long-sleeved grey jersey and black chinos; his hands were clasped comfortably on the table in front of him. His hair—shaved on the sides, with barely more on top—suggested he was still in the army. He sat looking past Vertesi to the mirror, its purpose surely not lost on him, and then, feeling eyes on him, he snapped his head towards the window and MacNeice.

MacNeice entered the room and Vertesi made the introductions. "Ms. Hughes, Mark Penniman, this is Detective Superintendent MacNeice." Penniman stood up and offered his hand first. He was at least an inch taller than MacNeice, with wide shoulders and pronounced trapezoid muscles that braced a wide neck. His grip was much stronger even than MacNeice had expected. Sue-Ellen didn't stand but offered her hand as well. MacNeice expected her handshake to be gentle—it wasn't. He wondered if this was a family trait or just something the United States military encouraged. He sat down opposite Sue-Ellen, and Vertesi continued his briefing about the homicide personnel assigned to the dock slayings.

In a soft-pink summer sweater, she was even lovelier than Vertesi had managed to convey—distinctly and wonderfully all-American. Only the dark shadows under her eyes betrayed her anxiety and loss.

"There are many questions we believe you can help us with," Vertesi said as he wrapped up. "But I know you're anxious to get to the viewing. I've asked DS MacNeice to brief you before we leave."

"Before I do," MacNeice said, "Mark, are you currently serving?"

"Yes, sir. I'm on leave to attend my father-in-law's funeral. I'm due to go back to my unit in Afghanistan next Tuesday."

"My condolences for your loss."

"Thank you, sir."

"Were you and Sergeant Hughes close?"

"Peas in a pod, those two," Sue-Ellen interjected, with obvious pride.

"We were both with the 2nd Brigade combat team," Penniman

said. "We served together overseas, made master sergeant together. I was the one who introduced Gary to my sister when he came home with me on leave."

"Gary and Mark got their stripes on the same day." Sue-Ellen was clearly struggling to keep the tone light.

"I appreciate that you accompanied your sister here today," MacNeice said.

"It's where I should be, sir. And, for the record, Sergeant Hughes was a soldier's soldier—if I make myself clear."

"Perfectly. I didn't want to overwhelm you both with people right off the top, but DIs Aziz and Williams are observing this conversation from the other side of the mirror. They will also play a role in the invesitgation."

Mark's face relaxed slightly now that MacNeice had put names to the invisible observers.

MacNeice added, "You'll meet them both in due course."

"Is it normal," Sue-Ellen asked, "to have such a large number of investigators on a homicide case?"

"We're also trying to find out who killed another man we found at the same time, also encased in cement."

"My sister downloaded a news article that said there were six altogether."

"Yes, but the other four had been there for more than seventy years. While we are researching those deaths, they don't have the same urgency as the two most recent."

"Understood."

MacNeice cleared his throat. "I don't really know how to prepare you for what you'll see at the morgue." He met Sue-Ellen Hughes's eyes. "Won't you reconsider the viewing? I can't see how it could be anything but hurtful for you to see what was done to your husband."

Her eyes welled up and her brother put his hand gently on her shoulder. "I do appreciate that," she said, "but I can't let Gary go without seeing him one last time."

MacNeice looked at each of them before speaking. "All right, I understand, but I think you should hear in advance what you're about to see. Please brace yourselves, as this description will be extremely painful to hear. Is that understood?"

She nodded as her brother, his jaw tightening, held her hands in his.

"Sergeant Hughes was mutilated. His face was sheared off, from the top of his skull to the neck and back to the ears."

For a long beat nothing registered on her face to suggest she'd actually heard him. But then she convulsed, pulling her hands out of her brother's grasp and covering her mouth to keep from screaming. Her brother gathered her in and she began to rock back and forth in his arms, sobbing into his chest. Penniman's own face seemed frozen, at first with shock and with anger. Vertesi got up and left the room, returning with a box of tissues and two paper cups of water that he put on the table in front of them.

When her sobbing subsided, she wiped her eyes, blew her nose and, with a shaking hand, took a short sip of water. After she set the cup back down, still shakily, she looked across the table at MacNeice. "There's more, isn't there."

"Yes, I'm sorry, there's more. His hands and feet and the tattoos on his arms were all removed . . ."

More tears fell down her face onto the table, and she struggled to catch her breath. Her hands rose as if to ask for his attention, but she couldn't speak and let them drop. She took several deep, steadying breaths and raised them again. MacNeice noticed the slim gold wedding ring. Slowly she let her hands fall. Minutes passed, and then she looked at her brother, patted his arm and nodded slowly. "Okay . . . okay . . . okay," she said as tears continued to spill down her cheeks. Her brother reached for more tissues and gently wiped her face.

"Ms. Hughes, Sergeant Penniman"—MacNeice's words came softly and without hesitation—"I urge you for the last time to reconsider viewing the body. Please let this meeting, and my words, be the worst of it for both of you."

Sue-Ellen put the heels of her hands to her eyes, pressing deeply for a moment before dropping them to her lap. She looked at her brother, who wiped another stream of tears from her cheek. "It has to be your call, Sis," he said. "Either way, I'm here . . ."

She looked from her brother to Vertesi, and then to MacNeice. "I have to say goodbye. It can't end here. If it did, it would never end." She looked again at her brother, willing him to agree.

"Take some time, just the two of you," MacNeice said, and he and Vertesi pushed their chairs back.

"No need," Penniman responded. "I know my sister, and it's her wish to see the body of her husband. If you can kindly direct us to the morgue . . ." He and his sister stood up slowly.

MacNeice nodded and said, "Michael will take you." He offered his hand to the brother, whose grip had softened somewhat. He turned to Sue-Ellen, who managed a nod before she and Penniman followed Vertesi out of the room. After they'd left, MacNeice sank back into the chair and closed his eyes.

"She's certain it's her husband?" MacNeice asked Vertesi when he got back, more as confirmation than a question.

"Oh yeah, oh yeah," Vertesi said. He looked spent. "He had a mole on the side of his chest—apparently called it his third nipple. But—and I apologize, Fiza—it was his penis that really confirmed it. They're back in the interview room, sir, but I don't know how much Sue-Ellen has left in her. Her brother had to hold her up, literally."

"Did they say anything, either during the viewing or outside, anything we should know about?" MacNeice asked.

"No. It was seriously grim." Vertesi fell silent. "I mean, on the way back, they tried talking old times—you know, like back to the beginning—but their hearts weren't in it. Good thing I'd stuffed my pockets with Kleenex."

"Let's get in there. If she's not up to it, we'll let them go."

MacNeice picked up his file folder and pad. "If they're comfortable with it, I want to split them up. Michael, you and Aziz with Sue-Ellen. Williams and I will take Mark."

MacNeice made the introductions. Penniman listened carefully but his sister's eyes kept welling up, and MacNeice didn't think she was really taking anything in.

"Mrs. Hughes—Sue-Ellen—are you up for this?" MacNeice asked. "We understand completely if you need to leave."

She wiped her face, straightened in her chair and met his eyes. "If I leave now I'm not sure I'll ever come back, Detective MacNeice. I want to help in any way I can. I want Gary to receive the justice he deserves. He'd expect that of me."

"All right, then. Thank you, and we will be as brief as possible."

MacNeice went to the video screen and raised it to reveal a wall-mounted whiteboard divided into two columns. The left one was headed *What We Know,* and the one to the right, *What We Don't Know.*

Below the first heading, he identified the images of the *Hamilton* and *Scourge,* the names of the couple from the Packard and the bodies in the two older concrete columns, and two photos of Bermuda Shorts—the close-up that Ryan had Photoshopped to remove the hole in his forehead, and a full-length shot that MacNeice had taken on site, also retouched. He pointed to Bermuda Shorts.

"This man has a .44-calibre entry wound in his forehead. We've doctored the images for this presentation so you can see what he looked like without it."

Under Bermuda Shorts were listed the three winning concrete supply companies and the loser, DeLillo Concrete, of Buffalo–Fort Erie. Following that was the Old Soldiers roadhouse in Tonawanda.

In the other column he wrote:

*Why did Sergeant Hughes leave the military?*
*What plans did he have for his future?*
*Who were his friends at the Old Soldiers roadhouse?*
*What work was he seeking?*
*What work was he qualified for?*
*Did he have relatives or friends in Canada?*
*Was he a gambler? Alcohol or drug dependent?*

MacNeice slid the marker into the tray and turned back to the room. "These questions aren't intended to cause more grief for either of you, and we have to ask them. Everything in the other column is what we have so far. Before we begin, you're welcome to ask anything at all about what you see here." He sat down, poured a glass of water and waited.

Penniman was staring at the photo of Bermuda Shorts. "That man wouldn't be a friend of Gary's under any circumstances." And that was all either of them could add or wanted to know about the first column.

They did a little better with the list of questions, though Sue-Ellen was barely holding it together. She said that her husband had begun to question America's role in Iraq, but it was when he was deployed to Afghanistan that he grew angry at both the role and the strategy. "I think Gary just burned out. There was a Catch-22 in place so that people kept getting rotated back: he kept seeing his troops get injured or killed, and it seemed there would be no end to it."

She blew her nose and wiped her eyes before continuing. "As for his future, it was vague. He decided to get out of the army and then think about what to do. Once he was out, he met up with some vets at Old Soldiers—I'm not sure he knew any of them before. I've never been there and I've never met any of them. After he disappeared, the investigators said no one at the roadhouse recognized him."

"I heard it was a biker hangout and that a lot of them were vets, but that's all I know," Penniman said.

"Gary wasn't a biker!" Sue-Ellen insisted. "He was there drinking beer. I worried that he had PTSD, and told him so, but he laughed it off. He was great with the kids, with me, but his benefits package wasn't enough to keep us going . . . so we argued about that . . . quite a bit." Her eyes filled and she stopped talking.

"You mentioned a security job? That he was going to meet someone about it?"

"Yeah. I mean, he was a martial arts specialist and a combat soldier, so in a way it made sense to me. But he didn't tell me anything more than that."

"Was he meeting this person at the roadhouse?"

"I think so, but it was like he was keeping something from me . . ."

"Did he know anyone or have relatives in Canada?"

"No, Gary didn't have any family. His parents have been gone for years and he was an only child. We were his family—me and the kids, and Mark and his wife, Tracy."

"And the army," Mark Penniman added.

MacNeice looked at the next question on the list and then finally just asked, "Did he have an abuse problem—drugs, alcohol, gambling?"

She flinched but answered. "Not drugs or gambling—never. Of

course he'd been drinking more since he got out—maybe too much—but he was never falling-down drunk or anything. He was a good man."

MacNeice said, "Mrs. Hughes, I think you've been through more than enough for one day. Would you mind if we had a brief word with your brother? I'd like to get his insights into what your husband might have been up to—if Sergeant Penniman agrees, of course."

Penniman nodded.

"All right, Michael will stay here with you, along with DI Aziz. Mark, would you please come with us?"

Aziz got up and went to sit beside Sue-Ellen as MacNeice and Williams led Penniman to Interview Room Two. The sergeant sat down facing the mirror.

"There's no one behind the glass this time," MacNeice said.

"I trust you, sir." He smiled, genuinely, MacNeice thought.

"Are you a martial arts specialist as well?"

"No, sir. I'm also special ops, like Gary was, but a different discipline."

"What discipline, if you don't mind my asking?" MacNeice had his pen in hand but decided not to use it; he laid it on the closed notebook.

"I'm a sniper."

"Do you work in a team?" MacNeice asked, trying to mask his surprise at how direct the statement was, as if he had been asked his astrological sign and responded, *I'm a Virgo.*

"I'm responsible for four teams—shooter/spotter teams."

"Would you cover Gary's platoons or were you out on your own?"

"Both. He was always getting up close, always the first to come to town. The local Ghannies around Helmand knew Gary, and I think they respected him. FOBs are hairy places—it's asymmetric warfare—and he was comfortable with that. I'm usually a thousand yards or more off the beaten path. In Iraq it was door-to-door, because the firefights there were mostly urban, so I was competing with Iraqi snipers for the rooftops."

"Just out of interest, when you're over a thousand yards away, what weapon are you using, and what are the targets?" Williams asked.

"M24—7.62-millimeter rifle. My spotter and I hunker down and look for opportunities. The best is another sniper, second best a Taliban leader, third, someone planting an IED. It was the IEDs that got to Gary. He was all army. We sure never talked about whether he liked the direction the Pentagon was taking. He just hated seeing his people blown away."

"Did he ask for leave?" Williams asked.

"You don't ask for leave—ever. I only got to come home for the funeral because my commanding officer took the call and told me to go. Gary'd just had enough, and leave wouldn't fix it, even if he'd asked."

"Do you think he was desperate enough to earn a living that he'd use his training for criminal ends? Could his attitude have changed that much?"

"Not a chance. Sir, if the recession hadn't hit, today Gary would probably be a carpenter building homes. He liked the work and he was good with his hands."

"Is there anything else you'd like us to know about your brother-in-law, anything that might help us?" MacNeice asked.

Penniman stared at him, then said, "I followed Gary from the Sunni Triangle to the Fallujah arms markets and into Afghanistan, where enemies and friends change loyalties every day. I've seen first-hand what he can do. All I can say is, whoever did that to him probably had to clean up a stack of bodies afterwards. He wouldn't go easy—you follow me?"

"I do."

Penniman stood up to indicate the interview was over. "You got what you needed?"

"Yes, I think we have," MacNeice said. He offered his hand. Once again, the Vise-Grip was on full crush.

# 28.

"**D**O YOU THINK Hughes was a one-man wrecking crew?" Vertesi asked.

"Four large men die. Two have their big, thick necks snapped, one gets his faced caved in by a size twelve, and the last has his throat slashed through to the spine—sounds like Special Forces killing to me," Aziz said.

"Yeah, it was the killing Olympics," Vertesi said. "But one guy who weighed—what, 180 pounds—against four guys who weighed 250 or so?"

"One guy puttin' an expensive education to use." Williams shrugged as if it was obvious.

MacNeice studied the whiteboard, placing what he knew and what he didn't in thought boxes. He said, "We've got bodies, competing concrete interests and—potentially—hired biker gangs for security. To secure what? We've got Hughes, who wasn't a biker. We need to tie the buried bikers to Hughes and to figure out if the bodies above ground were payback for killing him and Bermuda Shorts.

And if they were vets, why did they break their code of taking every comrade—or his body—home? Though if, as Penniman said, Hughes was always the first to come to town, perhaps he was too far ahead to support." He turned to his team. "Well, we can't ask Old Soldiers."

"Maybe we ask one of the local bikers—I mean, in a convincing way," Williams suggested. "That sounds like a perfect job for Swets. He knows these guys—at least, the ones still standing—though he'd have to find 'em first."

The desk phone rang. Ryan picked it up, listened and turned to MacNeice. "Sir, I've got Sheilagh Thomas from the university. She said you'll want to take this call."

Her voice in his ear was cheerful. "Mac, come out here this afternoon and I'll treat you to the best plonk B.U. can afford."

"It's a lovely idea—"

"Please, no buts, Mac. This is important and it won't take too much of your time. I'll open the bottle now and let it breathe—or gasp. See you soon."

Before he left the cubicle, MacNeice turned to Aziz and told her to start preparing for her first press conference.

"Detective Superintendent MacNeice?" A dark-haired young woman wearing a black T-shirt, knee-length khaki shorts and sandals greeted him inside the door.

"Yes."

"I'm Andrea Gomes, one of Dr. Thomas's grad students."

"Pleased to meet you, Andrea."

"I came to get you 'cause it's kind of a maze getting down to our lab."

He followed her up a flight of eight stairs, across a hallway buzzing with students and down another stairway to a corridor. At the end of the corridor they went through an exit door and down another set of stairs.

"I can see why you came for me," he said as they walked along a glazed-brick corridor.

"Yeah, it took me a few days before I could find my way. Now, though, I could probably do it blindfolded."

"I hope you'll never have to."

"Very funny, sir. Here we are."

They stopped in front of a lab door with a long, slim window in it.

"Dr. Thomas is in her office, just to the left of the door. I'm going to get some munchies." She smiled and walked back the way they had come.

Before opening the door, MacNeice peeked through the window to get a sense of the space. On the far wall there were large jars with specimens—of what he couldn't tell—on oak shelves that rose from the floor to the ceiling. There were no windows but an overabundance of fluorescent light. In the middle of the room were several pieces of equipment that looked high-tech, most of it covered in clear plastic, and six computer stations that made him think Ryan would be very comfortable there. A cluster of students was busy at one station, and none appeared to notice him peering in. He could see at least three bouquets of flowers; they didn't look store-bought but more as though they'd been cut from someone's garden and dropped into various pieces of medical glassware.

He opened the door and stepped inside. Baroque music rose above the hum of equipment and air conditioning. He thought it was Handel but wasn't sure.

Sheilagh Thomas was standing in her office with her back to the door, studying something in a large volume. Rising above the credenza in front of her was a bookcase that went up to the ceiling, and all of the books appeared to be immense. He looked back at the length of the lab. It ran for eighty feet or more and seemed to be broken into sections, or perhaps disciplines. At the far end was a row of much larger equipment and in between were six stainless steel specimen tables, four of them occupied.

"Impressive, isn't it," Thomas said, coming out to meet him.

"I have no idea what I'm looking at, but yes, it is. The only things I recognize are the flowers and possibly the music—Handel?"

"Close. Henry Purcell. The flowers come from a farm near my house; most of them grow wild. In the absence of daylight and fresh air, it's the best I can do for my students. Would you like a tour?"

"I would very much, but not now. I have to get back downtown."

"We're building a stack of rain checks greater than the annual rainfall in Dundurn, but I understand. Come in and we'll get straight to it—but over a glass of wine, I insist. And sometime soon you'll take me to dinner and I'll show you that I have more in my wardrobe—well, admittedly not much more—than lumberjack shirts."

He smiled, noticing that her linen summer shirt was indeed a red, grey and black plaid.

The clutter of her Land Rover was nothing compared to her desk. It was piled high with more huge leather-covered books, bound documents, large manila sleeves with X-rays in them and at least ten Styrofoam cups with unintelligible markings on them—mostly numbers and letters. At the far end of the credenza behind it were two wineglasses and a bottle of red wine sitting on a circular tray. Beyond it was a ceramic setter, its head held proud and high with a limp mallard between its jaws, marching out of some marsh cattails.

"Let me clear a space . . ." She picked up a stack of books and put them on the floor behind her desk. A green blotter covered her desk, and on it, nearest the telephone, were doodles—all of bones. She moved the Styrofoam cups to the opposite end of the credenza, next to the skull of a small animal. On the bare brick walls were anatomical drawings that looked centuries old and a framed photograph—he guessed from the 1920s—of an elegant young woman standing next to a large stone fireplace, holding a pipe to her lips as she lit it with a stick from the fire.

"My grandmother. Something of a rebel."

"She's beautiful."

"Quite." She went on to say that the family had money, position and power, but her grandmother left it all shortly after that photograph was taken and moved to Kenya to be a nurse. She stayed there till the Second World War and returned just in time to treat the wounded returning from Dieppe. Many were Canadians, of course."

"Was she the one who inspired you?"

"Very much so, yes. Even when she was in her eighties, I would go over and sit by that fireplace as she told me stories and smoked her pipe."

"Did she ever marry?"

"No. She'd had an affair with someone during the war who was killed in France. She died without revealing who he was. My mother was the product of that affair."

"Tragic, and probably not uncommon," MacNeice said, and she nodded.

The lab door opened behind him and Andrea appeared with a large plastic bowl filled with what looked like potato chips. She placed it on the desk. "They're organic sweet potato as well as parsnip chips sprinkled with sea salt—we're crazy about them. Hope you like them, Detective." She looked over at Dr. Thomas and asked, "Need anything else?"

"No, thank you, Andrea, that's lovely. We'll be out shortly."

Handing MacNeice the wine, she said, "A surprisingly lovely Pinot Noir from Niagara. Chin-chin. Sit down for a moment, Mac."

He did, but even as he toasted her and sipped his wine, he was worrying that he needed to be gone, and he knew that she could see his mind was elsewhere. She set her own glass down.

"Well, let's get down to it. Harry and Arthur. The scrapings we took from the concrete and the bones suggest they were dumped together, in 1928 or '29. We started modelling the faces on the computer and noticed straightaway that the modelling wireframes were interesting."

"In what respect?"

"The cheekbones. It seemed like a wild guess, but we said aboriginal."

"Local?"

"We think so. One of my post-docs noticed a similarity in the cheekbones and jaw to the painting of Joseph Brant—a Mohawk—that hangs in the common room. Then we had a breakthrough; hence my call and this rather decent Pinot. I can tell you for a certainty that they both died in 1929 and both had served in World War One."

"How did you determine that?"

"We did a chemical scan of their leg, arm and rib bones, and in one of the column fragments there was a shred of flesh stuck to the concrete where a hand had been. In each scan we found a trace chemical that we've now identified as mustard gas. These men were both in the trenches."

"That means we may be able to track them through Veterans Affairs."

"You could, but you won't have to. We know who they are." She popped a chip into her mouth, crunched, then smiled triumphantly. "Andrea went through all the missing-person mentions in the *Standard* for 1928 and '29. On March 31, 1929, there was a small article mentioning two Indian high-riggers who had failed to show up at work for a week and whose belongings were still in the Barton Hotel room they had rented by the month. What made it newsworthy wasn't that they'd gone missing—that wasn't uncommon at the time—it was that both had been decorated for valour during the second Battle of Ypres."

"Ypres Salient . . . where the Germans first used mustard gas."

"Very good, MacNeice. These two were cousins on their mother's side, Charlie Maracle and George Marshall. They were both awarded medals of valour—Charlie a Military Cross, and George the Military Medal and bar. We haven't researched for descendants yet . . . Care for a bit more wine?"

"No thanks, but I definitely wouldn't call it plonk."

"Come along, then, the stars of our molecular anthropology lab, led by Andrea and a couple of the undergrads, are going to present what they discovered when they extracted genetic material from the bones of Charlie and George."

Halfway down the lab a laptop was connected to a projector that lit the white concrete blocks of the exterior wall. The students had gathered around, waiting for the two of them to appear. Further on, the skeletal remains of Charlie and George were also waiting, on the stainless steel tables. On cue, someone killed the fluorescents.

The show was lucid, precise, thorough and thrilling: it felt as though the students were opening a time capsule. The chemical analysis was dense but comprehensible, and the animated reconstruction of the damaged skull was magical, but that was just the beginning. Using National Archives photographs taken at the time of the young men's medal honours, Andrea and her colleagues had skilfully employed a computer modelling program called Tracer to morph the young men's faces onto their skulls. Noses, jaws, eye orbits, foreheads—everything fit into place. The skeletons had been placed on a metric grid, photographed from above and morphed onto images of the uniformed soldiers to confirm that they matched in body type. Charlie was six feet, George five foot nine. Finally, they presented the *Standard*'s "Indian Heroes Missing" article, highlighting a paragraph that read in part: "Both men were respected high-riggers on the city's

tallest tower—Dundurn's amazingly modern Pigott Building—
and outspoken advocates for establishing a union to protect high-
riggers' rights."

The Chevy moved with the traffic down Main, a steel bubble filled
to overflowing with Ellington's "Solitude." He parked on the far
side of the lot and watched a pair of dark-eyed juncos trading places
on a serviceberry tree. For no reason he could identify, he remembered his father, a master of Celtic gloom, standing on the dock on
a hot day in August thinking about winter and telling him that the
days were getting shorter and by how many seconds.

His cellphone rang as he reached the door. "What is it?" he
asked.

"Just got an email, came in to the division server," Wiliams said.
"You close?"

# 29.

I T WAS SENT from a house laptop at an Internet café called WebWORX, near the university. *Saw your press conference. Know your man. Ask a demographer.* Signed *X-Dem.*

"I've pulled up the organizations in Dundurn that do demographic research," Aziz said. "Apart from the university, there are only two in the city."

"You think it's the slasher talking to us through email?" Williams asked.

"No, our man has an agenda," MacNeice said. "I'm not certain what it is exactly, but this would be tempting fate."

"I think you're right." Aziz glanced down at her watch. "Though all that may change in forty minutes from now."

"What are the names of the firms?" MacNeice asked. For just this minute he didn't want to think about Fiza tempting fate.

"Accudem Associates Limited and Braithwaite Demography Incorporated, both in the west end," Aziz said. "Shall we split up?"

"I was going to visit the Waterdown OPP detachment, give them a heads-up that I'll be interviewing one of their citizens—Sean McNamara."

"Not just yet, Michael," MacNeice said. "I've demanded search warrants to seize the financial records of ABC, Mancini and McNamara."

"That'll rattle some cages—especially Alberto's. Pa tells me he's tight with the mayor." Vertesi was actually smiling.

"Someone hired muscle and paid for it. How they put that expense on their books will take some forensic accounting, but it probably wasn't tucked away under 'petty cash.' While we're waiting for those warrants, we can visit Accudem with photos of our suspect and his bike, and then we'll go out to Braithwaite. But let's stick around until Fiza does her press conference."

Williams went over to Aziz's desk and leaned against it, his brown eyes fixed on hers. "I've got another thought about our slasher," he said. "Maybe you can use it."

"I'm all ears," Aziz said, smiling up at him.

Taking his cue, Williams began to pace, holding an imaginary microphone. "Okay, in grade nine we had a teacher, Miss Dodd, who did a variation on show-and-tell she called 'Storytelling 101.' Two months into the year, a kid named Georg—with no E on the end—joins our class. He was Hungarian, son of a guy connected with the Hungarian government somehow. For his first show-and-tell he brings this flag, all stained with blood. It was his grandfather's, who had carried it during the 1956 uprising when he was killed. Fantastic stuff. Dried blood, almost brown—seriously cool to a ninth-grader."

"Is there a point?" Vertesi asked.

"Lemme finish. So next time, Georg puts up his hand and gives his topic, which he says is 'Public/Private.' Miss Dodd's all over this. He goes up to the front of the room, takes the teacher's chair and stands on it. I'm in the front row, sitting next to Sophie Levy,

Chantal Davidson—a sister—and Judy Jamieson, the sweetest girls in the class."

Williams had them all by now, even Ryan, still facing his computer but with his hands still and his head down, listening.

"Georg looks out at all of us. He's got a sheet of paper full of typewritten notes. Dodd's at the back of the room leaning against a bookshelf when Georg smiles, bends over like he's bowing, then drops sweatpants and gotchies to his ankles and straightens up. His pecker is hanging six feet from Chantal's face—"

"What the hell!" Vertesi exclaimed.

"Exactly. He starts to read this manifesto—all the world's problems would be solved if we could see each other's privates in public—but it's hard to hear him because he's drowned out by the girls, who are covering their mouths, laughing or screaming these horror-movie screams, and the guys yelling stupid shit from behind. Miss Dodd launches herself off the bookcase, hollerin' something I can't remember, and the bookcase topples over as she's running between the desks, and Georg is reading somethin' I can't hear and everyone's looking at his dick hanging there. Dodd slams into him and gets slapped in the face by it as she's pullin' up his sweatpants.

"Georg is as calm as can be—he just keeps reading. Somebody's yellin', 'Ho-ly-shit-fuck-no-way!' behind me and Dodd tears Georg off the chair, and it goes skidding across the floor and smashes a plaster bust of Shakespeare that was sitting like a shrine on the table by the window, and *wham*—they're out the door and gone."

"So what happened?"

"So, the paper he was reading from fell at my feet. There's pande-fuckin'-monium breaking loose in the room and I'm sitting there reading this manifesto. He wanted us to understand that power comes from the groin—all subjugation, all violence, all rape, all of everything that's evil. He had this whole thing mapped out.

At the end of it he was going to ask that we all stand up and take our clothes off—even Miss Dodd!"

"What happened next?"

"Nothin' happened. She came back in the room ten minutes later, her face almost purple, tore the paper out of my hands and went out again. A few minutes later the bell rang to end the period, and we all walked out. We never saw Georg again—ever."

"So what's your point?" MacNeice asked.

"My point is . . . well, two things. The slasher"—he waved a hand dismissively at the whiteboards—"has a manifesto, a mission. Point two, he's got a dick thing, even if he ain't using it—at least not yet."

Aziz just shook her head. Finally she said, "It's profound, Montile, and I will keep it in mind."

"You make that shit up?" Vertesi asked.

"My man, you can't make that shit up!"

Vertesi's desk phone rang and he picked it up. He listened to it for a moment, then cupped the phone and said, "Sir, I've got Mark Penniman on the line. He's going over to Old Soldiers and wants an idea of what questions you need answers for."

MacNeice took the handset. "Hello, Sergeant."

Penniman said, "I'm about a half-mile from Old Soldiers and I need some instructions about what I'm looking for."

"Sergeant, this isn't your fight. We'll contact the local—"

"With respect sir, this *is* my fight. And Gary'd expect my ass to be on the ground where the action is, whether that's in Afghanistan or Tonawanda. Kindly tell me what I'm looking for."

MacNeice turned and stared at the whiteboard while he considered. "What I say now, Mark, is off the record."

"Understood."

"We think we've discovered the connection between Gary, Old Soldiers and the project on our waterfront. Four bodies were dug up recently around here that bear the marks of a specialist—we think Sergeant Hughes."

"Go on."

"You say Gary wasn't a biker and we believe you. But he spent time in Old Soldiers, and there are both veterans and bikers there. What we need to know is, are they organized, and if so, do they hire themselves out for security? Did they suffer some losses recently, and about two years ago? But I have no idea how you would go about asking these things without arousing suspicion."

"Understood, sir. Anything else?"

"I wouldn't advise mentioning Sergeant Hughes by name, or your connection to him. The Canadian club we believe they ran into is Damned Two Deuces—D2D MC."

"D2D, roger that. Okay, I'm pulling into the parking lot. I can see what you mean. There are"—there was static on the line for a moment—"eighteen Harleys."

"Were you ever a biker?"

"No, sir. I built a scooter out of a lawn mower when I was in high school, but that's the closest."

"Be careful, Sergeant—"

"Sir, if there are vets there, we were all trained by the same boss. I'll be okay."

The line went dead and MacNeice hung up.

"Shouldn't we be calling in the local police or state troopers?" Aziz asked. "The last thing Sue-Ellen needs is a dead brother."

"Trust me, that boy can take care of himself," Williams said.

"I'm sure that's what both of them thought about Gary," she said.

"He's fresh out of combat; Gary wasn't. I think if a cockroach sneezes in Old Soldiers, he'll hear it."

"Probably say 'Gesundheit,'" Vertesi added, smirking a little at his colleagues.

"Well, my two macho men, I hope you're right," Aziz said.

No one had the machismo to point out to Aziz that she was about to do the equivalent of walking into Old Soldiers—live and in front of the media.

MacNeice checked his watch and said to her, "Five minutes until we leave, twelve before it begins."

If Aziz was intimidated by standing on a platform in front of television and still cameras—the clacking storm of the latter drowning out Wallace's introduction—it didn't show. When she spoke, every word and breath she took was recorded. At one point she raised a hand to push a strand of black hair away from her eye, and the racket sounded like June bugs. Surprised by the suddenness of it, she hesitated, then continued, her voice never wavering.

She spoke for roughly four minutes, presenting her clinical assessment of the slasher, then paused and asked for questions. Responding to reporters from news sources she'd never heard of, Aziz answered every question professionally and with ease. If she felt the weight of responsibility clawing at her gut—Mayor Bob Maybank was standing so rigidly behind her that MacNeice thought he might pass out—her poise never faltered.

Only one question, from a reporter in the front row, appeared to faze her: "Are you concerned that your being a female Muslim police officer and criminologist might make you a target for this man?"

The cameras clacked to a crescendo as they zoomed in for Aziz's answer. It was, of course, the very heart of the matter, and the question she'd hoped someone would put to her. She let the question sink in for a moment, focusing the media horde's attention like a professional. "No," she said, "I am not concerned."

The follow-up question came fast. "Why not?"

"Because I'm not a woman alone on a stair, a path or the beach.

I'm an armed detective, surrounded by my police colleagues. Thank you."

She took a step back and the Deputy Chief introduced the mayor, who spoke about the fine work of the force and of DS MacNeice's leadership on both investigations. MacNeice's announcement of a connection between the bodies discovered at the biker retreat in Cayuga and those found in the bay generated no follow-up questions from the media, who all still seemed focused on Aziz and the slasher.

It wasn't till they were leaving City Hall by the back door that Aziz's whole body seemed to sag.

"Keep breathing, keep walking. You've achieved exactly what you were going for, and maybe better. The black suit was perfect for the occasion."

"Well, that's good, because it was all I had to wear. I packed so fast I wasn't thinking!"

As they settled into the Chevy for the drive out to Braithwaite Demography, MacNeice said, "Now the hard part begins—waiting."

# 30.

THE FIRST THING that struck Mark Penniman was the smell of stale smoke. Most of the world had been sanitized, its smokers banished to the shadows outside bars and restaurants or forced to huddle night and day under the canopies of office towers and bus stations. Everywhere, it seemed, but Iraq, Afghanistan and Tonawanda's Old Soldiers roadhouse. The years of spilt beer and lit and dead cigarettes was such an assault on the nostrils that it forced him to stop inside the doors. Penniman adjusted to the darkness as the music rolled over him—Creedence Clearwater Revival, "Have You Ever Seen the Rain?" He walked down the short hallway, past the cigarette and chewing tobacco vending machines and the "Be All You Can Be," *Platoon, Full Metal Jacket, Saving Private Ryan, Band of Brothers, The Hurt Locker* and *Restrepo* posters. The visual cacophony of the images forced Penniman to look away, down at the worn and stained red runner. Every combat soldier he knew who had thought beyond how cool it was to fire weapons and vaporize ragheads knew how contradictory all that was, and how the further from the dust and boredom, the terrible suddenness of killing and hoping you won't get killed, the better it all looked. And yet he and Gary had been redeployed—happily—so many times he'd almost forgotten. Somewhere deep inside, he knew that they, and those others who survived and went back again, loved it—loved war. Until they didn't anymore. And he wanted to keep it as simple as that—Gary stopped loving it, but he still did.

Penniman took a deep breath and slowly, silently exhaled, the way he did before pressing the trigger. Then he stepped through a doorway edged in the Old Glory bunting to survey the room.

The bar was on the left. Three men sitting at the far end looked over their beer and cigarettes at him. The bartender, who'd been speaking with them, glanced his way before turning back to his friends. Whatever he said made all three laugh; Penniman assumed it was at his expense. In the far corner were two pinball machines and a shoot-'em-up video game with a toy M-16, its sound bursts adding a bizarre staccato to Fogerty's raspy vocal. Along the windows opposite the bar was a long table with benches on both sides. The curtains were made of dark brown camo canvas that allowed in only a horizontal sliver of light from the Old Soldiers neon sign. Blue smoke drifted above six big men; like distracted cattle their heads turned to check him out while their bodies remained hunched over large glasses of beer. They were dressed in black T-shirts, leather vests and black jeans. *Traded one uniform for another*, Penniman thought.

The door to the washroom swung open and a tall, lanky young man walked out. He had a limp, not pronounced, favouring his left foot. The young man nodded his way and took his place at a pinball machine.

*So we've got ten men but eighteen motorcycles outside. Where were the others?* Penniman scanned the back wall of the bar and saw a door marked PRIVATE next to the washroom. A slice of light defined the bottom of the door—they were inside. He made his way to the bar and studied the display above the bottles of bourbon, whisky and vodka. A long, narrow and faded battalion photograph, Second World War by the looks of it, hung slightly off level. Bookending the photo were two M1 Garand rifles, their straps grimy with dust. Above them, more bunting that looked as if it would fall apart if someone tried to clean it, but there appeared to be no risk of that. To the right, a large box frame contained service patches, and beyond it were more framed photos, presumably of the great battles in Europe and the Pacific.

Next to the door marked private was a giant poster of a Hummer in factory-finish camouflage under the headline HUMVEE INVINCIBLE. It almost made Penniman laugh out loud. The vehicles that arrived in country were quickly modified by those forced to depend on them. They welded extra metal panels— cannibalized from dead Hummers—to the sides and bottom in an often futile attempt to provide more protection. Going out on patrol, these overburdened vehicles looked more like *Mad Max* than General Motors. And when they hit an IED, it just meant they didn't bounce as high. *What the hell were you doing here, Gary?*

The bartender made his way slowly towards him. "What you drinkin', bud?"

"Draught, thanks."

The bartender's meaty paw took hold of the eagle topping the draught handle as he glanced again at Penniman. "You just out or still in?"

"Still in."

"What brings you here?"

"I was passin' by and saw the sign. I thought I'd come in and see what old soldiers look like. These guys old soldiers?" He swivelled on the stool and looked at the others. No one seemed interested in him anymore.

"Most, yeah. Call it truth in advertising." He put down the glass in front of Penniman, its foam overflowing onto the bar in front of him.

"Thanks. All army?"

"All army all the time, brother. You?"

"Yeah."

"Stationed?"

"Helmand province."

"Tonawanda ain't Helmand province."

"I'm here for a funeral."

The tall kid with the limp dodged around the scattered circular tables and wooden chairs and stepped up to the bar, nodding again to Penniman. He asked the bartender for bourbon.

"You ain't got the freight, Weasel."

"You know I'm good for it, Wayne. I get my cheque next week."

"Shit, I do know that! You'll get your ass in here on Tuesday and drop"—he turned, lifted up the cash register change tray and looked at a small stack of receipts—"two hundred and forty-five bucks."

"You know I'm good for it. C'mon, stop bustin' my balls."

"I'll cover him," Penniman said. "Give him a bourbon."

The bartender shrugged, snapped up a glass and turned away for the bottle, poured a shot and set the drink in front of the kid.

"Thanks, pal. I mean, Wayne knows I'm good for it, but thanks."

"You a vet?"

"Yeah, been out now for . . . I think it's like three and a half years."

"Noticed you were limping."

"Yeah, yeah. I mean, nothin' special. I took a round in the left foot. Lost four toes."

"That's a ticket home right there."

"No shit. Looks weird, though." The kid had knocked back his bourbon and was staring at his empty glass. "I definitely avoid the beach, heh-heh. I got one big toe, that's all."

"Why'd he call you Weasel?"

"Name's Wenzel—it's German. I dunno, it's only here I'm called that."

"So you don't mind."

"Naw, they don't mean nothin' by it."

"Maybe." Penniman emptied his glass. The bartender picked it up and held it in front of Penniman, his head cocked.

"Thanks, I'll have another one."

"Who you with?" the kid asked.

"With?"

"I can tell you're still in."

"Oh, right. Army, 2nd Division."

"No shit? I mean, you fuckin' with me?"

"Why would I do that, Wenzel?"

"I was with the 2nd Division in Iraq. That's where this happened!" He looked down at his foot.

"Where in Iraq? When?"

Wenzel screwed up his face as if he was in pain. "I was hit on patrol near Fallujah, that's it. Yeah. One minute I'm walking along, smiling at the kids, then, you know—*ffft, ffft, ffft*—and I'm on my ass in the road with my boot open and blood sprayin' everywhere. It was summer over here, I remember. My mom sent me pictures from Virginia Beach; I had 'em on me."

"You from Virginia Beach?"

"Naw, man, we're from West Virginia. But she loved the beach . . . She died last year."

"Sorry to hear that."

The bartender was standing at the end of the bar, and he and the other three men were watching them now. Penniman kept it as casual as he could, nursing his beer and looking at the mirror. He could see the bartender approaching, and downed the last of the second glass of draught.

"You got some business here?" the bartender said.

"Another beer, if that's what you mean. Wenzel, you up for another bourbon?" Penniman said, looking at the young man.

"Does the Pope shit in the woods?" he said, sounding uncertain that he'd gotten it right.

"Probably not, but I'll take that as a yes. Bartender, another bourbon, please."

"First, let's settle up on what you've had."

Penniman took out two twenties and put them on the bar. The bartender took one, turned to get the bourbon and poured another glass. He took the empty beer glass and filled it to the brim, put it in front of Penniman and walked back down the bar.

"I've been in friendlier bars," Penniman said.

"Yeah, well, these guys got their reasons . . . So, you still in Iraq?"

"No, we moved on to Afghanistan, just about the time you came home, I guess."

"No shit. Man, I lost touch with everybody so fast . . ."

"Pissed off?"

"Naw, naw, not that. Shit, I loved the army. No, I guess it felt . . . like being kicked off the baseball team and sent home. I got nothing, man. I got a small pension, a Purple Heart and this shithole." He looked around the bar with blurry disdain.

"It's not so bad. A lot of big bikes outside—one of them yours?"

"Naw, my money's used up just makin' it from week to week. Sometimes I ride with them, though."

"More bikes than guys in here . . ."

"The rest are in the office at the back. The bikers actually own this place. Good guys, mostly."

"Nice clubhouse."

"Sure, yeah. Like, on weekends, man, there's . . . I've counted forty bikes out there. Regulars too . . ."

"Forty. Now that's an army in itself right there."

"Seen their colours? OSMC. Two crossed swords under a skull. So cool, man—gold and black."

"OSMC's too close to USMC for me. You a member?"

"Naw, man—this here foot . . . It's as tough to be a member here as staying in the army. But I've ridden with them."

"You mean like down to the mall?"

"Yeah, right. These guys can fuck you up, man, and I ain't talking teenyboppers down at no mall."

"How'd you end up here? I mean, in Tonawanda and not in West Virginia."

"Oh, I did go home. I was there after I got out of hospital. But after a while I heard that my sergeant had left the army and was here. Shit, man, I was on the next bus."

"He's a good guy?"

"The best. Bester. Bestest. I'da bin shot to pieces on that road, man. Like zippers tearing up the dirt—they had me. Sarge took out the two snipers on the roof and a guy in a doorway—it was like a fuckin' movie. He drags me into a house, a guy runs at us out of nowhere, Sarge does this karate move—*boom,* down he goes—he was dead, man. Then it's off with the boot, on with the field bandage. Next thing I know, I'm waking up and there's a pretty woman feedin' me Tropicana through a straw."

"You were lucky."

"Wasn't luck—it was Sergeant Hughes, man." Wenzel's eyes were glassy. Penniman couldn't tell whether it was from remembering or the bourbon—probably both.

"Still see him?"

Wenzel was about to answer, then glanced at the table by the window and realized that all the men were staring at them. "Aw, man . . . sorry. I shouldn't drink so much . . . I starts runnin' my mouth and shit. Thanks for the drinks, though . . . And hey, man," he said under his breath, "watch your back." Wenzel stood up unsteadily and offered his hand.

Taking it, Penniman said, "You mean over there or here?"

The kid leaned closer. "Both." Wenzel let go, straightened himself and called out to the bartender, "See ya, Wayners. You too, guys . . ." Then he limped towards the front door.

The bartender came over and retrieved the empty bourbon glass. "Get what you came for?"

"I don't follow you."

"Sure, bud. You want another one?"

"No thanks. I'll just finish this and be on my way. He seems like a good kid," Penniman said, nodding towards the front door.

"Weasel? Why, what was he saying?"

"Nothing much. I asked him about the limp and he talked about how much he loved the army."

"He gets the mouth shits when he drinks too much."

"I didn't think so."

"In case I get someone in from Helmand province, what's your name?"

"My name's Bud. I thought you knew that."

The bartender stared at him.

Penniman emptied the glass, retrieved the second twenty, pulled a ten from his pocket and slapped it on the counter. "Tip's for you, and the vets." He studied the men at the end of the bar and those at the table for a moment. Turning back to the bartender, he said, "Interesting place you got here. Might look you up when I get out. Not too many vet-friendly bars around anymore."

The bartender put the ten in his pocket but didn't answer.

# 31.

THE LOBBY OF Braithwaite Demography Incorporated was faux British all the way, with dark green panelled wainscoting topped by white and cream vertical-stripe wallpaper. There were hunting prints from the nineteenth century on every wall except the one behind the receptionist, where a large BDI hung in brass serifed letters.

As they sat in the deep leather chairs waiting for BDI's president to appear, Aziz said, "I thought demographics was a new high-tech discipline run by math and computer geeks, but this looks like a men's club in London. I feel naked without a cigar and a newspaper."

"I'm not sure they'd let you into that kind of club," MacNeice said, "naked or otherwise."

"Yes, well, quite."

MacNeice laughed.

A young woman pushed open the heavy oak door, nodded to the receptionist and said, "Dr. Braithwaite will see you now.

Please follow me."

They followed her into another world, one of glass and steel. Offices around the perimeter defined an open inner space, roughly square; at its heart was a carousel of six flat-screen televisions hanging from the ceiling, tuned to various channels. Below them, at four narrow rows of white tables, people sat staring at desktop computers. Without exception, they were young. If they were curious as to who was being led through, they did a fine job of covering it. Most were wearing headphones and many were watching one of the overhead screens, which were also visible to the people in the glassed-in offices.

The assistant opened a door in the northeast corner; the glass of this office had been coated with a film that made it translucent. Presumably the boss needed privacy more than a view of the flat-screens. Not to worry—it turned out he had his own grid of four screens on the wall of his office.

A man of medium height and weight stood up from his desk and smiled as they approached. "I'm Roger Braithwaite, president and CEO of BDI." He had pale skin and rosy cheeks, a close-cropped beard and short hair receding from his forehead.

MacNeice introduced himself and Aziz. They shook hands and Braithwaite gestured for them to sit, not in front of the desk, where there were chairs, but at a pine harvest table that was centred on the exterior windows. Outside was a screen of mature fir trees, beyond which MacNeice could see the Chevy in the parking lot. Braithwaite smiled, jostled a large stack of papers into shape and moved it off to the side before putting his hands together as if he were sitting in church.

Aziz put a large envelope on the table and pulled out several photos of the young man from the emergency ward, as well as his motorcycle.

"You know why we've come. And with this many televisions, you may already have seen these images," MacNeice said.

Avoiding his eyes, Braithwaite picked up the photos.

"Mr. Braithwaite, I believe you know this man," MacNeice said.

Braithwaite put down the photos, sat back in his chair and looked out to the trees and then back at the two detectives. "Yes, I do."

"His name, please."

"William Dance. He is—or rather, was—a demographer here. A quite brilliant young man." He smiled.

"You saw the press conference where these images were first introduced?"

"Yes, I did, on one of the screens behind you."

"Why didn't you come forward?" Aziz asked.

"I'm sure you can appreciate why, Detective."

"Actually, given what we suspect this man has been doing, I cannot appreciate why at all."

"When did you leave the firm?" MacNeice asked.

"William graduated at the top of his undergrad class, did his MA and then came to work for me. He was with us for just over three years and left almost nine months ago."

"What happened?"

"We're not entirely sure. His parents had a cottage on one of the Muskoka Lakes, and both of them were killed in a traffic accident up there. Understandably, William appeared to be devastated. I told him to take all the time he needed, and he did—three months of it. Then he called and said he wasn't coming back. No explanations."

"Do you have his address?"

"His old one. He was living with his parents, but he's moved out, which I found out only when I went by to see if I could persuade him to come back. I ended up talking to a neighbour who saw me standing by the gate, and the neighbour said that William was long gone, that he'd cut himself off, even from old family friends. Also that he'd likely come into a considerable amount of money from his father's estate. No one knows where he went."

"And you're certain these are photos of William Dance?"

"Oh, absolutely. And that's his motorcycle—no question. It was the bane of our collective existence. He loved that thing, called it 'The Avenger' for some reason. So far as any of us knew, he didn't know how to ride it without making a terrible noise."

"So where is his parents' place?"

"It's 6 Spring Lane, a cul-de-sac out past the university, on the edge of the ravine."

"Do you know if anyone on your staff has stayed in touch with Dance?"

"I doubt it. But several members of the executive team, my assistant and a few of the researchers in the pit—sorry, out there at the long desks—worked with him."

"We'd like to talk with each of them as soon as possible. Detective Aziz, will you call Vertesi and Williams and get them over here?" Turning back to Braithwaite, MacNeice said, "We'll need you to help organize this, as well as find us a private space to conduct the interviews."

Braithwaite nodded. "That entire wall of offices is interview rooms—we do a lot of them for our research. You're welcome to set up in any one of them."

Braithwaite called in his assistant and asked her to organize the staff. When she left, Aziz went with her. MacNeice sat down again and took out his notebook.

Braithwaite stared at his hands on the table in front of him. "What's happening is so grotesque . . . We'll help in any way we can. I apologize for not coming forward. I should tell you that his neighbour on Spring Lane said William chased him away from the door when he went over to offer condolences. He actually screamed at this chap to go away and slammed the door. That was the night he disappeared."

"So you had no clue he was unstable?"

"Well, I knew he was an odd duck."

"What exactly do you mean by that?"

Braithwaite again put his hands together as he struggled for the right words. "He's very . . . interior, if you know what I mean. In my experience, demographers, and mathematicians, tend to be somewhat odd that way. But with him there was something else— arrogance, perhaps? But William was always pleasant. We're all in a state of shock to think that he might actually have anything to do with . . ." His voice trailed off, as if he was too decent to comment on young women being slashed to death.

Of Dance's private life, Braithwaite said he knew nothing. "I mean, I met his parents occasionally at social functions when his father was CEO of Sterling Insurance. I knew he still lived at home—but so many young people do these days." He gazed at his television screens, though they weren't on—out of habit, or seeking inspiration?—before dropping his eyes to MacNeice. "He smiled a lot, you know, even when we were under intense pressure. William was so opaque . . . but there were many occasions when I thought how marvellous it would be to have several more people on staff just like him. You see, many are good at the math and some even shine in comparative analysis, but he had the ability to see it all as if it wasn't just data but a narrative spread out before him."

With all four of them involved, the interviews with BDI staff lasted just over two hours. When they were done, the four detectives sat in the interview room to review what they'd heard. While most of his co-workers thought Dance was a brilliant demographer and a benign presence, some said they found it—in the words of one young woman—"a bit unnerving" that he smiled so much. That young researcher went on to say that she assumed he was religious. When pressed to explain, she added, "Well, he had that fundamentalist

Christian thing, you know . . . like those women in Bountiful who are all married to the same guy and always smiling. It was creepy."

According to another, Dance was a vegan and used that as an excuse not to go out with his co-workers, preferring instead to take his bagged lunch and tear off on his motorcycle—no one knew where. The only recreation he'd engaged in was video games on the office computers after work. "The ones I spoke to hated playing with him," Williams said.

"Why?" Vertesi asked.

"Because he always won! Those games should be intense fun—lots of furrowed brows, yelling and laughing. But not for Dance. He was quiet, smiling the whole time. Once during a game, this one guy I interviewed said he asked Dance why he was always smiling, and his answer freaked him out. Dance said"—Williams looked down at his notes—"'I wasn't aware I was smiling. This is war. What's there to smile about?' The guy said Dance was dead serious, and smiling as he said it."

"That boy should spend more time in front of a mirror," Vertesi said. "Now that we have his name, we'll get the motor vehicle registration for the Yamaha. With luck, they'll have a current address."

"Time to get out of here," MacNeice said, looking at his watch—7:08 p.m.

"I'll make some calls on that Muskoka traffic accident," Williams added. "Shouldn't take long, boss. We'll join you at the house in max . . . three-quarters of an hour."

Turning out of the parking lot, MacNeice and Aziz headed for 6 Spring Lane. Williams and Vertesi went back to Division to ensure that the face and name of a person of interest in the slasher killings—William Dance—was released to police forces and media across the province.

# 32.

"IT'S LIKE YOU were invisible, walking across that beach," He said to his friend in the mirror.

"I know. I can't explain it, but I think there's something in the way I walk—unassuming, focused, but at the same time distracted—part of the landscape, a person who wouldn't catch your eye."

"But the blood—you were covered in it!"

"Doesn't matter. No one noticed me."

Billie Dance turned to pin the photo from Samora Aploon's cell-phone on the wall next to those he'd taken of her behind the counter of the Burger Shack and several others of her walking along the beach with a book or papers and her tray of food. "I like how these all look like spy photos."

Samora wore the same T-shirt in each, the one with the happy typeface and a cartoon of a shack that didn't look anything like the real building. "She went down like a tree."

"It was a noble stroke."

Stepping back, Billie leaned against the wall of the living room. It was furnished with a sofa from a second-hand shop on Parkdale and a chair that he'd picked up off the street. The cane seat was torn through, but he'd put a piece of plywood across it and secured it with duct tape. He looked at the images on the wall.

"They look good together."

"Yeah, Samora—that great cellphone death shot—next to Ghosh . . ."

"Major freak-out when this hits the Web."

"Major."

"When do we tell the world what this is all about?"

"Okay, a history lesson: we don't tell the world. We leave that to our adversaries. Eventually they'll figure it out. Our actions will be our proclamation. No words."

"The new Knights Templar."

"Exactly. And it was two hundred years or so before they were finally put down. I don't need two hundred years—I've got 3G broadband. The Knights only had runners and pigeons."

"Drag about Lea Nam. These scouting shots look lonely—missing that splash of red."

Below the photos of Samora and Ghosh were newspaper clippings touting Nam as an Olympic prospect as well as a brilliant student. "We're in no hurry. It'll be better the second time around, and you know she'll be waiting for it."

"What's next?"

"No, who's next?"

He swung about and pointed to the opposite wall, which was stained from an ancient roof leak that had streaked and bubbled the faded floral wallpaper from the ceiling to the floor.

"The entrepreneur?"

"Yes, the entrepreneur. The scouting's done—we're ready." He was looking at a photograph of an elegant young woman emerging from an office building, briefcase in hand, putting on large and stylish black sunglasses. Below were six underground parking lot photos of a silver Mercedes 300 parked in the same reserved space, with individual times printed on the bottom of each image—8:10 to 8:53 a.m. and 6:47 to 7:35 p.m.

"A breeze."

"No, not so easy. It's the first level down, there are cars coming and going—it could be tricky."

"What about doing her at the apartment?"

"Security's too tight. This is the best option. There's no camera at the entrance or on the parking level—just rape phones." Billie walked over to tap the print. "They've got a barrier but no booth. We take our ticket, and on the way out we dodge the barrier and vanish."

"So, morning or night?"

"Personally, I'm a morning guy."

"I like mornings."

"She may be the prettiest yet."

"Maybe, but I don't care about that."

"What does she actually do?"

"In India, where she comes from, they can do things faster, better and cheaper than anything we can do here. We're undereducated but we think we're not; we're lazy and uninventive but think we're brilliant. Narinder Dass was named one of the top ten CEOs under thirty—see here . . ."

"Oh yeah, nice photo."

"Runs a company staffed in India that makes every Canadian call centre redundant. No great loss, you might think."

"That's what I was thinking."

"You've got to understand. It starts with handling all our Q&As on credit cards, then it moves on to everything else."

"At least they stay where they belong."

"No, they don't. Look, they speak English better than most Canadians, and better than any Chinese. You don't hear about call centres being run out of Beijing, do you?"

"No."

"We've had millions of Indians already emigrate here, but that number is just a trickle of what we will have. How do you think Narinder Dass got her money?"

"From over there?"

"For sure—India's now a superpower . . . And look at that smile—who can resist that? It's like having a Bollywood movie star right here in Dundurn. She's doing social events, running in marathons; soon I bet she'll even run for office."

"I see your point."

"Yes, well, we're going to cut the line. Disconnect it. Hang up, Ms. Dass."

"Call failed."

"Exactly."

"Did you watch that press conference?"

"No, why?"

"Why?! It was about our project. I'd say we've got a new candidate—a Muslim."

"What does she do?"

"Detective, criminologist . . . Bottom line, she thinks we've always felt inadequate. I think she's calling us a coward."

"No shit, that's rich. I don't think Samora or Taaraa would have agreed."

# 33.

**D**EFINED BY A low fieldstone wall, the house sat deep in a large lot, barely visible through a dense cover of trees and landscaping. MacNeice parked the Chevy adjacent to the large electronic gate that guarded the driveway to the red-brick and greystone mansion. The curtains were drawn and it was difficult to tell the place had been abandoned—difficult, but not impossible. He could see flyers and newspapers scattered on the stone walkway behind the iron side gate.

A small stand of oak, birch and maple trees on the grounds appeared to have been lifted from the forest and ravine beyond— roughly a mile from where Lea Nam had been attacked. Several large rocks were strategically placed among them, and under a large pine, two grey squirrels were foraging on the ground. MacNeice surveyed the scene as he got out of the Chevy, closing the door behind him. He opened the trunk, took out his old Samsonite briefcase and approached the gate, Aziz trailing him.

"You look like a travelling insurance man with that," she said.

He smiled briefly. "I suppose I am, in a way." Though right now he hadn't been doing so well at ensuring the lives of Dundurn's young women.

"I'll check the side," Aziz said, picking up a small branch. She walked along a path that ran between the stone wall that bordered the grounds and the line of old-growth trees that led to the edge of the ravine.

MacNeice tried the side gate and was surprised to find it unlocked. He waited, watching Aziz until she turned back towards him. Scanning the forest beside the path, he looked for one thing that didn't look like the rest: a clump of darkness in the leaf and shadow pattern, a misfit patch of colour, a shivering branch or bush, a startled bird or squirrel calling on an otherwise still day . . . but nothing pulled focus.

Pushing through the gate, he stooped to check the dates on two newspapers—early February. Counting another seven, he concluded that Dance had cancelled the subscription. MacNeice put the briefcase on the ground and sat on one of the large rocks, trying to imagine the family that had lived here. The place seemed as cold as the stone beneath him.

The neighbouring house—a greystone heap—was another fifty yards beyond the stone wall and set even further back. In its garden, several concrete deer wandered about, eating the grass or looking up surprised and ready to scamper off into the forest. There they stood, year in and year out—lifelike and lifeless.

Tossing the stick away, Aziz came through the gate. "They've got a big pool and a hot tub in the back garden. Both still have winter covers over them, with lots of fallen leaves left over from last autumn." She sat next to him on the rock, picked up a pine cone and turned it slowly in her hands. "Fascinating things, these . . ."

"They are," he said, looking down at it, "very mathematical—the entire golden mean in that one cone. From nautilus shells to the

Parthenon to pine cones . . . What do you think happened to Dance?"

"You mean, why do I think he snapped?" she said, lobbing the pine cone over to the next rock, where the squirrels gave it only passing interest.

"Yes."

"Well, I don't think his sickness has anything to do with his parents getting killed. I think he must have been ill for a long time. Perhaps their deaths were the trigger for this . . ." MacNeice noticed that Aziz was careful to suppress any disgust she felt for William Dance. "It's his use of the Internet, not the killings, that will guarantee him a chapter in the texts on psychopathy," she added.

MacNeice looked up at the facade looming over them. "Maybe Williams is right. Maybe it is a 'groin thing,' and the Web is the fastest way to build a following—his version of standing on a chair in front of the class and dropping his pants."

Moments passed in silence before he said, "Hear that bird? Not the crows off to the right, but the one calling from down in the ravine—high, sharp, short calls."

She listened for several seconds, then said, "Yes, what is it?"

"A downy woodpecker. If it comes closer, you might hear him tapping on a tree."

"When did you develop a love of birds, Mac?"

"I think I've always loved birds, but I'd have to credit Kate's family in Suffolk for teaching me about them. It seemed like everyone I met over there was a birder." They listened, but the calls grew more distant before receding altogether.

"Now that we have a face and a name, I'm going to recommend another press conference, to allow you to speak directly to Dance."

"Ask him to surrender."

"If you're willing. Otherwise, I can do it."

"In for a penny . . ." she said, somewhat cheerily.

A car approached. From the squealing of brakes, MacNeice knew it was Williams. In a moment he and Vertesi appeared at the gate.

MacNeice stood up and scanned the forest again, looking for any sudden movement. Aziz smiled, thinking he was looking for the woodpecker.

"Nice digs," Williams said, looking up at the house.

"News?" MacNeice asked.

Vertesi went first. He'd spoken to the provincial police corporal who was first responder at the accident that killed Dance's parents. It had happened on an unusually warm afternoon the previous November. They were leaving their cottage near Lake Joseph in their Land Cruiser and had stopped at an intersection with the highway. The father was driving. A witness said the left signal was on, indicating they'd turn south towards Toronto and Dundurn, but the driver missed several opportunities to cross when the highway was clear in both directions. Inexplicably, he shot out instead into oncoming traffic. Their vehicle was T-boned by a Dodge Ram carrying two 3,600-horsepower marine diesel engines. The impact fused the two vehicles together, and they clawed eighty yards out of the highway before grinding to a stop in the ditch.

"The driver of the truck—the OPP officer said he must have been doing at least eighty when they collided—was cut in half by one of the engine blocks when it tore through the cab. The autopsy revealed only that Mr. Dance had no alcohol or drugs in his system, and as far as they could tell, he hadn't had a heart attack or stroke. Police concluded that he wasn't paying attention."

This news was greeted by a long pause. It would have been natural to express some sympathy for the horrific demise of the Dances, but the moment passed without comment. Perhaps, MacNeice thought, it was because William was their son, their responsibility, and ultimately their catastrophic failure.

"We've also got the bike's plate number, but it's still registered to this address," Vertesi added. "Oh, and a uniform's on his way with the warrant." He looked over at Williams. "Your turn."

Williams turned to Aziz and said, "You're a media darling, darling. The Deputy Chief came down to the cubicle and left a message: *The National* wants an interview tomorrow at 6:00 p.m. The TV network's promoting it as a major segment called"—he looked down at his notebook—"'The Mind of a Serial Killer.'"

He also said that Ryan had found six more women who had been featured in the *Standard* over the previous twelve months. Two of the six had moved away and one had since gone bankrupt, leaving a Chinese doctor, an Indian entrepreneur and a Nigerian immunologist—all accomplished, all in their late twenties or early thirties.

Williams counted on his fingers. "A Bangladeshi, a Korean and a South African . . . probably the one with the least to worry about is the Nigerian." As if Dance were trading hockey cards—*got it, need it*—building his collection.

"That makes me rather special, I should think," Aziz said under her breath.

"Why's that? Oh, right—a Muslim born in the Middle East." Vertesi nodded, embarrassed at missing the obvious.

"We'll call a media conference for ten tomorrow," MacNeice said.

"If Dance is payin' attention, he might realize we're trying to provoke him to come after Aziz," Williams said. "He might just stick to his game plan and go after the next one on the list."

Either way, MacNeice thought, they wouldn't have long to wait. His attacks were frequent enough that another one could be expected within the next forty-eight hours.

"Unless he's superconfident and not rattled by what he hears. What do you think, Mac?" Aziz asked.

"I think we're in uncharted territory. So far Dance has been free to act at will, isolating and working his way down a list of brilliant young women. Now he's being challenged. Does he accept the challenge or ignore it?" Regardless of what he chose to do, MacNeice decided to assign a plainclothes unit to each of the three new candidates—and Aziz. To hell with staff shortages and strained resources.

He scanned the forest again, and seeing nothing out of place, he led them along the path and up the four steps to the house, where MacNeice opened the briefcase on a stone ledge. He took out three thin steel rods that looked vaguely like short barbecue skewers and knelt in front of the door, where he inserted them one by one into the keyhole.

"Shhh, the master's at work," Williams said.

"That's right, be quiet." MacNeice moved the rods about inside the keyhole, listening and feeling. A minute later he stood up, put the rods back in the briefcase pocket, retrieved his camera and closed the Samsonite. "Right. There'll likely be a security system, so be prepared." He turned the heavy brass knob.

The door opened and the beeping began. "I've got this one," Williams said, sprinting down the hall and disappearing through the door to the basement. In fifteen seconds the friendly beeps turned into a loud *whurp-whurp-whurp* that continued for another three seconds before it stopped. Williams appeared at the doorway and took a bow.

"I'm not going to ask where you learned how to do that," Vertesi said.

As they put their gloves on, MacNeice directed Williams back to the basement and Vertesi to the first floor. "I'll take the second," he said. "Aziz, you do the third. If and when the security company calls, I'll answer. Take your time; be neat but thorough. Let's find out as much as we can about Billie Dance before Forensics arrives."

What he saw as he searched the second floor filled him with dread—not any specific horror, just the sheer banality leaching through the space and over every surface and object. There were framed images—decades of mother, father, son—that looked more like stock photographs than an authentically happy family of three. The furnishings were expensive and vaguely Edwardian but couldn't be taken seriously as either antiques or family heirlooms. The place was like a hotel—a hodgepodge of fake respectability.

The house was a showpiece, in which the lives of the family who'd lived there appeared to play as much or as little of a role as a hall chair, or the photo that he imagined had graced the Christmas card from Sterling's CEO—*From my family to yours. Season's greetings and a prosperous New Year.* Had he time, MacNeice bet he would find the actual card somewhere in a drawer.

Of the three bedrooms and two baths on the second floor, only the master bedroom looked at all lived in. It still had the parent's belongings—clothes, shoes, jewellery, brushes, bric-a-brac—and a fine layer of dust to reflect the months during which nothing had been disturbed. The drawers were neatly divided, the top ones hers, the bottom ones his. The contents of the walk-in closet—his clothes on the left, hers on the right—were all tastefully conservative. For him, a row of brown and black dress shoes, two pairs of tennis shoes and one pair of golf shoes. For her, flats, mostly blue, grey, brown and black, and two pairs each of sneakers and tennis shoes—but nothing for golf.

The study, which appeared to be his, had framed photos on almost every surface except the desk. They showed a man giving awards, presumably to individuals who'd met or exceeded their sales targets, and several more of him at company functions wearing a tuxedo and standing next to his wife—a handsome couple. As for the desk itself, nothing; the drawers had been cleared of everything but staplers, pens and pencils, a calculator and several empty pads or notebooks. The correspondence, bills, cheque-book, legal papers and computer or laptop were gone, if they were ever there.

Certain there was nothing to find, MacNeice headed for the basement. On his way past Vertesi, he asked, "Anything?"

"Zip, zilch, nada. They were serious drinkers, but boring." Vertesi was opening a drawer in the liquor cabinet. "It's all like an upscale Howard Johnson's—executive-level living." The dining room had a large mahogany table and eight matching chairs; a sideboard filled with expensive stemwear, crystal tumblers and several decanters; and a rolling cart that boasted an array of spirits—heavy on Scotch—mostly half full. Next to the fireplace stood a sleek Bang & Olufsen stereo, with two tower speakers on either side of the front window. A quick scan of the music revealed someone's passion for male crooners.

Aziz had climbed the stairs to the attic only to find it clean—"Who cleans an attic?" There were a few banker's boxes of files and two more of awards bearing the father's name. There were also two boxes of blue Christmas decorations and a trunk that contained what appeared to be Mrs. Dance's wedding gown and veil lying on a cluster of mothballs. There were no boxes for William Junior—no yearbooks or pennants or school jackets or sports equipment, nothing to indicate that he had actually grown up there.

MacNeice descended the stairs and followed the sound of Williams humming "Amazing Grace."

"Welcome to the kid's room," Williams said when MacNeice appeared. He was holding up a samurai sword. Pointing with it, Williams said, "On that shelf you've likely got damn near every samurai movie ever made, and over there—where the oil stain is on the exercise mat—are tools and bits for fixing his bike. The door down the hall leads to the garage. How's it upstairs?"

"Like nobody lives here anymore."

"Yeah, well, this was lived in . . ." Williams said, fanning through the books on the shelves below the videos.

MacNeice scanned the spines. Math, computer science, the science of demography, chess, chaos theory, the Crusades, the Knights Templar, Dungeons and Dragons and a substantial number of video games that appeared to mirror the books' subject matter.

"It's *Fantasy Island* for geeks—oh, except for the ever-popular *Mein Kampf.*" Williams handed him the book from the bottom shelf.

MacNeice flipped through the pages, checking the handwritten notes in the margins, the twisted wisdom underlined with shockingly straight lines. The spine of the book told the story—so well worn it was close to breaking. He put it back on the shelf and opened the closet door.

It was a drill sergeant's dream. Six pant hangers, each with a neatly hung pair of chinos, size 32 long. Next to them, four madras shirts, long-sleeved, in shades of blue, and next to those, eight pale blue button-down cotton shirts. On the shelf above were T-shirts in white, black and dark blue, all neatly folded and stacked. On the floor were several pairs of brown and black penny loafers and two pairs of white Converse high-tops—but no hiking boots.

In the adjoining room there was a large tatami mat and a small shelf with candles, incense and a ceramic Buddha. On the wall was an illustration—front and back—of a nude Chinese male with the pressure points, veins and arteries drawn as if they were surface-mounted on the flesh. MacNeice wondered how Dance squared this side of his personality with *Mein Kampf.*

He backtracked to open the door to an empty garage. There were tire tracks in the dust and old oil stains from an automobile. The garbage bins were empty and tucked neatly along the far side; a robin's egg–blue bicycle with big fenders and white-walled balloon tires leaned against one wall. Both tires were flat. Williams came up beside him and peered into the garage.

"Where's the mother's car?" MacNeice said.

"She had one?"

"We're out in the middle of nowhere. She'd have to drive to buy groceries or gin."

"I'll get onto Motor Vehicles."

At 8:17 p.m. the forensics team arrived. MacNeice and Williams stepped into the cool of the evening to find Aziz and Vertesi waiting on the stone path. Aziz held up a small plastic bag. "I picked up some of the mail, but Michael says there's another stack of it in the dining room."

"Forensics will bring it in for us," MacNeice said. Someone cleared his throat off to the left, presumably to get their attention.

"Michael, that's likely the next-door neighbour, wondering what's going on over here. Get a statement from him. I'd like to know what kind of relationship William had with his parents and to see if the neighbour has any idea where we'd find him, or whether he knows someone who might."

Vertesi walked between the trees and vaulted easily over the fieldstone wall. MacNeice carried his briefcase to the Chevy, locked it in the trunk and then stood staring into the woods again. Nothing.

Aziz and Williams soon joined him. "See anything, boss?" Williams asked.

"Just wondering if he was watching us."

"I thought you were looking for birds," Aziz said, looking up at him.

MacNeice smiled.

"You think he'd have the balls to do that?" Williams asked.

"I'm certain he would. I'd go so far as to say I thought I could feel him watching us earlier."

"Well, in that case, let me check it out." Williams made sure his sidearm was free and took out his Maglite. Stepping over a fallen branch, he sang softly, "If you go down to the woods tonight, you're in for a big-motherfuckin' surprise . . ."

"Straight ahead fifty yards or so, to where the ground falls off into the ravine," MacNeice directed.

They watched Williams pick his way through underbrush and fallen branches, sweeping his Maglite back and forth. MacNeice wasn't worried about his being attacked by Dance—even if he was the right colour, he was the wrong gender.

Watching the bright cone of light recede in the distance, Aziz asked, "What did you see in that house?"

"Feel, not see. I can't define it . . . a vibe. Strange." It wasn't haunted, but the whole house had a sad quality, an absence of love. He had felt it outside, sitting in the garden, and everywhere inside. He could hear Vertesi making his way towards them over the unraked leaves of the mini forest.

"Where's Montile headed?" Vertesi asked, as he hopped the wall again to rejoin them.

"Just checking. What'd the neighbour say?"

"He was curious, all right. Hadn't seen the news, but unlike Braithwaite, he always thought the kid was weird. His name is Howard Matheson, a wealth manager. He has no idea where Dance has gone."

Matheson had described the parents as pleasant but not social; they'd moved in about twelve years before, after Dance retired as CEO of Sterling. He had stayed on as chair of the board, but other than coming in for board meetings, he and his wife spent most of the year up north, leaving the house to their only child.

"At least the guy was honest," Vertesi said. "He told me he learned much of what he knew about them from their obits."

"Dance Senior was—what, an actuary?" MacNeice said, watching as Williams made his way back through the forest towards them.

"How'd you guess?" Vertesi said.

"Dance Junior—extraordinary skills in mathematics and data. Just a guess."

When Williams emerged from the forest, he switched off the flashlight. "Someone has been there," he called. "The ground five feet or so below the ridge is torn up. I can't say whether it was an hour or a day ago, but recently."

# 34.

**P**ENNIMAN BACKED HIS twenty-year-old grey Suburban behind the 24/7 pizza stand on the corner and waited. Ten minutes after he had left the bar, two heavies came out of Old Soldiers and climbed on their Harleys. They turned south up the service road, riding slowly side by side. Penniman waited till they were almost out of sight, then followed them. A half-mile later he could see Wenzel walking along the gravel shoulder on the opposite side. Penniman eased onto the shoulder without hitting the brakes and rolled to a stop. He reached into the glove compartment, retrieved an M9 Beretta and snapped in the clip.

Up ahead, the bikers had pulled a U-turn and stopped so that they hemmed Wenzel in. Unsure what to do, the kid backed down into the ditch as if he was going to make a run for the bush. Then, maybe realizing how futile that was, he stopped. Caught between them, he stumbled back onto the shoulder, his hands raised. As the bikers climbed off their machines and came towards him, Penniman put the truck in gear and moved off the shoulder. When he was within fifty yards, he crossed the road, driving towards them on the gravel shoulder. He stopped as one of the bikers grabbed Wenzel and held him so the other could punch him hard in the face. Wenzel's nose exploded and blood ran down the kid's chin. The biker was about to hit him again when Penniman hit the horn. The biker spat in the dirt towards him and threw another punch, to Wenzel's stomach. Penniman stepped on the gas and rammed the bike then drove over it, grinding the machine under his front wheels. Inside the Suburban it sounded like a beer can being crushed by hand.

The biker holding Wenzel screamed, dropped the kid and rushed towards Penniman, swearing and waving his arms as if he needed oxygen. The second biker headed for his saddlebag, presumably for a weapon.

Stepping out of the Suburban, Penniman pointed his sidearm at the nearest of the bikers and fired a round into the gravel between his legs. Both men stopped dead. Wenzel stumbled to his feet, squatted and puked into the dirt. Groaning, he sat down on the ground, spitting a mixture of blood and vomit.

The one whose bike lay crushed and leaking fuel into the ditch screamed, "You are a fucking dead man! You are so fucking dead!" Up close Penniman could see that both of these men had been sitting with the bartender at the end of the bar.

"Get up, Wenzel. Into the truck—now," Penniman ordered. Wenzel staggered towards the passenger side, climbed in and slammed the door behind him.

"You fucking shit, you'll pay for this," the second biker threatened, his eyes on Penniman's gun.

"Get whatever you were going for out of the saddlebag, now. Move."

The biker hesitated.

"The next round will be into your gas tank, so either go get it now or stand clear."

"I'll get it. Fuck, I'll get it!" He unbuckled the strap and removed a .44 Magnum. For a fraction of a second he was clearly considering taking the chance; then he dropped the gun on the ground.

"Not on the ground, grunt. That is a precision instrument. You'll hand that to me, and I think you know how."

The biker picked it up by the barrel and walked slowly to within arm's reach, then passed it to Penniman butt first. "You boys were having fun back at the bar, I think at my expense."

"We spotted you as a faggot—a fucking army faggot."

"So let me get this straight. Here are the two of you—dressed in black leather with little fringes on your pants and your motorcycles all dolled up with bags, more fringes and shit—and you think *I* look like a faggot? You truly are sorry fucks. I'm going to head back home now. I'll drop off Wenzel somewhere safe. Do I have your approval to do that?"

"Fuck you."

"Last thing—get out your cellphones."

Both bikers hesitated.

"Do it now." Penniman pointed the weapon at the motorcycle's gas tank.

"Okay, okay—fuck!" They took out their cellphones and held them out to him.

"I don't want your phones, for Christ's sake. Throw them into the bush." He fired at the bike; the shot tore a hole in the black leather seat. Both men threw their phones as far as they could.

"I will personally skin you alive, you fuck," the second biker said.

"Pathetic. Mount up, boys. Take the hog that's still standing back to the pigpen."

Slowly the men backed away from him, then climbed onto the

bike. As they rode off, the one on the back yelled, "We'll come back for you, fucker!"

Penniman climbed into his truck, backed it off the Harley and pulled away, heading towards the Peace Bridge, and Canada.

# 35.

"WHAT DO YOU think they'll find?" Billie asked, closing the door behind him.

"Squat. My books—math mostly, some history, stuff on the Knights Templar. They'll get my prints and probably my DNA, but that would only be a problem if I was trying to get away."

"What do you think of the Muslim criminologist?"

"She took a chance walking along the forest there. Probably thinks that Glock on her hip will protect her."

"It would, wouldn't it?"

"If she had a chance to use it, but she won't."

"Anything else?"

"Yeah. The other guy is a bigwig cop—I've read about him. He holds the record for solving homicides, at least around here. It was cool how he kept scanning the forest—slowly, like a predator with a heat-seeking scope. We ducked below the edge just in time."

"It was cool too, how he got inside."

"Yeah, cops and crooks—they all use the same tools. But there was something else about him . . ."

"What?"

"When they were sitting on the rock, didn't you notice?"

"Well, yeah, they were talkin' and stuff."

"But not the way a detective superintendent talks to a detective inspector. He's her superior officer . . ."

"I didn't notice anything."

"Don't you think they were very familiar with each other?"

"You mean, like he's fuckin' her?"

"I don't know, but something's up with them that isn't cop work."

"So, do we hit her first or the Indian with the Mercedes?"

"You know, the one thing that makes demographers like Braithwaite grind their teeth at night . . ." he said, looking at the photo of Narinder Dass on the wall.

"Old beady-eye?"

"BDI, yes. They can't stand chance—the roll of the dice, the flip of the coin. They hate chance, even if it's a one percent risk."

"Why?"

"Just because it's chance! He measures trends from facts and predicts facts from trends. If you flip a coin—especially when you mix that in with measured choices like Ghosh and Aploon—it royally fucks up the stats. BDI hates that. My guess is Braithwaite tipped them off to go to the house."

"So should we ride out and do him?"

"No, forget that. I'm into colour. Braithwaite's lame, but his shit is probably as white as he is. I say we flip a coin—heads we do the Muslim, tails we do the Indian."

"How fuckin' cool is that! I love it."

"Yeah, me too."

"Glad you didn't ride the Yamaha."

"I'm many things, but stupid isn't one of them."

"She's good-looking too . . ."

"This one? Yeah, I guess so, but that doesn't interest me."

"I know, sure, but I'd rather be doing beautiful women than fat, ugly ones."

"For the aesthetics, yes, I agree. But strictly for the aesthetics."

## 36.

**D**RIVING BACK TO Division, Aziz sorted the mail she'd
picked up from inside the door. It was a mixture of bills
and letters from former employees and friends sent to
William Junior, offering condolences. There were five from Wes
Young Toyota. The leasing department was asking for back payment on the beige 2010 Toyota Camry registered to Dance's mother.
The first had arrived when the payments were in arrears by two
months; from there they got increasingly threatening as the months
went by with no response from Billie.

MacNeice looked at his watch as they entered the empty cubicle—9:23 p.m. "Do those letters include the ownership and licence
plate numbers?"

"Yes, you want them?" She offered the letters.

"Hang on to them and we'll use the info in tomorrow's press
conference. But get it into the system too, in the unlikely event that
he's driving around town."

By the time MacNeice had tracked Maybank down, it was 10:12

p.m. Vertesi and Williams had come and gone, Williams agreeing to take Aziz to the hotel and pick her up in the morning. The mayor was on edge. The unions were upset because they'd heard rumours about links between the concrete suppliers and biker gangs, after Maybank had gone on record to say there was no connection between the bodies in the bay and the contractors on the project. The media had been sniffing around trying to make a story out of it, and if they did, the unions would shut down the project, and the deadlines he'd guaranteed to the city's provincial and federal partners would be blown.

He didn't mince words, loudly telling MacNeice that this was exactly the situation he had brought him in to avoid. When he finally ran out of steam, he asked why MacNeice was calling so late.

MacNeice explained that Aziz was leading the press conference the next day and that they had identified three more potential victims—there was no telling which, if any, of the women Dance would go after. But he would likely attack someone in the next day or so.

"You think he's got a fucking list? Does she realize the danger?"

"Of course she does. For all these women, including Aziz, I need cover." MacNeice waited for the mayor to respond but heard only heavy breathing. "Bob, I can't promise this will flush him out, but I want him to either try for Aziz so we can stop him, or feel so pressured he gives himself up."

"What's the likelihood he'd do that?" Maybank sounded hopeful.

"Low to very low."

"So you're really just screwing with his head and using Aziz for bait."

"Basically, yes."

"You're a colder fucker than I ever realized."

"Perhaps. Okay the units, Bob, and if this works, I promise you

I'll stand beside you and face the music on everything. You can dump it all on me if you need to."

"Oh, trust me, that's a given! We go back a long way and I've never asked you for anything, ever—but I need this project to go ahead. You've got your units, but don't let me down."

"I'll do my best."

"Better than best, Mac. Way better. For your colleague's sake, I hope you know what you're doing."

The mayor's comment stayed with him on the drive home, throughout dinner and even as he sat looking out to the garden with a grappa, watching the bats zip through the light from the window. MacNeice didn't know what he was doing. He was, at best, improvising. At worst he was relying on someone who only days before had been a university lecturer, who claimed she hadn't lost her touch with a Glock 17. Worst of all, he knew Aziz assumed she'd have time to use it. He wasn't convinced.

He turned away from the bat races as Art Pepper's heartbreaking solo in "Loverman" came on the stereo. That's when he noticed the light bouncing off the wall in the hallway—a car was speeding up towards the cottage. He set the grappa glass on the windowsill and stood up. He heard the car stop and idle outside, its door opening and shoes moving quickly across the gravel. Something about the gait suggested Vertesi. He opened the front door just as the young detective was about to knock.

"It's Mark Penniman, sir. We gotta go. I'll tell you on the way." Vertesi ran back to the car, turned it around and opened the passenger door, waiting for MacNeice.

"Sir, did you bring your piece?" he asked as MacNeice climbed in.

"I did. Start talking."

Vertesi tore down the hill. Putting his red grille flashers on, he sped along Mountain Road to the Queen Elizabeth, heading for

Niagara. He told him about Penniman and Wenzel, the confrontation on the service road, the run to the border, and Penniman flashing his army ID to the American customs agents, many of whom were vets. If anyone had asked him to wake up his passenger it would have been over right there, because the kid was covered in blood, his eyes blackened and his nose broken.

"Where are they now?"

"The honeymoon suite of the Niagara Paramount." Penniman had told the desk that his wife was coming in by train and he wanted to get ready for her. The suite was the only room left in the hotel. He retrieved Wenzel from the underground garage and took him up fourteen flights of stairs.

MacNeice looked off to the distant escarpment, a ridge of black against the blue-black night. "Has it occurred to you, Michael, that we're living a miniature War of 1812?"

"I don't follow."

"Troops crossing the border and fighting it out for territory over here—where troops crossed the border and fought it out two hundred years ago."

"Happy anniversary, you mean?"

"More or less. My best guess: things got out of hand. Bikers were hired as muscle in case something happened, without anyone knowing that the other side had done the same. After that, it spun out of control."

# 37.

I T WAS 1:49 a.m. when Mark Penniman opened the door to room 1421—the Shangri-La Suite—for them. They shook hands and stepped in. Penniman remained in the doorway to see if anyone had followed them.

Shangri-La was red from top to bottom, except where the mirror on the ceiling reflected the bed. The walls were flocked, red on red, in the floral patterns of the *belle époque*; under their shoes was a hot-pink shag carpet.

"You boys are wonderin' where they get this shit from, aren't you." Wenzel stood up from the long burgundy sofa, smiling at the two detectives as they stood there with dropped jaws.

Penniman closed the door. "Wenzel Hausman, this is Detective Michael Vertesi, and his commanding officer, DS MacNeice."

MacNeice offered his hand to Wenzel and studied his face. The eyes were ringed in black, his nose was swollen, the nostrils still bloody.

"I know, I look like shit, sir. This face's seen better days." Vertesi sat down on the sofa, took out a digital recorder, switched it on and placed it upright on the heart-shaped Plexiglas coffee table. Wenzel sat in front of the recorder and leaned forward as if he was unsure it would pick him up from a distance.

"Before we begin, as a foreign national, you can refuse to speak to us," MacNeice said. "But should you agree to provide us with information concerning the death of Sergeant Gary Hughes, you will be considered a witness and we'll do all we can to protect you. You won't likely be able to return to New York State if the presiding judge determines there's a risk in your doing so. Is that clear?"

"I told Wenzel that might be the case," Penniman said, pulling up an upholstered chair, its back also shaped like a heart.

"Yeah, I understand," Wenzel said. "But shit, I got nothin' to go home to now. If I did, they'd finish what they started on that road . . . for sure man, for sure."

"Sergeant Penniman didn't bring you across the border against your will?" MacNeice watched the young man for any hesitation in his voice or manner.

"No, man. Shit, if it weren't for him I'd be suckin' dirt in a ditch. Those fuckers wouldn't stop till I was done."

"Wenzel, what was your former rank and unit and where did you serve?"

"Private Wenzel Hausman, rifleman with the Army's 2nd Division, stationed in Iraq. Honourably discharged." He smiled as if he had passed a test; his teeth were still rimmed with blood.

"And the sergeant you served under?" Vertesi asked.

"Sergeant Gary Hughes." Wenzel took a sip from a miniature bottle of Coke—it was clearly painful to do so.

"I understand you learned that Hughes had left the army and was living in Tonawanda," Vertesi said.

MacNeice watched the young man's face. Battered though it was, he still showed an innocence that had likely always made him vulnerable.

"Yes, sir. Like, most of the time I was out of it—I mean, West Virginia's out of it by definition, and I had no prospects there. I stayed at home a lot. But one of the guys in town, he'd been overseas too, and he told me Sarge was back, and man, I was outta there. I called Sarge when I got to Tonawanda, and he picked me up at the station."

"What did you think he could do for you?" Vertesi asked.

"I didn't know. But he took care of us for two years, and I thought I could get a start-over with him."

"Any idea what that would look like?"

"None." He laughed, and then had to cough.

"That sounds nasty, Wenzel," MacNeice said.

"Shit"—he took another swig of Coke—"that's nothin', man. I thought that fucker's second punch tore somethin' . . ." He pointed to his stomach just below the ribcage.

"We can bring in a doctor," MacNeice offered.

"Naw, I'll be okay."

"Did Hughes introduce you to the Old Soldiers roadhouse?"

"Other way round. I got a furnished two-room in the basement of a house off the service road, about a half-mile from where Sergeant Penniman found me. Mostly I'd call Sarge like once a week or so, but he was with his family. So's I got to walkin' down the road for a little beer 'n' bourbon, and before long, like, I'm there most of the time—day, night, weekends. I'd play the machines and shoot the shit with the guys."

"You knew it was owned by a motorcycle gang?"

"Yeah, oh yeah. But I thought, like, they're army too. So, no big deal."

"Why did you introduce Sergeant Hughes to the roadhouse?"

"Once I found out they were doing security jobs, you know, I asked if they wanted a couple guys—you know, thinking I'd score a job too. Well, they laughed at me. So I told them about Sergeant

Hughes an' how the brass in Iraq kept shoving him forward like he was Rambo or somethin'—shit, way outta the box. So they say, 'Bring the fucker in here; we wanna meet him.'"

"Was this security for rock festivals and drag races?"

"Yeah, but other shit too. Business stuff. They never talked much about it around me."

"So Hughes became a regular." Vertesi wasn't asking a question, merely confirming for the recording.

"Sort of, but, ya know, he'd sit at the bar with me, like we were separate from those guys—the Old Soldiers Motorcycle Club, I mean."

"Did he work security for them?"

"No, that's the thing I was tellin' Sergeant Penniman on the way here. They led him on with promises of the bigger stuff and never came through."

"How long did they string him out?"

"Not all that long, but when you're showin' up and drinkin' and waitin' it seems long, man. Sarge wasn't happy."

"What happened then?"

"So a guy in a suit shows up—big fat guy, Eyetalian lookin'."

MacNeice noticed Vertesi smile.

"In he goes to the office, and after a while Sarge gets called in. He grabs me and we get to the door—*boom*. Jake—he's the OSMC leader—slams his hand on the door frame, *wham!* I stop, think I'm goin' to piss myself. Hughes takes Jake's hand and peels it off the door, like some weird Jap Jedi move, you know—the guy's almost crying—and Sarge says, 'Wenzel's with me. We're a team.'"

Wenzel's eyes welled up and he grabbed the Coke to take a swig and cover the tears, but it was empty.

"Got it," Penniman said. He went over to the minibar and retrieved another miniature Coke.

Wenzel cleared his throat. "So, yeah, then we're in the room.

There's a couch and a desk and some chairs. The guy in the suit looks at Sarge, then at me, and just nods to Jake behind the desk."

"What's his full name?" Vertesi asked, pen poised over his notebook.

"Don't know. They just call him Jake . . ."

"And the guy in the suit?" Vertesi asked.

"Luigi. No last name, just Luigi."

"What happened then, Wenzel?" MacNeice asked.

"So the job is security for Luigi is up here in Canada, some kinda business. There'd be twenty members of OSMC; I'd ride with them and Sergeant Hughes would go in a car with Luigi. This meeting was on a Wednesday and we'd ride that Friday."

"Ride where?" Vertesi asked.

"Shit . . . somewhere past Niagara, a town down that queen's highway. I can't remember the name."

"St. Catharines?" Vertesi suggested. Wenzel shook his head.

"Grimsby," MacNeice said.

"Fuck, yeah! Shit, I remember now, thinking, *Grimsby—that's grim!* To live in a town called *Grim*-sby . . . they can't have happy teenagers there, man. I mean, Iraq was Grimsby—big-time Grimsby."

"Did Luigi ever say who he was working for?" Vertesi was trying to refocus him.

"Not when we were in there, but the money was great, man. They were going to give Sarge ten thousand and I was gonna get fifteen hundred. Here's the thing about him: He says to them, 'How much are the other soldiers getting?' And Jake says, 'Three thousand.' So Sarge says, 'Wenzel takes the same risks; Wenzel gets three thousand.'"

"What was the job?" Vertesi asked.

"So, there's a quarry near *Grim*sby owned by American Eyetalians. Then there's Eyetalians from Dundurn and more

Eyetalians they thought might show up—I don't know where from. Luigi was there to make a deal. The thing is, we don't know which ones Luigi's workin' for. I was sober as shit in that room, so I know what I know. Luigi looks at Sarge and says, 'Your job is to stand beside me, and your job'—he's looking at Jake—'is to spread out and cover the meeting.'"

Vertesi pressed him. "Again, he didn't mention the names of the people he was meeting?"

"Negative. But we stop in Niagara, on the Canadian side, in the underground parking lot of a hotel, and these guys come out and we load up with firepower and ammunition, so I know we're not goin' there to play checkers."

"Do you recall which hotel?" MacNeice asked.

"I was too shit-scared to notice. But I wonder if that was where we lost Sarge and Luigi. We were supposed to be right on their tail, not an hour behind. I think that was when they got so far ahead of us, when we stopped to get the guns."

"What happened at the quarry?"

"Nothin'—absolutely nothin'. We all pull up like the cavalry an' there's no one there. We roar around the site and there's no sign of Luigi and Sarge."

"And then?"

"Well, there's a security shed with an old man who's so scared, man, seein' all these crazy fuckers . . . and two of our guys go in his shed for five minutes, maybe less. Then they come out wavin' a piece of paper and off we go. I ask the guy I'm riding with—he was the brother of the one who split my nose—where we were going, and he says, 'Shut your hole, Weasel.'"

"Can you describe the landscape?" MacNeice asked.

"Oh yeah, like we were heading up this ridge and up there it's all flat country—farms an' shit—and after a half-hour we're parked in the trees near a huge farm with a shit-high fence . . ."

"You were on the escarpment," MacNeice said softly.

"Sir?"

"It's called the escarpment," Vertesi explained. "What did you do while you were waiting near the farm?"

"Jake's on his cellphone walking along the road and the guys are takin' leaks and drinking shots of somethin'—they didn't offer me none. Then Jake comes back and says, 'We're going in hot.' And these guys are pulling Uzis and sawed-off shotguns outta their saddlebags and I'm like, 'Oh, shit, man, I'm not into this . . . '"

"Was the gate to the property closed or guarded?" MacNeice asked.

"Neither—and that scared the shit outta me too. I'd seen enough in Iraq to recognize a setup."

"So you went into the property ready for a firefight," Vertesi clarified.

"*I* wasn't ready! Nobody even gave me a piece. I'm just meat on the back of a Harley."

"And then?" MacNeice asked.

"Yeah, well, there's like a house there and a couple of barns— new ones—and we get almost to the house and the shit hits the fan. All the fire's comin' from the doors and windows of one of the barns—but we were goin' so fast we're committed. Two guys went down right away; the rest of us blew past the house and the barns. There's only like, eighteen bikes now and we're spraying the side of the barn. Then my biker gets hit, so the bike is skidding around in a circle 'cause he's cranked the accelerator—we both get thrown off. His neck's opened up. I pressed hard on it, but I got no bandages—nothin'—and there's still people shootin'."

"So you're down beside a dying man," Vertesi said.

"He's gone. I back away to the treeline and hide in the bush. The shooting goes on for about another five minutes and then it just stops. I can see three of our men down; a couple more are hit, one holding his arm, the other his leg—but the shooting fuckin' stops. Then it was so weird. A couple of our guys pick up the three bodies and they all ride out to the gate, where all of a sudden there's an eighteen-wheeler waiting."

"Jake's cell call," MacNeice said.

"Yeah. Six guys come out of the barn. They watch OSMC loading up bikes and bodies at the end of the road until they all drive off in the truck. I stay in the woods till dark. I can hear, like, a saw or somethin' in the barn, but I'm so scared I sit there and wait it out."

"What did you think was happening?" Vertesi asked.

"Shit, I don't know. But it went on for a while. Then two guys come out and back up a van, and four others go into the other barn. That's when I seen it. They drag out a big body—it was all wrapped in plastic, but it was Luigi. I recognized him 'cause he'd been wearing these freaky shorts and socks and a fuckin' loud, bright shirt when we left Tonawanda, and you could see it through the plastic. They threw him in the van." Wenzel took a swig of Coke. "Then, I don't know, they bring out another body. But I'm like, eighty yards away—I can't make out what's wrong with it. It looks weird; through the plastic you could see it had no feet. But it was Sergeant Hughes, for sure—I could see his black jeans and T-shirt. They throw him in the van. Then a guy comes out with a garbage bag and walks around behind the house. The two guys drive away. The three left at the barn turn out the lights and lock the door, and they're carrying weapons, two each at least. And then it's quiet, like I'd dreamed the whole thing. I wait till they go in the house and then I skirt along the treeline till I find a culvert that goes under the road we came in on. I washed the blood off my hands in the water there."

"Did Hughes have a weapon?" Vertesi asked.

"No, sir. He refused to carry a weapon."

"How did you make it back to the States?" Vertesi asked.

"I hitched a ride with a family from Ohio. They were heading home from up north. I told them I'd gotten lost on a bar tour with some vets and was stuck with no money, only my driver's licence."

"They took pity on you," MacNeice suggested.

"Yessir. I lucked out, because their kid was a marine in Afghanistan. They told the border officer I was their son and I'd lost my passport when my canoe tipped on some lake."

"How did you square your reappearance at Old Soldiers?" MacNeice asked.

"I told them the truth. And that I came back to tell them that Luigi and Sergeant Hughes were both dead and that Sarge had been cut up somehow."

"Did they buy that?" Vertesi asked.

"More or less. They were always suspicious of me after that, but not worried, 'cause they thought I was a cripple or stupid and maybe that I'd be good for somethin' someday. Plus, I paid my bar bills."

"Why would you go back there, Wenzel?" MacNeice asked.

"For starters, I had nowhere else to go. But I was too scared not to go back—they woulda had me down as a snitch, and hunted me down."

"OSMC lost three men that day?" Vertesi asked.

"Yessir. Two others injured, but not bad."

"What did they do with the bodies?"

"Nobody ever told me and I didn't ask. Either they got them over the border somehow or maybe they buried them at sea in the lake."

"Any idea of how many casualties on the other side?" MacNeice asked.

"No. I know some were hit, but they had the cover. If they kept going they'd have cut our men to pieces. For some reason they stopped and let them clear the field."

"Why would they do that?" Vertesi asked.

"Fucked if I know. Maybe not wanting a larger war . . . I remember thinking it was like the Indian wars or something, you know, where there's a moment when you collect your dead? The war's still on but you clear the field of battle."

"Did you get paid?" MacNeice asked.

"Fuck, no, man. I don't know if anybody got paid."

"And you didn't think to call your sergeant's wife, or the authorities . . ."

"No way—I'd be dead. I'm only talkin' now because I know they were going to kill me anyways."

"Were you part of the raid a few weeks ago?" Vertesi asked.

"No, man. I didn't even know that was goin' down. I mean, it got weird around the bar, but nobody said anything. Two guys never came back to the bar, is all I know."

Looking at Penniman, MacNeice asked, "Have you told Mr. Hausman what happened to Sergeant Hughes?"

"I have, sir. He knows what I know."

"If I knew what was going down in that barn, sir, I swear on my mother's tears I woulda found a way to go in for him. I swear—"

"I believe you would, Wenzel. I believe you would." MacNeice said.

"What happens to me now?"

"We'll take you to Dundurn and put you up in a hotel under twenty-four-hour protection. The American authorities will be informed in the morning"—MacNeice looked at his watch—"about four and half hours from now. I expect the local forces will pay a visit to Old Soldiers. We'll get someone in to look at your nose and chest and get you a clean set of clothes. Sergeant Penniman will go home in the morning and report for his deployment back to Afghanistan," MacNeice said. "Right?"

Penniman, who was opening a tall tin of Guinness, didn't look up.

# 38.

AZIZ WAS WEARING a pale-blue blouse with her black suit. Her shoes had heels, modest compared to most, but nonetheless they gave her an additional two inches. However, it was her eyes that were most transformed—they were highlighted with brown-black liner. She looked more dramatic than MacNeice had ever seen; the line extended a quarter-inch from the outside corner of each eye, curving slightly upwards—as erotic as it was exotic. Though he knew he shouldn't be thinking that way.

As they walked across the parking lot to City Hall, Williams trailing them to cover their rear, MacNeice glanced so frequently at Aziz that she asked, "What, is it too much?" Concern flashed across her face.

"No, certainly not. I'm just adjusting." He changed the subject and spoke about the order of the presentation. He would recap what they knew about William Dance, from the Yamaha to the Camry, from his work with BDI to his disappearance following the death of his parents. "I'll review the attacks and the damage done and finish by saying that we've launched a province-wide manhunt involving hundreds of police."

"Not strictly true, is it, boss. I mean, I haven't seen anyone," Williams said from behind them.

"Electronically speaking, it's true," MacNeice said. "Then I'll turn it over to you, Fiza. Have you considered what you'll say?"

"You know I have." Aziz smiled briefly and he saw the real genius of the makeup. Her lips and eyes smiled together, as if the curves in the corners of both were in harmony—though he didn't think there was much to smile about.

Outside the rear entrance to City Hall were more mobile news units than he could remember ever seeing, and through the doors, more flat black power cords snaking to the media room than there was space for walking. Approaching the double doors, MacNeice could see that it was standing room only, and he steered Aziz to the anteroom from which the mayor made his entrance. Inside, the mayor's communications officer, Julia Marchetti, nodded at MacNeice and Williams but studied Aziz curiously.

"Mayor Maybank," Marchetti called, and the mayor, who'd been speaking to Wallace, spun around with his *Vote for Me* face on. His jaw dropped, but he recovered quickly. "My goodness, Detective Aziz, don't you look lovely."

Then Wallace came forward, obviously struggling for something to say that would be politically correct. "Yes, Detective Inspector, you're very—"

Aziz saved him. "I'm going for exotic, sir. And you needn't worry—you won't be seeing me like this again."

Wallace smiled awkwardly, perhaps unsure of what she meant.

Williams led the four of them into the conference room, then made his way back to the media riser, scanning faces on the off chance that Dance was crazy enough to show up. MacNeice stepped to the microphone and gave a clear and restrained update of the investigation. On cue, the screen behind him faded from the city's heraldic logo to images of Dance, his motorcycle, the Toyota Camry. He showed the student ID photographs of Taaraa Ghosh, Lea Nam and Samora Aploon and stated that anyone knowing the whereabouts of Dance had an obligation—enforceable by law—to contact the authorities. Failure to do so would be met with severe consequences. The phone number and Web address came onscreen, where it would remain for the rest of the conference.

When he introduced Aziz, MacNeice made a point of putting her in the same category as the three women so savagely attacked: an immigrant known for her accomplishments as a Canadian citizen. He noticed that his stomach tightened anxiously as he did so. He picked up his note cards and took his place beside the mayor.

There was a buzz in the room beyond the whirring, clacking and flashing of equipment. People were leaning this way and that to get a better view or to say something to the person next to them. Aziz cleared her throat and adjusted the principal microphone to her height, ignoring the cluster of seven others taped to the podium.

"I am standing before you as a homicide detective and criminologist. I'm also standing before you as a Lebanese Muslim, a woman—like those who've been brutally attacked, a woman of colour. I'm here not to offer more insights into the mind of William Dance but to make a direct appeal to this young man."

She took a moment to scan the faces before her. Some had pen and notebook in hand, others were kneeling, trying to get their microphones closer without obstructing the view of those behind them.

Aziz took a deep breath that was heard throughout the room, then looked down, not to study her notes—she had none—but to focus clearly on what she'd say next. When she lifted her eyes again to the room, she scanned each of the journalists' faces. She didn't want any of them going away not having been seen by her. She wanted each to be her collaborator.

"In my lifetime—my parents' lifetime—Lebanon has known war. War interrupted by peace, but always the certainty of another war. I know that my parents chose Canada because of many things: Pierre Trudeau and the multicultural society; the dream of a country where we, as Muslims, could live peacefully next to people from every other race and creed in the world. The certainty of peace drew them here, and keeps me here."

For several seconds there was no other sound in the room but her breathing.

"The suspect we are looking for didn't choose Canada. He was privileged enough to be born here; his parents and their parents before them were born here. He has been blessed with a life that these three women and I would never have known *if we hadn't chosen to be here.*"

She looked down again, this time to control her emotions. When her eyes returned to the room again, she was all cop. "William Dance, as Detective Superintendent MacNeice has indicated, the steel net of law enforcement is descending swiftly around you and on top of you. You are a smart young man, smart enough to know how this will end. I appeal to you now to turn yourself in, to call the number listed on the screen or to make your way to any of the police divisions in the city."

She looked directly into the television cameras on the riser at the back of the room, trying to focus through them on Dance, sitting somewhere, watching her. "There's no need for further shedding of blood—neither yours nor that of the women you've been intent on destroying. And while there's no going back, you can go forward. I urge you to end this and surrender today. Surrender—now."

———

"What do you think?"

"Masterful manipulation."

"Yeah, she's making a good point . . ."

"No. No. No. She's missing the point! Of course I know how this will end, but I'm not concerned about the ending." He quietly recited the Templar code: "A KT is a truly fearless knight, secure on every side, protected by the armour of faith. He fears neither demons nor men, nor," he added, "Muslim women."

"But they've identified the bike, the car . . . they've got a call out for us."

"They've probably also figured out my target list. Any dummy could do that."

"Yeah, well, I guess. Man, that was one sexy Muslim, though . . ."

"Done up for the occasion. Yes, she's impressive." Billie Dance was studying the images on his wall. News clippings of Aziz without makeup would soon share space with those from today, as she was certain to be front page, above the fold, in the daily papers. His eyes scanned the images of his first three women, pausing on the razor-torn flesh and the deep, precise punctures. He smiled briefly at the symmetry of each stroke. "Time to flip a coin. Call it."

"Cool. Okay, heads we do the Muslim, tails the Indian. Best two out of three?"

"Nope, one flip is all you get." He pulled a quarter out of his pocket and flipped it high into the air, catching it on the way down and slapping it hard onto the back of his left hand. Pulling his hand away, he said, "Heads."

"No, it's not! I saw it; it was definitely tails. Tails for the Indian."

"Chance. The beauty of chance . . . Get it?"

"Well, yeah . . . no, actually. I think you were going for Aziz all along, so why flip?"

"Just fuckin' with chance." A flash of a smile.

"She got to you. I think she got to you."

"Maybe . . ."

"She'll be covered by MacNeice. See him watching her when she was speaking?"

"Like I said, they've got something going that ain't police work."

"She's also armed."

"Yes, but she's not going to have time to use her weapon. Now that she's opened up to me, I'm going to open her up."

"Big time. She's got those Arab tits—for sure hers are plump and have those blackberry nipples."

"I hate it when you go off on that shit. We have a code!"

"All the same, though, she's a sweet piece. Full bush too, I bet—Muslims probably don't allow shaved pussies."

"You are sick, you know that? I'm starting a revolution, a crusade, and you're talking about pussy and nipples and shit."

"Nothing sick about that, Billie. Why couldn't we—you know—do her, before we *do her*?"

A minute or so passed before Billie responded. "Ah, what the hell—I bet there were Knights Templar like you, Crusaders too. A little bit of rape keeps the troops keen for more fighting. I should research that—the number of rapes per knights in the field at any given time."

He muted the television as Deputy Chief Wallace began fielding questions, and picked up his paintbrush. He dipped it in a can of black and began to apply it to the tank of the Yamaha. "Don't know why I didn't do this before . . ."

"Yeah, man, and the silver fenders look cool too. It's not a great paint job, though."

"I know, but fuck, I'm not entering bike shows with it. Now that I have different plates, it's like I'm riding a brand-new horse."

"How we gonna isolate her?"

"That's the challenge, or, as Pop would say"—Billie changed his posture to deliver his father's golly-gosh epithet with sneering contempt—"*Why, that's the opportunity, son.*"

"Dontcha miss him at all?"

"Miss him? . . . That hadn't occurred to me. I miss my mother. The dumb fucks that did the autopsy didn't notice he was full of cancer. I think he was waiting for that truck."

"Murder-suicide, you mean?"

"A double homicide and suicide, you mean. That other driver died too. You know, long before he was diagnosed, when I got my master's degree, he said to me, 'These are your salad years, William. Don't ever grow old.'"

"Salad years . . . hmm."

"This was a guy with a lot of talent who ended up running an insurance company . . . definitely no dressing on his salad years. To his credit, though, he knew a suicide would cost me my inheritance. Somewhat ironic, since I've taken a vow of poverty."

"Sad fuck."

"Whatever. Hey, what's this?"

On the television screen, a photo of Aziz filled the frame. Billie reached for the remote and hit the Mute button.

" . . . tune in this evening at six p.m. when Dr. Aziz is interviewed for our special, 'The Mind of a Serial Killer.' That's tonight at six. Thank you for watching this broadcast. I'm Kelly Forrestal."

"We've made that Arab a star!"

"Doing her will be like doing ten nobodies. It couldn't be better."

# 39.

"**N**O SHIT, THAT babe is your partner?" Wenzel was sitting on the edge of the bed with the remote control in his hand.

"Strictly speaking, I never refer to her as a babe, and I'd prefer it if you didn't either."

"Shit . . . sorry, I gets hoof and mouth disease. It won't happen again."

Vertesi was lying on the twin bed nearest the door, where he'd spent the night, seeing as how no one else was available to babysit. To be certain he wouldn't miss the press conference, however, he'd asked the front desk for a wake-up call at 9:30 a.m. He was still in bed, propped up by foam pillows, as Aziz took the podium. He'd been suprised that MacNeice could pull off his presentation so effortlessly, having had, at best, three hours' sleep. Though maybe that lack of sleep added to his air of gravity.

Looking over at Wenzel, Vertesi smiled. The kid had taken a shower and cleaned himself up as soon as they got to the room, but he still had raccoon eyes and an off-centre, puffy nose. The good news was that he hadn't been coughing and it seemed that he had no problems sleeping. Vertesi was fairly certain that whatever damage the beating had done to his chest and stomach wasn't severe enough to require medical attention.

Shortly after the wake-up call, a cop had delivered a bag containing new clothes for Wenzel: sweatpants, a knock-off Leafs jersey, sweat socks, underwear, a toothbrush and toothpaste, shaving foam and a razor. Wenzel was now decked out in his Canadian regalia.

When the press conference wrapped, he started channel surfing. Vertesi got up, showered and dressed. When he was ready to leave, he told Wenzel to order breakfast from room service and watch TV till either he or MacNeice came back for him. He told him not to answer the door; there was a cop on duty outside, and he would open the door and bring in his food when it arrived. "Just sit tight, eat, drink and watch movies. Got that?"

"Yeah. Basically I'm on holiday with Dad's credit card."

"Your dad let you do that, did he?" Vertesi said, sliding his weapon into the holster attached to his belt.

"Naw, I didn't know my dad."

"What size shoes do you wear, Wenz?"

"Oh, eleven, but I'm okay with these," he said, looking to where his shoes lay by the door.

"You'll never get the blood off them. The City of Dundurn will spring for a new pair of Nikes." Vertesi knew the city wouldn't pay for them too; he'd pick them up himself.

When MacNeice and Aziz got back to Division after the press conference, Ryan flagged them down as they walked into the cubicle.

"I got a lead in Rhode Island on the couple in the Packard—a guy who's in his mid-nineties. He was a ventriloquist in the Borscht Belt, which my Google search says was in the Catskills, also called the 'Jewish Alps.' I got his son on the phone first, and when I asked if his father was healthy, he said, 'Ya mean, he still got his marbles?' I felt busted, so I copped to it and said, 'Well, yes, more or less.'"

"What'd he say?" Aziz asked.

"He says, 'Sonny, he's not only got his marbles, he's got his bowling balls—whaddya think of that!'"

"Sounds painful . . ."

"He says, 'Dad can remember all his tours from 1932 to 1957 but he can't remember where he keeps his Depends.' So we agreed that I'd call at five before the old guy went down for the early-bird special."

"So what have you got?" MacNeice asked.

"Okay, the ventriloquist's name is Al Katzenberg, but his stage name was Alley Katz. His dummy was a big ginger cat named Mort."

Ryan's fingers skipped rhythmically across the keyboard; MacNeice wondered if he had a melody in mind. An audio file appeared on the screen. "I've edited out most of the *What? Whaddya say? I don't understand yer accent?* So here you go—it's pretty clean. He's a sharp guy, so if I blew any questions, let me know and I'll get him on the phone again."

"How old is this man?" MacNeice asked.

"Ninety-four. Running time's just over four minutes. A warning, though—his language is X-rated."

There was a beep, then nothing for two seconds, then the sound of a phone being picked up. "Mr. Katzenberg?"

"Call me Katz." The old man's voice was strong, a bit raspy but not weakened by age. "You are Mr. Al Katzenberg the ventriloquist?"

"Whaa? Are you a fuckin' moron? I just told ya, call me Katz! Who's this jerk-off you put me on with here, huh?" In the background they could hear a male voice saying something about

Canada and Chas Greene.

"Mr. Katz, I'm calling from Dundurn Homicide in Ontario, Canada."

"Dundurn? Remind me, is that near Montreal? I killed 'em in Montreal."

"No, it's between Toronto and Buffalo. We're investigating the death of Chas Greene, sir, a long time ago—"

"Who? Chas! You call him Chas?" Then, to the person in the background, "This putz talkin' about Greenblatt?" The answer came clearly, "Yes, Dad, he's callin' about Chaim Greenblatt."

"Then why didn't he say so? Fuck, this call's costin' a shitload, ain't it?"

Ryan's voice: "Sir, we're covering the call. Did you know Mr. Greenblatt?"

"Stop callin' me sir, goddammit. You a fuckin' limey?"

"Sorry. No, Mr. Katz, I'm Canadian."

"Yeah, well . . . sure, I knew the little shit. Knew his fuckin' dummy too—what was his name . . ."

"Archie."

"Fuck! Don't tell me that; I coulda got it. What's yer hurry anyways?" And aside, "This kid's getting on my tits, Murray."

"Sorry."

"Stop apologizing, fer chrissakes. Now gimme time to think here . . . yeah, so, Archie . . . Yeah, me 'n' Mort killed 'em one night in Jersey City. Killed 'em! We did the Catskills—everybody did—then we'd hit the road . . . Jeezus, we'd be gone for almost a year—"

"But you toured together?"

"Fuck, ya idiot, no! Do you think he'd want me killin' him an' Arch every night in every bum-fuck club in the country? No, we just knew where each other was, 'cause we had the same agent."

"Oh yes, Irving Schubert, in Brooklyn."

"Yeah, Irv. So Irv married my sister Flora and . . . Well, I kept tabs on Chaim—little shit even had Irv trained to call him Chas. So after I killed 'em in Jersey, I says to Irv, 'Get me in every house that takes Greenblatt, but I wanna be there two weeks after.' Ya know why two weeks?"

"No. Was it because you wanted the audience to forget about Chas and Archie?"

"Jesus Christ, are all the cops in Canada dumb? No, the opposite—I wanted them to remember the two of 'em fondly, give 'em time to let the memory mellow . . . Ya follow me now?"

"I think so, Katz. So, do you recall playing Dundurn two weeks after Chaim?"

"Near Toronto? Yeah, fulla smoke—a shithole town, that it?"

"I guess so."

"You guess so? You fuckin' live there, doncha?" To his son he offered, "You got one dumb fuck on the phone here, kiddo." And the son's answer: "Pa, it's a murder investigation. Just cooperate with him."

"You see, Katz, Mr. Greenblatt's body was recently brought up from the harbour here. He was in the trunk of a Packard with a dead girl. He'd been down there since the thirties."

"He was pussy mad, that putz—always chasing. Nice car, though, I remember that. He had flashy taste. A girl . . . lemme think here . . ."

There was a beep on the recording and Ryan hit the pause button. "It gets good here. It took about five minutes till he remembered, but he did."

"Glad you took out all the salty bits, Ryan." Aziz smiled.

"Yeah, he's sharp and has his marbles all right—some razor blades too. Has a thing about Chaim changing his name, even though he did too," Vertesi said.

"But he kept the Katz part," Aziz said.

"You'll see, though, he comes around." Ryan pressed the key. They could hear the old man shift in his squeaky chair, then what sounded like a muffled fart. Ryan raised his thumb and smiled broadly to confirm that it was.

"Yeah, so I remember now. Didn't hear a peep about Chaim going missing till I got to Buffalo following his bookings, only to find out that he blew the gig. He never showed up—never showed up anywhere after that, neither."

"But no one said a word in Dundurn?"

"Not then, no. But the next year, when I was out on tour, I hit there again—Christ, that place smelled like shit—I can still smell it."

They could hear him taking a deep breath.

"So I asked the club owner about him."

"Do you remember his name?"

"You think I'm senile, you little schmuck?"

"No, but it was a long time ago."

"Not for me, kiddo. It's like yesterday—well, okay, like last week. Yeah, so the guy's name was Dressler. He also owned Club Lucky in Niagara Falls—same format."

"Dancing, big bands and comedy?"

"Of course, yeah, but dinner too—good dinners."

They could hear him turn away from the mouthpiece as he added,

"Not like this farkakte dive."

"And he remembered something?"

"Not exactly, no. He said one of his dance girls went missing at the same time as Chaim . . . a pretty girl . . ."

"Rosemary McKenzie."

"That her name? Anyway, I says to him, 'Figures. Chaim loves girls—shiksa or yid, the prettier the better.' Then Dressler says something like, 'Not that one, I hope. That one is reserved, and if

Chas's got his pecker in her, Archie's gonna be a fuckin' orphan.' At that point I think I said something like, 'Well, don't look at me, I'm a fairy.'"

He laughed out loud; so did his son.

"I used that in a routine at stags—huge laughs."

"Did Dressler say whose girlfriend she was?"

"Everywhere we played there was the mobs—Italian mostly, but also Irish and even Jews—so ya could take yer pick. Best strategy always was to play the gig, take the dough and get to the next gig. Yah know—what's yer name, anyway?"

"Ryan."

"Yeah, well . . . Ryan, here's the point. There's girls everywhere, but the pretty ones are always taken. And in those days a smart guy knew that—but Greenblatt wasn't smart, and neither was Archie."

"Did you ever play Dundurn again?"

"Sure. What the hell, there were only a few of us. Yeah, if I was honest I'd say Chaim and me, we were pretty much even, talent-wise, but Mort definitely had the edge on Archie."

"People like cats, I guess."

"No, kiddo, that wasn't it. People thought Mort was human, that Archie was human—that was the whole fuckin' point. Mort had the edge because cats are smart, but he was human! Haven't you ever seen a ventriloquist, son, a good one?"

MacNeice heard deep sadness and resignation in the old man's voice. "Sorry to say I haven't."

"Hear that, Murray?" And from a distance, "Yes, Dad, it's a tragedy."

Ryan pressed a key and the audio bar disappeared from his screen. "That's all I got from him. But his son did say that if his father remembered anything else, he'd call and let me know. And just after I spoke to Mr. Katzenberg, I got lucky."

Ryan turned back to the computer and tapped the keys until a series of images piled up on the screen. "This is Dundurn's paper from December 3, 1937. On the right is a sidebar article about a missing local girl, Rosemary McKenzie, and how police had been interviewing her family and friends, including"—he brought up the next screen—"an ex-con by the name of Freddy O'Leary. The article quotes several 'unnamed sources' who identified Freddy as Rosemary's boyfriend."

He clicked the keyboard again. "And here are three photos of Freddy. The first one is his mug shot; he was arrested for assault and battery of his mother three years before Rosemary went missing." The photograph of a handsome young man, smiling at the camera as someone held a number in front of his chest, was oddly disturbing.

"Strange eyes," Aziz said.

"An ex-con . . . He looks more con than ex—probably explains why people didn't rush to identify him as Rosemary's boyfriend."

*Click, click.* The next image was Freddy on the street on January 16, 1938. "The guy he's walking with was gunned down in the north end two days after this photo was taken. He was Freddy's boss after Freddy got out of jail for beating his mother senseless." With a cigarette dangling from his lips, O'Leary was glaring at the camera. His topcoat had blown open, revealing a tight, dark double-breasted suit, starched collar, tie and tiepin. He was wearing two-tone shoes.

"Same creepy eyes."

"Yeah. Would you actually hire this guy or trust him?" Ryan asked as he clicked a key and the next image joined the other two onscreen. "This is a police crime-scene photo from July 2, 1945. Freddy had his throat cut outside the steelworks on Burlington Street; he was found there by the morning shift." No longer handsome, Freddy's face had grown puffy, his body bloated.

"Now there's a boy who's let himself go," MacNeice said.

"Gotta weigh 220 at least, I think," Ryan said.

"Maybe he missed Rosemary more than he thought he would," MacNeice said. "Was anyone ever charged with his murder?"

"No, but police reported at the time that it was a mob slaying, that Freddy was suspected of being involved with an Irish gang trying to take over the local steelworkers' union."

MacNeice walked over to Ryan and held out his hand. Looking somewhat abashed, Ryan extended his, and they shook. "You have a real knack for asking the right questions, Ryan," MacNeice said. "That was excellent police work." Not to mention comic relief.

# 40.

I T WAS 1:12 p.m. when MacNeice and Aziz arrived at the hotel. MacNeice dismissed the uniform sitting outside, taking the key from him. Inside, Wenzel was sitting on the bed, watching *Cops* on TV. "Thought it would get me in the groove."

MacNeice introduced him to Aziz and handed him the box of Nikes from Vertesi. They were basketball high-tops; Wenzel put them on, then awkwardly pretended to jump for a layup. The missing toes didn't help. "You guys have been real good to me; I 'preciate it."

"Today we're going to go out to the farm so you can take us through what happened and where. Are you up for that?"

"Sure, sure . . . I guess." He didn't look sure; he looked scared.

"Wenzel, there will be four detectives there, plus a uniform in a cruiser to guard the driveway."

He still looked scared, but once they were in the Chevy he seemed to brighten up, quietly rubbernecking on the drive through Dundurn and up the mountain.

Finally he piped up. "Saw you guys on TV this morning—you were great. Sounds like ya got your hands full, between this and the serial slasher dude . . ."

"Very true," Aziz said.

When neither detective commented further, Wenzel busied himself with humming and looking out at the suburban tracts that soon gave way to tidy acres of farmland. When they approached the farm with the tall fence and razor wire, he went quiet. As they passed the cruiser at the gate, he slid down in the seat and didn't look out the window again.

Williams came over to the car as MacNeice parked the Chevy. Vertesi appeared in the doorway of the large industrial barn. "Swetsky was tucking into a Phat Burger when we left Division. He said if you don't mind, he's going to sit this one out."

"Not a problem. I think he's probably had enough of this place."

"It is creepy," Aziz said, opening the door for Wenzel.

"Standing out here ain't the half of it. Wait till you see the machine shop," Williams said.

Catching Vertesi's eye, Wenzel did a little shuffle, pointing down at his shoes. "Thanks!"

Vertesi gave a thumbs-up and smiled.

"Wenzel, why don't you show us where you were when the shooting began." MacNeice laid his jacket over the headrest of the front seat and closed the door.

"Yessir. Well, folks, follow me—" He suddenly limped away, rattling on like a tour guide, telling them how OSMC came tearing up the driveway, showing them the exact spot where it all started. He waved his arms around to indicate the field of fire and then headed for the second barn. Thirty feet beyond it he stopped, turned around, then stepped sideways to recall his position precisely.

"Shit, they never fixed the wall of that barn . . . Maybe they're proud of those holes." There were hundreds of bullet holes and several from shotgun blasts, mostly clustered towards the front. "I was right over here." He walked over a little rise and pointed to where his biker went down. "You see this little hill? I was lying back here—that's where I stayed till it was over." He was about to lie down to demonstrate, then realized he'd get his new clothes dirty, so he simply squatted to explain why they didn't see him when they came to take the dead biker and his bike away. "Fuckers didn't really care where I was at, neither."

"If the shooting had stopped, why didn't you go with them?" Aziz asked.

"I didn't know at that point who I was more scared of, my guys or the ones in the barns. Anyways, I thought it might be a trick and the locals would never let us walk outta here. Honestly, though . . . I'd had enough of shootin', no matter whose side I was on."

"And the culvert where you escaped?" MacNeice asked.

"All the way across that field. Just this side of the forest, at the end, there's this culvert. It comes out the other side of the road we came in by."

"So the fire was coming from the windows and doors of this barn?" Vertesi pointed.

"Yeah, but also from the doors of the first barn and—maybe, I dunno—from the farmhouse too. Our guys were givin' 'er too, just spraying those barns . . ." He waved his arm like a garden sprinkler.

They stepped inside the second barn, where the smell of manure—they must have hauled away dozens of shot-up animals after the murders—hung in the air. The cattle stalls, wooden beams and their supports were chewed up by gunfire, and the light pouring in through the bullet holes divided the space with dust-defined zigzag lines.

Back at the first barn, Wenzel stopped at the entrance. "Mind if I wait out here, sir? I don't want to see it."

"Sure," MacNeice said. "I understand. Do you remember where they took the plastic bag?"

His shoulders slumped. "Yes, they went behind the farmhouse. I don't know where exactly, but I could still see one of them at the back edge of it, so I think it musta bin close by."

"Do you want to wait in the car, Wenzel?"

"No, sir, I'll just sit in the sun here by the door." He sank down and leaned against the warm metal wall with his legs outstretched. As MacNeice left him he was half-singing something to himself that sounded like "Ring of Fire."

The three detectives followed MacNeice into the barn, walking past the rows of heavy equipment and recreational vehicles, back to the drain, which was still open, and the variety of cutting tools still sitting where Swetsky and crew had left them. They examined the workbench that ran the length of the back wall. Williams and Vertesi showed Aziz the shrink-wrapping machine that had been used to wrap the bodies, both those that were buried and the two that had been carried away. MacNeice stood quietly behind the drain, looking around and trying to imagine what it had been like for Hughes. He said a silent prayer, shook his head and walked over to a rack of shovels and spades.

"Montile, grab a couple of these shovels. We're going to do some digging."

Halfway to the entrance of the barn, MacNeice suddenly felt uneasy. "Something's wrong," he said, and stopped.

They were twenty feet from the open door. "Aziz, go over to the far side of the barn and stay there. If I'm right, call it in."

"Boss, there's a uniform out at the road and this place has been locked down for weeks—" Williams said, leaning the shovels quietly against an ATV.

MacNeice wasn't listening. He remained focused on the open door ahead.

"Vertesi, check the back way out of here. If it's open, stand by. If it's locked, come back here and take cover." Vertesi drew his weapon and ran to the rear of the building, trying to figure out what had set off MacNeice.

"Take the safety off your sidearm, Montile, and stay to the left, behind the sliding door. Don't show yourself till you have to."

They walked slowly towards the entrance. Williams held his weapon in front of him with both hands as if he were about to make a chip shot with a nine iron.

The afternoon sun cut an angled shaft deep into the barn; cluster flies flew in spiralling circles, chasing the tiny specks of dust floating harmlessly in the light. As he stepped out of the shadow, MacNeice raised his hand and Williams stopped moving. He struggled to hear what MacNeice was hearing, but apart from cicadas and a crow calling somewhere in the distance, he couldn't make out a thing.

As his eyes adjusted to the brightness, MacNeice called out, "Wenzel, let me hear you."

Wenzel didn't respond. MacNeice looked over to Aziz, who had her Glock drawn and her cellphone in the other hand. Pointing to the wall beside the door, MacNeice said softly to Williams, "Over there." Once he was in position, MacNeice took several deep breaths, raised his own weapon and approached the door from the left.

The first man he saw had a chrome-plated pistol tucked into his belt. He smiled at MacNeice and casually urged the detective forward with his index finger. Beside him stood a mountain of a man with a shotgun levelled in MacNeice's direction. Both of them were in black; the one with the pistol wore tight black leather pants with small silver disks on the outside seam, in the style of a Mexican desperado. He was short, slender and good-looking.

"Come, *monsieur,* join the party. Be smart, now, and drop the gun."

"I don't think so," MacNeice said. "But I'd be grateful if your friend dropped his."

"Bruni? No, no, that's not going to happen. But come, come— you'll reconsider, I think so."

MacNeice kept his weapon pointed at the first man as he stepped further into the sun. To his left, in front of the barn, Wenzel was on his knees. Beside him was the uniform from the cruiser, a gag in his mouth. Two more men held shotguns to their heads.

"Now—the weapon?"

"No, I insist your men drop theirs."

"*Ah, oui?*" He took out his shiny pistol and fired at the uniform, hitting him in the thigh. As the cop fell sideways with a muffled scream, the shooter looked back at MacNeice. "My name is Frédéric—it's French. Will you reconsider, *monsieur?*"

From somewhere in the barn they heard a tinkling melody— Ravel's *Bolero*. MacNeice could hear Williams fumbling for his phone, but the music repeated twice before it stopped. MacNeice shrugged. Frédéric, who was shaking his head at the absurdity of it, said, "Shit *merde*, I hate that piece. Stupid music, stupid movie too, eh? I joke, but . . . tell that fool to come out here."

"Williams, come on out. Train your weapon on the big guy."

Williams came around the corner trying not to look embarrassed. He stood several feet away from MacNeice and levelled his weapon on the centre of the big man's chest.

"What do you want, Frédéric?" MacNeice asked.

"What do I want? What do I want?" He glanced at Bruni and shrugged. "You and your friends are on my property, and this"—he pointed his weapon at Wenzel—"this . . . Maple Leaf, I think he's not with you, am I right?"

"Wrong."

"He's a *mouchard*—a rat, I think. Yes, I think so. A rat. Do you know what we do with rats in Montréal?"

"I can't imagine. You realize there are more of us here, Frédéric?"

"I know. I know they're calling for the SWAT team, but this will be over before they arrive."

"So far you haven't killed anyone. Don't start now."

"*Monsieur*, the rat must die. *Alors*, fire that thing or put it down."

MacNeice took two more steps towards Frédéric. "Drop your weapon, and tell your friends to do the same."

Williams wasn't sure it was a good idea, but he stepped towards the big man, certain that with the size of him at least he couldn't miss, wishing at the same time he was holding something with more punch than his standard issue.

"You are amusing. First, I'm going to deal with this Maple Leaf rat—they spread disease, you know." He walked over to Wenzel, put the barrel against the kid's head and pulled back the hammer. "Bruni, *s'il vous plaît, fais le compte—à partir de trois*."

"I will stop you before he gets to one, Frédéric. Don't do it." MacNeice took another step towards him and held his weapon with both hands.

"*Oui*, maybe yes—and Bruni will stop you. Are you ready to die, *monsieur*?"

"Why would you risk a life sentence when you can stand down now?"

"This property is *énorme*. We will be gone but you, sadly, will stay."

"Mr. MacNeice, sir, please don't let him do this, please." Wenzel was crying, his eyes squeezed shut.

"Ah, *splendide, mes amis*, this is Monsieur MacNeice. I must say, though, I'm not impressed." He looked at his watch, buried in the middle of a heavy black leather band. "*Alors*, no more talk. Say *au revoir au petit mouchard*. Bruni, from three."

"*Trois* . . ." The mountain's voice was so high-pitched that if you weren't looking at him, you'd swear he was female.

Frédéric looked down at Wenzel, who was whimpering, drool spilling from his lip into the dirt. He was whispering, "No, please, sir, don't . . ."

"*Deux . . .*"

MacNeice steadied his weapon, pointed at Frédéric's head and started walking towards him. "Put it down, Frédéric, put it down now." Bruni followed him with the shotgun, the barrel levelled at his midsection.

"*Un . . .*"

Frédéric turned towards MacNeice, smiled and opened his mouth to say something when his face exploded, spraying flesh, blood, hair, bone and brain matter all over Wenzel and the exterior wall of the barn. His body pitched forward violently, knocking Wenzel onto his back. Bruni swung around to fire at the attacker, and seeing no one, turned back—but it was too late. Williams's shot slammed into his chest. Dazed, the big man staggered backwards with the shotgun raised. Williams fired again, hitting him in the chin, snapping his head back. Bruni slammed down hard on the pavement. The biker who had been covering the wounded cop ran for the farmhouse, while the other one crouched at the corner of the barn as if he was still trying to spot the first shooter. MacNeice moved quickly towards him, stepping over Frédéric's legs.

"Lay it down—it's over."

The biker hesitated, then slowly placed the shotgun on the ground. MacNeice kicked the piece away and said, "On your stomach, hands behind your back. Don't move."

Vertesi came racing around the side of the building, heading towards the farmhouse, weapon in hand. Aziz appeared at the barn door and, spotting Vertesi, yelled, "Michael, where are you going?"

"I've got him." Vertesi leapt up onto the porch and disappeared into the house, the screen door slapping shut behind him.

"Aziz, cuff this one. Take care of the uniform and Wenzel."

Williams was taking the shotgun from Bruni's hand when MacNeice tapped him on the shoulder, pointing to the farmhouse. He and Williams ran to the door. Once inside they stopped and listened—it was dead quiet.

Williams pointed upstairs and MacNeice grabbed his arm. "Wait," he said softly, putting his hand to his ear. "Listen."

There was a faint rumbling of footfalls moving fast.

*What the fuck?* Williams mouthed the words.

MacNeice's eyes widened. "There's a tunnel!"

They tore down the stairs. In the basement they listened again: the rumbling was coming from the rear of the house. They rushed into the back room and saw a heavy oak shelving unit full of preserves; it had been pulled away from the wall. Behind it an open steel door revealed a concrete tunnel with caged lights set at intervals along the ceiling. They took off running and were just approaching a dogleg turn when three loud shots echoed towards them. The first was from a shotgun, the other two from a sidearm. Pellets from the shotgun ricocheted off the wall ahead of them and rattled menacingly towards them on the floor.

As they turned the corner, an acrid smell filled the air. A hundred yards in the distance they could see two bodies. "Fuck!" Williams shouted and began running faster, easily pulling away from MacNeice. "Vertesi, you crazy motherfucker, you better be alive!"

MacNeice was out of breath when he reached them. Williams was squatting beside Vertesi. Beyond them there seemed to be blood everywhere, but none on Vertesi.

"He's deaf, boss. He can't hear a thing," Williams said.

MacNeice looked at Vertesi, who smiled that little-kid smile all the women loved and most men envied. MacNeice patted him hard on the shoulder and looked up the tunnel.

The fourth biker was lying dead on his back in a pool of blood. The shotgun was behind him in the middle of the floor.

"Take Vertesi back. I'm going to follow this tunnel to the end." He stepped over the biker, avoiding the blood. It was another hundred yards or so before he reached a steel door with a small peeka-boo cover and grate. He slid the cover aside and looked out into forest. Pulling the bolt, he stepped outside with his weapon drawn. The four bikes were parked in a shallow gully surrounded by trees. Only a narrow path leading up to the road could possibly give it away, and it was obscured by brush. MacNeice walked up to the road and looked back towards the farmhouse. It had to be a quarter-mile away.

Things had happened so fast he hadn't thought about the shot that killed Frédéric until now. He hadn't heard it, not even a delayed, muffled *pop*. MacNeice walked along the perimeter of the chain-link fence until the meadow sank and he could see the first barn to the right of the house. As he tried to recall the angle, he could see uniformed figures running back and forth, several cruisers, ambulances, two firetrucks and a SWAT van in the driveway; he hadn't even heard them arrive. He could still make out where Frédéric had fallen.

Walking further along the road, he looked for fresh tire tracks on the mud and gravel shoulder. Fifty yards on, he found them. The vehicle had pulled into an old, tire-rutted driveway used to stack firewood and fallen timber from the property. He looked at the tread marks, pushed his fingers into their zigzag grooves—they were still moist. He stood between the tracks trying to picture the vehicle. They were too wide for a sedan. *It must have been an SUV*, he thought. There were no footprints near the tracks, no broken twigs or disturbed leaves. *Light-footed*, he thought, as he crossed the road.

MacNeice began working out the geometry. The distance to the barn had to be more than six hundred yards. He looked down in the ditch for evidence of a shooter: depressed weeds, scuffed dirt, a fresh shoe or boot print. He was about to retrace his footsteps when he spotted something standing on the edge of the road like a tiny soldier. MacNeice squatted and looked closely at the narrow two-and-a-half-inch brass shell. Inside, the shooter had placed a tiny yellow buttercup, taken from a clump growing in the nearby ditch. Within a second of Frédéric's head exploding he'd thought he'd figured out who the shooter was—now he was certain. Putting on a latex glove, MacNeice picked up the shell and nestled it inside the second glove, then slipped both into his pocket and walked back along the road towards the farm.

He found Vertesi sitting on the steps of the farmhouse. "Can you hear me?"

"Yes, sir, I'm okay now—just big-time ringing in my ears."

"Good work back there. But why did you take off alone?"

"With respect, boss, you went out there with nothing but a handgun."

"I thought I could talk him out of it—I was mistaken. That tunnel was his insurance, the reason for his bravado. We would have been six dead people, and no suspects."

"Swets is on his way. He couldn't believe he missed the show. When I told him there was a tunnel, he asked where it was, and when I told him it was behind the preserves in the basement, you know what he said?"

"No."

"Palmer polished off three Mason jars of peaches over the two weeks they were bunked down here, and he never noticed it."

"And what did you say?"

"I said he was probably on his cellphone all the time." Palmer was notorious for conducting the business of his romantic life while on the job. "But I also pointed out that you couldn't spot it even if you were standing in front of it. I only found it because the guy didn't take the time to close it behind him."

"How's the young cop?"

"He's gonna be fine—the bullet tore through the muscle on the outside of his thigh. He's embarrassed that he fell asleep in the cruiser. Frédéric actually tapped on his window with that chrome piece of his."

"What's his name?"

"Tyler Wosniac, third year on the force."

"He won't make that mistake again. Have you got your cellphone?"

"Yessir."

"Do you have Sue-Ellen's phone number on there?"

"Yes."

"Good. Call her."

"Like right now?"

"Right now."

MacNeice sat down on one of the chairs that had been retrieved from the barn and watched as Vertesi punched in the call. "Hello, Sue-Ellen, it's Michael Vertesi. The boss wants to—" MacNeice was waving at him to stop. "Sorry, Sue-Ellen, just a second." He cupped the phone in his hand and looked at MacNeice. "What should I say?"

"Ask if her brother has shipped out. If he didn't, I want to leave him a message."

"He was supposed to go this morning, wasn't he?"

"I know. Just ask the question."

Vertesi asked. His eyes widened as he heard the answer; he shook his head and mouthed *no* at MacNeice.

"Okay, ask her to give him this message: 'Thanks for being there.'"

"That it?"

"No. She should also wish him good hunting."

Vertesi repeated the message verbatim. After he said goodbye, he looked quizzically at MacNeice.

"Tell you later. How's Wenzel?"

"Aziz has him over in the field, just walking and talking, trying to get him settled down. He's pretty messed up—in every way, actually—he pissed himself."

"Another set of clothes is in order. Get him back to the hotel and make sure his minibar is stocked with bourbon."

"Will do."

"What about Williams?"

"He's gone behind the house with two uniforms to dig around for the plastic bag. Oh, by the way, he returned that call—the one that went off in the barn. It was from Ryan. The state police have closed Old Soldiers and taken four members, including the owner, into custody."

"Perfect. And our surviving biker?"

"He's over there in the back of the cruiser but he hasn't said anything. His Quebec driver's licence says he's Gérard Langlois."

"Good. I want him in the interview room in a half-hour."

"Will do, sir. The guy without a face was Frédéric Paradis."

"Freddy Paradise . . ."

"You're thinking it was Penniman who took him out?" Vertesi asked.

MacNeice met Vertesi's eye. "As far as our reports go, it was an unknown assailant, likely a rival biker. Understood?"

"Understood, sir. Helluva shot—went right through the wall and killed an all-terrain vehicle." Vertesi walked off towards the uniforms clustered around the cruiser.

MacNeice went looking for Aziz and Wenzel. He spotted them walking along the treeline. Wenzel carried a stick and was swiping at the weeds that lined the path. They were lost in conversation and didn't hear MacNeice coming up behind them until he snapped a twig underfoot. Wenzel jumped out of his skin.

"Sorry, Wenzel, I didn't mean to startle you."

"Ah, jeez, man—I mean sir. That was pretty freaky back there, so I'm like, really on edge, ya know?"

"I do. I thought you showed great courage, Wenzel."

"Courage? I was so scared I pissed myself."

MacNeice wanted to tell him there was no shame in that, but he doubted the kid would believe him. Looking at Wenzel's gore- and urine-stained clothing, he said, "We'll get you some new gear."

Wenzel looked down at himself. "Shit . . . well, I was always a Blackhawks fan anyways."

"Aziz, you're okay?"

"I am, boss, I am."

"Good. In half an hour you and I are going to interview the last of the bikers."

MacNeice retrieved his jacket from the Chevy and put it on. He took one last look around the place before getting in the car; Aziz was already doing up her seatbelt. He drove slowly past the big men in body armour carrying heavy weapons.

Aziz noticed that several of them stared as they went by. Through her open window she heard one of them say, "That him?" and the answer, "Yeah, that's him." Aziz had to admit she was also wondering why MacNeice had taken such a risk.

Hidden hunkered down in the barn, she could barely hear them speaking—there were no raised voices—but she had almost screamed when Paradis shot the young cop, so afraid was she that he'd hit MacNeice. Then she'd heard his voice, just as calm as before. She'd called dispatch again and whispered, "Get that bloody SWAT team out here! Send a goddamned helicopter if you have to, but do not, under any circumstances, call any of the cellphones of this team."

Glancing at MacNeice, she saw that he seemed lost in reverie, as calm as if he were on a Sunday drive in the country. She shivered, a delayed reaction to how close they'd all come to disaster.

No report had signalled the arrival of the fatal shot. From where she was, she hadn't even heard it tearing through Paradis's skull, only the *bang-bang* of it piercing the barn wall, then slamming into the engine block of a new ATV not four feet away from where she was crouching.

As they turned right on the concession road, Aziz said, "Wenzel couldn't stop talking about you. Apparently you reminded him of Hughes, being so calm and all. He peed himself when you started marching towards Frédéric with your weapon pointed at his head."

MacNeice stopped at a light and watched as a young woman wheeled a stroller past the Chevy. Had he thought Frédéric would actually execute Wenzel? Absolutely. He was equally certain that Bruni would unload the shotgun into him, though he didn't want to say any of that to Aziz. Instead he said, "Neither of those men would have backed down, not Frédéric or Bruni." Even though the light had changed, he waited till the woman and her stroller were safely on the other sidewalk.

He knew what he'd done was risky, but there was no another strategy that had a chance of saving Wenzel's life. Had he stayed in the barn with his team to wait for the SWAT vans to arrive, at the very least Paradis and his men would have been down the tunnel and away, leaving two corpses lying in the dirt and no one knowing who'd done it or why, or how they'd managed to escape. If he'd opened fire from inside he'd have initiated a gun battle, echoing battles the farm had already seen. Though the bikers had more firepower, his team might have prevailed, or at least held out until the SWAT team arrived. However, Wenzel and Wosniac would be lying dead in the dirt.

"What made you think they were out there?"

"I don't know. Wenzel was singing to himself when we went in, and he stopped. He's a fidgety kid, nervous about being here; he should have been pacing or tossing stones or singing Johnny Cash songs—hearing nothing at all seemed strange."

"Sixth sense."

"Just observation."

"What do you think the biker will tell us?"

"Depends on how rattled he is. What I want to know is why Quebec bikers are riding with D2D. We know that farm isn't registered to Frédéric Paradis, but he acted like the lord of the manor. Of course, I also want to know if he was the one who butchered Hughes and shot Luigi."

"That would be grim justice . . . Frédéric's face exploding."

"Yes . . ."

"You think it was Penniman, don't you."

"That shot was at least six hundred yards—I'm certain of it." He shoved himself up in the seat and reached into his pocket with his right hand. Pulling out the latex gloves, he handed them to her and drove on in silence as she retrieved the shell with the wilted buttercup in it.

She held up the casing, turning it around in her fingers. "What in God's name is this?"

"I don't know. It's a calibre I've never seen before. He set it up on the road like a lead soldier."

"I saw Paradis when they bagged him—there was nothing left, just a hairline and a jawline . . . and part of one ear." She stared at the shell. "What calibre do you think this is?"

"I don't know. Remember Ferguson from last year?"

"The Brit engineer who gave you the name of the Bulgarian assassin?"

"He'll know."

"Why not just give it to our forensics team?"

"Because I think Sue-Ellen Hughes has suffered enough."

Aziz took a deep breath and sighed. "Well, I never expected the day to turn out this way . . . from Dance to this."

They were cresting the escarpment. Dundurn stretched out before them, all green and grey under a cloudless sky; the lake and bay lay cool and shimmering in the blue beyond. The view never failed to give MacNeice a small hiccup of joy; it always suggested home and—somewhat ironically—peace. He turned onto the Jolly Cut and dropped the Chevy into second gear, letting it sink slowly into the city.

# 41.

A S THEY PULLED into the division parking lot, Deputy Chief Wallace was on his way out. He flashed his headlights so that MacNeice would stop. Rolling down his window, he said, "Join me for a minute, Mac." He backed up into the closest spot and waited for MacNeice to appear at his window.

"I'm on my way to Cayuga; the media's already there, waiting for a statement," Wallace said, "so give me a statement."

MacNeice began at the beginning, told him all he knew and what he didn't know—the long-range shooter, the basement tunnel—and said a cop had been shot in the leg but otherwise there were no other injuries to their side. Not wanting to get into it right then, he left out the details of his standoff with Paradis.

"Okay, where can I find you after this?"

"We're interviewing the surviving biker upstairs. That'll take some time."

"Aziz has that interview—she gonna make it?"

"No, we'll have to cancel."

"Don't bother. I'll do it, and offer an exclusive on the biker slayings. That it?"

"That's it."


Wallace didn't appear to be in a rage when he returned, but he was. In less than two and a half hours he'd been given three disturbing reports about the events at Cayuga, including the fact that MacNeice had almost got the American kid, a young cop, Williams and himself killed. He hauled MacNeice into an interview room, demanding to hear his version of the events. He didn't sit down, so neither did MacNeice.

MacNeice insisted that the standoff with Paradis was unavoidable given the circumstances, but that he had done his best to protect Hausman, the cop and his team.

"So who killed him?"

"Unidentified. I was about to fire when it happened. I assume it was revenge."

"Is that the truth?"

"Yes—it was a spectacular shot. Paradis probably identified himself as the target the moment he fired into our officer's leg."

"My opinion, Mac, is that you could have ended up dead, along with your whole team. I think it was pure luck that it didn't turn out that way."

"Luck had a lot to do with it, I agree. But the risk I took was calculated."

"I saw that fucking tunnel. Tell me how we had Swetsky and his team out there for two weeks and they missed it."

"I would have missed that tunnel, and so would you. Short of tearing the place apart—which Swetsky had no authority to do—he wouldn't have found it."

"Okay, fine. Look, to be honest with you, I'm really just

wondering if you have a death wish."

"Actually, I don't." MacNeice said it as if he'd considered the point—and realized he had, more than once.

"Well, there's an officer nursing a leg wound in Dundurn General who thinks you might. He described you as 'freaky cool, but freakin' crazy.'"

MacNeice shrugged.

Wallace began pacing. "I've already been told what the headline is for tomorrow's *Standard*. Interested?"

MacNeice studied the Deputy Chief's face, which seemed a lot calmer.

"'Mysterious Sniper Saves Six Lives.'" Wallace was nodding as if his head had come loose. "How d'ya like that?"

"I don't mind it—it's true. And an alliteration like that isn't something you see every day."

"You're still saying you don't know who the shooter was?" Wallace was leaning against the wall, his eyes levelled at MacNeice.

"I am. Whoever it was got away clean. They had to be somewhere out by the road when they took the shot. Once the shooting started, we were too preoccupied to find out where the sniper was."

Wallace pushed himself off the wall and walked over to the two-way mirror. He looked at his reflection and groaned, rubbed his eyes and ran his fingers through his hair several times before he turned back to MacNeice. Pulling out the chair Langlois had used, Wallace sat down heavily. "Okay, tell me what you got out of that biker."

When MacNeice walked back into the cubicle, the detectives and Ryan all stopped what they were doing.

"We cool?" Williams asked.

"Yes." He turned to Aziz. "Have you filled them in on the Langlois interview?"

"I didn't. First, I think you should see what Williams found behind the house."

Williams held up a plastic Baggie that at first looked empty. But then MacNeice noticed something round and solid weighing down its corner: a simple gold band—Gary Hughes's wedding ring. "It was still on his finger, boss. Everything but his face and forearm flesh was there—hands and feet, and this too." He picked up a larger bag and took out Hughes's wallet and passport, then another, with another wallet and passport. "Luigi Vanucci, of Buffalo, New York," he announced.

In Hughes's wallet there was twenty-three dollars; in Vanucci's, two hundred sixty-five, in American currency. No Canadian—but then, they hadn't come for the shopping.

"Strange they didn't boost the cash," Williams said. "Maybe they're superstitious about blood money." From the wallet he pulled out a snapshot of Hughes with his family. It was difficult to look at—everyone smiling at the camera from a picnic table. All these artifacts had been shrink-wrapped together, then stuffed in a garbage bag and buried five feet under the vegetable garden. "The tomatoes above it were doing really well."

When MacNeice asked how he'd found it, Williams smiled. "I found a metal detector on top of some larger equipment in the barn." He had gone looking behind the farmhouse and, in less than five minutes, the wedding ring triggered the detector. When he got back to the division, Williams had tried to find out if Vanucci had any family, without success. He scanned the driver's licence and passport and sent them down to Buffalo Homicide.

Vertesi had taken Wenzel back to the hotel with his new gear. He was feeling better and running up room service and movie rental charges.

"Okay—Gérard Langlois. Fiza, take us through it." MacNeice consulted his notebook and on the whiteboard wrote the names

Langlois had given them—Quebec bikers—under the heading *Jokers MC*. He put a vertical line next to them and added *Luigi Vanucci* and *Gary Hughes*.

He drew another line and printed *D2D*. Aziz described how the Jokers and D2D were partnering on security jobs across Ontario and Quebec, based on the notion that two clubs were stronger than one, but also to eliminate any conflict between them. Presumably it also gave them better odds in competing against the larger clubs.

Langlois had started riding with Jokers MC six months after the first shoot-out at Cayuga, the one with the Old Soldiers in which Hughes and Luigi had been killed. He missed the second one because he'd gone home for his mother's funeral in Dorval; he even provided the name of the funeral home in case MacNeice and Aziz didn't believe him. He'd said Frédéric Paradis was ruthless and ambitious, the "grand marshal." His leadership had begun long before the first shootout. Langlois remembered Bruni once telling him how he'd cut the face off an American and fed it to the pigs. When Langlois asked him why he'd done that, Bruni said the guy had killed four D2D bikers—it was *un cadeau* from Frédéric to D2D. Langlois believed the story and said that Frédéric would have had to order it; Bruni would never have done it on his own, because "that big *bête* didn't have a brain."

"Can we believe this guy?" Vertesi asked.

"Aziz told him what would happen if he didn't cooperate. He's tough but not stupid—he knows there are as many bikers inside the system as on the street," MacNeice said. "The fact that Langlois survived the day's events at the farm will immediately put him under suspicion. If he cooperates with us, we'll at least give him a new identity and offer to relocate him."

When asked the whereabouts of the D2D bikers, he told them that, as far as he knew, there were five hiding in Montreal and the rest—another six or seven—had gone underground somewhere in

Ontario or as far away as Vancouver. He had no idea who'd originally hired the Jokers or why, but when Aziz asked him why they came back to the farm, he stalled, said his English wasn't very good—not true—then asked her to repeat the question.

Finally he told them there was supposed to be a lot of money stored somewhere at the farm, and Frédéric needed it. No one else but Paradis knew where it was hidden. Langlois doubted that the D2D crew knew anything about the cash stashed there—the relationship wasn't that cosy.

So Frédéric and his crew had been watching the farm and were about to go in when MacNeice's team had arrived. Given that they had the element of surprise on their side, the bikers decided to risk it. They could see that the cop was falling asleep behind the wheel; Frédéric and Bruni handled him. The others had waited for half an hour in the tunnel; when they emerged, they saw the cop and Wenzel sitting in front of the barn and Frédéric smiling, pointing a gun at Wenzel's head.

Langlois, of course, claimed he had no intention of shooting anyone but that he had no doubt the other three would—especially Frédéric, whom he described somewhat loftily as a "*sadiste classique.*" Bruni was hopped up on steroids and energy drinks. "He said it was good that the second shot took out Bruni's neck, because he would have kept coming after the first one," Aziz said.

"Amen to that," Williams, said, wiping Cayuga dust off his shoes. As a result of the shooting, he'd spent two hours with Internal Affairs and was only now starting to breathe normally.

"Assuming that was the end of the interview," MacNeice said, and checked his watch. It was past eight and he was exhausted. "This is the end of me." He stood up, grabbed his jacket and looked across at Aziz.

"I'll make sure Aziz gets to the hotel, boss," Williams said. "I've already checked—there's a cop assigned to sit outside her door."

———

MacNeice drove out of the parking lot, merging with the late evening traffic gliding along Main Street. He didn't turn any music on. As he approached the cottage, he saw a red Corvette parked in his driveway. Pulling in behind it, he could see through the tinted rear window that someone was in the driver's seat. He checked the licence plate—PATMAN—before swinging his car back and around so that he ended up sitting three feet from the driver's window.

He lowered his own window and waited. In a few seconds, the darkened window slid down.

"Pat Mancini," MacNeice said.

"You know me?" Mancini looked surprised.

"Your plate's a giveaway. What are you doing here, Patman?"

"I watched Wallace on TV tonight, put one and one together and thought you'd be looking for me."

"Do I have a reason to?"

"No, no. That's why I'm here—"

"It's late, Pat. Let's meet at the division tomorrow morning."

"No way, man. Nobody knows I'm up here, but they'd sure as hell know if I showed up at the cop shop."

"Who'd know?"

"Oh yeah, like I'm going to fall for that shit . . ."

"Back up your car and get out of here."

"I just want to talk to you."

"Thirty seconds."

"Fuck, man . . . Okay, look, I know your man Vertesi probably suspects me in this thing out at Cayuga, but I had nothin' to do with it, okay?"

"Fine, then you have nothing to worry about. Get going."

"Why are you such a hardass?"

"Because it's late, you're at my home, parked on private property—my property. It's time for you to get out of here."

"I can give you some shit on this, I can."

"If you're serious, I'll be at your office tomorrow morning before nine."

"I can't talk there either, man—no fucking way."

"Because of your father?"

"No, because of the guys inside, and out. This is a small business—I mean, the whole concrete industry is. People talk."

"What would they have to talk about?"

"What I say to you can never come back to me, agreed?"

"What have you got to tell me?"

"I need your word, man. Don't fuck with me—I need it."

"Pat, I'm not empowered to make deals."

"You gotta, or I'm outta here—and I mean gone."

"I promise you, I'll do all I can to keep you out of it."

"Not good enough. I need your word."

MacNeice sighed. "You have my word."

Mancini looked around, peering into the night. "Can we talk inside?"

"No one followed you here."

"Yeah, no shit, but they may have followed you."

"Get into my car and slouch down. We'll go for a drive over the bridge."

As quickly as he could, Mancini slipped out of his car and into the passenger seat of the Chevy.

As they headed north on Mountain Road, MacNeice asked him, "How did you know where I live?"

"It wasn't hard to find out. You have a gravel driveway—that gravel came from somewhere . . ."

"All right, so I'm listening."

Mancini spoke in a slow monotone as if he'd rehearsed what he was going to say. He started from the beginning for him—which was hockey. When he was playing in the NHL, he had been sent down to Junior A for a while to help him focus on his game, out of the limelight. On game day at the local arena, he'd buy marijuana from one of the guys on security. That was in Montreal, and the Jokers controlled security at the rink. "When I heard the Deputy Chief announce the death of Frédéric Paridis, I knew I had to talk to someone," Mancini said.

As the Chevy climbed the Sky-High Bridge, Mancini told MacNeice that he and another player had begun scoring more than bud from the Jokers: the bikers owned a string of Ukrainian dancers who weren't exactly dancers in the strictest sense.

"Prostitutes, you mean, Pat?"

"Yeah . . ."

Those women would have been expensive, but when MacNeice asked him how much they cost, Mancini said, "That was the thing—Freddy didn't want money. He said, 'We'll pick it up some-where down the line, when you're back on Broadway.' So, you know, that was good, but Broadway didn't last all that long and then I was out of hockey altogether."

"But you still owed Frédéric."

"Big time. And he had this motherfucker of a guy—like Lou Ferrigno without the weird speech thing, though this guy sounded like a girl. He bought it today too, I heard."

"He did. What did they want from you?"

Frédéric wanted security jobs. He'd done a deal with D2D and had hookers and dope lines from Windsor to Quebec City, but they were always on the fringes of the large gangs. Frédéric was certain Pat Mancini could get them better connections.

"Why would he think that?"

"I dunno. Maybe 'cause I'm Italian and I went back to work in my pa's concrete company."

"You mean you were bragging to him about being Italian?"

At first Mancini denied it, but then he admitted Paradis had told him that once, when he was stoned, Mancini had been going on about his family's mob connections. Mancini had no recollection of ever having done so. "I swear on my grandfather's grave, I don't think I would have—"

"Even if you didn't, Pat, he had you because you were too out of it to remember what you said." Mancini was staring out the window over the dark horizon of the lake; the bridge lights caught the thin stream of a tear coursing down his face. "He was still supplying girls and grass?"

"Yeah, quite a bit."

"What did you provide in return?"

"Information. I thought I was giving him a line on solid security jobs, but I guess I told him about the concrete deal going down between ABC and my dad for the harbour project."

"You guess you told him?"

"I told him."

He'd also told him about DeLillo and how they'd got beaten out of the deal and might be looking for a fight with ABC. MacNeice was waiting for it, but Mancini did not mention McNamara. When MacNeice asked him what else he was getting besides women and dope, Mancini said he had no interest in harder drugs and had even cut back on the grass. Women, however, were a serious addiction.

"So you may not have told him anything about mobs in the beginning, but to maintain a steady supply of 'dancers,' you fed him full of Mafia stories, right? And the Italian concrete business on both sides of the border, all with the idea that he could supply security?"

"More or less."

"Who'd he work for?"

"I swear we never got into that. We both agreed that the less I knew about what happened after I handed over the information, the better."

So Mancini had told stories about competing Italian families and left Paradis to draw his own conclusions—and he had. Mancini had no idea who Paradis was offering muscle to, including his own father, and he didn't want to know.

"So why come forward now, Pat, now that Frédéric's dead?"

"You think that fucking frog was working alone? No way. He's got a brother for one—Joe. For all I know, his brother is nuttier than he was."

"Perfect. Joe and Fred Paradise, like names out of a Raymond Chandler novel."

"I don't know who Raymond Chandler is, but I wouldn't joke about that shit with him."

After Mancini had gone to work for his dad, Paradis would send the Ukrainian girls from Montreal on the train. They'd spend a day or two in Dundurn and then be back on the train again. In return, Mancini had provided enough truth along with his fantasy mob world that Paradis felt he was always on the edge of a major break-through—getting the nod to provide expensive muscle to the Mafia.

"I was away when that OK Corral gunfight happened," Mancini said. "I didn't hear about that—not from Paradis, not in the news—until today. I'm shit-scared. I love the dancers . . . okay, I'm guilty of beautiful women, but not the rest of this shit. No way." Mancini was watching the vehicles passing by, studying the occupants for any possible threat.

"How much does your father know?"

"Nothing. My dad would be sick if he knew what his favourite son was up to." He insisted that Mancini Concrete was as straight as they come and that his father had worked hard to be the most stand-up guy in Dundurn.

"Are you going to continue in the business?"

"I don't have any talent for concrete. I mean, I'm a hockey player—sorry, I *was* a hockey player. What do I know about concrete? The guys there see me for what I am: an ex-jock, and now Daddy's boy."

"That's a very raw assessment, Pat. Do you mean it?"

"Oh yeah. I got the game-shits when I watched that press conference. My pa saw you on TV earlier when that other cop, the Muslim one, spoke about the mangia-cake slasher. He said, 'There's a good man.' That's why I came looking for you."

As they passed Princess Point, MacNeice asked him what he was going to do now. Mancini said he had a duffle bag full of gear in the back of his car and he planned on leaving right away for L.A., where a friend of his played for the Kings. He figured he'd lie low but he didn't have any idea how long it would take for the Paradis family or D2D to forget about him.

"I can stop you from doing that."

"I know you can, but will you? I've been straight with you."

"So far, I believe you have. You're sure there's nothing you're not telling me?"

But for the hum of the engine, there was no sound in the car for several seconds.

"McNamara," Mancini finally said.

*Finally*, MacNeice thought. "What about them?"

Another long silence as the nighttime landscape drifted by in horizontal streaks on either side of the Chevy.

"I told Freddy that I thought the Irish were trying a power move on the project."

He insisted there was no evidence for it, other than a phone call McNamara had made to his father when Pat was in his office enjoying an espresso. He was on the sofa ten feet away but said he could hear Sean McNamara yelling at his father over the phone. When he asked him about the call after he hung up, Alberto handed him a chocolate wafer as if he were a kid. "Just business with our Irish friends . . ."

"When you and your dad met with Vertesi, you said something about your family knowing how to take care of yourselves. What were you referring to?"

"Shit, man, I was just crankin' him up. He's such a sincere guy, and Pa likes him. I think it was a line out of a gangster movie."

"So what if Joe Paradis comes looking for you and finds your father instead?" MacNeice asked.

Mancini had been staring out the passenger window again, and now he turned to look at MacNeice. "Good shot." He paused, then said, "Am I more of a risk to him here or in L.A.?"

MacNeice explained patiently that if Pat skipped town, his family would be the only logical target for revenge or demands for financial compensation. The motorcycle club from New York wouldn't go away, and neither would the locals. Going to California might take him out of it, but not his parents, brothers and sisters, aunts and uncles. "Even though you were the one getting the girls, your family could end up paying the bill."

They passed by Division in silence. Mancini began tapping the armrest with the tip of his middle finger. It wasn't a rhythm, just erratic tapping as the buildings slid by. They went straight across town like that, moving with the lights and the traffic and the finger-tapping. They crossed Parkdale and the vacant lot that long ago had been an outdoor dancehall where a young woman in a party dress spent her last night dancing for dollars. They passed the Dairy Queen and McDonald's, the car dealerships and all-night coffee-and-doughnut gas stations.

MacNeice turned right on Mountain Road South and, a few hundred yards later, right again into the lane leading up to the stone cottage. He pulled in beside the Corvette, turned off the ignition and took out the key. He looked over at Mancini, who was still looking out at nothing in particular and tapping the side window with the knuckles of his right hand.

"What are you going to do, Pat? Stay, or cut and run?"

"You're crazy, you know that?" He snapped his head towards MacNeice.

"Believe it or not, that's the second time I've been told that today."

"Oh, I can believe it, I can believe it. All right, I'll stay. But not for long—you gotta wrap this up fast."

MacNeice couldn't help smiling at the irony of Pat's plea. Having started the fire in the first place, he was desperate to have it put out before it consumed him.

Mancini was studying his face and correctly interpreted the smile. "Okay, yeah, well, I know I got this—"

"Don't sweat it, Pat. I'm here, as it says on the company cars, to serve and protect. What I need to know is, what can I count on you for?"

"You get these guys locked up or, like today, dead, and I'll testify . . . Fuck, man, I'm a hockey player, not a soldier."

Another ironic statement, but this time MacNeice made sure his face didn't betray him. The soldier found in the bay had only been trying to provide for his family—by taking a so-called security job that Pat had unwittingly created.

Mancini got out of the car and leaned in to shake hands. "I know you'll come through for me. Pa never makes mistakes about men—except maybe me."

"Pat, don't give up on yourself just yet. It took a lot of courage to seek me out. Stay low, and stay away from women and dope, agreed?"

Mancini smiled for the first time. "I will, I promise . . . but I have to ask, have you ever had a Ukrainian dancer?"

"Goodnight, Pat."

MacNeice stood watching as Mancini eased the overpowered red machine tenderly down the rough road to the highway. Then he opened the door, put down his keys and gently smacked the bum of the girl in the photo.

Approaching the cut-off that would lead either to the Peace Bridge and America or over the Sky-High home, the red Corvette suddenly sliced across the lanes and powered down the ramp towards Niagara.

*That isn't an easy decision,* he told himself. *I've grown up giving my word—to my father, to coaches, to owners, to fans. I've put body and fucking soul behind my word. I even gave my word to MacNeice. But fuck it, just plain fuck it! I've given enough. It's time for me.* Merging with the late-night traffic, he cranked up the classic vinyl channel on his satellite radio and howled along with Hendrix.

Then, somewhere between Secord and Vineland, worms bored holes in his resolve. MacNeice's logic—about who would pay the cost if he bolted—was killing his case for disappearing. Pat swung off the Queen E at the Vineland exit, looped around and joined the sparse traffic heading for Dundurn and beyond. The guitar licks of "Hotel California" argued for a slower speed, so he set the cruise control to 70 mph and took the middle lane.

As he approached Secord, another car fell in behind the Corvette. It was late and there were lots of road to choose from, but it closed the distance and sat fifty feet behind him. He studied the headlight pattern and the reflections off the grille. *It's not a cop, unless they're driving Mustangs now. Don't panic, Pat.*

Mancini slid into the slow lane but left the Vette on cruise control. At first the Mustang maintained speed in the middle lane, then it suddenly accelerated. Mancini could feel his chest tighten as he waited to see what it would do. When it came alongside the Corvette, the Mustang slowed to match his speed again. He resisted the urge to look across the short distance. Easing his car closer to the shoulder, he could sense that the Mustang was edging closer, straddling the lanes. Mancini gripped the wheel with both hands and looked across at the other car, which was now no more than two feet from him.

The passenger in the Mustang lowered his window, pointed an index finger at him and lowered his thumb, letting his hand recoil. Then he smiled—a wide, menacing smile set in a massive head.

Mancini slammed the accelerator down and the Corvette responded, pinning him to the seat, its rear end grinding onto the gravel shoulder before correcting again on the pavement. The Mustang dropped back in his rear-view mirror, but by the time the Corvette hit 110 mph, it had closed the distance to seventy yards.

*This is my world. I know how to do this: every rink is divided into invisible lanes, every player—like every car—an obstacle. This is my world, fucker.*

Mancini changed lanes, flashing past cars and sliding around eighteen-wheelers like they were rubber cones.

*Come on, bring it on! When I'm in the zone, no one can touch me. Bring it on. I've deked past the heavies . . . Keep your head up, Patman. You own the ice—keep your fucking head up!*

He looked in the rear-view and checked the side mirrors. The Mustang wasn't as quick to weave, but once it was in the open he could see its lights shaking crazily as it closed the distance. At 125 mph the Corvette opened the gap again, but only for a few seconds—the Mustang cleared a pair of RVs and was gaining again.

Approaching the Sky-High Bridge, Mancini could see the Mustang's lights jiggling in his side mirror maybe a hundred feet behind. His chest was tight but he felt exhilarated, pumped—as if nothing could touch him. He adjusted himself in the seat, relaxed his hands and held the accelerator to the floor.

*Shoulda' done this long ago. Bring the game to what I do best. I can see everything. The net, the lanes, the players—I can even see the players behind me. I can measure their speed, their legs, their instincts for the game. There is no noise . . . I can hear my heartbeat. I can breathe easily.*

The Corvette started climbing the bridge, leaving the land below. As if they were tethered by an elastic band, the Mustang fell behind—150 feet—and then the elastic contracted and the gap closed again. Mancini held the pedal to the floor. The speedometer rose to 184 mph as he raced towards the top, the peak of the bridge. He felt supremely capable of outrunning, outdriving and outdistancing his opponent. He was certain the other driver's heart was red-lining, while his was actually slowing down. He smiled, realizing that he was still breathing easily. For the first time in a long time, he wasn't afraid—wasn't faking or lying—he was back in the game. Mancini took the time to glance over at the city and then laughed. Dundurn was jiggling too.

Less than two hundred yards from the top, in one of those strange coincidences, a David Bowie classic came on the radio. It suddenly occurred to him that at this speed the Corvette could probably lift off. He re-established his grip—not too tight, not too loose.

*Ground Control to Major Tom . . .*

And he knew he was safe, that he was home free, that his legs were steel pistons. Anticipating the launch, sinking further back in the seat, Mancini laughed out loud, then sang along. "Ground Control to Major Tom . . ."

Sixty yards, and the iron superstructure above seemed to zip by like a lightspeed spaceship, the Mustang's lights now at least a hundred yards behind. The wind jolted the suspension, but the Corvette held the road and screamed higher, only steel and sky ahead.

*Take your protein pills and put your helmet on.*

———

The phone rang before the alarm went off. It was Vertesi. "Have you heard the news, boss?"

"What news?" MacNeice said, looking over at the clock radio, only to realize he'd forgotten to set the alarm. The time was 8:49 a.m.

"Pat Mancini. His car blew up on top of the Sky-High Bridge around 1:30 this morning. Bits of him and the car ended up in the canal—what's that, 120 feet or so below?"

"Christ, no—" MacNeice pulled himself up in bed.

"Yeah. They've closed off the Toronto-bound lanes and are using the other side as a two-way. Crews have been up there all night. They even found part of the car's roof on the lift bridge, and that's hundreds of feet away."

"Do you know what caused the explosion?" MacNeice got out of bed and headed into the kitchen. He turned on the espresso machine, opened the grappa bottle and poured a shot into a cup.

"They think it was plastic, probably a pile of C4 right under the driver's seat. There wasn't any structural damage to the bridge but it tore up the asphalt pretty bad."

"Who's with the family?" MacNeice cradled the phone on his shoulder, put the cup under the spout and pressed the button for a double shot of espresso.

"Far as I know, only their priest and family. I'm going to pay my respects at nine. I can wait if you want to join me."

"Who's on the bridge?" He swirled the coffee and grappa together, then drank it down.

"DS Whitman and a couple of guys from the east end. Firefighters were there first, and there's a bomb unit and a forensics team. Divers go down around ten this morning."

"I'll go over to the bridge. You go alone to the Mancinis. Keep it respectful but let him know I'll want to speak with him today."

"Any thoughts on why Pat was blown up?"

"Let's talk about it at Division."

The coffee helped MacNeice shake off the fuzzies from his heavy night's sleep. He was amazed that after the events of the previous day he had slept so dreamlessly. Nonetheless, he still felt bone-weary.

# 42.

**M**acNeice arrived on the bridge thirty-four minutes later. As he got out of the Chevy he was immediately whipped about by the wind.

What remained of the Corvette was laying on a flatbed, covered with a tarpaulin. Judging by the low, ragged profile, it was just what was left of the chassis. Other pieces had been collected and put in a van, and whatever was left of Pat Mancini had been taken to Richardson's lab. *Not for reassembly, though,* MacNeice thought. All the king's horses and men couldn't put Pat Mancini together again.

Detective Superintendent Harvey Whitman's hair was blowing wildly off his forehead and his pants and shirt were pinned to his body. He was wearing black aviator shades, and his eyebrows were pulled together so tightly that only the deep vertical furrow in the centre of his brow kept them apart.

"Check this out . . ." Whitman walked over to the torn asphalt. The surface had been ripped open for twenty feet or more, a long oval of melted highway. "That fucker was moving! Forensics figures he was topping 170 to 190 at this point—any more and he would have been airborne right about here. Which is funny, 'cause all of a sudden he was airborne! I'da parked the fucker and run like hell."

"If he knew it was there, he would have too."

"You think he was out joyriding?"

"No, I don't think that young man and joy were on speaking terms. Were there any witnesses?"

Whitman said no, at least none that had stopped. When the fire-fighters arrived, there was a lineup stretching back two hundred yards. Drivers wouldn't go any closer, as there was burning wreck-age from Mancini's lane all the way over to the other side of the bridge.

MacNeice looked up at the bridge's superstructure. "Isn't a traf-fic camera mounted up there somewhere?"

"Yep. We've called Highways and they're checking to see if there's a live feed. But traffic isn't usually an issue at 1:30 a.m., so it was probably down."

"Anyone gone to check Mancini's place?"

"Yeah, I went over around four this morning. He's got the pent-house of a condo overlooking the lake in Burlington. Apart from a small bag of weed, so far we've found nothing unusual. Lots of framed pictures of himself playing hockey, a few large photos of Ferrari racing cars, leather furniture, king-size waterbed, a weight room with a stationary bike an' shit—bachelor's pad all the way. We sealed it."

"Any contents of the car left intact?"

"They found a canvas handle from a duffle bag, but that's it. Everything was either blown up or blown away." Whitman looked off to the lake, where ribs of narrow whitecaps headed angrily to shore.

"Do you know how it was triggered?"

"Not yet. Forensics guys aren't optimistic either. What wasn't up here when we arrived—which isn't much—is down there." He leaned casually over the edge; MacNeice stayed several feet back from the rail. "The current's a bitch down there. I used to dive off at this end and surface about thirty yards down the canal."

MacNeice's cellphone rang; he looked at his watch—9:52 a.m.—before putting the phone to his ear. The buffeting of the wind made it impossible for him to hear or be heard. He held the phone to his mouth and yelled, "Hang on," then ran back to the Chevy. As soon as he was inside, he said, "Go ahead—what have you got?"

It was Williams. "I connected with Buffalo Homicide last night; got a good guy, Demetrius Johnson—a brother. Anyway, Johnson got on it right away and called me about ten minutes ago. Luigi Vanucci had a house in an exclusive neighbourhood on the outskirts of Buffalo; he lived alone and didn't mingle with the neighbours. Johnson said he rented the house furnished, then one day a couple of years ago, he left and never came back. The house sat empty for four or five months, till a new guy moved in. He got all this from a woman across the street. The new tenant is a stockbroker. He's clean, Johnson says, *if you can believe stockbrokers are clean.*" MacNeice could tell that Williams was reading from his notebook.

"He's checking tax records to see how Luigi made a living, but the neighbour said someone told her he owned a security company. Johnson hasn't spoken to the owner of the house yet but thinks he'll reach him later on today."

The Chevy rocked and lifted in the wind. MacNeice looked out over the city and thought about Pat Mancini. "Great work, Montile. Have you heard from Vertesi?"

"Yeah, man, he's at the father's house. What's it like up there?"

"Nothing left to see. What didn't disintegrate in the explosion is either in the canal or, with this wind, somewhere out on the water.

The rest was bagged and tagged. There's just a long, nasty tear in the road to fix."

"Sorta simplifies our go-forward from last night, though."

"How so?"

"Well, I mean, at least we know now that Mancini Concrete was on one side of the fight at Cayuga."

"Maybe not . . . but we'll talk when I get in. Is Aziz there yet?"

"Yeah, I went over and picked her up. It's just the two of us. We were gonna call you but we figured you were sleeping in, and Aziz thought it was a good idea to leave you alone. Ryan'll be here in a half-hour or so."

"So will I. Check in on the Old Soldiers investigation, Montile. See if they have any records from that office at the back of the bar—a business card from a security company with Luigi's name on it, something . . ."

"Yup, I'm on it. I'm actually diggin' this cross-border copping. Demetrius wanted to know if I was from the Caribbean. He couldn't believe that my family goes back generations in Canada—and in a place called Africville."

"How did he know you were black?"

"You know, sir. You just know."

After MacNeice ended the call, he sat for a moment looking out at the city before going back to confirm that he'd be getting a report from Whitman and any footage from the cameras—if they had been recording.

Driving around the line of cruisers blocking the ramp to the bridge, he looked at the cops redirecting traffic to the opposite side and thought about the ride the night before. Was there anything he should have noticed that would indicate the threat on Mancini's life was greater than he imagined it to be? It was possible that his car was rigged while it sat on the gravel outside the cottage. Was the C4 in place before he arrived and detonated from a follow-car with a phone call, or was it on a timer? Who tipped off the bomber? And why now? Had Pat Mancini died because he'd spoken to a cop?

As he turned into the division driveway, he noticed Vertesi pulling in behind him. They parked beside each other and got out their cars.

Vertesi spoke as they walked towards the building. "Yeah, well, they're all really shaken up. His mother had to be taken upstairs; she had just calmed down when I came in and when she saw me, she started crying so hard she fainted—I guess because I was still alive. There were at least twenty people in the house—sisters, brothers, kids, cousins; a few of them I recognized from church or school. Mr. Mancini's face was so pale it was grey. He doesn't understand why anyone would do this, and he kept grabbing my lapels, begging me at one point, saying, 'You must find the people who did this. I need to know who did this to Patrizio.'"

MacNeice held the door for him and they climbed the stairs together.

Stopping in front of the second whiteboard, MacNeice took off his jacket and threw it on the back of his chair. He wrote Pat Mancini's name next to Vanucci's and Hughes's and stood back, studying the board. Then he turned to his three detectives. MacNeice told them about his drive with Pat Mancini, and how a love of weed and women had forced him into a lie that had carried him away and gathered momentum until it came crashing home with Wallace's press conference.

"He told me he knew nothing about how Paradis was using his information, and I believed him—he was too shattered. I want to speak with Pat's father before we upset the family with a warrant. Michael, I'll want you there with me. While I hope it won't be necessary, depending on how that meeting goes, we'll seize their records as well."

"Phew . . . that's gonna hurt," Vertesi said.

"I know that," said MacNeice. "But two of the concrete companies used bikers as security specialists, and by doing a forensic audit of the books we may able to find out which two—and also discover who provided the concrete for the tunnel."

"What about the money Paradis stashed somewhere at Cayuga?"

"Swetsky will be granted an unlimited warrant to literally tear that place apart. He's already scheduled an excavation of the barn's drainage system."

"What do you want to do with Langlois?" asked Aziz.

"While Michael and I are paying a visit to Alberto Mancini, you and Williams rattle him. Tell him about Pat Mancini, that we're going for broke, that we have nothing to lose—he's just the unlucky one who's still alive. And even if he doesn't say a word, the remaining D2Ds and Jokers will assume he has, so the best strategy for him is to tell us what he knows."

Mancini Concrete was closed for the remainder of the week, but Alberto had asked MacNeice to come to his office, not his home. A man who introduced himself only as Pat's uncle met them at the door. Of medium height, he was slim and elegant; he offered a solemn handshake. His black suit and black satin armband seemed out of place in an office covered with a thin film of concrete dust. Walking past Pat's desk, Vertesi tapped MacNeice on the shoulder and pointed to the Ferrari. MacNeice could easily imagine how painful it had been for Pat to sit there, pretending to be in the concrete business, waiting for the train to arrive from Montreal.

Alberto Mancini stood to greet them. His bearing impressed MacNeice, his grief betrayed only by the redness around his eyes. MacNeice kept the condolences brief, which seemed to be appreciated by the older man, who then gestured for them to sit in the chairs in front of his desk.

"May I offer you something? Coffee, water, something stronger?" He pointed to the trolley with its crystal decanters and bottles of spirits.

"We're fine, thank you." MacNeice looked over at the uncle, who had come in and taken a seat on the sofa.

Mancini caught his look. "My brother is a partner in this company, and he's also Pat's favourite uncle. I asked him to be here."

MacNeice nodded. "As you wish. First, I want you to know that your son came to my home to see me last night."

Mancini straightened in surprise and glanced at his brother.

"He was frightened—though he was not seeking protection," MacNeice explained. "He needed to speak to me."

"I don't understand. What would he want to speak with the police about?" Mancini poured himself a glass of water from a stainless steel carafe on his desk.

"How much do you know, sir, of your son's lifestyle?"

The question hung in the air for a few seconds as Mancini drank the water. When the glass was empty, he studied it for a moment, then put it down slowly on a leather coaster. He met MacNeice's gaze. "Like any father of a young man, perhaps not much. But Pat was a good boy—"

"I believe he was. But when he was a hockey player, he became involved with a motorcyle club in Montreal called the Jokers."

"I don't believe it," Alberto Mancini protested, but his tone was tentative. MacNeice could see that he wasn't being honest with himself.

"He was trading information for women and marijuana."

"He was a hockey player, Detective MacNeice. What information of interest to a biker gang could he possibly have?"

"Your son had an active imagination. He either pretended to be an Italian with mob connections or he was tricked into believing he'd made such a claim."

"That's a joke—and this is not a day for joking." The old man crossed his arms and stared defiantly at MacNeice.

"I'm not one given to joking, on this or any other day. The events reported yesterday by Deputy Chief Wallace were unknown to your son, but the individuals involved were not. Your son told Frédéric Paradis, one of the bikers who was shot yesterday, about the deal with ABC. He told him about an argument you had on the phone with someone from McNamara."

Alberto Mancini looked again at his brother and lifted his chin to indicate he should go. The younger man stood up, straightened his jacket and left the room, closing the door quietly behind him.

"Go on, please."

"There isn't much more. Pat was frightened and wanted to leave the country. I persuaded him to stay and he agreed to do so because of the potential threat to you and your family if he left."

"I see . . ." Mancini stood up and walked over to the drinks trolley. "Please join me in a grappa."

"I will. A short one." MacNeice said.

"*Si, grazie mille.*" Vertesi added.

"*Prego.*"

Mancini picked up a tall, slim bottle and poured three shots. He handed them their small glasses and then, toasting them in silence, emptied his glass and set it on the desk before he sat down again. MacNeice and Vertesi followed suit.

"What do you want to know from me?"

"What was the conversation Pat overheard in this office, and who was it with?"

"Anything else?"

"Yes. Pat didn't think he was right for the concrete business and felt that everyone but you understood that—"

"He wasn't, and I did know that. But . . . I hoped he would learn." He used his hands to help him make his point. "No one aspires to be in the concrete business, but it's a good business. It's been good to our family. I wanted to leave it to him."

"And your brother?"

"He's a partner—actually he's not much older than my son—but I control two-thirds of Mancini."

"And my first question . . . ?"

"Even though we won two-thirds of the bay project together, McNamara was at a disadvantage because of the distance they had to truck their concrete. They were losing on every ton because of fuel and labour, in addition to the penalty the government imposes for the environmental costs."

"Did they blame you for that?"

"They saw two Italian-owned companies and called it an Italian conspiracy."

"Who were you speaking to on that call?"

"The owner, Sean McNamara. He's my age; we started out more or less at the same time. Friendly foes—it's a competitive business."

"Do you know who won a job to supply a large amount of concrete to a farm property in Cayuga?"

MacNeice watched his face for any flicker of recognition. He saw none.

"No."

"Did you warn ABC about McNamara, or indicate in any way that McNamara felt resentful about your having an exclusive contract?"

"I did. They had a right to know."

"Did anyone other than yourself know that McNamara was upset?"

"Well, anyone in concrete could guess. But here, other than Pat, only Gianni Moretti knew about the call." Seeing the next question in MacNeice's face, he added, "Gianni's desk is next to Patrizio's. He's the most senior here—he's been here for twenty-one years."

"What was Gianni's relationship with Pat like?"

"I don't understand, Detective."

"How did Gianni feel about Pat coming back to Mancini Concrete and getting a desk right beside his with no experience in the business?"

"Ah, yes, I see. I think Gianni was disappointed, yes, but in me, not Pat."

"Disappointed?"

"He felt I favoured my son over him. Of course, that was true—I did. I asked Gianni to teach him all he knew about the business."

"But that didn't happen."

"No."

"Pat suggested that he found out where I lived because of the gravel that was used for my driveway. Who in this office would know about that?"

"It may have been our gravel, but your contractor would know that better than I."

"My contractor, as I recall, was Menzies Paving and Stone."

"Menzies is our customer, so our order desk would have a record of it."

"Is there one person who collects all the orders from the desk?"

"Gianni."

"One last question: have you ever needed to hire additional security?"

"For what?"

"To protect you or your assets, Mr. Mancini."

"No, not ever."

"We will be bringing down a search warrant to seize your books for the past three years. We'll try our best to minimize the disruption to your business. I trust you understand."

"Well . . . I don't understand at all. Our books are absolutely in order; this is a business built on integrity. But do as you must. When will this happen?"

"Today." MacNeice stood up and held out his hand. Before the old man took it he pressed a button beside his telephone. The door opened and the brother reappeared. "Thank you for taking the time to meet with us, sir. I apologize again for the intrusion."

"Find who did this, Detective."

"I promise you, we'll do our best." MacNeice turned towards the door.

"Goodbye, Mr. Mancini," Vertesi said. "My father and mother would like to pay their respects today."

"By all means. They should come by the house, Michael."

As the brother led them through the office to the front door, MacNeice glanced at Gianni's desk and made a mental note to have it searched. At the door he turned to the brother. "I'm sorry, what is your name?"

"Roberto, Roberto Mancini."

Looking back at the desks, MacNeice asked, "Is your office here as well?"

"No, I'm an accountant; I work uptown. My partnership responsibilities are to oversee the books, advise on financial matters, do the taxes."

"Do you have a card?"

"Yes." He pulled out a silver holder and handed cards to MacNeice and Vertesi.

"So you work closely with Gianni?"

He seemed surprised to hear the name spoken with such familiarity. "Yes, yes," he said. "Gianni Moretti."

"And the records are here and not at your office?"

"Yes, they remain here. I keep duplicates for tax purposes, but the day-to-day paperwork is here."

"Thank you, Mr. Mancini."

Vertesi waited till they were in the car and out of the yard to ask, "What made you decide to go for seizure, boss?"

"At first, only Gianni Moretti. But after that exchange at the door, I've got two reasons: Moretti and Roberto Mancini."

"I don't follow."

"Neither may have been too happy about Pat Mancini coming back and taking the pole position without earning it."

"You think one of them might have tipped off the Irish about ABC coming to a meeting with muscle? His own uncle?"

"That, or someone called ABC and told them about the Jokers and D2D. Also, one of them might have known Pat was coming to speak to me, and tipped off the bikers."

"Pat probably trusted them both, especially his uncle . . ."

"Yes. And because he knew he had no intention of staying in the concrete business, he wouldn't have considered himself a threat to either of them."

"If that's true, it's good that the place is closed till after the funeral."

"Except, if I'm right, Roberto now knows that we're coming to seize the books. I want Gianni's computer seized along with everything in his desk."

Vertesi took out his cell and made the call. "Two cruisers will be there within five minutes."

# 43.

FOLLOWING THE ANNOUNCEMENT of Pat Mancini's death in a fiery unexplained explosion on the bridge, television news reran the Cayuga press conference from the day before. Behind the Deputy Chief on the screen were two coroner's vehicles and a SWAT van; in the distance several figures dressed in black were walking between a farmhouse and a barn. For the cameras the Deputy Chief gave a recap of the history of violence at the farm and mentioned that the Dundurn Police investigation, under the leadership of MacNeice and Swetsky, was straining the resources of both teams of homicide detectives. Then he announced that the investigation had taken "a new turn with the death of gang leader Frédéric Paradis and two fellow members of the Jokers Motorcycle Club from Montreal."

"This seems like the perfect time to do her, Billie."

"You mean, because she and everyone else is distracted by the biker dudes?" Dance said, turning off the television.

"Exactamundo! We could take her at the hotel after a hard day of biker-bashing."

"Hmm . . . I've thought about it. There is a balconey right above hers. We could get into that room and rappel down to her floor."

"Fuckin' A! She'd be our first bed job. Probably doesn't sleep naked, but we'll check out her ya-yas anyway."

"Have to be fast, quiet—not wake up that cop sleeping outside her door. Hotel security's useless. It could be done . . ."

"Let's do it. They'll talk about this one forever."

"They would. On the other hand, we wouldn't get to shove their noses in the shit, would we?"

"I don't follow you, Billie. They've got a cop outside the door; she'll be sleeping. We can leave her opened up and naked on the bed. How sexy cool is that!"

"Very sexy . . . but think about it. They'll blame the cop outside, they'll blame MacNeice for not securing that upper level . . . I want the blame to go much further—I want it to cover this whole fucking trash can of a country. And I want her profile to be bigger. They cancelled that psycho series interview last night—that would have put her on televisions all across Canada. I want her to be a star . . . We can wait till she is."

"So what? We do Narinder Dass?"

"We go underground for a while. Break the schedule and we'll break their certainty there's a schedule we're following."

"The best screw-up for demographics is a broken pattern."

"Precisely. When I unzip her, she'll be our *star*—our name and hers will be linked together forever. Even her parents won't be able to think about her without thinking about us."

"Man, you are the Templar Wizard of Oz."

"I am—and that's spelled A-W-E-S."

# 44.

MacNEICE RECOGNIZED THE black limo parked illegally in the handicapped spot outside Division. He told Vertesi he'd meet him upstairs, then walked over to the mayor's car. The driver got out, smiled briefly and opened the back door.

"Is this a social call, Bob?" he said, climbing in beside him.

The mayor pushed the button to close the tinted glass screen between them and the driver, then said, "I was on my way to a lunch meeting when I took a call from Alberto Mancini—you had just left. What the fuck are you up to?"

"My job, Bob. And you may get a call from ABC and McNamara before the day's out."

"Christ almighty, we're drowning in bodies and fuckin' intrigue when we should be celebrating the boldest initiative in the city's history! When I called you—"

"When you called me, you asked me to keep this quiet. I told you you can't keep homicide quiet, and now—"

"But what the fuck is happening, Mac? Pat Mancini was a local hero, for chrissakes. Who'd wanna blow up that kid?"

"I should be able to answer that question very soon. Tell me the specific problem you want me to solve."

"Mancini's a friend of mine. He's offended by the search and seizure of the company books. Apparently two cruisers showed up right after you left with their lights flashing, blocking the entrance to the yard like it was *Crime Busters* or something."

"I believe someone in Mancini's operation placed the call that resulted in Pat's execution on the bridge. But, if it's any consolation, we're also hitting ABC-Grimsby and McNamara, and hopefully the state police are doing the same at ABC–New York."

"Mac, is all this really necessary?"

MacNeice reached for the door handle. "I'll see you later, Bob."

"Wait, wait. Before you go, as friends, I wanna make something clear—I don't give a rat's ass about McNamara and ABC. D'you know why?"

"They're out of voting range?"

"Exactly. But Mancini has just lost a son and he carries a lot of influence locally. You get my point, Mac?"

"Yes, but it pales next to Pat Mancini's being splattered all over the bridge and feeding carp in the bay while we sit in your limo worrying about votes. So if there's nothing else to say, Bob, let me do my job." He looked over at Maybank, who was still fuming but could only manage to wave MacNeice away, the way one would a wasp at a picnic.

MacNeice stepped away from the limo and watched it loop around the parking lot and onto the street. As he was walking to the door, his cellphone rang. He looked down at the display and saw Harvey Whitman's name.

"You're in luck," Whitman announced. "Highways called back. The summer student who was supposed to shut down the video equipment on the bridge—he forgot. I asked them to isolate the footage leading up to and after 1:30 a.m. It will arrive electronically in the next hour or so."

"Good news. Anything else?"

"Yeah, well . . . The divers went down over an hour ago. The first ones to come up found pieces of the car—only because they were red. So far, no pieces of Pat. Oh yeah, I sent Forensics over to his penthouse, and except for the weed we found, the place was clean. You having any luck?"

"Well, I'm pissing people off."

Whitman laughed. "Always a good sign, Mac."

Williams was fuming about a call he'd received from his Buffalo Homicide contact: the state troopers had been forced to release the Old Soldiers and lift the lockdown on the roadhouse. The judge basically told the district attorney to come back when he had evidence that crimes had been committed in the state of New York, and to let other jurisidictions—meaning Dundurn, Canada—know they should do the same.

"I'm not surprised, Montile," MacNeice said as he took off his jacket and sat down to look at the whiteboard. "We've got to produce the evidence and present Wenzel as a witness. But sitting in jail here for a while should at least cool out the club. They know we're watching."

More positive was the second interview with Langlois. When he wouldn't say anything more about his colleagues, Aziz finally told him about the death of Pat Mancini. Langlois dropped his arms, moved his chair in closer and put both hands on the table as if playing a major chord. It turned out that Langlois knew about Pat's appetite for Ukrainian girls, and he seemed surprised that the detectives didn't know the girls weren't just for Pat. He was the one who shepherded the girls from Montreal to Dundurn. On four occasions when he arrived with them at the penthouse from the train station, it wasn't Pat who opened the door but another man, whom Pat introduced as his Uncle Roberto. The girls would stay the night or—twice—the whole weekend. Langlois would show up early in the morning on Monday to take them back to the station.

"Right. Williams, pick up Roberto Mancini for questioning. If he isn't at Mancini Concrete, you'll likely find him at the family home."

MacNeice turned to Vertesi. "Can you organize an interview and a lunchtime raid for the books at McNamara?"

"The officers are ready to go when we are, so I'm on my way." He swung around to call the Waterdown detachment of the Ontario Provincial Police, who would supervise the operation.

Taking the business card out of his pocket, MacNeice turned to Aziz. "I want the forensic accounting team to retrieve the financial records for Mancini Concrete, on file at Mancini Group Financial, 1 James Street South, Suite 1200."

"I can do that," Aziz said, picking up the phone.

As Williams stood up to leave, the tinny refrain of Ravel's *Bolero* broke the tension in the cubicle. "Shit! Sorry, boss, I haven't had time to change it . . ." He stepped out into the corridor to take the call.

"Ryan, there's some footage from the bridge coming in to my computer. Can you open it up for me, please."

"Yessir." Ryan rolled his chair over to MacNeice's desk. Within a minute he said, "Yup, here it is. I'll send it to the Falcon and have it up in no time."

Williams came back smiling—it had been his new best friend Demetrius Johnson on the phone. Johnson had met with Vanucci's landlord. When the big man vanished, the landlord had waited three months before emptying the house for a new tenant. Since the place was rented furnished, that meant clothing, personal effects, his computer and office files. They were all in a Sekurit container and the landlord was more than happy to hand over the contents, as it was costing him money every month to keep them. Williams had arranged to meet Johnson on the American side of the border, at Martin's Real Italian Restaurant, to be briefed and get copies of any paperwork that might prove useful to them.

"When does he want you there?"

"Tonight at six."

MacNeice gave the okay and said he'd square it with Wallace. Then he added *Roberto Mancini* and *Gianni Moretti* to the whiteboard lists.

Ryan swivelled about. "Okay, sir, black-and-white overhead footage from the Sky-High."

"You know what we're looking for. I want to know about any cars behind Mancini's Corvette. Make it as clear as possible."

"It makes my job easier that they've got a time code on the bottom. Give me five." Ryan pushed the joystick forward, watching the numbers tumble through time.

Aziz pressed the hold button and turned around. "When do you want to hit their offices?"

"Within the next two hours, or sooner."

She turned and relayed the message. When she hung up, she said, "Check this out. While I was waiting on the phone I googled Roberto Mancini." MacNeice rolled his chair next to hers. On the screen were several photos of Roberto and his wife, Angela, as well as their two kids. "One big happy family."

"Not for long," MacNeice said. "It's going to get ugly. Roberto was sharing the women, and he probably provided the lion's share of the tips. Pat didn't know enough about the business ever to fake it—I think he was just the messenger. Roberto knew Pat wouldn't betray him, and he didn't. Even when Pat was telling me everything, he was still protecting his favourite uncle."

"Still, it's hard to believe he'd be that foolish. Look at his wife—she's beautiful, and the kids are adorable. He's close with his brother by the sounds of it. Do you think he knew they would kill Pat?"

"Can I be brutally unsentimental?"

Aziz nodded at him.

"With Pat out of the way, Roberto becomes the logical heir when Alberto retires; he already owns one-third of the business. And with Pat gone, he doesn't have to worry about his nephew eventually taking over a business he has no talent for or interest in, putting Roberto's one-third share in jeopardy."

Before Aziz could respond, Ryan swung around. "This is seriously nasty stuff. Brace yourselves." He waited for them to slide in beside him. "Okay, check the time on the bottom of the screen. I'm paused at 1:28:24 and the image takes in about two hundred yards, judging by the stripes on the road. The Corvette will appear in the speed lane here"—he pointed to the left side of the large monitor—"in about one-tenth of a second. I've slowed everything down so you can make sense of it. In real time, it's just a blur—that car was off-the-charts fast. Ready?"

"Ready." MacNeice watched as the Corvette entered the frame. Even in slow motion the front end of the car was blurred, as if it was pushing the speed of light. At mid-frame an elliptical flash grew until it filled the whole screen. "My God," MacNeice said.

"It's not over, sir."

The strong prevailing wind blew ragged holes through the cloud of smoke and fire as another car appeared at the top right of the frame. "I'll pause it here for a second. Judging by its speed as that second car enters the frame, it was locked on to the Corvette, maybe a hundred yards behind." The car was three lanes away from the Corvette. "But watch." Ryan released the image and the second car slid down towards the bottom of the frame, where he paused it again. "It maintains speed. He doesn't even slow down to see the damage. If the Corvette is red, then this car—it's a 2011 Mustang—was dark grey, blue or black." He released the image, the smoke cleared and the fire scattered into several sites of burning debris.

"Is there any way you can enhance that second car?" MacNeice asked, pushing his chair away.

"They're using great technology, and the lights on the bridge don't over-illuminate the objects . . . I'll give it a shot."

Sergeant Ray Ryu of the Commercial Investigations Branch met Vertesi at the door of the OPP detachment in Waterdown. Three white SUVs sat idling in front, five cops in each.

Vertesi and Ryu shook hands and Ryu said, "You'll come in my car. You can tell me what you know on the way over. It's an eight-minute drive."

"You work out of Waterdown?"

"Toronto, but my wife and I live here. She's a teacher at one of the local high schools."

Vertesi looked out the back window of the unmarked car and wondered what impact the parade of white SUVs, cruising quietly through town with cherry lights on their hoods and headlights flashing, would have on the quiet streets of Waterdown. "Not exactly discreet," he said.

"Taxpayers gotta have their show, Detective."

Vertesi was just wrapping up an abbreviated overview of the case as Ryu pulled over at the gate to McNamara's yard. The SUVs filed through one by one, parking like horses in front of a saloon. He liked the style but wondered how effective it was when several men came out of the concrete-block structure and stood with their hands on their hips, laughing at the whole affair.

"This shit always happens. It's gonna go like this till it flips over. Our guys are bigger than theirs, and they got guns and know how to use 'em. We'll stay in the car for a while. Enjoy the show . . ."

As the police marched in carrying stacks of flattened banker's boxes, the energy of those standing outside sagged, and one after the other they followed them inside.

"See what I mean—the flipover?"

"Yep."

"I remember you from last year, Vertesi. You took some buckshot out by the lake—"

"That was me. My claim to fame."

Neither of them looked at the other as they spoke, their eyes glued to the aluminum storm door of the building.

Soon a young female officer stepped out and waved briefly in their direction. "That's our cue. I'll let you take the lead on this— you okay with that?"

"I'm okay."

Sean McNamara, a pug of a man, sat behind an ancient oak desk. The trappings of his office revealed the differences between him and Alberto Mancini. He'd mounted a large stuffed fish over the window that looked out on the working side of the concrete business, and on the walls were several framed colour photos of cement trucks with the McNamara logo—a shamrock—emblazoned on their sides. The floor was covered with indoor-outdoor carpet worn to a dull grey-green, the path to the desk trodden down to its black nylon roots. Vertesi could feel the plywood subfloor give way with every step. There were stacking chairs for the guests and an old overstuffed leatherette office chair for McNamara. He had an ashtray with several cigars butts in it and was sucking on another as they approached the desk. If he was upset, he didn't show it.

"You two the heavies?"

"I'm Sergeant Ray Ryu of the OPP Commercial Investigations Branch, and this is Detective Inspector Michael Vertesi, of Dundurn Homicide."

"A little off your beat, ain't it?"

"A little, yes," Vertesi said.

"So what can I do for you?"

"We're investigating the deaths of several people linked to the concrete business. The investigation has led us to your firm."

"Bullshit."

"Well, I'll take that comment for what it's worth."

"Ya mean you'll take my comment as meanin' fuck all."

"You said it. Sir, we're aware that you knew of the exclusive arrangement between Mancini Concrete of Dundurn and ABC-Grimsby to supply the mayor's waterfront project."

"So?"

"We understand that you placed a call to Alberto Mancini and alleged a conspiracy between Mancini and ABC. Is that correct?"

McNamara stood up, looked out the window at the squat grey towers and dusty sheds of his business, and took a long drag on the cigar. Exhaling, he pointed the stogie to the concrete works beyond. "I built this—me. I din't have any family to support me. Just me."

"I don't follow you, sir." Vertesi said, though he knew exactly where McNamara was going.

"I employ ninety-four people in this town. I've earned my success. They'd spit in your eye if they knew what you was up to here, ya know that?"

"I'm concerned about only one individual at the moment, sir—yourself."

McNamara smiled and took two more puffs as he continued to admire the view from his window. He rocked back and forth, toe to heel, heel to toe. Then he turned and sat down again. Vertesi thought he was going to go whole hog and put his feet up on the desk, but he didn't. Instead he rolled his chair in close, leaning on his elbows on the desk, the cigar in the centre of his mouth. He kept puffing leisurely, the smoke escaping on either side. It was all

Vertesi could do not to laugh. After a few more puffs, he took the cigar out of his mouth, picked a bit of tobacco from his lip and flicked it onto the floor.

When he looked up and noticed they were both smiling, he said, "You think I'm funny? Let's see . . . a chink cop and a wop cop. You think you scare me? You have no fuckin' idea, the two of you." He swung his chair around and glanced back to the yard, where his business was continuing as usual. "Take the fuckin' computers—they're a pain in the ass anyways. Computers mean shit to concrete, and to me, you stupid fucks."

"Forgive me, Mr. McNamara," Vertesi said, "but you're acting as if you just got called by central casting to play the part of a tough Irishman. But I know you were born here, just like me and Ray. So are you ready to have a serious discussion?"

"Fuck you, dago."

"We can do this somewhere else . . . you do understand that, sir?" Ryu said. "And just so you're fully aware, we didn't come here to charge you with hate crimes, but I'll be more than happy to do so if you continue with these slurs."

"Oh, yeah, sure." McNamara let out a hoarse howl of laughter and stared at Vertesi for several seconds, tipping his head this way and that as if confronted by an exotic animal. "I was born in forty-three. That date mean anything to you, Vertesi?"

"No, should it?"

"My dad landed with the Allies in Sicily that year, about a month after I was born."

"Your point is?"

"When I was old enough, I asks him, I says"—McNamara leaned into the desk again, stabbing the air with his cigar—"'What was it like to invade Italy, Dad?' An' ya know what he says?"

"Haven't a clue."

"He said, 'It was all flies, fleas and fuckin' Eyeties.' Ain't that great? Flies, fleas and fuckin' Eyeties." McNamara laughed so hard he rocked back and forth in his chair.

Vertesi wanted to shove the cigar down his throat, but he'd learned a lot from getting shot—basically that he needed to control his temper when this very button was pressed. He let the moment pass, watching McNamara settle down and take another long puff on his cigar before he said, "My grandfather was there too, and he tells a somewhat different story. He said that your dad and all the rest of them pissed their way through the streets, shit in the alleys and churches and tried to fuck every Italian girl they came across. Funny isn't it, Mr. McNamara—you and your dad were both born in Canada, not Belfast, but here you are, smoking that shit-ass cigar and pretending you're playing an Irish gangster like James Cagney."

McNamara was caught mid-inhale. He started coughing, then laughed so much he had to stand up to keep from spewing out whatever smoky sludge lined his windpipe. When he'd pulled himself together, he pulled up his trousers and smiled, this time genuinely, across the table. "Kid, I like your style. Cagney, is it? Why, I never . . . That's the tops!" He laughed again, the way he might do with his grandkids—God forbid the man had grandkids! Vertesi thought.

"Okay, let's talk about what you two are here to do to my modest little enterprise in the heart of lovely Waterdown." He ground out the cigar in the ashtray, where it stood smouldering among the others—a tiny stogie Stonehenge.

"For starters," Vertesi said, "did you hire the Damned Two Deuces Motorcycle Club and their Quebec partners, the Jokers, to represent you at the negotiations in Grimsby with ABC?"

"Yes, sir. Next question." McNamara nodded and adjusted his shoulders, keen to get on with the game.

"Why?"

"Because I was told ABC had no intention of doing an honest deal with me and they were bringing in some gang from New York to kick my Irish—my Irish-*Canadian*—ass."

"Who told you that?"

"This ain't gonna be pretty, Detective Vertesi."

"I'm not here for pretty."

He laughed again. "You sure as shit aren't. Okay, I got a call from Roberto Mancini."

"Seriously?"

"Fuckin' A—seriously. It was a 'thought you should know' conversation. He says I should speak to D2D. I didn't know what Mancini was up to, but I sure as shit wasn't going to Grimsby to get beat up."

"How much did you pay D2D?"

"First of all, turns out I wasn't dealing with D2D. Oh, they was here, but it was that swaggering little French fucker Freddy Paradis, who just got shot, who did the deal—with this huge piece of shit who came with him—I guess to impress me."

"How much?"

"I gave him seventy-five hundred, with a promise to double it if the problem"—he waved his meaty hand in circles—"went away. And it did, so I coughed up the second seventy-five. That was it. End of story."

"Till the news yesterday."

"Yeah. I never bin the shiniest penny in the purse, but I didn't know shit about those killings till yesterday. I had a problem, I paid to have it taken away, and it was end of story."

"You heard what happened to Pat Mancini?"

"Sure. Look, I liked that kid. I rooted for him as a player, I surely fuckin' did. But he didn't know squat about this business, likely never would . . . Still, I don't know why he was lit up top a the fuckin' bridge. You don't get much higher than that around

Dundurn. We sent a huge bouquet to the family. I got nothing against 'em really—Eyeties, I mean. And earlier, wit' you . . . shit, Eyetalians 'n' Irish got more in common than startin' with an I. Am I right?"

"Can't think of what that would be, Mr. McNamara, other than knowing what being occupied by foreign troops is like. Nope. The food, wine, women, art, history, contributions to the world—they all tip in Italy's favour, I'm afraid." Vertesi wasn't smiling, and McNamara studied his face, waiting for some indication of intent. Vertesi didn't give him one.

"Christ, you're a cocky fucker. But when you climb down from yer golden chariot, Ben-fuckin'-Hur, maybe you'll explain Sylvio Berlusconi to me."

Vertesi smiled at last. "I take your point."

"If you two have finished with your Old World one-upmanship, we've got an investigation to wrap up." Ryu stood up and buttoned his suit.

"Last question," Vertesi said. "The biker farm in Cayuga had a long concrete underground tunnel that ran out to the woods. Are we going to find the invoice for that on your books?"

"Wasn't us. Look, you take the shit you need, boys—I'm not worried. If what you wanted to know about was D2D and the Jokers, I've already given it to ya." McNamara stood up and shook Ryu's hand. As they walked the beaten indoor-outdoor path to the door, he put his hand on Vertesi's shoulder and said, "I like ya, kid, honest ta shit I do." And, in his best Cagney voice, he added, "Good luck wit yer investigation, eh?" They shook hands, and Vertesi and Ryu headed for the front door.

"Elvis is leaving the building," Ryu said to the receptionist. The SUVs were being loaded and the staff were outside again, watching the show. "Come on, we're outta here."

In the car Ryu asked, "So, did you get what you came for?"

"Yes, I did. And I was surprised when he turned around just like *that*"—Vertesi snapped his fingers—"I actually liked the second version of McNamara."

"I'm sure he doesn't get called on his shit every day. It was a bit tense there for a while."

"Yeah, the old country comes to the new country carrying all that failed shit that made them leave the old country in the first place—and hands it down through the generations."

"Tell me about it. What was all that Cagney stuff about?" Ryu asked as he drove out of the yard.

"You don't know James Cagney?"

"No."

"No, I guess most people these days don't. Well, in the thirties and forties James Cagney, a cocky little Irish-American actor, played a cocky little Irish gangster. My pop loved to watch those old movies on weekends; it was a great break from always seeing Italians as the thugs and crooks."

"So McNamara was doing Cagney?"

"Yes, but so can I, and so can my dad."

Ryu pulled into the detachment parking space they'd left earlier and said, "We'll keep this team together, do the forensics and hopefully have a report for you within a week." Vertesi nodded his thanks and got out of the car.

Leaving Waterdown, Vertesi cut south on Plains Road so he could drive over the Sky-High Bridge—he wanted to see where Pat Mancini had died. Both sides were already open, though the damaged lane appeared to be closed for resurfacing.

The sad thing, he thought, was that no one would be able to lay wreaths or leave photographs or trading cards or tear-stained messages where he died. But Vertesi knew he'd never cross the bridge again without thinking about Pat Mancini lighting up the night sky.

# 45.

LOOKING THROUGH THE sidelight of the interview room, MacNeice saw Roberto Mancini pacing back and forth in his black suit and armband. Williams sat like someone watching a tennis match he wasn't all that interested in.

"Montile's silence must be unnerving for Mancini," Aziz said.

"If we had the time, I'd let it go on for another half-hour—but we don't. Ready?"

"As ever."

"We're not going to have him alone for long. Pat's father probably has counsel on the way here."

As MacNeice and Aziz came in, Williams stood up and Roberto stopped pacing. Aziz held the door for Williams. He left without speaking but winked as he passed her. Aziz winked back at him before stepping into the room.

"Have a seat, Mr. Mancini." MacNeice pulled out a chair and sat down, as did Aziz.

"I'd rather stand." He began pacing again.

"Mr. Mancini, that wasn't a request. Sit down now."

Mancini looked at them, attempting to gather his dignity, then did as he was told. He crossed his arms, but MacNeice noticed that his left leg was moving furiously up and down. He spoke without looking at either of them, his eyes fixed on the fake wood grain of the table. "This is an outrage. I will have legal representation here shortly, and until then I will not say another word."

"As you wish, but I have a lot to say to you. With me is Detective Inspector Fiza Aziz, who is also a doctor of criminology."

Mancini looked at her briefly, then returned to his fascination with the table.

"Roberto, I suspect you know why you were brought in today, but you likely don't know that we're here to help you." The man's foot stopped bouncing for a moment. "Your relationship with your nephew, as we understand it, was very close. You were, of course, of a similar age—what, five years apart?"

Mancini did not respond, just ran a finger along the table's fake grain.

"I'm sure that Pat's taking on the role of an executive at Mancini Concrete made his dad happy, but I'm curious to know how you felt about that."

Roberto withdrew his hand and smiled weakly in MacNeice's direction. Shifting in his chair, he faced the door as if expecting to see his lawyer appear.

"Aziz googled you earlier, Roberto—you have a beautiful wife and family. You have every reason to be proud of them."

"I am." He smiled at Aziz and looked back to the door.

"You see how easy that was, Roberto. I'll be more specific: we are actually trying to protect you."

"I am a respected member of the community," Mancini said. "I don't require your protection—but you may shortly require your own."

"If you'd been watching the news as Pat was, you'd know that you and your family are in very real peril." Mancini crossed his arms but didn't turn away from the door.

MacNeice was prepared to wait until he responded. After thirty seconds of silence, Mancini shot a look his way—he was clearly waiting to hear what came next.

"Roberto, do you speak Ukrainian?"

The blood ran out of the young man's face. He closed his eyes and took a deep breath.

"I want to assure you that our interest is not in the nights you spent at Pat's with two Ukrainian dancers but in the price you paid for that pleasure. As a respected member of the community, what you do in the privacy of someone else's bedroom is not our concern."

Mancini's eyes flooded and tremors shook his body, but he made no sound.

"You see, Pat believed that he could enjoy the carnal delights of these women by simply trading—or inventing—information to serve the purposes of those who were supplying the women."

Mancini stood up and looked through the sidelight for help, then started pacing again.

"Sit down, please. We won't be long."

Roberto loosened his black silk tie and sank into the chair.

"Are you sure you don't want to say something?" MacNeice asked.

Mancini leaned forward and put both forearms on the table, but he didn't speak.

"I'll continue, then. When the Jokers MC entered the picture in Dundurn, the game changed for Damned Two Deuces—stop me if you know all this—"

Mancini stared down at the table again; his shoulders were vibrating because both his feet were bouncing.

"Pat was trading mostly bogus information for sex—he died for it. What were you trading? Your financials and your computer are being seized as we speak, Roberto, and while the specifics may not appear on the books, are you sure there isn't some correspondence buried deep in the hard drive of your computer?"

Mancini slapped the table and shot a look to the door just as a face MacNeice didn't recognize appeared. There was a knock and the door opened.

The lawyer was wearing a three-piece grey suit and carrying a thin alligator-skin briefcase, which he laid on the table in front of him. "I'm Jacob Goldman. I've been retained to represent Mr. Mancini, and I request that no further questions be asked without my presence and consent. I will instruct my client which questions he will answer—have I made myself clear?"

Aziz and MacNeice stood up and offered their hands. Goldman gave them both a brief handshake and moved to sit down beside his client. "Take your briefcase off the table," MacNeice said, and remained standing. Goldman looked at him, confused, but seeing that MacNeice was serious, he shook his head and removed the case.

"Shall I review our conversation so far for Mr. Goldman's benefit, Roberto?" He waited for a response but could see that Mancini's face was frozen. Again he chose to wait him out.

Goldman looked at his client, then at MacNeice and Aziz. Uncertain what the issue could be, he said, "Yes, Detective Superintendent, please review everything you've discussed with my client."

"No." One word, spoken softly. When Roberto Mancini looked up at MacNeice, he was weeping, tears dropping onto his pristine white shirt. "Jacob, I don't need you, not at the moment. I'm sorry for the inconvience—"

"Roberto, don't be foolish! I don't know what's been going on here, but I can assure you, it will cease immediately."

"No. Please go. I'll call you." Roberto didn't look at his lawyer, letting the tears fall as he focused on MacNeice.

"Detectives, I need a few moments alone with my client, please," Goldman insisted.

"No, Jacob, I'm telling you to leave."

"If there has been any coercion in this," Goldman said, picking up his briefcase, "I can promise you that I'll sue both of you personally, and the Dundurn police force." He opened the door, looked back and shook his head again for emphasis before walking away.

Roberto waited for the door to close, then said, "Go on . . ."

"Before I do, I must tell you that this conversation will be recorded and that I have to question the wisdom of your dismissing counsel."

"Your question is duly noted," Mancini said.

"As you wish. Our witness, a member of the Jokers, has given us an idea of what you paid in return for the dancers, but we'd like to hear it from you."

"Is there any way, any way at all . . ." Mancini had started to cry in earnest. Aziz retrieved the box of tissues and placed it in front of him. He took several, wiped his face and blew his nose. "My family—do they have to know about this?"

MacNeice said, "We need to know the extent of your involvement, Roberto—all of it—before we can determine what, if anything, can be kept quiet."

Aziz spoke for the first time. "Judging by the images we saw online, you have a family that would hopefully stand by you . . . if you were completely honest in your efforts to assist this investigation."

"May I have some water?"

"Of course." MacNeice left the room and walked down the hall to the servery, where he filled a large paper cup from the cooler. He was about to return when his phone rang. He lifted it to his ear.

"It's me, boss. I'm just about to leave for Buffalo. Demetrius is just finishing the Vanucci boxes now. They've also downloaded what was on Luigi's computer."

"This is perfect, Montile. It means we don't have to attempt a search and seizure of ABC's American offices."

"He told me not to come in a company car, so I went home and got my passport and the Grey Sickness."

"The Grey Sickness . . . Oh, your BMW?"

"Yeah, she looks tired but runs like a teenager. How's it going with Mr. Smoothie?"

"He's dismissed his counsel; I think he wants to cooperate."

"That's the ticket. Good luck, boss—I feel like we're closing in on something."

Through the interview room sidelight, MacNeice could see that Roberto's head was buried in his arms on the table and Aziz's hand was on his forearm. She was saying something to him. MacNeice waited till she sat back again before opening the door.

"Here you are."

Mancini took the cup, drank half of it, wiped his face again and dropped the tissues in the wastebasket Aziz had placed beside him. "Pat and I were like brothers, did you know that?" He wasn't expecting a response and spoke before any could be offered. "We grew up together, we played hockey as kids . . . I went on to study business and accounting in university. Pat was so much better than I was in sports; it made sense for me to get a career."

"When did you learn about the girls and the deal he'd made to get them?"

"He invited me over to the penthouse. I thought he wanted to watch a playoff game."

"And they were already there?"

"Yeah, the first time. I had five nights with them that year. Then we slowed it down, mostly because the economy tanked and we couldn't invent anything believable to trade with. But once the mayor's project on the bay got going, we were back in business."

"What did you tell your wife?" Aziz asked.

"I had—I mean, I have to travel on business. Not the concrete business, but financial clients I have in Winnipeg and Thunder Bay."

"Did he tell you what the price was that first night?"

"No, he told me after they left. I was still in bed, so the guy who picked them up assumed Pat had had a two-on-one."

"And when he told you?"

"Well, Pat . . . He told me the story of Frédéric, the pot and the girls and the Mafia stuff."

"How did that sound to you?"

"Well, first I was scared shitless. I would have paid for the sex, but Pat was like all gung-ho. I said, 'Pat, you're living in a penthouse in Burlington and I'm a fucking accountant in Dundurn. We don't know squat about the Mafia.' And he goes, 'Well, ye-ah, but these frogs don't know that! They think, *Italians and concrete— gotta be the Mafia.*' Then he smiled and said, 'There'll be two new girls here next Thursday.'"

"When did he introduce you to Frédéric?"

"That Thursday. He was waiting for me at Pat's. I thought for sure he was going to spot me as a fake, but, I don't know, maybe it was the language thing . . . Anyway, I just started telling him about some of the deals we'd done at Mancini Concrete, and he was, like, smiling and shit. Then he shakes my hand and says we have a contract and asks if I want anything to sweeten it, like dope or coke. I said no. A half-hour later the girls arrived with another biker."

"How did you provide the information?" Aziz asked.

"Mostly by phone but sometimes by email. Frédéric wanted me to open a Facebook account and use Skype to stay in touch with him."

"Did you?" Aziz asked.

"No, I told him that I'm not very computer savvy. It was all . . . too easy."

"So we know Pat's father told ABC about McNamara being angry about the exclusive contract they'd given Mancini Concrete."

"Yeah, I heard about that." He emptied the water cup and held it gently in both hands.

"Did you tell McNamara that ABC was bringing muscle to the meeting at the quarry?"

"Yes."

"Why?"

"Well, to me it was a game, though the reward was real. I told McNamara that ABC was bringing in a private security team from New York and Pat told ABC that McNamara was showing up with a motorcycle gang."

"And you never considered the consequences?" Aziz asked, somewhat incredulously.

"We knew as much about motorcycle gangs as we did about the Mafia. I think we thought there might be a brawl or a standoff but it wouldn't come back to us. To Frédéric it looked like a good paying gig, a chance to collect on some of what we owed him."

"Did you know anything about what happened when Frédéric's men arrived at ABC-Grimsby?" MacNeice asked.

"No, we just supplied the information and didn't know what he did with it. Then, when the deputy chief did that press conference, Pat freaked. He called me and asked what the fuck we were going to do.'"

"You weren't frightened or concerned?"

"When I heard that Frédéric and that huge fucker—sorry, Detective"—Aziz waved her hand dismissively—"when I heard that both of them were killed in Cayuga, I thought the worst of it was that we wouldn't get the girls anymore. And that was okay too, because I wasn't doing a great job covering it at home . . ."

"Did Pat tell you about Frédéric's brother?"

"Yeah, but I didn't know whether he knew anything about Pat and me."

"Did anyone else know about you and Pat and the bikers?"

"Not specifically, no."

"Plain English, please—who knew what about your deal?"

"Gianni probably put the pieces together. He sits next to Pat."

"Did you speak to Gianni about it?"

"No, not exactly."

"Again, in plain English, what did you tell Gianni?"

Mancini swallowed hard. "I told him Pat had a little action on the side with D2D—getting paid by getting laid."

"But you didn't mention your involvement," Aziz said.

"No, I couldn't afford to. Pat was single—no one minded if he screwed around . . ."

"Did you give Pat my home address?"

"No, Gianni did. You have a gravel driveway; we supplied the gravel. Gianni called me and said Pat went looking for you."

"And you called D2D and told them."

"No, no, no—I wouldn't do that. Pat's like a brother to me!"

"Then . . . ?"

"Gianni was the only one who knew about the biker deal."

"Unless he told someone in turn . . ." Aziz offered.

"He wouldn't. He didn't get where he is by shooting off his mouth. He wouldn't."

"Maybe not to you, but would he do that to Pat?"

Mancini looked down at the paper cup, twirled it nervously and began weeping again. He looked up to both of them and tried to speak but couldn't. He pushed the cup aside and covered his face.

"This seems like the right time for a break. I'll make the espresso." MacNeice stood up.

"No, let me." Aziz stood up and picked up the paper cup. "And I'll get a refill."

For several seconds after she left, neither man said anything. Mancini kept his eyes averted from MacNeice, who sensed there was something else he wasn't saying. He could see that right leg bouncing again. When Aziz returned with a tray of coffee and water for all three, Mancini appeared relieved by the distraction and sipped eagerly. MacNeice reached over and touched Aziz's thigh under the table. She looked casually in his direction and he nodded slowly towards Mancini, who was now swirling the crema in almost empty cup. When he had drunk it down, he looked up at MacNeice.

"What is it, Roberto?" MacNeice hadn't touched his coffee.

"Sorry?"

"What is it you're not saying?"

Mancini pushed his empty cup aside and drank some water. He looked at both of them in turn. "Gianni asked me what he should do with the information."

"What information?"

"That Pat had gone looking for you."

"And you said?"

"I—I told him to call D2D. The local guys were still around, living in a house in Aldershot."

"You gave him the number."

"Yes."

"So you didn't call them yourself but you told Gianni to. Did you consider what the outcome of that might be, Roberto?"

"No . . . well, yes. I thought they'd rough Pat up, scare him, you know. He needed it. He didn't have that much to lose, but I sure as hell did. He needed to settle down till this blew over . . . I thought they'd just scare him."

MacNeice said flatly, "You thought Pat was an immature kid who just needed a good beating. You thought he was naïve."

Mancini was sobbing openly. Moving his hand to wipe his face, he spilled the water. He tried to mop it up with the tissues, and when that proved insufficient, he put the sleeve of his fine suit in the puddle and swirled it around till the cloth was wet and the table was dry. "Pat was always spoiled, you know," he finally managed to say. "He was beautiful, a gifted athlete, smart and funny—but he had no street sense. None!" Anger flashed across his face. "That's why his game was cut short, you know. He thought it was all about putting the puck in the net, not watching out for who was gunning for your head."

"I think you were both naïve," MacNeice said. He drank his shot of espresso and slid the cup aside.

"Yeah . . . maybe. Yeah, I guess so. This was a game too."

Aziz's question was direct. "Just for clarification, Roberto—if they had beat up Pat, do you think his head could have survived another concussion?"

His eyes widened as he looked at her. It was clear he hadn't considered the consequences of a severe beating for a young man who had had to quit the sport he loved because of damage to his brain. "I . . . didn't think. No . . . look, I just didn't think. Pat was panicking, talking about coming clean. I told him that was easy for him to say but that I was the one with all the risk—my business, my family . . . I know you'll think it's wrong, but . . . my reputation."

"The time to consider all those things was the first time you showed up at Pat's penthouse," MacNeice said slowly.

It seemed as if the full weight of his actions had just hit him. Roberto covered his face again and sobbed for two or three minutes, gasping because he was crying so hard.

When he finally calmed down, MacNeice spoke. "I can imagine how difficult this has been for you. We have only a few more questions."

"Were you jealous that Pat was asked to take an executive position at Mancini Concrete?" Aziz asked.

"Jealous? Oh, I see—because I own one-third and my brother two-thirds."

"And when he stepped down, you'd still only have one-third but Pat would have two."

"No. Half the time I don't feel I deserve the third I have. No, I wanted Pat to win . . . I always wanted him to win."

"Didn't he tell you he had no interest in concrete?" Aziz asked.

"Sure. But he didn't have to tell me—it was obvious."

"So . . . ?"

"My brother Alberto is brilliant; he knows what he's doing. Gianni could have taught Pat. It's a good business and it's not like he was trained for anything else. That was the idea, and, I think, once Pat grew up a little more, he'd get into it."

"Once he was finished sowing the wild oats you never had a chance to," Aziz said.

"Yeah . . . well, yeah." Mancini hadn't missed the biting irony.

"And Gianni Moretti—was he thrilled to be the tutor of a reluctant pupil?" MacNeice asked.

"Not exactly. Pat was a joke to all the guys in the office, but the Mancinis have been good to them. Gianni was the right guy to teach him. Once he did, Pat and I would have been unstoppable building that business together. He had the charisma and I have the money sense."

"Might Gianni have allowed himself to believe—if only from his years of service—that he would be the right person to assume a leadership role?"

Mancini seemed surprised to be asked the question. "He's not family. He'll always have a great job there, but this is about family."

"What number did Gianni call?" Aziz asked.

He fiddled with his phone and then handed it to Aziz, who wrote down the number before handing it back to him. The moment Roberto touched it, the phone rang.

"Don't take that call," MacNeice said, and Roberto, who didn't appear keen to anyway, turned the phone off.

"What's going to happen to me now?"

"It's a good question, Roberto. Your actions have caused the death of your nephew, disgraced your family and betrayed your brother's trust in you."

Mancini flinched and blinked several times.

"The question of charges, however, is a little more complex. You and Pat ignited a tragedy that has destroyed the lives of several individuals, both American and Canadian, and not all of them were violent gang members. As an accessory, you are culpable in all of those deaths."

"I understand . . ." he said, his voice betraying fear.

"Roberto, we both respect your decision to dismiss your counsel and speak openly." MacNeice glanced over to Aziz, who nodded slowly in agreement. "But I encourage you now to call your lawyer and your family—and no one else."

"And the media? What will you say?"

"The answer to that, and the charges that may arise as a result of your statement, will come from the Crown Attorney. For now, neither of us will be saying anything to the media."

MacNeice stood up heavily, thinking of the real victims—Gary Hughes, Luigi Vanucci, Sue-Ellen Hughes and her children. Even Pat Mancini.

"What should I do now?" Roberto was weeping again, but this time he just let the tears fall. MacNeice watched them splash on the table and let Aziz answer for him.

"For now, Roberto, just let this interview sink in. If you accept the extent of human suffering you've contributed to, then you'll find, I hope, some way to take responsibility for what has been done to your family, your nephew, your brother's family, and the others whose lives have been ruined. You are not a victim in this tale, so don't allow yourself the luxury of thinking that you are."

He was wiping his eyes with his shirt cuff, trying to say something. They both stood silent, waiting. Mancini shook his head a few times, coughed and at last got it out. "I'm so, so profoundly sorry for all of this. . . . I know something else too—I could have stopped Pat, that first night. I could have. He looked up to me, thought I was where he was not." He wiped his face and blew his nose with the last of the tissues. "I didn't, because it was just . . . just . . . so wild!" He shook his head. "And I wanted to have that too, you know, to be a wild boy like Pat . . . just once."

MacNeice offered his hand. "Thank you for your honesty. If you're smart, you'll take Detective Aziz's words to heart." They shook hands and MacNeice left.

The door opened again and a uniform appeared. Aziz waited while Roberto pulled himself together, then followed the two down the hall to the elevator. Mancini stepped in and turned to face her. Maybe it was the steely blue lighting, or perhaps it was just the end of a gruelling afternoon, but he looked decades older. The elevator doors closed and Aziz stood for a moment, watching the sliver of light between the doors descend, before walking slowly back to the cubicles.

# 46.

"**R**YAN, YOU'VE BEEN a bit neglected in all this," MacNeice said, sagging wearily into his chair.

The young man looked over his shoulder and smiled. "I do have something that just came in from Forensics on the Dance case." Ryan opened a file on his computer and a scan appeared of one of the pieces of mail left at the Dance residence. He tapped the keyboard and the envelope filled the screen.

"What is it?"

"Addressed to William Dance, Senior, and it's dated"—with his cursor he circled the postal cancellation—"last November 14. It's from Chedoke Health Centre—you know, the private health centre where executives go for exams and treatment. So I called Chedoke and asked for the head of the accounts department. And I said—sorry, sir—that I was a detective working on a case involving the Dance family."

"That kind of thing could end up costing you your job, Ryan."

"I realize that, sir. That's why I said my name was Detective

Inspector Michael Vertesi." Reading MacNeice's smile correctly as approval, he cut to the chase. "In the end they sent me—or rather, Vertesi—two documents, sir."

Ryan clicked the keyboard again and was suddenly in Vertesi's email. "The first is a letter from Charles Pepper, the CEO of Chedoke Health Centre, and the second is a copy of an invoice for magnetic resonance imaging scans of Dance's chest and stomach. The MRI bill is $7,074.21, and it has a bold line of type indicating that Mr. Dance's next series of scans would be in April—long after he died."

"Must have been serious if he wasn't willing to wait in line with the public for his MRI. And the letter?"

Ryan opened the letter onscreen and enlarged a paragraph so MacNeice could easily read it:

*Bill, it is with a heavy heart that I write this note to you, both as an old friend and former colleague and in my capacity as Director of Chedoke Health Centre. After the tests we conducted, the several oncologists we've consulted here and at Dundurn General concur with the diagnosis that Dr. Philip Martin of CHC gave you late last month. Our collective conclusion suggests that, if the proper chemotherapy protocol is begun immediately, you may survive six months or possibly even a year. We are equally certain, Bill, that you will not survive more than a few weeks without this treatment. I write this as a follow-up to our meeting here on November 9, only to stress my personal concern and commitment to you.*

MacNeice sat back when he was done. "November. Not much traffic in Muskoka, and on a clear day a Land Cruiser idles at an intersection, waiting to turn onto the highway until the exact moment a speeding truck is approaching. It suggests that Dance's father had no intention of undergoing chemotherapy."

Ryan nodded.

MacNeice gave him a gentle slap on the shoulder. "Good work. Print out the letter and the invoice." He was taping them up on the whiteboard when Aziz returned.

"What's that?"

"Dance's father may have committed suicide in Muskoka."

"Lord—if he did, he took his wife and the driver of that truck with him. Are all the males in the Dance family crazy?"

The telephone on MacNeice's desk rang and he slid across to pick it up. "MacNeice."

"Mary Richardson. I have two representatives of the U.S. military here. They have the necessary documents required for me to release the Hughes remains, but they want copies of the DNA and pathology reports that were completed here. I want your approval before I release them."

"Is a member of the family with them?"

"No, they came alone. They are, however, bona fide bureaucrats—though I should keep my voice down. Junior is entertaining them. He's been trying to reassemble the pieces of the young man blown up on the bridge."

"Christ, Mary!"

"Sorry, gallows humour. Would you like to speak to one of these chaps?"

"Yes." He turned and looked at the army portrait of Hughes.

"Detective MacNeice, it's David Farrody, senior claims agent for the U.S. Department of Veterans Affairs. Is there a problem with releasing this information and the remains of Sergeant Hughes?"

"None whatsoever. Will the remains be returned to his family for burial?"

"The remains will be housed in a local mortuary until the date can be set for a proper funeral."

"When Sergeant Hughes's hands were discovered, his wedding ring was still on his finger. Shall I send a patrolman down with it?"

"Ah, no. Our task is to retrieve the body and return it to the States. Anything else should be dealt with directly by the deceased's family."

"Thank you. Can you put Dr. Richardson back on, please?"

"Certainly."

"Release the remains, Mary, and give them copies of whatever paperwork they've asked for."

"Shall be done."

MacNeice put down the phone and picked up his jacket.

"You heading out, boss?" Vertesi asked.

"Just home for a workout to clear my head. I'll be back. Are you okay for an hour and a half?"

Aziz answered first. "I'm fine. I'll write up some observations on the Mancini interview."

"If you decide to take her back to the hotel, Michael, make sure you take her right to the door, and check the room before you leave."

Aziz didn't bother to insist that she'd be okay getting back on her own. She just smiled at Vertesi.

"Jeezus, I'd almost forgotten about our psycho," Vertesi said.

"I haven't. He's overdue." MacNeice left the cubicle.


Merging with the traffic streaming by on Main Street, he replayed the interview in his head. The look on Roberto's face as he spoke about being wild—*just once*—had been, for MacNeice, the most revealing and raw moment of the session. It was like chaos theory: a harmless flutter of butterfly wings that ends up consuming so many people. That small moment of giving in had consumed both

Pat and his favourite uncle, leaving their families to sift through the ashes looking for explanations.

Cresting the last rise before home, his heart quickened when he saw a vehicle waiting in his driveway. This time it was a black Porsche Cayenne with black-tinted windows and Quebec plates. As he pulled in beside the SUV, he unhooked the straps restraining his weapon. He lowered his passenger-side window, turned off the ignition, drew out his sidearm and pointed it at the SUV's window. Seconds passed, but he kept the gun levelled at the black glass.

Eventually the window slid down to reveal a large, smiling face looking back at him. Before MacNeice could say anything, the barrel of a shotgun slid into view, and the driver's smile broadened to a toothy grin.

"Get out of the vehicle," MacNeice said.

The driver pursed his lips and shook his head slowly. He gestured with the sawed-off piece for MacNeice to turn around. As he glanced to his left, MacNeice saw the barrel of a handgun six inches from his ear on the other side of the window. The person on the end of it tapped it twice on the glass. MacNeice looked back to the driver of the Porsche, who smiled again and nodded slowly up and down. There was a sharper tap on the Chevy's window. MacNeice laid his weapon on the seat and got out of the car with his hands up.

He stood facing a short, wiry man with slicked-back hair that was greying at the temples; he was wearing a turquoise linen shirt open at the neck and baggy black linen pants. A small fleur-de-lis tattoo sat high on his right cheekbone; little blue dashes trailed down to it from just below his eye, presumably suggesting a falling French tear. MacNeice heard the heavy thump of the SUV's door and the crunch of big boots on gravel.

A huge man with dark, wavy hair appeared from behind the Chevy, wearing loose black denim jeans and an untucked white cotton shirt. MacNeice realized he must be looking at Bruni's older brother. No longer smiling, the man carried his weapon angled loosely over his shoulder. He motioned for MacNeice to walk to the entrance of the cottage; the smaller man led the way and opened the door as if he lived there. MacNeice followed him inside.

He found their boss sitting comfortably in the living room with a glass of MacNeice's grappa. The bottle, with a second glass, sat on the table next to a nickel-plated handgun identical to Frédéric's.

"Please, join me, *Monsieur* MacNeice." The man smiled, stood up and offered his hand. He was wearing a dark grey-blue suit, a pale blue-green shirt and black suede shoes.

"You would be Joe Paradise."

"*Oui, c'est moi.* Though personally I prefer the French—Joseph Paradis. Yes, I am Frédéric's brother. Please sit down . . . your grappa is superb, by the way." He nodded to his men, who turned and went back outside, closing the door behind them. "Please, *monsieur*, sit down." He smiled, poured a grappa for MacNeice and another for himself, and sat down again.

"What do you want, Joseph?"

"Please—" He offered the grappa to MacNeice, who took it. "We have much to discuss, I think."

MacNeice pointedly considered the distance from his hand to the weapon. Joseph noticed.

"*Ah, oui*, the weapon." He put down his grappa and picked up the gun. "I am not here to harm you, *monsieur*. If I were, you would have been harmed already, yes?"

"I take your point."

"Of course. Take the weapon. Go on—you hold it." He handed the shiny piece to MacNeice. "I am here to discuss the situation we are both in, *vous comprenez*?"

"In that case, why don't I put this down over here—" MacNeice put the weapon on the coffee table next to *Birds of North America*.

"As you wish. Now let's enjoy the moment. Chin-chin, MacNeice."

MacNeice sat down across from him and lifted the glass, toasted him back. He drank slowly, watching Joseph relish the taste of his very fine grappa.

"My brother died the way he lived—violently. You were there; I want you to tell me about it."

"He was about to shoot an innocent young man, having already wounded a police officer. With him were three men. One, I believe, was the brother of your colleague outside."

"*Oui*, it's true."

"One of the four survived and he's in police custody. It appears that D2D and the Jokers have cut him loose. Why is that?"

"Not yet, *monsieur* . . . *S'il vous plaît*, tell me more about Frédéric's death." He put the small tumbler to his nose and inhaled.

"Frédéric was determined, I believe, to kill all of us. If it weren't for an unknown assassin, he would have."

"Ah, yes, the sniper—was he yours?"

"No. We don't know who shot your brother. He was at least six hundred yards away, and by the time we found his position he was long gone.

"Not a police officer?"

"Most definitely not."

"This is a beautiful home." Joseph looked around the room. "I can tell that you love this place."

"I do, very much."

"*Oui*, it shows." He finished the last of his grappa and put the glass down. "I've never liked grappa—'Italian screech,' I called it—until now. Thank you for introducing me to something new."

"Why are you here?"

"Frédéric and I were orphans. I took care of him since he was fourteen."

"He was an extremely violent man, Joseph. Did you teach him that too?"

"*Touché—mais non.* As you can see, I am not violent. My world is, but I remain . . . calm within it."

"But you supported him?"

"In this adventure, no. He wanted to make his own way, without me. I was happy to see him go."

"You're not aware of what happened in Cayuga because of Frédéric?"

"I had not spoken to my brother for some time. We were sending girls here by train—among many other interests, I run an escort service in Montréal—but he was buying and selling dope on his own. I gave that up long ago."

"Was he competing with you?"

"*Oui et non*—I let him. I don't care to do business here; I don't need to. The Jokers in Montréal have a niche. We don't ruffle the feathers of the police or the Angels, you understand? If you choose to be violent, you have to be more violent than anyone else, and even then you cannot win."

"Yes, that must require a delicate balance."

"We are close to being legitimate now, but Frédéric wanted a different life—to run everything from pot and ecstasy to cocaine. He called southern Ontario his Wild West. Within six months, however, we in Montréal will be as clean as McDonald's."

"A young man came to my home yesterday. After he left me, he was blown up on the bridge. Do you know anything about that?"

"*Oui,* of course; I saw the news. I believe you know who was responsible, *non?*"

"I suspect it was the remnants of D2D."

"*Oui,* as I do."

"If I asked you about a dark late-model Mustang, would you

know anything about it?"

"Do I look like someone who drives a muscle car, *monsieur*?"

"Frankly, no, but you may know someone who does. Let's put it another way . . . do you know who rigged Pat Mancini's car with explosives?"

"Two people." He sat up and leaned forward. "Shortly I will leave here, MacNeice. We'll go back to Montréal, and I want this escapade of my brother's to slide into the past."

"I'm not sure I follow you . . ."

"This meeting never took place."

"I think I understand."

"You are looking for Randall 'Bigboy' Ross. He has some expertise with C4. He doesn't drive a Mustang but his associate, Perry Mitchell, does. They followed Mancini here. When you went for a drive, they—how do you say?—*modified* the Corvette."

"And they are D2D?"

"*Oui.*"

"Did you know about it?"

"No, I started asking questions today. You've had a busy day, and so have we."

"Where can I find them?"

"Langlois gave you the address in Aldershot. Be careful—*explosives plastiques* are in a crawl space in the basement."

"How do I know you're not setting them up—or me?"

"You don't. Do you think I am?"

MacNeice finished his grappa. "No, I think you're telling the truth—but I'd like to know why."

Joseph smiled, stood up and looked out at the forest. "I loved my brother, but I knew it would end this way—so did he. As he and Bruni grew more violent, we grew more civilized." He turned back to MacNeice. "I don't own a motorcycle and neither does Pascal—that's Bruni's brother. And I loathe leather pants."

"And Pascal . . . any thoughts of revenge for the killing of his brother?"

"No. Frédéric and Bruni were *deux gouttes d'eau*—in English, ah . . . two peas in a pod—though Bruni took up most of the room. He was addicted to cocaine and steroids. The last time Pascal saw him, Bruni tried to kill him."

"Did you come for the money that was hidden out at Cayuga?"

"I don't need Frédéric's money."

"Do you know anything about the killings there?"

"I didn't know, and he wouldn't have told me. I am out some money, yes—for the girls—but I can live with that; we will be selling the escort service soon. I will leave you now, and I trust you won't make a call to stop me when I do."

"Other than the weapons and the break-and-enter, do I have a reason to?"

Joseph smiled and picked up the shiny handgun. "The weapons are registered, though it's true that Pascal's is modified—for travel. Nothing was stolen or broken in your home, *monsieur*, and it wasn't difficult to enter."

"I'll have to do something about that."

"There is no need—we won't be back." He tucked the gun under his belt and held out his hand. Shaking it, MacNeice caught a glimpse of a heavy Rolex on his wrist.

Walking towards the door, Joseph paused. "If I was going to steal anything, *Monsieur* MacNeice, I'd take that photograph—*très, très jolie.*" For a long moment he looked closely at the nude girl on the stone beach.

They stepped out of the cottage together; his men were already sitting in the Porsche with the engine idling. Joseph walked around to the passenger side. "*Bonsoir*, MacNeice, and thank you for the grappa—and also, *bonne chance.*" Climbing into the front seat, he said, "*Allons-y! Revenons à civilisation.*" The door shut with a

solid *thunk*, and the shiny black Cayenne swung out of the driveway and rumbled off slowly down the lane.

MacNeice retrieved his handgun from the Chevy and went back
inside. He placed the palm of his hand on the bum of the girl and
said, "Thank you." After putting the glasses in the sink and the
grappa back in the cabinet, he checked the kitchen door and every
window—all locked. He stood on the threshold of his bedroom
and considered changing into his workout gear, then, his heart still
racing, he walked out of the cottage, locking the door behind him.
He punched in the division number before descending the hill to
the highway.

"MacNeice," he said when he heard Ryan's voice on the hands-
free. "Is Aziz still there?"

"Yessir, and Vertesi."

"Thanks, Ryan. Put Aziz on."

"How's the workout going?"

"I'm coming back. Call and get Swetsky and Palmer together—
we're going to Aldershot."

"Do you want the SWAT team?"

"Yes, but hopefully we can avoid a gunfight. Anything from
Montile?"

"He tried to reach you five minutes ago. I told him to call your cell."

"I'll be there in eight minutes."

MacNeice was walking across the parking lot when his phone
rang.

"It's me. Turns out Luigi documented everything. We've got
emails and hard copies going back and forth to ABC. Demetrius
read one of them to me where this ABC executive is giving Vanucci
fifty grand and the authority to secure Grimsby against any threat
from McNamara or his thugs. Apparently Luigi wanted everything
spelled out, so he asked this guy why not give the job to the local
authorities in Canada—"

"Good question."

"Exactly. Demetrius read that letter too, something about comparing our local government to theirs, and that if they were the same, ABC would be trashed before they showed up . . . I've got three boxes of documents, mostly photocopies of the originals, as well as two CDs of what was on the computer."

"Is that all of it?"

"That's it. There's enough here for them to take down the Old Soldiers. One thing's for sure, though—Wenzel won't have a life in Tonawanda anymore."

"When this is over, I think the safest place for him is back in West Virginia. Well done, Montile. Get back here as soon as you can."

"Thanks, boss. I should be there in under an hour."

MacNeice felt so buoyed by the news he jogged to the back door and sprinted up the stairs.

Vertesi's head appeared above the office landscaping. "He's here."

"Swetsky and Palmer are on their way back," Aziz said. "They should be here in ten or fifteen minutes. We've got SWAT backup. Two men who have just arrived are in position among the trees, about two hundred yards in front of the house."

"They've got a camera equipped with a 300-millimetre lens that they can hook up to a laptop, so Ryan will be getting images pretty soon," Vertesi said.

Ryan was clicking away at his keyboard. "They've locked on to me, sir. Give me a few seconds and we'll see."

"Swets also wanted you to know he has something for you," Aziz said.

MacNeice said, "It's all coming together. Montile will be coming home with the Vanucci Rosetta Stone—all the paperwork and emails confirming that the Old Soldiers were hired on behalf of ABC." MacNeice picked up a marker and started adding the new information to the board.

"Fantastic," Vertesi said.

"And there's more—I met Joseph Paradis."

"What! Where?" Aziz was so startled she stood up.

"In my living room. He was waiting for me and drinking my grappa. He offered me one."

Vertesi couldn't take it in. "Jesus Christ!"

"Yes, exactly."

"What'd he want?" Vertesi asked.

MacNeice explained, down to writing on the whiteboard the names of the two men Paradis said had planted the bomb.

Aziz wasn't focused on the info. "How'd they get into the cottage?"

"I have no idea. There's no damage to anything, and with the exception of the front door, everything that was locked remained locked. They appear to have simply walked in."

"Time for new locks," Vertesi said.

"Okay," Ryan interjected, "here are some images of the place. First one's a long shot." He clicked the keyboard and a two-storey white frame house appeared through a screen of trees. There was a single-car garage off to the right. Behind the house to the left was a rundown barn and a grain tower missing its conical roof. The driveway led straight off the concession road to the side of the house, where a black trailer was parked.

"Is that a horse trailer?" Vertesi asked.

"More likely a motorcycle trailer," Ryan offered. "You could get a half-dozen hogs in that thing."

"Looks like corn behind the house," Aziz said.

"A lotta corn."

"Next," MacNeice said.

"Same shot but much closer. He's moved off to the right of the forest for a clear shot—low, like he's on the ground in the weeds." The house had a small covered porch with two chairs on it, and several more—they looked like kitchen chairs—were on the front lawn near a small fruit tree. All the windows had the blinds pulled down.

"Next."

"Close-up of the barn." While some of its vertical boards were missing, the structure looked sound, especially the lower level, a stone base that rose eight to ten feet above the ground—likely an old stable.

"That could be a problem," Vertesi said. "If we hit the house, we might take fire from the barn."

"A tactic these men like to use," Aziz said.

"Next."

"Two vehicles arriving. One's a Dodge Ram pickup with a trailer hitch, and the other—ta-dah!—a late-model dark blue Mustang." Ryan lifted his feet and did a three-sixty spin in his desk chair. "I need a couple of minutes to upload the last two images."

"Good one, Ry."

"There's no way to surprise them—they'll see us coming," Aziz said.

"In daylight, yes, but the night's on our side. No street lights or much ambient light out there—let's check the weather reports and the phase of the moon."

"First-stage crescent moon tonight, sir," Ryan said.

All three detectives stared at him. "How the hell do you know that, Ry?" Vertesi asked.

"Dirt bikes, computer technology, the cycles of the moon— they're all my things. I've been studying the sky since I was a kid looking through a telescope with my granddad. Nerdy, I know."

"Not nerdy at all," MacNeice said.

"Well, maybe a bit . . ." Vertesi said.

"Weather's overcast, threatening rain, sixty percent chance of thunderstorms overnight," Aziz said, staring at her screen.

"Perfect," MacNeice said.

"Here you go—two more images." Ryan nodded towards the Falcon's large monitor. Two more cars had arrived in the driveway. "First one's a ten-year-old Lincoln Town Car, the second a beefed-up Jeep Cherokee. She's riding too low for hauling firewood, so I'd say she's been chopped into a low-rider. Next shot is the family reunion." He clicked the keyboard and the photo appeared.

Four men and one woman had emerged from the house to greet the six men who'd emerged from the cars. Everyone, including the woman, appeared to be wearing black.

"That would be the hairdresser. It's her name on the deed to the property . . ."

"Fiza, call the surveillance team and tell them to stay low. No more photos unless the status changes. Otherwise, strictly cellphone eyeball reports—I don't want the glow from that laptop being seen."

"Will do." She swung around and slid her chair back to the desk. "Do I tell them what the plan is?"

"One more in, sir. Here it comes." Ryan slid away from the screen.

Two children were bolting out the front door. The camera had caught them in mid-air, jumping off the porch—two boys, one perhaps four, the other five or six.

"Not good," Vertesi said.

"Not at all," Aziz added, reaching for her phone.

"At the moment, just tell them to stay low and keep reporting," MacNeice said.

MacNeice was taping the last of the Aldershot photographs to the whiteboard when Swetsky came around the corner of the cubicle.

"Whaddya got here, Mac?" Swetsky put his massive arm over the top of the whiteboard.

"Where's Palmer?" MacNeice asked.

"He said he had to see someone first. If we need him, I'll have his ass back here in ten minutes."

MacNeice nodded. "These are photos of D2D's Aldershot crib. Do you recognize any of the people in this one? Ryan enlarged and sharpened the image."

Swetsky leaned in for a better look. "Uh-huh, yeah, oh yeah. These three were out west—nice to see they've come home. I don't know those two. The girl is Randy Ross's girlfriend, Melanie Butter."

"Butter, like . . . ?" Vertesi said.

"Yeah—spreads real easy." Swetsky regretted the pathetic joke immediately. "Aw, Jesus, sorry, Aziz."

"No problem, Detective," Aziz said sharply as she picked up the phone.

"Sorry, Mac, I keep thinkin' she's one of the guys," Swetsky said quietly.

"Yes, you do, and she's not." His voice was sterner than he'd intended. "Ms. Butter has two kids out there."

"They're hers, not Ross's. Their father was T-boned on his Harley by a freight train at a rail crossing in Tweed a few years ago."

"I remember that. He tried to beat it to the crossing," Vertesi said.

"Darwinian, ain't it," Swetsky said. "What's the plan?"

"We have SWAT backup, and once Montile gets here we'll have the six of us plus the two in the forest. We've just found out that Randall Ross and Perry Mitchell, the guy who owns that Mustang"—MacNeice tapped the photo—"likely killed Pat Mancini."

"Yup, that makes sense. Bigboy earned his chops planting explosives in a granite quarry up north."

"The house is sitting on a concession road with visibility in every direction. There's a stand of trees across the road—where our men are—but coming at them in daylight would be a disaster. Ten men, the woman and two kids . . . we don't want a bloodbath. Those kids and their mother, at least, have got to come out of this walking and talking." MacNeice studied the boys jumping off the porch, as if they didn't have a care in the world.

"How we gonna guarantee that?" Swetsky said, looking over at him.

"I'm not sure yet. But they've gathered together for a reason, and I don't want to miss this opportunity."

The Jokers, with three dead and one in custody, had to be finished in Dundurn. If there were any others, they'd likely headed back to Quebec. "We can set up roadblocks out of sight of the farmhouse in both directions. If any of them leave, we can pick them up. The problem is, the moment they see us they'll alert the farmhouse, and then we're into a gun battle, or worse."

"Just a thought—surely ten men can't all stay in that house overnight. Some of them are going to leave at some point this evening," Aziz said.

"Good point."

"So, sooner than later's what you're saying?" Swetsky said, sitting down.

"I'm with Mac—I don't want an exchange of gunfire. But I can't think of a way to prevent it," Aziz said.

"Tell me more about Melanie Butter," MacNeice said. "Is she steeped in the biker culture or is she a hairdresser whose fatal flaw is her choice of men?"

"I only met her once, at her salon in Burlington. She had photos of her kids clipped onto the mirror. No tattoos, at least that I could see. She looks like someone who cuts hair. She most definitely didn't have a hate-on for cops."

"It's a long shot, but do you think we could get Melanie on her cellphone, tell her what's about to happen at the farmhouse?

Suggest that she take the kids out to get some snacks so they'll be out of the way when we sweep in?"

"A Hail Mary pass," Vertesi said, miming throwing a long ball.

"Yes, with the clock ticking down. If she outs us they'll be gone in a flash, and we'll have to stop them on the road."

"It ain't hard to get her number; I know the woman who owns the salon." Swetsky pulled out his cellphone.

MacNeice looked at his watch. "It's 8:38 now. Montile will be here soon. Assuming Palmer's as good as his word, he'll be here too . . ." MacNeice looked at Swetsky for confirmation.

"He'll be here, and if he isn't, I'll put him on report." The big man's jaw tightened.

"Right. Aziz, let the SWAT team know we'll meet in the parking lot of LaSalle Park, which is roughly five minutes from the farmhouse. From there we'll use cruisers to set up roadblocks on both ends of Concession Road 2. Have the firefighters and EMS arrive in the park at 9:45 so we don't overlap. I'll call Ms. Butter at 9:35 and, depending on her reaction, give her some time to get out. Either way, we arrive at the farmhouse at precisely 9:45 p.m. Questions?"

"Who goes in first?" Vertesi asked.

"The SWAT team will cover the terrain from the house to the barn and the garage. We'll position ourselves on the lawn. I'll try and talk them out peacefully. We'll be wearing armour and stay behind our vehicles."

"Keep an eye on Ross—he really does know how to blow things up." Swetsky walked over to the whiteboard, where he tapped the image of the farmhouse. "I wouldn't put it past him to have that driveway peppered with IEDs."

"Right, so we'll put the SWAT van on the grass. Ryan, make sure we have prints of these images with the names of the actors Swets gives you."

"IEDs in Aldershot . . . what's next?" Vertesi said, shaking his head.

"Aziz, find out the status of the department helicopter."

"For what?" Vertesi asked.

"Your boss wants light on that farm." Swetsky smiled.

"Minimum, we'll hit the house with our headlights and the SWAT van floodlights."

Aziz dialled the number.

"How do you rate our chances of pulling them out of there without a fight?" MacNeice asked, looking at Swetsky.

"Zero to ten percent, though the new guys may have some influence. D2D has been almost destroyed. They gave over leadership to a psychopath and a bunch of them died. If they're trying to rebuild and stay out of the limelight, smoking Pat Mancini was a mistake. Maybe the meeting's a gut check for the new guys . . . Mac, while Aziz is checkin' that chopper, take a walk with me."

Swetsky shambled down the exit stairs and MacNeice followed; Swets was so large it was difficult to imagine that anyone coming up could negotiate around him. At the bottom he swung the door open for MacNeice. "Over to my car."

"What are you up to, Swets?"

"Good Samaritan. Ever read that story?"

"Probably."

"It was about a relationship, not charity. He didn't feel sorry for the fucker by the road. He wanted to get to know him, to know he was going to be okay, and he was willing to put himself out to ensure that he would be."

"You brought me out here to talk religion?"

"Yeah, I guess so. I haven't been to church since I was sixteen. I got laid and didn't confess my sin."

"The clock's ticking, Swets . . ."

"Relax—I know. This is important." He popped the trunk. Inside was a large gym bag. "You remember what Langlois told you about why Freddy went back to the farm?"

"The money."

"We tore that place apart so thoroughly they might as well flatten it at this point."

"And?"

"So last night we're finishing our pizzas. I'm eating a pepperoni slice and I look at the circle of sausage in this sea of mozzarella—it was like *shazam!* There was this oil drum sitting near the back of the barn; I saw the guys rolling it around and Palmer said, 'Oil,' and left it at that. If we hadn't done such a great job trashing the place I might not have thought about it any more. But I go back to the barn on my own and I open up the strapping on that barrel." Swetsky looked like a very big cat with a canary in his cheek.

"And?" MacNeice prompted.

"It's definitely oil, but there's this thin wire going down either side. You can't really see it but you can feel it, hooked into the lip that runs around the waist of the barrel—invisible almost. I reach in and pull both wires and up comes this shrink-wrapped bundle. I pull it out, get a carpet knife from the workbench. This was inside." He pointed to the bag.

"The clock, Swets."

"Open it up."

MacNeice leaned into the trunk and unzipped the bag. It was full of thick bundles of hundred-dollar bills, multiples of Sir Robert Borden looking off to his left, each bundle held together with an elastic band. MacNeice shot back as if the bag were full of snakes.

"Each bundle's ten thousand, and there's over eighty of 'em in there."

"And what—you needed help bringing it in?"

"The guys that knew how much was there are both dead."

"I'm going to forget we had this conversation." MacNeice turned to walk away.

"Not for me, you righteous fucker—for the Hughes woman! Nobody knows I got this. We take out two hundred thousand and give it to her. The rest goes in as evidence and we make her life a little easier."

"I see . . ."

"Somebody takes it to a money-changer I know in Niagara. He'll wire it right into her bank account, assuming she has one."

"It's a crazy idea, Swets . . . Let's just get through the next couple of hours and we'll talk about it again. I'm sorry for thinking—"

"Hey, fuck, man! If the role was reversed I'da pulled my piece on you already." He zipped the bag shut and slammed the trunk.

They started walking back to Division, MacNeice's head spinning.

"Yeah, the oil drum's sealed up like it was before . . . though there's less oil in it." Swetsky laughed and slapped MacNeice on the back, so hard it made him stumble.

# 47.

"THE HELICOPTER ISN'T available because the Jesus nut is suspect. They've ordered a new part but it's not in yet," Aziz said.

When Vertesi asked what a Jesus nut was, Aziz admitted she'd asked the same question. "It's the big nut that keeps the rotor blades on. Sounds like a good reason not to fly tonight."

When Williams got back, they loaded up Kevlar vests, shotguns, ammunition and two bullhorns. They were getting into their cars when Palmer came loping over. "What's up?" he asked.

"Your call, Mac," Swetsky said and climbed into the front seat of MacNeice's Chevy.

"You are a liability, Detective. You'll sit this one out."

MacNeice opened the door to the Chevy and Palmer grabbed it from him. "What the fuck? What'd I do?"

"Take your hand off the car." MacNeice turned to face him and Palmer released the door.

"But—what's going on?"

"You'll read about it in the *Standard* tomorrow, like everyone else in Dundurn. You've put your personal life ahead of the men and women who count on you, Palmer, perhaps for the last time." He climbed in, started the engine and pulled away.

Palmer stood there with his hands out in a classic *What the fuck?* gesture as the two cars rolled out of the driveway. "That was probably what he looked like when the firefighter whose wife he was banging torched his motorcycle. I'll write him up tomorrow morning. With any luck he'll be on a desk by Monday," Swetsky said.

Aziz said, "Of course, now we're down one man."

"We were down one man even if he had made it. Would you want him covering your back?" MacNeice said, glancing in the rear-view mirror.

As they approached the Sky-High Bridge, the conversation in the car died away. The spot where Pat Mancini exploded had been transformed from an elongated elliptical scar to a neat dark rectangle of new pavement. MacNeice glanced quickly back at the city. The rust-red towers of the steel company had lights along their edges, but the massive buildings that housed the blast furnaces, pickling lines, coiler pits and God-knows-what seemed like black holes against the lights of the city. So too the bay, that featureless dark grey slab where pieces of Pat Mancini nestled deep in the bellies of fat, happy carp.

They were roughly two miles from LaSalle Park before he spoke again. "Get the spotters on the line, Fiza. I want to know if anything has changed. From now on, reports every five minutes, more if the status changes."

"Will do."

"Did you check the batteries on the bullhorn?"

"I didn't check them; I changed them."

"Perfect."

Aziz made contact with the SWAT team, then reported, "Nothing new, sir. Butter is alone on the porch, smoking. The kids are taking turns on a rope swing on a tree to the right of the driveway."

"Good sign. That means she's hasn't been invited to the meeting," Swets said.

"Let's hope she stays out there," MacNeice said.

In the park's parking lot, a dozen or so onlookers, some carrying soccer balls or picnic blankets and hampers, stood ogling or taking pictures of the cops with their cellphones. Getting out of the car, MacNeice approached the sergeant standing next to the two large black vans. "Don't worry about these folks, Mac," he said. "They've been told we're doing an exercise and a public relations tour, trying to drum up enrolment in the police academy." He smiled.

"That's reassuring, Sergeant Keeler. Did they buy it?"

"Oh, big time. Actually, it's not a bad idea. Sure, some of the kids want to touch the weapons, but other than that it does a worlda good to get out here and mingle. I'm not shittin' ya—it really does."

"Put the idea forward." MacNeice looked over at Keeler's men, who were standing in front of the second van. "They've been fully briefed?"

"Yes, sir. We have the images on board both vehicles. But I understand DI Aziz brought some printouts?"

"I wasn't expecting two units. Was that your idea?"

"This is a large assignment for us, which means lots of chances to learn. Let's go into my office." He climbed up into the van and MacNeice followed.

Inside the truck, a young officer in black Kevlar was working the computer terminal. The screen was mounted horizontally, with blocks representing the two SWAT units and the two unmarked cars.

"Jansen, this is Detective Superintendent MacNeice."

The young man looked up, snapped his hand forward and said, "Sir."

MacNeice shook the young man's hand and turned to Keeler. "Tell me the plan."

"We're aligned with yours. We'll take this unit to the front left of the driveway, where we have a sightline to the barn, well clear of the house. The second unit will stop here—off to the right—with a clear view to the side of the house and any activity near the vehicles or the garage." Jansen tapped the keyboard till thin red lines mapped the geometry of the sightlines. Mac's car was off to the left, angled to provide cover against any fire from the house while shining its headlights at the front door. Vertesi's car sat at an opposite angle on the other side of the driveway. Pale triangles of white pointed towards the house.

"The vehicle headlights will be augmented by our roof-mounted floods—three on each unit. Show 'em, Jansen." Jansen clicked the keyboard again and trios of white cones created a saturated path of light covering the house and the vehicles on the screen. "They better be wearing shades if they want to see us," Keeler said.

"Okay, it's anyone's guess how they'll react, but I want to give them the opportunity to surrender. So we'll put it to them first by loudspeaker. Clear?"

"Yes, sir. We'll wait for your signal—or theirs. If they start popping at us, we'll unleash."

MacNeice nodded. "Let's hope that doesn't happen."

MacNeice stepped out of the van. Before he could get to his car, the vans were already loaded up and turning about.

"Swetsky, you drive." MacNeice threw him the keys and got into the passenger side.

"Mac, I've been thinking. If her phone's inside the house, there's a risk someone other than Melanie will answer it when you call," Aziz said.

"It's a risk, but I don't see an alternative, do you?"

Swetsky was pulling out of the parking lot.

"No."

MacNeice pressed the button and Butter's phone started to ring. Swetsky pulled onto the northbound county four-lane that would take their convoy to the concession road. The phone rang several times, then went silent for a moment. "Hi, it's Mel. I'm not near the phone right now. Please leave me a message." MacNeice disconnected before the beep.

"Recording?" Aziz asked.

"Yes, and I think it would be a mistake to—" His phone rang. "MacNeice," he said.

"Hi. I'm sorry, did you just call me? I had the phone in my jeans but couldn't get to it in time." Like her phone message, the voice was cheerful, melodic.

"Yes, Melanie, I did."

"Do I know you?"

"No. I'm Detective Superintendent MacNeice, from Dundurn Homicide."

He heard her inhale sharply. "I'm calling to ask you to get your children away from the house immediately."

"Why? What's going on?" she whispered.

Aziz, listening to the spotter, said softly, "She's off the porch, Mac, moving towards the kids."

He nodded to indicate he'd heard. "The house is about to be raided. If there is any violence, I want to be certain that you and your children are out of harm's way. Do you understand?"

"Yeah, but how—What can I do, where can I go? My kids—they've got nothing to do—"

"I know that, Melanie. Can you get your car out of the driveway?"

"Shit . . . no, they're all blocked in. Mine's in the garage . . . oh, fuck . . . What's gonna happen?"

"Spotter says she's panicking. If anyone comes out right now it's—" MacNeice raised his hand to stop Aziz.

"Melanie, look across the road to the forest."

"Yeah. But what?"

"Take your kids."

Swetsky tapped his shoulder and pointed. He'd passed the cruiser at the intersection and was turning down the road towards the farmhouse. MacNeice nodded. "Tell them you want to go looking for the rabbits that live in that forest."

"Fucking rabbits?" she almost shrieked.

"Yes. Go straight to the far edge of the forest. There are two police officers there. When you get there, lie down and stay down. They'll tell you when it's safe. Do you understand me, Melanie?" He kept his voice calm and reassuring.

"Go to the far end of the forest . . . look for rabbits . . . stay down. Oh, God, if they catch me . . . fuck!"

"They won't. Go now. If anyone comes out, you and the kids are looking for rabbits. Go now, Melanie."

"Okay, okay." The line went dead.

"Rabbits . . . that's fucking amazing," Swetsky said.

"If it works."

Aziz sat forward suddenly with the cellphone pressed to her ear. "The front door just opened . . . Spotter thinks it's Ross—he's calling her . . . He's stepped off the porch and is walking across the lawn . . ."

"Do I stop?" Swetsky asked.

"Keep going."

"He's yelling at her. 'Babe, where the fuck are you going?'" Aziz looked around as the SWAT van loomed over the Chevy. She could see black-gloved hands on the steering wheel. When she looked up, the driver nodded down at her. She took a deep breath. "Melanie just said, 'Honey, we saw rabbits. We're going to look for them.' He's buying it, the spotter thinks."

"Rabbits . . . fucking rabbits," Swetsky said, shaking his head.

"He's gone back inside." Aziz exhaled. She handed MacNeice a Kevlar vest from the back seat. "Put this on."

MacNeice wriggled into it just as they crested a small hill.

"Farmhouse in sight. There's Melanie and the kids off to the left, almost to our men. Spotter's flashing me, probably wants to know what to do with them." Swetsky pointed at the narrow white beam.

"Tell them, Fiza," MacNeice said, noticing that Melanie was staring towards the approaching caravan.

Covering the mouthpiece, Aziz said, "I'm on it." Then, "Yes, get them to lie down beside you. Tell them it's a game. Make sure they stay put, no matter what happens. Right . . . you're all hunting for rabbits. I'm offline now." She put the phone in the pocket of her vest and unholstered her Glock 17. "Done."

"Good. Hand me the bullhorn. Remember, Swets, angle the car so the headlights are on the house."

"Got it. I'm coming out your side." Swetsky said, undoing his seatbelt.

"High beams."

"Check."

Swetsky swung the Chevy rudely into the shallow ditch, kicking up gravel as he spun it around. MacNeice and Aziz braced themselves to keep from toppling over, MacNeice focusing on the farmhouse. He saw the front-door blind shiver. Behind their car, the powerful SWAT vans bounced in and over the ditch and came to a halt, one on the front lawn next to the chairs, the other to the right of the driveway. Swetsky, Aziz and MacNeice were out of the car just as Vertesi's came to a stop. Twelve heavily armed men in battle gear bolted from the vans. Six ran for cover behind the vehicles parked in the driveway and the others took positions crouching outside the house, three on either side of the porch. One of the spotters came running up behind MacNeice and knelt beside Aziz at the rear of the Chevy. Keeler stood behind the lead van, ten feet away. He held his hand up to get the detective's attention, then dropped it.

MacNeice lifted the bullhorn. "You people inside—this is the police. There's no chance of escape and no need for bloodshed. Drop your weapons. Come out the front door with your hands on your heads and lie face down on the lawn. Do it now." He turned off the bullhorn and set it on the hood. The sounds of twilight—swallows, bats, crickets—and the low purring of the SWAT van's engine replaced the rush and rumble of vehicles and the rattle of armed men. The house was lit up like noon on a xenon day.

MacNeice saw someone moving behind a second-floor window. "They're taking positions inside—get down. I'll give it one more try." He lifted the bullhorn and flicked the switch "Randall Ross, Perry Mitchell, the rest of you—come out now! Hands over your heads—" The upper-floor window burst open and two shotgun blasts slammed into the driver's side of the Chevy, blowing out the windows. "Keeler, it's all yours!" MacNeice yelled.

On Keeler's signal, four members of the SWAT team fired tear gas into the front and side windows—the large shells tore through the blinds. MacNeice saw a running figure inside before a shredded blind fell back into place. On the driveway side of the house, someone opened up with an assault rifle on the SWAT team making their way along the far side of the vehicles. They had to sprint the three feet between the Jeep and pickup truck—the last member had just left the cover of the Jeep when he was hit.

With a deafening roar, from every window, shotguns, assault rifles and Uzis tore into the vehicles and ripped up the ground in front of them. The Chevy shuddered with the impact, slamming down onto its rims as the driver's-side tires were shot out. In a break between bursts, they heard one of the SWAT team scream, "Man down, man down!" If anyone answered, the response was lost as the onslaught resumed.

With the unrelenting fire directly above them, the team outside the house hugged the wall and waited for an opportunity to lob their stun grenades inside. Those behind the vehicles hunkered down, waiting for someone inside to stop to change a magazine so they could respond in kind. MacNeice realized the bikers hadn't been fazed by the tear gas. He yelled to his team, "Stay down, all of you," then crept past them to the rear of the Chevy, where he paused, took a deep breath and sprinted towards Keeler.

Several rounds zipped past him, tearing up the road, and something stung his leg. He screamed over the noise, "They're wearing masks!" The van was also taking fire and shuddering. He leaned into Keeler, his face so close that MacNeice's reflection filled the Plexi shield. "This is covering fire!" Keeler nodded. MacNeice made several downward jabbing motions with his left hand. "Explosives in the basement—they're buying time for Ross. Understand?"

Keeler nodded again. Through his helmet mike he yelled, "Six, eight and three, M84s through the basement, then first- and second-floor windows. *Go-go-go!*"

*Phwumph, phwumph, phwumph.* The stun grenades thudded through the windows and the firing from inside stopped. They could hear yelling from somewhere on the first floor, three loud, sharp bangs followed by bright flashes, and then silence. The tear gas puffed out of the windows—it looked as if the house was exhaling. The SWAT team were on their feet and advancing. Keeler pushed up his mask and called out to his men, "Move! Get in there now!"

There was a flash and an explosion from somewhere inside the house, and the blinds flew out of the window frames.

"What the fuck was that?" Keeler yelled. Turning to MacNeice and slicing his hand from side to side, he said, "It wasn't us. Not us!"

MacNeice realized what it was: Bigboy had screwed up. "Get your men back!"

"What?"

"Pull them out—fast! Do it!"

Keeler understood, yelling through his microphone, "Everyone away from that building! It's gonna blow! Go-go-go!"

The team that was heading to the side door, their weapons at the ready, looked back in Keeler's direction, hesitated and then scattered, running for cover behind the vehicles in the driveway. The six caught in front of the house saw Keeler and MacNeice waving frantically and started running towards the van and the Chevy. They were almost there when the house appeared to sag inwards from the roof to the ground, accompanied by creaking and snapping. A second later, with a deafening roar, the building tore skyward. It came apart as it flew up and then out in a disintegrating mess of glass, wood, plumbing, roofing, steel, cheap furniture . . . and bodies.

Everyone behind the vehicles got as low as they could, pressed against steel and earth. Those who hadn't made it to cover crawled like crabs under or behind the vans. Williams said later that he was standing by Vertesi's car, his jaw dropped like a kid's, watching the house head skyward—"It was better than a movie"—when Vertesi grabbed his Kevlar vest and screamed three words at him—"*What goes up* . . ."—then pulled him to the ground.

And so it came down—the heaviest debris first, stabbing and slamming into the ground, punishing the vehicles, digging into anything soft and richocheting off anything hard. Next the glass and wood and lengths of twisted pipe slashed into every surface, looking for something to hurt. No one could say with any certainty how long this hellish hail lasted, but at some point it ended, and people began emerging from their hiding places.

Particles of insulation, upholstery, clothing, pillows, blankets and carpeting were floating everywhere like snowflakes, completely disinterested and in no hurry to come down. It made the air seem alive, almost magical. Both headlights of the Chevy were shot out, but when the artificial snow drifted into the remaining lights of the SWAT van, MacNeice thought he could hear the chorus of "White Christmas."

Beyond where the farmhouse had stood, several small fires were burning, lit by debris that had ignited before it blew apart. Two of these fires were very close to the cornfield. Keeler yelled to his men, "Keep your masks on! Get those fires out!"

MacNeice turned to check on his team. Aziz, Swetsky, the young cop from the forest—all stood up tentatively, wide-eyed. He looked quickly over at Vertesi's car. They weren't up yet but he saw a hand waving and heard Vertesi yell, "We're okay."

"Everyone, put something over your nose and mouth! Do not breathe this air!" MacNeice said. Aziz and Swetsky came out from behind the car, their jackets covering their mouths and noses; their wide eyes told the story.

"Miller. Miller! Get these people some face masks. On the run, now!" Keeler yelled.

"How's your man?" MacNeice asked.

"The round tore through the side of his hip. He'll have physio ahead of him, but he'll survive; they've got a field pack on him. He was almost taken out by the refrigerator. It landed behind the Jeep, a foot from his head."

With their masks on, the detectives stepped over the scattered debris to see what was left of the house. One porch column remained, still anchored to its base—the only vertical remaining. The concrete foundation was intact but the furnace block had gone up and come down again several yards from its original position. The water heater had landed on the motorcycle trailer, breaking its spine. There was no fire, no smoke in the hole that had been the basement; it was as if it had all been sucked into the sky. While the tank was nowhere to be seen, heating oil covered the basement floor, swirling about with the water gushing from the severed main.

Three members of the SWAT team were using extinguishers to kill the small fires. They could hear the cruisers, EMS vehicles and firefighters beating their way along the road towards them. Amid the debris around them were several shreds of viscera—ugly, but none of it recognizably human.

To the young spotter, MacNeice said, "Go and get Melanie and the kids, but keep them away from the house."

"No problem, sir. Man, I never—"

"Me neither, son, me neither. Go on now, make sure your partner and Melanie and the kids are all okay."

The young officer took off at a jog, jumping over the wreckage like a cross-country runner over hedges.

"I'll go with him, Mac. She'll be pretty shaken up," Aziz said, walking around the shattered remains of life on a country road.

A firefighter ran up to MacNeice and Swetsky, looked at the hole in the ground and said, "What the fuck did you guys use on this place?"

"It was self-inflicted," Keeler said, coming towards them.

"Fuckin' effective, whatever it was."

"You can take over killing those small fires. I've got a man down over in the driveway—is there an ambulance on the way?"

"Is he it?"

"Some cuts. Otherwise, everyone else is fine." The firefighter went down to the driveway, still shaking his head. He hollered to several others to follow him.

Keeler stepped closer and said in low voice, "There are large pieces of those bikers in the driveway and behind the house—the force of the blast went backwards and took them with it. Mac, we've gotta shut this site down or people are going to be trampling on some pretty grisly stuff."

"Good call, Sergeant. Pull your people out and tape it. We'll let the firefighters mark the remains. And get a retrieval team in here."

"I'll call it in," Swetsky said, "before the coyotes get here for easy pickin's." He took the cellphone out of his hip pocket and headed off towards the road.

The Lincoln, Mustang, pickup truck and Jeep had taken the brunt of the gunfire and the explosion; each sagged on its house-side rims, leaning submissively towards the hole in the ground. The glass in the vehicles was shattered and most of the metal on the house side was torn up. Pieces of plumbing, steel framing and even wood trim stuck out of some of the vehicles—they looked like animals speared to death in some bizarre nighttime hunt. By contrast, anything that hit the SWAT vans had basically bounced off, leaving the heavy metal surfaces looking ball-peened. Mac's Chevy hadn't been spared. Dozens of rounds had hit the front and the driver's side, pocked the steel, torn through the upholstery, taken out all of the glass and shredded the house-side tires. A sizable chunk of chimney had folded the hood. MacNeice wondered whether his CD collection had survived, and how long it would take to get the car roadworthy again. He patted the damaged hood the way a cowboy would a horse before putting it down—except MacNeice wasn't willing to say goodbye to the Chevy.

His cellphone rang. He checked the number, then answered.

"What in God's name happened?" Wallace asked. "I've got people telling me you could see that explosion from the mountain!"

"The bikers triggered explosives in the basement. I don't know how, sir. We were taking fire. Non-lethal M84 stun grenades were thrown or fired in. There was a pause, and then suddenly the whole place went up."

He told Wallace how he'd tried to talk the men out and about his doubts that everyone inside was as committed to a gun battle as the two who had killed Pat Mancini. He also told him about the mother and her kids.

"Fuck it, MacNeice!" Wallace said. "So ten bad men got blown up. I get it—you didn't want that to happen. Still, I'm not crying. I'll deal with the press. Keep that goddamned road closed. No photos till it's cleaned up!" Wallace hung up.

MacNeice put the phone back in his pocket and looked up to see Aziz coming up the road with her arm around Melanie Butter, the boys trailing behind. He walked towards them.

"Melanie, I'm DS MacNeice. I deeply regret the way this ended."

She had her hands in front of her lower face and was looking beyond him to the devastation. "I . . . Randy wasn't . . . Why'd you have to do this? Why?"

"We didn't. There were explosives in the basement and something happened. We didn't use explosives."

"Oh my God, where are all those men who were in there?" She tried to push past Aziz but the detective held her back.

"They're gone, Melanie. Gone . . ."

The two kids were looking around for something familiar. One of them picked up a chair that had been blown onto the road and sat down on it. The other went over to him and pushed his butt onto the chair next to his brother.

"But . . . all of them? Gone?" She was holding on to her head as two EMS teams approached from behind.

"Can we help?" the first paramedic to reach them asked.

"Yes," Aziz said. "This is Melanie Butter. She lived here with her two sons. Can you take care of them?"

"Definitely, Detective, that's what we're here for. But what about you, sir?"

"Me?" MacNeice asked.

"Yes, sir, you're losing a lot of blood." She pointed to the back of his right leg.

"God, Mac, you've been hit!" Aziz said.

"I forgot. Yeah, I felt it—like a hornet sting, when I was running."

"These guys will take care of you." The paramedic had an arm around Melanie, ready to lead her away. "Come with me, dear. You're going to be fine."

Her partner turned to the kids. "Wanna see inside our ambulance? There's some really neat stuff in there. Come on, we'll take a look." He took each boy by the hand. "Watch out for broken glass and stuff."

A young man from the second team said, "Sit down on that chair, sir. We'll take a look at that leg."

MacNeice sat down obediently and the first attendant pulled up his pant leg. The second opened a case. "You're lucky, sir, it only grazed the muscle. You need stitches to avoid scarring, but the muscle will heal. It'll be fine."

"Good to hear, good to hear." But MacNeice wasn't really listening; he was staring at the devastation. The firefighters had placed several portable lights around the site. Everywhere they found human remains they were placing yellow flag markers. There were a lot of markers.

"We'll clean and patch it up for you, but you should really come to Emerg now or check in at the hospital tomorrow."

"Okay, I will . . ."

"I know the sound of that *okay*. I'll make sure he does," Aziz said, smiling at MacNeice.

MacNeice was still trying to figure it out. "I think Randall was down there rigging something. I think the stun grenade disoriented him and made him drop it."

"Mac, the stuff in the basement was inert. It took Ross being down there to bring it to life."

"I know, but all those men . . ." Firefighters were placing markers as far away as the barn.

"Yes, ten Damned Two Deuces thugs with assault rifles and explosives. They weren't the local cricket team."

"Cricket team—" He winced at whatever they were now putting on the wound. "Isn't that eleven men?"

"Details, details," Aziz said, resting a hand on his shoulder.

MacNeice looked up to see several bats doing crazy aerobatics above the wreckage, their radar probably confused by the specks of debris floating in the air. Far out beyond the cornfield he saw the beginnings of an electrical storm—flashes of lightning testing the ground for weakness. He said, "Retrieval better get here soon."

"They will. Swets used the threat of coyotes. Let me make sure Melanie and her kids are taken care of, then I'll see how we can get back to Dundurn. Is there anything you want out of your car?"

"My keys, the CDs from the glove compartment, and my briefcase from the trunk."

"Okay, don't move. I'll be right back."

The young paramedic stood up and his partner repacked the bag. "Okay, sir, that should do it. You've lost a fair amount of blood, so no heavy drinking or jogging tonight." MacNeice rolled down his pant leg and thanked them. Standing up, he noticed that his shoe was soggy with blood. Realizing there was nothing more that he wanted to see, he sat down again. Maybe it was the power of suggestion, but he felt lightheaded.

Aziz had disappeared among the people and vehicles. There were firetrucks, ambulances, police cars and now department tow trucks parked everywhere. A frenzy of stuttering emergency lights shone up and down the road, illuminating the forest canopy in red and blue. MacNeice tried to imagine what the farm had been like when it was built—full of fresh hope and rugged enthusiasm for growing and nurturing a life on the land—but he couldn't keep the image in focus. He gave up when he saw a firefighter squat nearby to put down another yellow marker.

# 48.

SWETSKY DROVE THEM back in one of the cruisers that had been blocking the intersection. MacNeice sat up front; Vertesi, Aziz and Williams were in the back. As the devastation and flashing lights disappeared from view, MacNeice turned off the matter-of-fact dispatcher and looked out at the dark landscape. An awkward silence filled the car.

After a few miles, Williams asked, "Butter and her kids going to be okay?"

"I think so," Aziz said. "The paramedic gave her something to calm her down and they're going to her mother's place in Oakville. I told her we would need her to come in for an interview, but not for a day or two. I called her mom for her, and she was very concerned. So Melanie will be fine, I think . . . I hope."

"I'm glad," Williams said. "You know, as long as I live, I'll never forget that house going up . . ."

"What do you think happened, boss?" Vertesi asked.

"Initially I thought there must have been natural gas in the basement and the stun grenade caused it to explode. But now I think Ross must have made a mistake when the stun grenade hit. Other than that, I just don't know."

"Musta been a shitload of explosives down there."

"Indeed . . ."

The car fell silent again until Swetsky said, "You gotta be relieved it's over, Mac."

"Yes—if it is—I am."

As the car rolled on, MacNeice tried to catalogue what remained to be done on the case. There were the Vanucci papers to examine; charges to be laid against the Old Soldiers by the New York authorities; Wenzel Hausman's safe return to West Virginia before he bankrupted the city with charges for room service, the minibar and rented movies. Payback for Roberto Mancini had already begun and would likely be harsher than any sentence a judge might bring down. Swetsky would pursue any stragglers from D2D and the Jokers, but those members who'd escaped were probably already wearing the colours of rival gangs. And there was the return of Gary Hughes's wedding ring.

And William Dance. He couldn't forget Dance.

As the car climbed the Sky-High he looked out over the sleeping city, resisting the urge, as they reached the top, to look towards the eastbound lane—though he sensed that all three in the back seat were looking. The big man was about to pull off onto Lakeshore when MacNeice said, "Swets, do me a favour. Keep going to the Mountain Road exit and drive me home."

"Are you okay, Mac? The EMS guy said you should go to Emerg." Aziz said, leaning forward, close to the separating Plexiglas.

"I'm fine . . . just tired." The cruiser fell silent again.

It was 11:43 when Swetsky pulled up outside the stone cottage. MacNeice opened the door and got out. The back door opened and

Williams, then Aziz, got out; she handed him the leather CD case, the briefcase and keys.

"See you in the morning?" Aziz said, climbing into the front seat.

"Yes, bright and early. Thank you, Fiza, John, Michael, Montile. Get some rest." Looking over to Swetsky, he said, "When you drop her off, make sure you walk her to the door and then go through the room. Make sure the officer is posted there." Swetsky nodded. MacNeice tapped the roof of the cruiser and waved, but didn't look back.

In the bathroom he undressed, washed the blood off his foot and leg and put on a T-shirt. He retrieved his cellphone, emptied the pockets and threw the torn and bloodied pants into the garbage pail under the sink. With the lights turned down, MacNeice poured a double grappa and sat at the window looking into the night. His thoughts went back to the farmhouse, to the bikers inside and the question of whether the new men had been as eager to fight it out as the rest. The trailer hadn't taken any fire, he realized, because the bikes inside would be their escape after Ross blew up everyone outside. He wondered if the new men had known anything about the basement crawl space. Did Melanie Butter know? He couldn't believe she did, not with her sons living there.

The pain in his leg was starting to bother him. He had a strange feeling that the wound was leaking blood, but when he checked, the bandage was holding. He distracted himself by thinking about Swetsky's proposition concerning the money from the oil barrel. MacNeice suspected that military death benefits would serve only to keep Sue-Ellen Hughes comfortably poor. Two hundred thousand would give her the breathing room she needed to create a new life for her family.

But it troubled him. If it was the right thing to do, then why do it on the sly? Then it hit him—the money was dirty, but the gift of it didn't have to be. He smiled, poured himself another grappa and grabbed his cellphone off the table.

"Bob, it's Mac."

"Christ, it's late!"

"I know."

"Did you watch the press conference?"

"No. Why?"

"Wallace lavished praise on you and your team, SWAT team too. He's turning into your biggest fan . . . Are you okay?"

"Yes, yes, I am. Are you?"

"You mean with the Mancinis?"

"To begin with."

"I got a call. They're very grateful to you and wanted me to tell you. Apparently Roberto Mancini even acknowledged you and Aziz, though maybe to save face somehow—and that's not going to happen."

"He and Pat had no idea of the consequences."

"Good thing you were able to get that girl and her kids out of there tonight . . ." He could hear the mayor yawning.

"It was lucky."

"So what the hell are you calling about, Mac?"

"Sorry, were you in bed already?"

"Yes, but that doesn't matter now . . . What's going on?"

"We can talk about it tomorrow."

"Fuck off and tell me! Otherwise I'll be awake all night wondering what's going through your mind now."

"Swetsky discovered over eight hundred thousand dollars in an oil drum out at the barn in Cayuga. It was the stash Frédéric Paradis came back for."

"A lotta money . . . So?"

"You remember Sergeant Hughes's wife, Sue-Ellen."

"Of course."

"Well, we've just released the body of her husband—with the hands and feet—to officials from the U.S. Department of Veterans Affairs. They'll give her Gary's death benefits, but for the past two years she's been living on handouts from her parents and whatever she could scrape together from welfare for her and the kids."

"What's your point?"

"No one but you, me and Swetsky know what was in that oil drum. Take two hundred of the eight hundred and give it to her. The rest can go into the city's budget, or to the *Hamilton-Scourge* Project—I don't care."

At least half a minute passed before the mayor responded. "How could we even do that?"

"Take out the two hundred, turn it into U.S. currency and give it to her when we return her husband's wedding ring—it was still on his finger when his hands were discovered buried in the garden—"

"For chrissakes, stop with the gore! You'll give me nightmares."

"I want you to say yes. And we won't do it unless you do."

"Can I decide tomorrow?"

"No, we're into it now—decide now. Make this woman's life easier, Bob. You'll never be able to tell anyone but you'll know we did the right thing."

"You've been drinking that grappa shit again."

"I have, yes, but my mind is clear . . . I'm waiting for you."

"You're nuts, you know that! Okay, skim off two hundred—I'll back you. Now can I get some sleep?"

"And Bob—nightmares aren't so bad. I have them all the time."

"Goodnight, Mac. Thanks for what you did out there, and I'll see you at the ribbon-cutting down at the dock. It's gonna be a really big deal." He hung up without waiting for a response.

MacNeice sat looking out the window at the twinkling lights of Secord. Suddenly two small, round silvery mirrors turned his way from a branch midway up the closest maple tree. MacNeice gasped.

Like that, the disks disappeared, then reappeared again. Standing up, he limped over to the window in time to see a barn owl glide away through the trees. He imagined he could hear its wings as it set off—*va-whumph, va-whumph, va-whumph*—but he knew its true power was that it hunted silently. He kept watching till it was swallowed by the night. More wing than bird—he wished it had stayed. The grappa had helped with the pain, but MacNeice's leg was still throbbing.

He started humming an old song, letting his breath form a fog circle on the window. When he came to the chorus, he stopped humming and spoke the lyrics out loud: "What a long, strange trip it's been . . ." Tears filled his eyes and spilled down his cheeks as he turned away from the window. He coughed to clear his head, finished the grappa and went to bed.

Morning came too early. Wallace was the first to call, letting MacNeice know that Aziz was going to be on *Jane in the Afternoon*, a local interview program broadcast live to network television and beamed across the country. Its success rested on the shoulders of Jane Tierney, a smart, attractive, engaging and insightful former foreign correspondent. Jane had been slated to host the program Aziz had missed because of the shootout in Cayuga. This would be a one-on-one along the lines of the cancelled "Psycho" segment.

Stalling as he tried to wake up, MacNeice asked if the events in Aldershot would override William Dance as a story. Wallace said no, though apparently Jane's producers had told him they were going to approach Melanie Butter for a feature interview. "This is exactly what the producer said," Wallace recounted. "'Speaking for our audience, the bikers got what they deserved, but the hairdresser and her kids—now there's a story.'"

"I'll call Aziz."

———

MacNeice went over to the whiteboard to stare at the ugly reality of one case and the sad remains of the other. Looking over at Aziz, he asked, "Are you ready for today?"

"I think so. I've studied all my notes several times."

"Where are Vertesi and Williams?" he asked.

"Michael brought me in this morning, then he went over to Montile's to retrieve the Vanucci papers from the BMW. They'll be here shortly."

Feeling weary from the night before and in constant pain from his leg, MacNeice went into the servery to make coffee for himself and Aziz. He was resisting the task of writing up the events in Aldershot. The actions and images weren't likely to fade anytime soon, and he was reluctant to reinforce them in his mind with words.

MacNeice sat down with the espresso and studied the printout of Dance smiling up at the security camera. He wondered why he had strayed from his schedule, but was grateful he had. He hoped that the young man was hunkered down because he knew every cruiser in the city had onboard photographs of him, the motorcycle and his mother's Camry. Though the three women his team had identified as potential targets were still under protection, it didn't mean they were on Dance's list, or that his list didn't include more. And then there was Aziz.

She was at her desk, transcribing speaking points for her interview. He looked at his watch. "In approximately two hours," he said, "you're going to be on national television. Is there anything you need help with?"

"I'm just trying to clear my head of last night and yesterday afternoon with Roberto Mancini . . . I'm okay. I think I'll just reiterate what I believe to be the case—that William is a desperately sick individual who should surrender immediately." She put her pen down and turned to him. "Why? Do you have anything you want me to say?"

"Just be careful, Fiza."

"I'll be fine, Mac, but thanks." She smiled and went back to her notes.

Vertesi and Williams wandered in together carrying the boxes from Buffalo. Williams sat down theatrically, flinging his arms out in both directions. Vertesi went to make himself a coffee. When MacNeice announced Aziz's upcoming live interview with Jane Tierney, Vertesi said, "Yeah, tell me about it. In the span of half an hour I heard about it three times on the radio, and it was on television this morning, following the news about last night."

"Network's driving traffic to it," Williams said. "They had a shot of Fiz from the first press conference with the headline—are you ready?—'Hunting a Serial Killer: An Exclusive Interview with Dr. Fiza Aziz, Criminologist and Detective.'" Williams emptied his box onto the desk, put it in the corridor and returned to empty the second one. "How are we playing it today, boss?"

"You and I will escort Fiza to and from the interview. Michael, I want you to return the sergeant's wedding ring to Sue-Ellen and let her know that the Veterans Affairs agents collected his body for burial in the States."

"Okay. That it?"

"No. You'll take two hundred thousand dollars to a currency exchange in Niagara and have it wired to her account. You'll need to call her to get her account information."

"Whoa! Did we do a collection?" Vertesi asked.

"In a manner of speaking—it's a gift from Frédéric Paradis. When Swetsky gets in, he'll tell you where to get it converted."

"This on the up and up?" Williams asked.

"Approved by the mayor himself."

"What do I tell her?"

"Insurance was taken out on Gary for doing that job. We were able to collect it for his beneficiaries. However, the payment needs to remain confidential and she should not speak about it to anyone."

"No problem. Whose idea was it?"

"Swets."

# 49.

"**W**HAT ARE THE plastic sleeves for?"

"Authenticity. What do you think of my design skills—convincing?" He held up a colour output: KT COURIERS, in huge red letters with a black drop shadow above a bogus phone number.

"Cool, but what for?"

"See this heavy-duty double-sided tape? Well, one goes on each side of the bike's gas tank and the other on my backpack. We're in the courier business. Nobody ever checks the names, and we're as common as dogshit."

"KT—Knights Templar—and the Third Reich colours . . ."

"Nice you noticed. Nobody will get that either."

When he was alone, Billie almost never smiled, but the thought of people missing the significance of "KT" and the colours made him grin. "Most people miss most things—that's our greatest advantage."

"Dude, the Knights Templar logo was two guys on a horse—but

I guess that looks a bit gay."

"Yeah, it worked a thousand years ago, but now it would just make people laugh." He took off the taped-together sunglasses and beat-up Yankees cap.

"I don't know . . . MacNeice is a piece of work. I mean, look at that blowout last night—he's pretty sharp. You really think you can beat him?"

"He looked smart last night, sure. But even a broken clock gets the time right twice a day. So, yeah, I can beat him."

"Where were you?"

"You mean, when I went out dressed like a poor person? I took a bus ride."

"No shit. Where'd you go?"

"Scouting. The whole city's buzzing about the blown-up bikers, and MacNeice and his detectives are getting all the praise. It couldn't be better even if I had planned it."

"Better how?"

"They're all distracted, worn out after the big game! And our little brown Muslim is going on television this afternoon. She'll be a superstar after this. It'll be really tragic—cut down, 'gory in her glory.'"

"What are those drawings you left on the table?"

"The floor plans for division headquarters. Amazing what you can find on the Internet if you know where to look."

Billie picked up a small blue metal cylinder the size of a mouse— a mouse with two wire tails, one white, the other red. "Surprised you haven't asked me about this."

"You had three of them yesterday . . ."

"True. But I've already deployed two of them."

"Where?"

"Oh, that's a surprise."

"What about this one?"

"Not going to need it. We'll leave it here—a keepsake." He tossed it onto the table next to the silver helmet. Its reimagined swastika had been covered by a two-inch square of paper sporting the red and black KT.

"And this?"

"That's part of the surprise. The red wire receiveth and the white taketh away. And this transponder"—Billie picked up the silver remote control—"this is their god." He put it in his pocket and finished installing the black tank on the chassis of the Yamaha. When he was done, he stood back to admire the look of it.

"It's beautiful, in an ugly kinda way."

"You sort of read my mind. It's ugly, in a beautiful kind of way."

"They're not going to let Aziz just go walking around the city like she's a tourist."

"I know, I'm counting on that. Otherwise it wouldn't be so much fun." He tapped his pocket theatrically.

Across the street from the two-storey house was another house identical in every way, except for the old man sitting on the concrete porch. As always, he braced himself when he heard the Jap motorcycle crackle to life. He knew it would be only a few seconds before the guy tore out of the narrow laneway and down the street to the intersection a hundred yards away. From there he would hear the bike all the way to the bridge that crossed into Dundurn, six blocks away. Each time the guy left he thought about calling the city to complain about noise pollution—*Can't I have some peace and quiet, for chrissakes!* He never called, but after almost five decades of shift work on the steel company's pickling line, all he wanted was his peace and quiet; he was owed at least that. He didn't own a television, a radio or a computer. He didn't read the *Standard* or the *Globe*—he didn't want to know about the state of the economy or the war in Afghanistan. He subscribed to *Hockey News* and *Reader's Digest*, which gave him all the excitement he needed.

Maybe, he told himself, as the engine crackled menacingly in the laneway, it was because he lived in a suburban dead end of four identical wartime houses and they created what was referred to as a canyon effect when it came to noise. Two were owned by retired factory workers like himself, forgotten but for mail and bills and garbage. His neighbours, however, never spent time in town during the summer, preferring the cool breezes of lake this or lake that, so the newcomer wasn't a problem for them. Maybe, he thought, Harold Crescent's being anchored to the main road by two vacant one-storey industrial units made it a sound canyon for the motor-cycle. As his mind drifted to wondering who the hell Harold was, it dawned on him that, with his neighbours up north and both corner buildings sporting FOR LEASE OR SALE signs out front, he was alone on the block with this motorcycle man. While he described himself with pride as a hermit, his heart quickened and he felt anxious about his solitude for the first time.

The bike tore out of the lane with a terrifying squeal. The rider—whom he'd never seen without a helmet—paused there to line it up on the road before launching. "Ah," the old man said under his breath, "the silver helmet today—he's got an appointment. I hope he gets smacked by a semi." He saw the helmet snap towards him as if the rider had heard him—a ridiculous thought, given the racket—but he looked down at his *Hockey News* just in case. Glancing above the pages, he noticed that the bike had changed colour. It sounded the same but it was now silver and black, not orange, and the rider was wearing jeans and a checked shirt instead of his fancy biker jumpsuit. The engine rose to an ear-piercing whine, the front wheel lifted off the ground and the bike screamed away on its rear wheel, first gear carrying it to the intersection in less time than it took to sneeze. As it had since the guy moved in six months before, the sound of it faded when it tore up to the highway.

The old man went back to sipping his coffee and reading about the latest trades, hoping that someone would eventually complain or a mishap would solve the problem for everyone.

Uptown, the new carpool Chevy rumbled heavily out of the parking lot close behind Williams's car. As it bounced from the driveway ramp onto the street, MacNeice heard Aziz groan. She was draped over the driveshaft hump and had taken the impact in the ribs. "Sorry," he said. "Not used to this car yet."

"No problem. I wasn't prepared for it, that's all. Does it have a CD player?"

"No."

"Is it okay to sit up now?"

"Stay put if you don't mind. I'll warn you if I'm going to hit another bump." MacNeice maintained a space of about twenty feet behind Williams.

"I know I'm pushing him, Mac, but I'm trying to save lives."

"We're almost there. We'll do this as a team." MacNeice slowed to a stop behind Williams. "Wait till I open the door for you."

The television station's street-front entrance in a quiet neighbourhood made it possible to drive right up to the front doors. Williams got out quickly and appeared at the side of MacNeice's car as he opened the door for Aziz. "Nothing unusual on the way over—didn't see a Camry, and no motorcycles."

"Good. Make sure the hallway's clear." After Aziz got out, MacNeice did a slow three-sixty around the entrance, watching for anything or anyone that appeared out of place.

"We're clear," Williams said when he returned.

MacNeice casually released the harness on his weapon. "Okay, straight in. You'll go into makeup, do the show and we're on our way in an hour."

# 50.

JANE TIERNEY'S FIRST questions were about the bikers. Aziz offered no further details than what had been revealed by the Deputy Chief the night before, and reiterated that every effort had been taken to avoid a firefight. Then up on the studio monitors came a video recounting the two slasher murders and the attempted murder of Lea Nam. The question that MacNeice knew would be coming was the first one asked. Sounding infinitely compassionate, Jane Tierney leaned forward in her chair and asked Aziz, "As a detective, a criminologist and a Muslim female, are you at all concerned that speaking out as you have, puts you at risk?"

Aziz had been told to look for the light on the camera to know which was active, the close-up or the wide-angle shot. It was to the close-up lens that she addressed her answer, in a steady and measured voice: "I believe, having studied his previous attacks, that this individual isolates his victims so that they are vulnerable to him. He attacks without warning, and he's not a man who wants to be confronted by someone with a weapon—someone who's an equal in combat."

"Are you suggesting there's something cowardly about these attacks?"

"Without doubt. A man in black who hides his face, slashes young women and flees on a motorcycle? Yes, he's a coward, but that's typically the case. Stand-and-fight serial killers are rare to non-existent."

"*Coward.* That's something I believe we're hearing for the first time."

"I use the word advisedly, Jane. He will likely attack again, and it's all about power—that's his mission."

"I'm sorry to press you on this, Detective Aziz, but would you not say—as a professional young woman of colour, a Muslim immigrant—that you are a perfect target for this man? And that speaking out only makes you more vulnerable?"

"If I'd taken to heart every instance in my life where my faith, sex, education or chosen field have made me vulnerable, I'd never leave my home. I'm not a victim."

"I must confess, when the idea of this interview came up at our production meeting, I was against it because I was certain we would be complicit if anything were to happen to you," Tierney said. "But hearing you now, I feel assured that you are going to be fine."

"Remember, I also have several experienced detectives—my partners—in my corner. I am seldom alone."

"Well said. Have you anything further to add about this individual?"

"It's possible, of course, that this individual is driven by a need for sexual fulfillment, but it's more likely, I believe, that he's so sexually repressed that that idea wouldn't occur to him. The investigation is well under way, and with the wealth of experience we have in the Homicide Department and the latest forensics technology, every hour brings us closer to an arrest."

"Do you believe there's any chance he'll surrender?"

"This is an extremely ill young man, and the best place for him is under psychiatric care. Yet, sadly, I think it unlikely that he'll surrender. But I can hope."

"Thank you for taking the time to come in, Detective Inspector Aziz. I know I speak for our audience across Canada when I say that I hope you and your colleagues in Dundurn bring this horror to a swift end."

"Thank you."

As Aziz waited for someone to unhook the lapel microphone, Jane Tierney said over the air, "Take care and stay safe." The comment rattled Aziz because it was so personal. If Dance managed to kill her, he'd add national significance to his cause—whatever that was.

She and Tierney shook hands and said goodbye during the commercial break, then Aziz joined Williams and MacNeice and walked out to the car. She was to ride back with Williams. Hunkered down on the floor behind the passenger seat, she looked over the console and asked, "How'd I do, Montile?"

"Well, my honest opinion is you're taking way too many risks." He glanced quickly back at her as he swung into traffic on Main Street.

"I'm not sure I know what you mean."

"You sure as fuck do know what I mean, Aziz. On air you said, 'He's not a man who wants to be confronted by someone with a weapon, an equal in combat'—end quote. *An equal in combat?* That's medieval horseshit. What are you trying to prove?"

They drove on in silence for several minutes, Williams scanning the rear and side mirrors for any tailing vehicles. Finally, as they were approaching the division parking lot, she said, "I'm drawing fire away from innocent women. I think that's my job."

"No—your job, Aziz, is to stay alive, to continue to serve and protect, not to sacrifice yourself. This cowboy shit is really pissing me off. You've seen what he's capable of, goddammit, and he's overdue."

"Cowboy? Sure, a female Muslim cowboy . . . How do you come up with this stuff anyway?"

"You know what I mean." He pulled in beside MacNeice's car, shut down the engine and turned to her. "I'm not kidding. This guy is off his head, and you're pushing too hard with this shit."

As MacNeice get out of the Chevy, he said, "Okay, wait for the boss, and then straight in."

As she climbed out, Aziz said, "Mac, Williams thinks I'm a cowboy for baiting Dance so directly. What do you think?"

"I agree with Montile." MacNeice scanned the parking lot. "Professionally—I mean, clinically—you must know that. Okay, in we go." They walked slowly across the lot towards the door. "If attacking you was irresistible to him before this interview, it's now something on a grander scale—a mission, I think was the word you used."

Still, she thought, she did not regret what she'd said.

As they approached the door, the lights and onboard sirens of both Chevys triggered. They stopped while both men tried to disarm the systems with their key fobs. "Get upstairs immediately," MacNeice said, opening the door and pushing Aziz through it.

He and Williams had taken only a few steps towards their cars when MacNeice said, "Shit! It's a diversion!" They ran to the door—it was locked.

Williams looked through the sidelight. "I think that thumbscrew lock has been turned. Christ, I didn't even know the thing worked."

"Can you see her?"

"No one there, boss. Maybe she's already upstairs. I'll call the front desk and get them to open it."

"No time." MacNeice ran to the first ground-floor window, pounding on it till someone came. Pointing to the door, he yelled, "The door's locked! Open it—fast!" Within seconds a burly uniform appeared in the sidelight and opened the door.

"That's never been locked before . . . sorry, sir."

MacNeice scanned the stairwell. "We don't have security cameras in here."

"Someone probably thought a staff entrance to a police station that never closes—"

MacNeice interrupted him. "Check all the offices and hallways on this floor. You're looking for Detective Aziz and an assailant. Williams, upstairs. Check floor by floor. Go!"

"On it." Drawing his weapon, Williams took the stairs three at a time.

The uniform was already through the door when MacNeice called after him, "What's down these stairs?"

"Dunno, sir. The holding cells are in the basement on the other side, but there's a concrete wall between them. Maybe the furnace room?"

"Okay, get going. Alert the desk sergeant. Lock down the building. Get people out on the perimeter, looking for a Yamaha two-stroke motorcycle."

"Fuck, the Dance kid! Right away, sir." He disappeared.

MacNeice listened for sounds of a struggle but heard nothing. He looked at the floor: no drag marks or blood. Moving down the stairs, he checked the hinged shackle on the fire door to the basement. The padlock lay on the step below. MacNeice drew his weapon, released the safety and pushed the door open.

Reaching into the dark, he felt for the light switch and flicked it—nothing. He considered bringing the entire division down to the basement, but that would only further unhinge Dance. He reached for his Maglite and realized it was in the glove compartment of his car, which he could still hear blaring in unison with Williams's. He closed the fire door behind him and waited for his eyes to adjust. The glow from a red exit light gave faint definition to his surroundings as he quietly stepped into the narrow corridor and stood still to listen again. Nothing.

He could see four doors, two on either side, and all of them steel. Light spilled from under each. He moved slowly to the one on the right and listened, ear to the door. Nothing. He rotated the handle and felt the latch give way—opening it quickly, he stepped into the division's storage room. Towers of toilet paper and paper towels in corrugated boxes, liquid soap, hand sanitizers and industrial cleaning supplies, all neatly arranged on grey metal shelving. He leaned into the adjoining wall and held his breath, listening for any sound from the next room. Nothing. MacNeice used a box of soap bottles to prop the door open, and with the added light surveyed the corridor again. *Three doors to go, and still not a sound.*

He moved further down the corridor. Listening again and hearing nothing, he gently released the latch of the next door—it was the office supply storeroom. The booking forms were neatly stacked alongside the stationery, interview pads, file folders, pens and pencils that together kept the bureaucracy of the city's largest division running. He stood in the doorway and listened. He heard a muffled cry but couldn't tell which of the two remaining doors it had come from. Stepping quietly across the corridor, he raised his weapon and tried the doorknob—locked. He moved towards the last door.

The sudden flashing lights and blaring of sirens had made Aziz jump. At first she was frightened, and then, feeling somewhat foolish, she was curious as to why both car alarms had fired at the same time. MacNeice had pushed her inside the door. A bike courier was there with his back to her, speaking on a cellphone, a helmet under his arm.

"Yeah, yeah, just finished here. I'm heading up to Mohawk . . . Yeah." It was the voice of someone accustomed to taking orders for a living, flat and monotonous.

Aziz was turning to look out the sidelight when he hit her and everything went black. She gasped, and a strange smell filled her mouth and nostrils. She was trying to reach for her Glock when her knees gave out and she pitched forward. She felt vaguely, and not unpleasantly, as if she were floating away.

Billie Dance had slammed his motorcycle helmet backwards onto her head to ensure that the chloroform-soaked sanitary pad inside would be most effective. As her knees folded, he hoisted her onto his shoulder and headed for the basement stairs.

The boiler room had two doors, dating back to when the heating and cooling systems for the city's largest division had been separate mechanical behemoths. Large galvanized ducts still spread across the ceiling before disappearing up to the floors above. Discovering the room on his scouting trip, he had admired the recently installed modern industrial heat pump, which took up a fraction of the room's real estate and gave him more than enough space for his purposes. On one side were four green lockers like those he remembered from high school, and on the other a small table with four mismatched chairs. The table was trimmed in chrome and had a worn imitation marble surface. Neatly arranged along the side against the wall were a deck of cards, a cribbage board—with matchsticks for pegs—and a metal jar top that served as an ashtray.

Billie laid the unconscious detective on the floor with her hands in front of her and tightened a plastic tie around her wrists. Then he threw a bungee cord from his backpack over the pipe of the sprinkler system and hoisted her up, looping the J-hooks of the bungee around the plastic tie that held her wrists.

Both doors had deadbolts on the inside—for what purpose other than his own, he couldn't imagine. He locked the far door but left the door directly in front of her unlocked, then turned to admire his captive.

Her head, encased in its silver bubble, hung forward. In spite of the fact that her feet just reached the floor, her body was limp, held upright only by the bungee attached to her wrists. "That will eventually pull your shoulders out of their sockets, Miss Aziz, but we're not concerned about such eventualities, are we?"

"Let's get a look at her, Billie."

"Okay, admire the view for a second . . ."

He removed the Glock 17 and holster from her belt and laid them on the table several feet away.

"I wanna see those titties, Billie."

"Okay, let's do her." Billie slid the knife out of its sheath, hoisted the blouse out of Aziz's trousers and sliced it straight up, sending buttons skidding across the floor.

"Yeah, man. Do the bra too."

"In time. Let me get the jacket off." He moved behind her and slit the jacket from the vent to the collar, so it hung in two pieces. Then he did the same to the blouse. He shoved the split sides up each arm and knotted them together above the silver helmet and her shoulders, which were now bare.

"Fantastic skin she has."

"Whatever. Okay, you ready?"

"Just do it."

Billie slid the knife between her breasts and popped it forward. The black bra came away and hung loose; Billie reached over and lifted it from each breast.

"Like I said, blackberry nipples . . . Beauty tits—on the small side, but firm. Lemme touch 'em."

"Not yet. I'm not done."

"Oh yeah, the bush . . . Let's see it."

There was a soft groan from under the helmet and Aziz moved

her legs slightly, searching for support, then sagged again into unconsciousness.

"Whoa, that was close."

"Don't kid yourself, man. I want this woman awake and looking at me when I open her up." Billie undid the belt and unzipped the fly on Aziz's grey trousers, then in one violent move yanked them down till they lay in a clump at her ankles. Aziz's body bobbed up and down.

"Yeah, man, black panties . . . So cool against her skin."

"Keep in mind we're ridding the world of another Muslim, dude, not falling in love."

"I'm just saying this is one beautiful A-rab, that's all."

The silver helmet rocked back and forth loosely and Aziz groaned again. She tried standing on her legs but they were still rubbery, and the bungee cord made her bounce several times.

"That's funny—she's like a jumping jack. Okay, off with the panties, Billie."

"No more beating about the bush, you mean?"

"Shit, man, you're so fast with a line."

Aziz groaned again, but Billie was listening to something else—the creaking of a steel door down the corridor. "He's here," he whispered.

"The panties, Billie—rip 'em off."

"He's outside," Billie whispered again. "This is gonna be good. Let's take off the helmet for her shining moment." He tore the silver bubble off Aziz's head, peeled the KT label from the back and slapped it aross her mouth before she could call out. She opened her eyes and blinked several times until she could focus.

She studied him wide-eyed. After glancing down at her body, naked but for her panties, she looked at him again, her eyes burning. She snapped her head back and forth and tried to move her feet to kick out, but they were caught in her suit pants. The movement only caused her to bounce up and down again, giving Billie even more pleasure. He moved about her with the blade in front of him. Resting the cold steel on her cheek, he leaned closer and smiled, then ran the cutting edge between her breasts and down to her navel, where he shoved the point in slightly. Aziz pulled back to avoid it. Billie pushed the knife further, until finally she was forced to relax and came down on the point of the blade. A thin trickle of blood ran down to her panties.

He leaned forward so he could speak softly in her ear. "You happy now, bitch? With my next stroke we'll see what you're made of." He stepped back and drew a line from her right hip across her left breast to the shoulder. "And you'll get to watch. So will your boyfriend, if he gets here in time."

With all her strength, Aziz forced herself downward and then pushed up with her legs, using the recoiling bungee to take her higher, and kicked out and struck Dance hard below the knees. It was crude but effective; he stumbled backwards as the door flew open. MacNeice stood in the doorway with his weapon levelled at the middle of Dance's back.

"Drop the knife, Dance!" MacNeice yelled at him. Billie regained his footing but was at least two feet from striking distance. "For the last time, now—drop it."

Billie moved swiftly towards Aziz, planting his right foot. MacNeice fired once. The round tore a hole through the backpack's KT logo, throwing Billie forward. He was still holding the knife as he slammed face first onto the concrete floor.

MacNeice rushed to his side, took the knife from his hand and used it to slash through the bungee. As Aziz fell, he held her upright. He removed the KT label as gently as he could from her mouth. They stayed that way for a moment, her arms still over her head, till she pushed away from him with her hip and held out her hands. He slit the plastic tie. She rubbed her wrists, then leaned down to pull up her pants.

Beside MacNeice, Dance was lying in a growing pool of blood. Deep red rivulets were coursing along the stress cracks in the concrete, and he was coughing and sputtering. Bizarrely, he seemed to be talking to someone.

Aziz shrugged her shoulders several times to loosen them up. Then, pulling her torn clothes around her, she walked unsteadily towards the Glock on the table. "Turn him over, Mac. Please do it."

MacNeice knew what was going to happen. He bolted the door, suddenly aware that the other door was locked from the inside— Dance had planned it so he'd walk directly into the action. He leaned over and turned Dance onto his back. Incredibly, in spite of the blood spilling from the gaping wound in his chest, Dance was smiling. And he was whispering something, even though he was fast running out of air.

As MacNeice stood up, Aziz approached. Seeing the rage filling her eyes, he stood between her and Dance. "Let me do it, Fiza," he said. "I can stand the guilt." He reached for her weapon but she shrugged him off.

Straddling the prone figure, she leaned over till she was face to face with William Dance. "You see me? You see my Muslim face? I'm still here." His eyes were glassy but he stared up at her. "But you . . . you are gone, Dance, and soon, I promise you, you will be remembered only as a vile mistake, a pathetic little creature—gone."

Dance's eyes changed, beginning to fade as the life flowed out of them. He coughed, and a mixture of blood and spittle spilled over his cheeks. When his mouth closed, the deep red line between his lips made the smile even more obscene. He managed a slow wink. The winking eye struggled to open again, only making it halfway. Aziz pushed off the safety on her weapon and first pointed it at his head, then scanned down the centre of his body. She fired a round into his groin. His body bucked violently.

Aziz stared at his face again. She wasn't aware of the pounding on the door. MacNeice could hear Williams screaming their names, and he reached over to retrieve her weapon. "It's over, Fiza. He's gone."

"Not yet, he isn't. Not yet. Look, the smile's still there." Without hesitating, Aziz fired another round, into Dance's mouth, shattering that smile. "No more smiling, William Dance." Then she handed her weapon to MacNeice, walked unsteadily to the opposite side of the room and leaned against the lockers.

Outside the door they heard someone shout, "Stand back!' A moment later a battering ram blew the door open, sending the deadbolt cartwheeling to a stop at Dance's feet. Williams rushed in with his weapon raised. Behind him it seemed as if the whole division was trying to cram through the door. "Get them out of here, Williams. Now!" MacNeice shouted.

After a quick glance at Aziz's shredded clothing, Williams turned. "Out, out, out—it's all over. Get out—now!" He pushed, grabbed shoulders and shoved the blue mass back through the doorway. Once he'd cleared the room he turned back and said, "I'll cover the door. Take your time." He stomped out and tried to slam the door, but it was hanging loose in its bent metal frame.

The voices outside were loud and agitated, but it seemed extra-ordinarily quiet in the room. There was only the smell of blood, spreading in a large Rorschach puddle around Dance's body.

MacNeice tucked Aziz's Glock into his belt, closed the harness restraining his own weapon and took off his jacket. He put it around Aziz's shoulders and held her arms gently, then pulled her towards him in a hug. She began shuddering but said nothing.

"We can stay here for as long as you like," MacNeice murmured, "but I'd rather get you away from this sight, this smell. We'll wait for EMS in an interview room upstairs."

"Montile was right," she said quietly next to his ear, the tremors in her body subsiding.

"The groin thing?" MacNeice drew away from her and held her face in his hands.

"Yes." She relaxed into him a little. Fearing she'd collapse, he held her up at the waist.

"Fiza, come on, let's get out of here. I'll take you up the back stairs. We'll get you patched up and do our debriefing with SIU."

"Okay." She looked down at the corpse—the eyes, one still half-open, were splattered with blood and finally unseeing.

"Williams," MacNeice called, "clear that corridor. Give us a path to the back stairs and a clean T-shirt from the weight room."

"Yes, sir." They could hear him moving people down the corridor as complaints rose above his voice. Ten seconds or so passed before they heard, "Boss, it's all yours."

MacNeice did up two buttons of his suit jacket to cover her chest and put his arm around her. Sidestepping the pool of blood that had finally stopped growing, they left the room.

Williams was waiting for them. "He wired the cars with transponders, boss. The Yamaha was on the other side of the building. No one noticed because he'd painted it black and silver." Keeping his eyes carefully averted, he held out his arm. "Here's a T-shirt, Fiz. You're now an official member of the tug-of-war team."

"I feel like one," she said, and managed a smile. "Thank you, Montile. And you were right."

"About what?"

"It was a mistake to push him. I apologize."

"Well, as a famous comic once said, all's well that ends swell." He led them to the foot of the stairs.

"Who said that?" she asked.

"Me." Williams did a slight bow. "I'll be right up with the EMS team."

———

MacNeice made sure Aziz was settled in the interview room before he went to make coffee. When he returned with two double espressos, she was wearing the tug-of-war T-shirt and had thrown her shredded clothing in the wastebasket.

"Sorry, Fiza, we'll need those for evidence."

She grimaced.

"You're allowed not to think for a little while, but then you need to start thinking again. Fiza, you've got to get your head together to talk to SIU." He put the coffee in front of her and retrieved the clothing from the bin, laying it on a rolling table in the corner of the room. Coming back to stand beside her, he said, "Show me your stomach."

Aziz tilted back her chair and lifted the T-shirt. The wound was an inch long and deep, but for the moment it had stopped bleeding. Her belly was pulsing rapidly, betraying her pretense of calm. The leaning back and stretching caused a fresh globule to track down the trail of dried blood to her waistband.

"It's right on the bottom lip of your belly button. It looks like a bad razor-blade cut, which is good—it's so fine it won't scar."

She let the T-shirt fall and eased her chair back onto all four legs. In the corridor they heard people approaching, and Williams appeared in the sidelight window. He opened the door a little. "EMS is here. And"—looking at MacNeice—"two suits for the incident report." He swung the door wide for the paramedics, stepping aside as they came through.

"Put the suits in the other room. I'll be with them shortly." MacNeice swirled the espresso in his cup to capture the crema, then drank it down. "I'll leave you to it then," he said to the paramedics. "Fiza, when you go in, just tell them what happened." He squeezed her shoulder briefly before turning to pick up the torn clothing. "When you've finished with your interview—which won't be long— I'll take you back to the hotel."

She nodded. "Okay, boss. Thanks."

MacNeice smiled and left the room.

Putting on her latex gloves, the solid young attendant with short-cropped blonde hair said, "Detective, would you mind just lying down on the table so we can see that wound?" Her partner, a burly man with red hair, smiling eyes and a Yosemite Sam moustache, squatted on the floor, digging into the large nylon medical bag. He was humming a tune that Aziz liked but couldn't identify. She lay down on the cool fake wood surface and let her eyes close as the two set to work. Feeling the woman's hand touch her skin, she opened her eyes and studied the ceiling-mounted fluorescent light, marvelling at the intricacy of the diamond-patterned plastic reflector and how it fractured and dispersed the light from the long, narrow tubes.

She heard the woman say, "Give me four swabs and four alcohol prep pads." The red-haired man with the cartoon moustache responded, "You got it," and returned to his humming.

She felt a sharp, hot sting and flinched. "Sorry, Detective," the woman said. "I forgot to say this would sting a bit. It's fairly deep."

She felt a faint tugging as the attendant taped the wound closed, and then the cool sensation of the alcohol pads as she mopped up the dried blood. Aziz realized that she had yet to look at what he'd done to her. Even though it wouldn't matter anymore to William Dance, she decided not to give him the satisfaction. Instead she closed her eyes again and focused on her breathing. Within seconds—they reported afterwards—she was asleep.

# 51.

AZIZ WAS IN the passenger seat, looking through the plastic bag of sleep goodies MacNeice had picked up for her after his interview—valerian, melatonin and two small bottles of lavender oil. "Do I do all of these?"

"Yes. Three or four each of the herbs and as much of the lavender oil as you can stand." He was driving west along King Street towards her hotel.

"What did they ask you, Mac?" she said, closing the bag.

"I'm sure it was exactly the same interview as you had. There was a stenographer, a union rep and a member of the Police Board. They're just doing their job."

"Those two shots are a problem, aren't they," she said, looking off to the passing streetscape.

"They are. There'll be a preliminary hearing, though, where we'll have a chance to explain ourselves." He made a left onto Osler Drive. "How are you feeling now?"

"Exhausted. I'd love a bath, but Doris—that was the paramedic

. . . Doris, and her partner Dave—said not to. They taped up the cut and said I should give it at least forty-eight hours before I get it wet."

"Makes sense." He pulled into the hotel parking lot and turned off the ignition. "If you'd like, I'll stay with you till you fall asleep."

"I'd like."

When they got to her room, she disappeared into the bathroom to get changed and re-emerged after a long time, wrapping the white terrycloth bathrobe over her pale blue pyjamas. She sat on the small sofa. "When I was getting undressed, I realized this could be as bad for you as for me. I'm so sorry I've put you in this position, Mac."

He turned on the bedside lamp and said, "Don't be. I'm an adult. I knew what you were going to do and I let you do it."

"You know, I actually fell asleep while they were patching my stomach."

"Shock."

"You think?"

"I think."

MacNeice went to the bathroom and filled a glass with cool water. He came back and handed it to her, then opened the valerian and melatonin and gave her four of each. Following his instructions, she swallowed the valerian with a gulp of water, then put the melatonin under her tongue and let it dissolve. He walked over to close the heavy drapes, and when he turned around, her head was resting on the back of the sofa and her eyes were closed.

"Come on, I'll tuck you in." He took both her hands and lifted her up gently; she groaned as she straightened.

"I imagine you're aching all over at this point."

"I am."

MacNeice pulled back the duvet, fluffed the pillow and took her robe as she lowered herself onto the bed. He could see how traumatized she was just from the effort it took for her to climb under the cover. Leaning over her, he smoothed the hair away from her face and kissed her forehead. He said softly, "Neither of us will ever forget what happened today, Fiza, but for me, what shines through the horror of it is your extraordinary courage."

She managed a smile before tears filled her eyes and spilled over her cheeks. He brushed them away tenderly with the tips of his fingers and tucked her in. Draping her robe over the back of a chair, he said, "I'll be over there on the couch. If you need anything, I'm right here."

Her eyes were closed as she said, "Thank you, Mac . . . for my life."

He turned out the light. "Go to sleep," he whispered.

MacNeice settled down to wait until she slept, his mind replaying the scene with Dance. He knew the incident report would raise red flags and the preliminary inquiry would question whether he and Fiza were fit to serve. Once Richardson had conducted her autopsy, SIU would ask them to account for the two rounds from her weapon.

The SIU might not be swayed by Dance's torture of her, by her being strung up like an animal, stripped and terrorized by a man intent on tearing her body apart, as he had done twice before to other women. Rather, they might take the position that Dance was provoked, cornered and slaughtered. It might be beyond the Police Board's collective comprehension that Dance had planned what unfolded in the basement of Division—with the obvious exception of the ending. If Aziz hadn't kicked out, if MacNeice hadn't opened the door . . . along with every other citizen of Dundurn, right now the board members would be mourning the loss of an officer who had given her life to save others.

Of course, MacNeice had his own questions, lax security at the division being chief among them—the parking lot, the deadbolt on the exit door, the stairwell without a security camera, the door to the front desk and offices with only a narrow wired glass window, the basement floor that no one but the maintenance staff—and Dance—knew anything about . . . Why were there deadbolts on the inside of the furnace room? How, when and where had a young man been able to plant transponders on his and Williams's cars? And how could a killer disguised as a bike courier linger in a stairwell within feet of several armed officers and not be noticed, especially when every cop in the region knew this kid's primary skill was not being noticed?

But soon the darkness in the room and his own fatigue had their way with him. He knew he'd dropped off only when he heard her calling him; how much time had passed he couldn't tell. "What is it, Fiza?"

"Nothing's working, Mac. Not the valerian, the melatonin or the lavender oil on my temples and hands. I'm burping and I smell like a flower, but I can't sleep."

"Well, I do have a last-resort solution . . ."

"We don't have any grappa."

"Not grappa."

"Narcotics?"

"No. Much more potent than sleeping pills—maybe because it takes work."

"I'm up for it."

"Kate's mom gave me a book once called *The Diary of a Cotswold Parson*."

"Bores you to sleep, does it?"

"Quite the contrary—it's fascinating. But what really intrigued me were the names of people and places—names I've never come across before, or since."

"How does that help you sleep?"

"I copied down the names as I read the book and memorized them. When I'm trying to sleep, I start reciting them. I've never made it through the whole list—maybe not even half of it—before I'm a goner. I don't know how I ever committed them to memory in the first place."

She sat up and turned on the bedside light. "I've got a pen somewhere here."

"Not necessary." He went over to the desk, where her laptop and portable printer sat. "I'll enter it on your computer and print it out. It'll take five minutes. In the meantime, count sheep."

"Tried that."

He turned on the computer, opened a new file and began typing: *Upper Slaughter. Crickley Hill. Aston Blank. Haw Passage. Mrs. Hippisley. Frogmill. Mrs. Backhouse. Giggleswick. Cleeve Cloud. Charlton Kings. Andoversford. Cricklade. Evenlode. Apphia Witts. Wood Stanway. Miss Gist. Chipping Norton. Cubberley. Birdlip. Nether Swell. Uley Bury. Over Bridge. Sharpness Point. Minchinhampton. Mrs. Vavasour. Mundy Pole. Chipping Sodbury. Lord Ribblesdale.*

He hit Print and, copy in hand, went over to her. "Okay, read it quietly to yourself, and focus on the words—they can be tricky."

"Ah, I love a challenge."

"I know you do, but this isn't that. This is just to read, pronounce each word softly to yourself and, if necessary, read it a second time."

He gave her the paper and went back to sit on the sofa. She began reciting the words, slowly at first and with too much articulation, as if she was making fun of the whole exercise. But by the time she reached "Nether Swell" and "Uley Bury" her pace had slowed significantly and her voice was a whisper. He heard her yawn then and waited for "Lord Ribblesdale," but it never came.

After ten minutes more of silence, he walked quietly over to the bed. The sheet of paper was still in her hand, which was lying flat on the bed beside her. *Never fails*, he thought, and clicked off her light. He felt his way back to the sofa, where he waited for another ten minutes. Then he crept to the door, cushioned the latch to keep it from making a sound and left the hotel room like a fifth-storey burglar.

Settling into the Chevy, he took several deep breaths before turning on his cellphone and the radio. He only had time to start the engine before both buzzed. He answered the cell. "MacNeice."

"Wallace. Wherever you are, get to a land line and call this number."

MacNeice wrote down the number on a scrap of paper, pulled over at a Main Street doughnut shop and walked over to the wall-mounted phone. Wallace answered on the first ring. First he wanted to know what shape Aziz was in, and then the specific details of what had happened in the furnace room, since Williams either didn't know or wasn't telling.

"He doesn't know."

MacNeice gave the Deputy Chief the top-line story of what had happened. He told him that Dance had ignored his call to drop the weapon and had started unwinding a blow that would have split her up the middle, just like his two previous victims.

"You fired the fatal shot."

"I did."

"And the other two?"

He was tempted to ask whether Wallace wanted an honest answer or one he could sell to the media. But then he decided to simply tell the truth. When he was done, he added that he'd seen first-hand what Dance could do—and what he'd already done to Fiza.

"Mac, she shot him in the mouth and the crotch. So what was it? Retribution, revenge? What?"

*Probably both*, MacNeice thought, letting a silence fall. But it might also have been simply to wipe that sick grin off his face and to let Dance know that stripping her and running the blade between her breasts had been a bad idea that came with a cost. There may have been another reason too, though it was one MacNeice decided he wouldn't talk about with anyone. MacNeice believed Aziz had misjudged her ability to defend herself, even though everything she had done to provoke Dance depended on it.

Wallace broke the silence, taking MacNeice's non-response as a yes on both counts. "It would have been better for everyone if you had done it, Mac. You could easily claim it took three rounds to knock that nutbar off his feet."

"I've got no comment on that, sir," MacNeice said. "But you might consider asking the mayor to conduct an independent inquiry into how a torture chamber could be set up in the basement of a division packed with cops.

"Shit, Mac, if you left the force you could get a job in public relations."

"I'm a cop—I am in public relations."

"Despite what's going on internally," Wallace said, "Aziz has become something of a media darling with this investigation."

"I'm aware of that."

"The kinky details of what happened down there are gonna be catnip for those fuckers . . ."

"Sir, all you have to say is that the matter is before the Police Board and you have no comment."

"Mac, you should be doing this job."

"Absolutely not. All I really want to do right now is my own job. But first I need some sleep."

# 52.

WALKING DOWN THE basement corridor to Richardson's lab the next morning, his pace slowed as he came closer to the big stainless steel doors. He dreaded opening them and finding Dance naked on the table; he'd seen enough of him clothed. Anyway, MacNeice had never been interested in the raw gore of an autopsy. He hesitated, took a deep breath and pushed the door open. Richardson was in her office and waved for him to come in.

Junior was wheeling out a gurney, the body—mercifully—under a white plastic sheet. The floor was wet and the ancient drains were sounding their last gurgling protests against what had been flushed through them.

"You already know the worst of it, Detective. His mouth and groin were smashed by a different calibre bullet than the one that tore through his chest. The latter was yours, I understand. It disconnected his aorta and shattered his heart. I assume, then, that the others were from Aziz's weapon. Please sit down, Mac."

He was aware of the *Goldberg Variations* playing softly as he sat down. She kept the light level in her office low, even intimate, in contrast to the ultra-white light of the lab.

"I can't fudge this report, Mac," she said. "The shots fired into his mouth and groin were unnecessary. If they were a *coup de grâce*, you'll have to explain the reasons. The best I can say is that they had nothing to do with the outcome. This young man was dead with the first shot."

"I know."

She could hear the weariness in his voice. Somewhat out of character, she offered, "Let me make you a spot of tea. I believe there's nothing so tragic or devastating that it cannot be improved by tea."

"I'd love a cup."

Richardson went over to a small counter that included a sink, bar fridge, electric kettle and teapot. He watched her as she conducted the lifelong ritual with ease and precision. He let himself drift with the music, wondering if it was Glenn Gould or some twenty-first-century player he didn't know—the sound was turned too low to hear Gould humming along with the piano.

"He was otherwise healthy, you know. Of course, I cannot speak for the blown fuses in his neural circuitry; his brain has been removed for others to study that. But he was a healthy young man. Milk and sugar?"

"Just milk, thanks."

She returned with the tea. The cups and saucers had small blue flowers on them.

"Bluebells . . ." he said.

"Bluebells and daffodils made spring bearable for me in England. No matter how much rain fell, one couldn't be gloomy when they were in bloom."

"We spread Kate's father's ashes on a carpet of bluebells in an ancient forest over there."

She put down her cup and glanced at her report, the business at hand reasserting itself. "Mac, I will emphasize that Mr. Dance was already dead when she fired those two rounds. I'm sorry I cannot do more—I have no doubt he deserved it."

"He did. And I could have stopped her. But I felt I owed her the chance to restore her sense of dignity."

"Professional detachment was absent, then, for both of you."

"You saw those women, Mary. You know what he was about to do to Aziz."

They fell silent then and drank the rest of their tea listening to the music. When he'd emptied his cup, Richardson offered more, but he declined, stood and shook her hand. "Thank you, Mary. You've been a good friend to my department."

"I'm a good friend of yours too, Mac," she qualified. "I cannot imagine anything you could do to alter that. When I testify, I will add a postscript to my report. I was a battlefield surgeon in the Bosnian war, and I've seen enough chest wounds to know that Dance was dead instantly; no amount of triage brilliance could have changed that. Therefore, Aziz's actions—which may be regarded as causing indignity to human remains—were irrelevant to that young man."

"Even though he was still smiling at her?" MacNeice needed to ask the question.

She sighed and put both hands on her knees. "When I was a child growing up in Wales, my grandfather raised chickens—mostly for eggs, but also for dinner. I was often in the barnyard when he chopped off their heads . . . You can see where I'm going, of course. Their bodies would run around crazily before dropping and the eyes in their severed heads would blink up at me and their little beaks would open and close . . . but they were most definitely dead."

"Very vivid."

"Death is vivid . . . and the dinners were divine." She smiled and stood up. Teatime was over.

# 53.

V ERTESI AND WILLIAMS were removing the images from the whiteboards when MacNeice walked in. They wanted to know how Aziz was, and then they wanted to know whether this would scare her away from police work.

"Quite the opposite, I think."

Vertesi stuffed the images and Aziz's torn clothing into a banker's box to be forwarded to the inquiry, and he and Williams rolled the whiteboards to the storage room. Ryan and MacNeice sat in silence, watching as they disappeared from view.

As MacNeice turned to his desk to write up the meeting with the coroner, the ground-floor admin clerk appeared with her cart. She said, "This came in for you by courier this morning, sir." She handed him a box and continued down the corridor.

It was neatly wrapped, and above his name and title it was sealed with a label that said KT COURIERS. MacNeice stood up sharply, put the box on his desk and stepped back.

"You okay, sir?" Ryan said, spinning around in his chair.

"I am. Though I feel as if I've just seen a ghost."

"What's up?" Williams asked as he and Vertesi returned.

"Dance just sent me a present." He pointed to the package on his desk.

"Sweet Jesus, what now? Should we be calling the bomb squad and evacuating the building?" Vertesi said.

"No, that's not his style. He was an up-close-and-personal killer. Anybody got a camera?"

"I've got my point 'n' shoot here, sir. It does a decent video too," Ryan said, reaching into his knapsack.

"Video it is." He waited for the nod from Ryan, then checked his watch. "The time is 5:18 p.m. Package arrived in the office mail distribution. Has been in the mailroom—I'm reading the department stamp—since 9:34 this morning. Dropped off likely by William Dance himself."

He took scissors to the top edge of the box and cut through the duct tape that surrounded it, leaving one side to act as a hinge.

"That suggests he would have spoken to at least two people: one to ask for the mail room and the person at the desk who took the package and signed for it," Vertesi said, pulling up a chair.

MacNeice spoke in a monotone for the video. "I'm taking off the KT label that reads 'DS MacNeice, best wishes from your S.S. friend,' which I assume is a reference to Hitler's S.S."

"That or your secret Santa," Williams deadpanned.

"You can't help yourself, can you?" Vertesi said, shaking his head.

"No," Williams countered. "I subscribe to the dictum 'No gag goes unspoken.'"

"Right. So the meaning is open to interpretation," MacNeice said, attempting to focus his team. He put the label on the desk and lifted the lid. "Inside there's an envelope addressed 'MacNeice.'" He took it out and placed it next to the label. "Underneath there's a memory stick on a black lanyard, a DVD and a handwritten address card for 8 Harold Crescent with a key taped to it. Below, a folded card with handwriting in capital letters—'A FEW OF MY FAVOURITE THINGS.' And finally, a packet of photographs held together with a rubber band."

He passed the memory stick to Williams and the DVD to Ryan, then picked up the envelope, opened it and began to read the letter. Ryan stopped recording.

*Dear Detective MacNeice*

*I'm sorry about your Detective Aziz but you know as well as I do she had it coming. It's not a pretty sight I know. No let me correct that—IT'S AN AMAZING SIGHT! The flesh just separates like you're cutting through caramel pudding. You'd never think it but it does. It's so beautiful. Not to you—I can understand that. You and Aziz had something special going on.*

*You were probably surprised that I made no attempt to escape or surrender, but consider this: all great movements begin with sacrifice—in this case hers and mine. And of course the other two. I knew both she and I would die swiftly so at least that's merciful.*

*You're a good cop MacNeice, but I'm a better killer. If I wasn't—and this is an extremely remote but nonetheless real possibility—I will be dead and Aziz will not. The odds however are so slight that they don't bear further consideration.*

*As for my "crusade" I've done enough for it to take hold—trust me—the demographics will prove me right. I have struck a match in a very dry forest. It's unnecessary for me to stick around and watch the blaze catch hold. It may not catch hold tomorrow or even next year but it has begun.*

*Crackle and burn. There'll be millions of people around the world cruising the net to see pictures of your gutted friend and me. Mine will be like Che. Not the politics of Che—just the pictures of him dead. I won't mind if you want to have your picture taken with a finger in one of my bullet holes like that Bolivian soldier did with him.*

*If I have one request it would be that henceforward I be referred to as the "White Assassin," because—quite justifiably I think—I removed several of the leaders and potential breeders that came here from the developing world. People like them will soon outnumber whites in this country. Check my research and you'll see I'm right.*

*I have left a few bibelots, some nuggets of wisdom, but other than that—nothing.*

*Goodbye*

*William (Billie) Dance*

*The White Assassin*

"Spreadsheets, sir," Ryan said, staring at his screen. "They're titled 'Racial Projections Based on Empirical Evidence,' and they seem to be indicating, by race or country of origin, how this country will . . . in fifty years . . . let me scroll down to the conclusion . . . Here we are—that the country will be left with a population that's only eighteen percent white, and twelve percent of those people will be in the Maritimes."

"Anything else on it?"

"There's a source list of his references and some kind of graphic modelling, province by province, as to how it's going to happen. Ontario and British Columbia lead the way, followed by Quebec, Alberta and so on. Whoa, he's even got a default. It says, 'If climate changes continue unabated, then Nunavut and the Northwest Territories will enter the equation and hasten the decline of the already small white populations in those regions, providing a differential reduction of 1.5 years on the forecast.' This guy was intense, man. Even if he wasn't a homicidal freak, he would still be a freak."

The clerk appeared at the cubicle again, looking as if she didn't want the task of delivering these particular four white business envelopes. She hesitated, not sure which detective she should hand them to.

"What are they, Carol?" MacNeice asked.

"SIU preliminary inquiry schedule, sir . . ."

"Give them to me, thank you." MacNeice looked at the names on the envelopes: DS MacNeice, DIs Williams, Vertesi and Aziz. Rather than passing them out, he tossed them on the desk.

"The memory stick is a diary of his attacks," Williams said as he scrolled down the document, "right up till last night. It ends with some gibberish about the Knights Templar having two hundred years to do what he's accomplished in less than a month, and that is, quote, 'to create a legendary movement intended to set things right.'"

"Knights Templar . . . KT Couriers," MacNeice said, glancing over at the label.

"What's in the letter, boss?"

MacNeice handed it to Vertesi and picked up the package of photographs. There were several scouting trip photos of Taaraa and Samora. Taaraa at the hospital, crossing the parking lot, walking along the street with Wendy Little, coming and going from the house at 94 Wentworth; Samora arriving at the Burger Shack, serving food and drink across the counter, at the end of her shift walking with a tray of food and her books to the breakwater where she would die. A piece of blank card separated these from images of the killings themselves—hastily shot close-ups of their staring faces in the dying moments of their lives, and two each of the wounds.

Then came another separating card, this one with a handwritten note: *Close Calls*. Research photos of Lea Nam running, stretching or leaving the gym after her workout, and several of Narinder Dass getting out of a Mercedes, walking to an elevator in an underground parking lot, or entering a building.

MacNeice checked his watch. "After the press conference, Montile, get over to"—he picked up the address card with the key and handed it to him—"18 Harold Crescent. I assume it was where he was living. Call Forensics and have them follow you there."

"No problem." Williams put the key and card in his jacket pocket.

# 54.

TWO WEEKS PASSED quickly. Far from retreating back to academe, Aziz took the plunge and arranged for her stuff to be moved back from Ottawa. Her old apartment was still empty, so she moved back in, grateful for once that the economy had been slow, especially in Dundurn. They kept her away from the media, which continued pushing the story of William Dance until at last it began losing ground to the upcoming launch event for the Museum of the Great Lakes. By coincidence, the launch and the inquiry were on the same day.

Wallace and Dr. Richardson had their interviews the day before MacNeice and his detectives were to be called. Though it was neither requested or required, the mayor had expressed his support of MacNeice and his investigative team by way of a written deposition, placing particular emphasis on the heroism of DI Aziz.

MacNeice was to go last, after Vertesi, Williams and Aziz herself. He looked at his watch—11:57 a.m.—and began making his way to the inquiry room two floors above. There was a uniformed officer standing at ease outside the door. "It won't be long, sir. So far they've been sticking to the schedule."

MacNeice nodded his thanks and walked over to the windows that overlooked the parking lot, to see if he could spot anything interesting in the trees. One minute before noon, the door opened and a shaken Aziz made her way to the stairs without even noticing MacNeice standing there. The uniform was called inside and came out a minute later to escort him in.

Before he followed he glanced back out to the treeline of the parking lot. Two crows were passing overhead; one dropped down to land on a young gingko tree, the branches swaying wildly under the bird's weight. MacNeice smiled.

Tent cards provided the names of each board member: Dorothy Peterson, Elizabeth Wells-Carpenter, Alice Yeung, David Hruby and Robert Crawford. He guessed that all three women were in their early to mid-forties. They were dressed in grey or black business suits, with only Yeung showing any colour—a jade blouse. The two men wore dark blue suits and looked like insurance brokers. A court stenographer sat behind her computer at the end of the table near the windows. Her face was a study in benign neutrality. In front of each board member was a notepad, a pencil, and a bulldog-clipped report that he assumed contained the details of the Dance case; each also had a glass of water and a cup of tea or coffee. They appeared relaxed and self-confident, as if it would be evident to any observer that they were the right people to tackle the task at hand.

Robert Crawford smiled broadly and introduced himself as chair. The pleasantries continued for almost ten minutes and included acknowledgement of MacNeice's service record and his many commendations. Crawford cited the documents of support provided by Chief Pathologist Mary Richardson and Deputy Chief Wallace, as well as the affidavit from the mayor. He spoke about the need to ensure that the facilities of all police divisions be assessed for their security and that deficiencies be corrected immediately where found wanting. He acknowledged MacNeice's personal courage in entering the basement and confronting William Dance—and that's where the flattery stalled.

The woman on the far left, Dorothy Peterson, spoke first. "DS MacNeice, why did you enter that basement alone?" She smiled, he thought, genuinely.

"I could have told Detective Inspector Williams to take the basement, but I didn't. The fact was, we had no time to ponder what to do; we had to trust our intuition and act swiftly. Dance set it up that way."

She was making notes without looking up. "Explain what you mean by 'Dance set it up that way.'"

"He wanted to die after he'd killed his last victim. If DI Aziz hadn't kicked out at him, that's exactly how it would have ended."

"You're certain about that?" She put down her pencil and looked directly at him.

MacNeice glanced over at the transcriber, who was also looking at him and waiting. He didn't answer.

"Detective?" Crawford prodded.

"Yes."

David Hruby took it from there. "We've been told by the pathologist that your shot was fatal."

"It was intended to be."

"I'm sure it was. Why then, was it necessary to fire twice more?"

"Necessary?"

"Yes. If you had already killed Dance, why was he shot a second and third time?" Hruby's tone was condescending.

"Once for Taaraa Ghosh and once for Samora Aploon."

"Is that supposed to be funny?" Hruby's face flushed.

"Let me answer the question I think you're asking. No, this

wasn't an execution."

"Was it not?" Dorothy Peterson asked.

"It was not an execution. My shot killed Dance as he lunged with his knife. If I hadn't shot him, DI Aziz would be dead."

"But you say that he set it up that way—effectively you executed him in the act," Peterson said.

"I told him twice to drop the weapon and he didn't. I shot him; I didn't execute him."

"So you believe there was no other way to stop him from killing DI Aziz?" Her pencil was poised again over the notepad.

"No."

"And the second and third rounds?" She spoke each word slowly for greater emphasis. Hruby looked up from his notes.

"After I cut Aziz down from where she was hanging, I gave her her service weapon and encouraged her to fire, thinking it would give her back her dignity, and knowing that Dance was already dead."

"Was her dignity such an issue?" the chair asked.

"Is it not for you, sir?"

"What do you mean?"

"If you had been stripped, hung up like a side of beef, sexually tormented and faced with the certainty that in a fraction of a second you'd be torn inside out, would survival not be your first concern?"

"Most certainly it would, yes."

"Yes. So, having survived that threat, having been cut down— free, but naked—would dignity then not be an issue for you?"

Crawford didn't answer but Alice Yeung took up the point. "Are you saying it was revenge, Detective?"

"No. Dance was already dead. This was an attempt to restore dignity. Aziz is a very fine officer; she had put her own safety at risk to capture him—"

Interrupting, Yeung asked, "Do you believe that what Aziz did—goading Mr. Dance into attacking her—was prudent? Was it a strategy that you, as her superior officer, endorsed?" She sat back and crossed her arms.

"I support Detective Aziz in all that she does. So yes, I endorsed it."

"You didn't feel it was cavalier . . . unnecessarily risky and provocative?" she asked.

"Aziz put herself in harm's way in order to ensure that women throughout this city, perhaps a woman such as yourself, wouldn't be harmed."

Crawford took another tack. "Is Detective Aziz well?"

"What do you mean, sir?"

"Is she stable? I understand she's back at work in your division."

"I do not allow unstable personnel to serve under me, sir."

"So she's stable?"

"Detective Aziz is a professional. She is, no doubt, still processing what happened in that basement, but if any of you required a homicide detective, I'd have no hesitation in recommending Aziz—now or in the future."

Elizabeth Wells-Carpenter turned over a page of notes and spoke for the first time. "Detective Aziz was until recently teaching criminology at a university. Can you tell us how and why she came back to work with Dundurn Homicide?"

"I believe the mayor addressed that in his recent press conference."

"And you agree with his version of events?"

"Of course I do."

The woman smiled at him and returned to her notes. Crawford looked at each of the members of the board in turn. Each nodded yes, whereupon he turned to MacNeice.

"Detective Superintendent MacNeice, speaking as the inquiry's chair, it is not the mandate of this board to prosecute or pursue DI Aziz unfairly. The documents of support we've received from the Deputy Chief and the mayor echo your own respect for her, as do those from your colleagues DIs Williams and Vertesi. However, there is a fact that we must consider: William Dance was shot twice after your fatal round. Why that was done—whether for revenge or perhaps so that Dance would at last atone for the grotesque deaths of two young women, as you seem to suggest—that sir, is a question worthy of consideration.

"If Detective Aziz, or you, were—shall we say—unbalanced through the course of this action, then some might question your steadiness under fire in the future. If Detective Aziz taunted Dance into attacking her, that could be interpreted in several ways. Was she personally, rather than professionally, caught up in this young man's twisted life? Was she crossing the line of responsible law enforcement, whatever her motives of justice were, by putting her life at risk—and your own, I might add—in a cavalier or unstable manner? As a visible minority herself, did she identify too closely with his victims?"

The chair's hands were crossed gently over each other and he looked calmly at MacNeice—as if he were explaining the rules of lawn bowling—before he continued. "If, as you say, she was given her weapon by you to fire those two shots into Mr. Dance's dead or dying body, then you are both responsible for something, and if it goes ahead, that may be the critical question this inquiry must resolve. I want to assure you, though, that this is not a witchhunt. This city is in your debt and in DI Aziz's debt. But as you and she were the only two to walk out of that furnace room alive, we need to probe what happened—and why. Do I make myself clear, sir?"

"You do."

"Very well. This is a preliminary hearing. What happens next will depend on the opinion of this board. It may end here or go further. Is there anything you'd like to add before you leave us, Detective MacNeice?"

MacNeice looked at each member of the inquiry panel. The smiling Wells-Carpenter was still smiling, Ms. Yeung still sat with her arms crossed and the others looked very relaxed about being on the other side of the table, with the exception of David Hruby, who still looked condescending.

"A while ago I was offered the position of deputy chief. I'd like to tell you why I turned it down."

"Go ahead." The older man sat back to listen.

"I am committed to serving this city and to training the finest homicide detectives in the country—in any country. They learn the skills of detection, of observation; they learn to trust their intuition—and each other, to interrogate and be thorough in every way. They gain a deep respect for the law; they work as a team, supported by each other's strengths and helping each other overcome their weaknesses. But by far—by far—the most powerful thing they learn from me, I hope, is empathy—empathy for the victim, for the family, for the city and, yes, for the killer.

"What DI Aziz did in the press conference and TV interview will remain for me and this team the finest act of empathy I've ever seen. It wasn't cavalier—it was courageous." He picked up his notebook and slid his pen into his jacket pocket. "Aziz didn't want Dance dead. She tried valiantly to bring him in unharmed—that's in the public record. I simply wanted him stopped, because I didn't think he would come in on his own."

MacNeice stood up. "So there you have it. This could have played out in so many ways: more women dead and all of us still hunting because Aziz did not put her own life at risk, or Aziz dead alongside Dance. That's what he wanted to happen—he wrote me a letter saying so."

Without warning, MacNeice slapped his hand hard against the

notebook. The noise startled everyone at the table, including the stenographer. "That's how much time I had to think about it, gentlemen, ladies—that long. When I cut Aziz down, I gave her her gun and that small bit of dignity, that small gift."

He nodded to each. The smiling woman wasn't smiling anymore. He reached across the table, shook their hands, then left the room and the building.

Big fat, creamy clouds raced across the sky. Tinged with September colours, they looked muscular but somehow fragile, uncertain. Lacking self-determination, their form would be whatever the wind decided it would be. He stood on the stone walkway looking up till four gulls flew by, riding the breeze, gliding high above Dundurn towards the bay. The city was quiet as MacNeice walked across City Hall Plaza. He was heading nowhere in particular, and for no reason he knew of, he began humming "Over the Rainbow."

# EPILOGUE

**T**HE RIBBON-CUTTING CEREMONY was set for 3:00 p.m. at the eastern wharf. Soldiers in period uniforms as well as members of the serving military of both countries lined the route from Burlington Street to the museum site. For MacNeice they presented a bizarre juxtaposition against the steel company's rusting behemoths, a backdrop of forgotten sentinels from Dundurn's industrial age.

Some distance to the east of the dock, public parking had been created. Once the dignitaries were comfortably seated at the bottom of the wharf, ordinary citizens from Dundurn and the Niagara region on both sides of the border were funnelled through metal detectors and invited to stand at the reinforced perimeter guardrail on the wharf above the site. When MacNeice stepped into one of the twelve industrial elevators that had been installed to aid construction—scheduled to begin a week later—it occurred to him that the public would have the best view.

Canadian and American security teams had been crawling over

the site for more than a week. They were now satisfied that it was safe to proceed with the event, though they would reveal very little to Dundurn's finest about what their contingency plans were if it went violently off script.

Politicians and VIPs from the United States, Britain and Canada were there, including the U.S. secretary of state, the British foreign secretary and Canada's prime minister. Before the speeches began there was a ceremonial flypast featuring an American F-15 and its Canadian counterpart, an F-18. They approached from the north and south, and once overhead they went vertical, roaring upwards in a corkscrew dance towards heaven, until all that remained was the delayed thunder and receding scream of their engines, two micrometallic glints flickering in the sunlight.

What followed was even more impressive. The pennant-festooned American destroyer USS *Arleigh Burke*, which had been in Dundurn Harbour for a week of public tours, unleashed a bone-rattling twenty-one-gun salute over the city. Though the ship was anchored at least two hundred yards off the eastern dock, the barrage was so deafening that most people smiled wildly, like kids on their first roller coaster, and covered their ears. Because the ship was floating sixty feet or more above them, every blast caused the red-carpeted floor of the site to vibrate, sending an uneasy shiver up the legs of the six hundred people sitting there.

The stage was at the north end—bayside—festively draped with red and white bunting and bracketed by the flags of Canada, the United States, Britain, Ontario and the city of Dundurn. Among the seated dignitaries were the major donors and partners, senior bureaucrats from three levels of government, museum directors and historians, a multitude of media from both sides of the border, project architects and engineers and the major contractors. Alberto Mancini, Sean McNamara and Peter Glattfelder, the American head of ABC Canada–Grimsby, and their wives were seated together.

Sue-Ellen Hughes and her children had also been invited. The mayor had insisted that she be acknowledged from the podium, and when the story of her husband made its way to the secretary of state, he insisted that an honour guard be drawn from Sergeant Hughes's battalion to formally present her with the flag.

In the last row, MacNeice, Aziz, Vertesi, Williams and Swetsky sat next to the Deputy Chief. On the other side of the aisle were Dr. Sheilagh Thomas, her postdoctoral students and Ryan—who was locked in conversation with the young woman who'd met MacNeice outside the lab. He hoped they weren't talking about computers.

Beyond them were members of the families of the Six Nations war heroes whose bodies had been found on this site. An elder dressed in beaded buckskin sat next to the prime minister on the stage, an eagle feather in his right hand. He would bless the project, on behalf of the First Nations of both countries, with a traditional smudging ceremony.

And so it began. A choir of two hundred schoolchildren—one hundred from each country—sang the national anthems of Britain, the United States and Canada. The elder rose and took the microphone. He spoke in Mohawk, and as he began the ceremony he walked slowly down the stairs and into the centre aisle, fanning the smoke with his eagle feather, spreading the pleasant smell of burning sweetgrass and sage. For several minutes it overcame an atmosphere that was vaguely marine and dank.

Then, as one would expect, the speeches began. Some were heavily scripted while others wandered on extemporaneously about history, peace and war. Mayor Robert Maybank spoke last, and his speech was by far the most compelling. He spoke about the history of Dundurn, about the glory days of steel, about the tragedies that had occurred off this very dock. But he was most splendid, most passionate, when it came to his vision for the Museum of the Great Lakes and the *Hamilton* and *Scourge*.

While not as deafening as the twenty-one-gun salute, when he was finished, people jumped to their feet to applaud him, while from above confetti and streamers showered down for several minutes, along with the cheers of more than three thousand spectators. Through the paper snow and swirling streamers, MacNeice could see Mayor Bob, his face shining, his eyes turned heavenward, arms outstretched—his greatest ambitions for Dundurn were finally coming resoundingly to life.

In the parking lot, MacNeice waved goodbye to Vertesi and Williams, then opened the passenger door for Aziz. She looked up at him and asked, "Where are we going?"

"For a drive. I'll show you the falls."

"I've seen Niagara a hundred times," she said, climbing into the car.

"Not Niagara—Ball's Falls. It's quieter there, and prettier. We'll get some peaches and sit in the park." He closed the car door.

"Why's it called Ball's Falls?" she asked as he made his way onto the QEW, heading for the Secord cut-off.

"The Ball family started a mill there a long, long time ago."

"Great name."

"It is. And the last of the Balls, the one who left it to the region—his name was Manley Ball."

"You're making that up," she said as she shifted in the seat to lean against the door, watching him.

"Fiza, honestly, to quote Montile, you can't make shit like that up."

He turned left on Highway 8, passing through Secord, passing the peach and pear and cherry orchards, passing the vineyards and the quiet towns that had once served hard-working farming families from Dundurn to Niagara, from the escarpment to the lake. He passed the awful sprawl of characterless condos and monster homes that every year erased more of that history, more of what mattered to him.

He stopped at a farm stall, parking in the shade of a century-old maple. "Wait here."

She watched him as he scanned the fruit, picking it up and examining each for bruises. He said something to the young woman in the stall, who laughed heartily and put the fruit in a paper bag. He gave her money, she gave him change—they were animated, enjoying the moment. Aziz thought to herself, *This must be what an ordinary life looks like . . .*

Returning to the car, he said, "I've got plums here and nectarines, but this peach is ready to eat right now." He lifted it out of the bag and handed it to her.

"It's perfect," she said, bringing it to her nose and inhaling deeply.

"Actually, that's what I said to her." He nodded in the direction of the woman at the fruit stand, who stood watching them, waiting, he suspected, for Fiza's reaction to the peach. When she saw them both looking at her, she smiled, waved and mouthed something to him.

"What's she saying?" Aziz was still holding the peach close to her nose, turning it slowly in both hands.

"I think it was 'good luck.' Next stop, Manley Ball's Falls," he said, fastening his seatbelt.

MacNeice powered the Chevy back onto the highway as Aziz bit into the peach.

# ACKNOWLEDGEMENTS

My partner in life, Shirley Blumberg Thornley, is the first reader of this book. She is an avid reader of mystery novels and an unerring barometer of authenticity. I'd like to think she rarely has to correct me in that regard, and while that's mostly true, it isn't true all the time. I'm human. So is MacNeice. Shirley knows him now—he is the other man in her life.

Anne Collins, my remarkable editor, takes veracity to another level and shows no hesitation in either praise or critique—though the reader will appreciate the fact that criticism always trumps praise. Anne's contribution and that of the book's copy editor, Gillian Watts, to my telling of this story is immeasurable. I am grateful, too, for the support of Marion Garner and Louise Dennys at Random House Canada. Bruce Westwood and Chris Casuccio of Westwood Creative Artists became early champions of this book and series, and I deeply appreciate their commitment to me.

Music is a through-line and back story for MacNeice, as it is for me. In my own collection—and passions—I have been guided by two great friends, Steve Wilson of Toronto and Richard Fleischner of Providence, Rhode Island. Together they have provided me with an incredible playlist. Not only do I write to the music, MacNeice listens in as he drives through Dundurn.

Doctors Dody and John Bienenstock, Dr. Rae Lake and Dr. Sarah Jane Caddick have—sometimes unknowingly—answered psychological, medical or scientific questions that have informed this story. I'm grateful that, no matter how bizarre the question, they all take me seriously—and thank you, Dody, for lending me *The Diary of a Cotswold Parson*. Scott Thornley+Company's Monika Bohan, Kirk Stephens, Carmen Serravalle, Mark Lyle and Melissa Hernandez have all contributed time and creative energy to this endeavour. Once again and without hesitation, Shin Sugino opened his studio for MacNeice. To Tim Seeton—thank you for your friendship and for bringing Merlin to life.

Finally, as well as Shirley, I'd like to thank my family for accepting, or tolerating, my absence (even when I'm present I'm aware that I'm occasionally absent, strolling the lanes of another city). Thank you to Marsh and Andrea, Ian and Christine, Daniela, Sophia, Ozzie, Charles and Kathryn—for your love and support, without which I'd be a poor man.

SCOTT THORNLEY grew up in Hamilton, Ontario, which inspired his fictional Dundurn. As president and creative director of Scott Thornley + Company (a strategic creative firm with clients in Canada, the United States and Great Britain), Thornley has worked with the pillars of the Canadian and international cultural and scientific communities in the field of applied storytelling. Having won over 150 international awards for design, he was inducted into the Royal Canadian Academy of the Arts in 1990. He lives in Toronto and retreats—as often as possible—to the southwest of France, where much of this book was written. *Erasing Memory* is the first book in the MacNeice Mystery series.

A NOTE ABOUT THE TYPE

*The Ambitous City* has been set in Sabon, an "old style" serif originally designed by Jan Tschichold in the 1960s.

The roman is based on types by Claude Garamond (c.1480–1561), primarily from a specimen printed by the German printer Konrad Berner. (Berner had married the widow of fellow printer Jacques Sabon, hence the face's name.)